Vulpini

VULPINI

Book One of the Remnants of the Old Gods Series

MEG PELLICCIO

KEY PRINT

Copyright © 2020 Meg Pelliccio.
All rights reserved.

The characters and events portrayed in this book are fictitious. Any similarity to real persons, living or dead, is coincidental and not intended by the author.

No part of this book may be reproduced, or stored in a retrieval system, or transmitted in any form or by any means, electronic, mechanical, photocopying, recording, or otherwise, without express written permission of the publisher.

First published in Great Britain in 2020 by Key Print.

ISBN-13: 9781838243005

Cover design by: Kadi Vowden-King

www.megpelliccio.co.uk

For Enzo

Chapter One

Tattered, faded flags swept back and forth under the influence of the wind; the flapping of the canvas like the beating of wings. Their golden emblazons were sun bleached to the point of being indistinguishable against the washed-out red of the streamers. Ayse sighed wearily, even in these cooler months the heat of the land felt close and claustrophobic. The city was too far from the shore for the stray breeze to bring its travellers any cool relief, instead, it only carried fragments of melodies from the minstrels within the city.

The gentle touch of the wind on Ayse's face was as warm as the breath from her own body, and she pulled at her blouse in a vain attempt of cooling herself somewhat. Dust arose in spiralling eddies from the sand strewn path like dancing spirits. The bustling city of Brankah had always been a place of festivities and commerce. It was built upon the crossroads of popular travel routes, and as such, the city had thrived under the constant arrival of travellers and merchants from all over the continent.

As Ayse reached the portcullis, she was confronted with stone-faced guards that were inspecting every traveller that entered the city. Ayse brought her horse to a stop as she stood beneath the main gate, allowing a guard to circle around her and inspect what little belongings she carried. He didn't bother to ask any questions and swiftly waved her on, already looking past her to the next wayfarer.

The chatter and noise of the city quickly became more audible as Ayse moved from the outskirts of the city and deeper into the market districts. Brankah had not changed since she had last visited; its streets were full to bursting point with all manner of people from merchants to conjurers. She dismounted at an inn, passing the stable hand the reins of her horse and a silver coin in one single hand movement.

Meandering through the maze of stalls, Ayse listened to the back and forth between vendors and customers. The hubbub of the city was a comfort after months of spending most of her time alone on the road. She had spent the last of the summer travelling to different cities and towns, using her less than honourable talents of pickpocketing and thievery to keep herself fed and warm. However, she could never stay long in any place where she was actively pilfering from the townspeople, and so she would continue travelling onwards to her next destination.

Contracts for thefts and information gathering had been thin on the ground of late, and so she had come to the one place where she knew she would find work that paid well. The autumn was well under way, and once winter hit it would be even harder to get by without real work. Ayse's plan was to stay close to Brankah, taking contracts as they came in, before finally moving onto greener pastures once the spring arrived in earnest.

Ayse branched down a side alley, the crowds of people thinning as she approached the Rubah District, the shadier underbelly of Brankah. The darkness seemed to thrive in such ill-mannered places. The shadows here were deeper and more mysterious than those in the rest of the city, almost as if the very surroundings were warning lost amblers to hurry onwards. Here the red of the buildings had become more of an unclean brown as a result of neglect. The structures all bore dirty and unkempt appearances, adding to the overall threatening atmosphere.

She stopped beneath the wooden sign of a tavern that was creaking in the slight wind. The battered plaque hanging above the door had seen better days, but she could still distinguish the words 'The Black Sheep' above an engraving that could arguably have been a goat more than a sheep. The tavern may easily have been mistaken as closed, as from a distance it looked as grim and abandoned as all the surrounding buildings. However, Ayse knew better than that. Peering closer she saw a dim glow through the darkened windows, the thick layer of grime upon the pane making it impossible to see inside clearly. She pushed open the large door, allowing an audible scraping sound to escape from the object as if in protest of being used.

The interior was even shadier than that of the building's exterior. A cloud of tobacco smoke engulfed the bar like a summoned mist, entrapping all the patrons in its soft embrace. All the lamps were dimmed beneath thick stained-glass cases, muting the overall lighting of the room. Most of the bar was bustling with drunken and chatty characters, juxtaposing the limits of the room where in the darkened recesses of the alcoves, groups of people huddled together and spoke in low whispers.

These people were not your average carousers. Although some seemed beyond any semblance of sobriety, all were individuals with a talent for appearing harmless, yet being fully functional should there be any sign of trouble. Their sharpened senses and heightened awareness were of a calibre that only thieves, frauds, and assassins possessed.

Ayse walked with feigned carelessness towards the nearest empty stall and took a seat. She didn't have to wait too long for the owner of the bar to approach her and take the seat that faced her own. He was a rounded figure of a man, his chubby cheeks and dancing bright eyes gave him the appearance of a friendly neighbour, but Ayse knew that hidden in the faded velveteen jacket that barely covered his mid-drift were daggers, poisons, and other deadly instruments. More than one unlucky patron who had wronged this man had received a tainted pint and drank their last inside the walls of The Black Sheep. The man placed a glass in front of her that brimmed with the customary house ale. It brought a wry smile to her lips as she considered his past reputation.

"It has been too long, Ayse," he greeted her with a warm smile. "You wouldn't believe the lack of talent we've had traipsing in here looking for work!"

Horace was a very animated man, his hands always waving wildly to embellish his tales. Ayse smiled warmly at him, he was one of the few people that she had continued to see on a somewhat regular basis in the past few years. She was very fond of the eccentric barkeep; he had proven to be an invaluable source of work and advice, and she considered him with the same regard as she would a dear uncle.

It was no secret that Horace favoured Ayse and gave her the lion's share of the good contracts when she was in town. While most people could safely assume it was due to Ayse's unparalleled talents, Ayse knew that the friendly man before her doted on her because he considered her to be as close to him as his own kin.

"Well then, there must be some jobs that are still in need of a suitable candidate?" Ayse enquired, sipping from the beverage before her.

"Indeed, there are." Horace shifted casually in his seat while his eyes quickly darted about the room to ensure there were no eavesdroppers. "However, they will have to wait as your assistance appears to be required elsewhere. A couple arrived a few weeks ago asking after you. They will hire *only* you. It is apparently a very delicate job."

"Delicate as in...?" Ayse was intrigued; she raised an eyebrow at Horace as she asked him, "Who were they?"

"Haven't a clue. They wouldn't divulge any information to me," he sniffed, clearly offended at this.

As the go-to man for hiring candidates such as Ayse, Horace clearly felt his position warranted a certain amount of trust and knowledge on the matters at hand. "Rather secretive couple, if I do say so myself, and *that* is saying something. Big strapping lad and a little woman. I'd bet good money they're gypsy folk. You can find them in Daringer's Square pedalling their tricks. They set up camp there the moment they learned you weren't around and have been raking in the coins ever since, waiting for your arrival."

Ayse didn't want to seem too eager to leave, but curiosity had begun to burn deep within her.

"Intriguing," she mused, her mind was already beginning to wander. "It's always nice to arrive to a welcoming party."

"Quite." Horace's restless hands began to play with the crumbs on the tabletop before settling on a splinter of wood that protruded from the table edge, picking at it with too much interest than necessary. He had been quick enough to see the flicker in Ayse's eyes as he had spoken to her, but when he finally realised that she would not be sharing her thoughts, he decided to continue on, "If this job is indeed... desirable, then let me know if you need any help, with equipment and the like."

His eyes fell on her, stern and unwavering. The flat line of his mouth gave his face a grim expression that was unusual for Horace. Ayse could not tell whether he was more perturbed by the fact that he was not a part of the mystery, or by the clientele that were offering it. Even the worst of Brankah shared the same stigma as the rest of the population that gypsies were untrustworthy and strange, the lowest form of travelling riffraff.

Ayse was sure she knew her guests based on his description. They hailed from the Vulpini tribe and she knew those particular gypsies better than any other outsider ever could. However, she had grown so accustomed over the years to the stereotype that people held of gypsies to even bother trying to object to the opinions of others any longer. Horace arose from the table, briefly putting his hand on her shoulder in a somewhat affectionate manner as he passed by her.

Ayse stayed awhile longer to make it appear as if she had at least made a decent effort to finish her drink, before embarking onto the streets of Brankah once more. Daringer's Square was one of the busiest parts of the city and, therefore, one of the best places for street entertainers to make the most money. Fortunately, it was easy to spot the couple she was looking for, as they were drawing the biggest crowd as a result of their impressive tricks. Ayse began to work her way through the large assembly of people to where the couple had set up their performance.

Everyone was deeply engrossed in the act before them, thrilled and delighted by the impossibilities that they were being confronted with. Ayse knew the act they were performing well; it was one of the main specialities of the Vulpini tribe whenever they plied their trade as conjurors or entertainers. Only one trade of many, after all, it was they who had taught Ayse her impressive thievery skills.

Vulpini children were taught from a very young age the delicacies of lock-picking, pickpocketing and more. As Ayse had been raised by the Vulpini tribe since she was a babe, she too had been afforded this special schooling to ensure she could make a living, even if it was a dishonest one.

The gypsy couple wore brightly coloured tunics that alternated between orange and white on the sleeves, bodices, and trousers, like that of a court jester's smock, but without the garish bells. No one in the tribe had ever liked the awful outfits, but it was a cliché costume that gave them the comical and friendly appearance that was expected of them when they presented themselves as performers.

Ayse watched Reuben, he didn't seem to have changed much in appearance or performance. The man was tall with sun-bronzed skin, his tousled blonde hair plastered to the side of his face from sweat as he juggled and spun, cavorting for the paying customers. His partner, a woman named Nell, was far more petite and slenderer; her size and playful manner leading many to believe she was much younger than she was. Nell's hair was a crimson shock of red, a common trait within the tribe.

Ayse remained unknown to the players as she stayed hidden in the captive crowd, continuing to watch their display with a pained familiarity. Reuben was rather flamboyantly helping Nell into an ornate wooden trunk with slit-like air holes.

After the locks were set, Reuben circled the trunk tapping the sides and top of the case with his knuckles to show that there was no way of Nell finding freedom from the container. As the trunk was placed on top of the hard-cobbled paving of the square, it ruled out any possible escape route from a trap door hidden in the base. Already a murmur was travelling through the crowd like a wave, gossipers guessing how the trick would play out, or speculating as to how it would be done.

Reuben stalked over to his prop baggage and withdrew a slim yet deadly blade. Its appearance was rewarded by gasps and further whispering from the audience. The sword was passed around the front row of the crowd, those that received it testing the authenticity of the weapon, checking that the metal didn't bend, break, or somehow disappear into the hilt. Ayse knew that this exaggerated showmanship was important in giving Nell the time needed to prepare for her part of the performance.

When it was once again in the hands of Reuben, he proceeded to walk over to the trunk and, without warning, he plunged it into the case, straight through one of the carved slits. The crowd held their breath, but there was no scream from within the trunk.

Immediately, the more arrogant customers decided that a small thing like Nell could have stuffed herself to one side of the trunk, avoiding the blade entirely. Accusations flew from the crowd, but Reuben was unperturbed, with a knowing smile he pulled the sword back out, gave an elaborate flick of the wrist and once again the weapon protruded from the case. This time, the blade went clean through the centre, buried in the casing up to its hilt. It was impossible for any person to dodge in such a confined space, even the slight figure of Nell.

The crowd fell into a stunned silence, the void of noise grew as people stared wide-eyed and mouth agape at each other. Before any alarm or notion of foul play could even be conceived, Reuben directed their attention back to the trick by withdrawing the blade and holding it aloft to reveal the lack of blood stain on the burnished metal.

Sighs of relief and hushed talk erupted amongst the audience, some even started to clap as they believed the trick to be finished. The applause only stopped when one viewer who felt tricked began demanding to see the woman inside the trunk once more. Obligingly, Reuben unlatched the trunk and flipped the lid. At that exact moment, Nell stood up and bowed with a flourish to the cheers of the astonished people of Brankah.

"Do you want more?" Nell shouted to the energetic crowd who responded with roars and cheers, excessively throwing shining coins towards the open pouch set before the performance area.

The shimmering mass of clinking metal rain fell to the floor, many of the coins missing the pouch entirely, and rolling all about the paving stones in a musical shower. With a dazzling smile, Nell resumed her position huddled in the trunk while her accomplice assisted in securing it once more. There was more bravado from Reuben to work the crowd and to allow Nell some time to prepare. Reuben then unlatched the case and lifted it to his chest with less effort than most would have deemed necessary, before flipping it over and completely upending the contents onto the floor in a white and orange blur.

Nell was gone. Only her clothes remained. There was another pause in the crowd, even some of the people passing by had stopped to stare speechlessly at the finale of the trick. The pile of tawdry fabric twitched and stirred into life. A black-nosed muzzle sniffing the air emerged from beneath an orange sleeve, followed by two golden unblinking eyes that stared at the stunned audience. Ayse took a moment to observe and enjoy the shocked faces of the crowd. It made her smile to think how the reality of the trick would completely astound them, considering how dumbfounded they were now in their ignorance. Sometimes the simplest explanation was the correct one, no matter how impossible it seemed.

The creature pounced from its nest to reveal itself, causing the crowd to rupture into applause once more. Ayse could already hear the onlookers discussing how Reuben could have possibly swapped Nell with a fox without any of them seeing it happen. However, they would never figure it out because Ayse knew for a fact that no exchange had been made. The fox that was skipping about amidst the new shower of silver, balancing on its hind legs and yipping in such a cavalier manner to please the crowd *was* Nell.

The whole of the Vulpini tribe were shapeshifters with the ability to transform into the guise of a fox. They were a very secretive people, forced to hide their true nature due to fear of persecution. Like other gypsies, the Vulpini were a travelling community that journeyed the length and breadth of Nevraah all year round. They made their money by hiring out their tribe members to those in need of thieves or spies, as well as their own small cons and tricks when they visited towns and cities.

No one outside of the tribe knew their secret, no one except Ayse that was. Ayse's childhood with the Vulpini brought her some pleasant memories, and although times were not always easy, she still appreciated every day that she had spent with them. The Vulpini had not only taught her all the skills that she had needed in life, as well as her professional expertise, but they had taught her the self-control and understanding of her own nature. However, Ayse was not a fox shifter like the others in the tribe — she was a werewolf.

Ayse knew how fortunate she was to have been taken in by the tribe. She couldn't even comprehend what it would have been like for someone of a shifting nature to come to terms with what they were alone.

Unfortunately, with the passing of the old chief, a new tribal leader had been elected, Solomon. He was a severe character who was hard and practical. He had decided that once Ayse was old enough to fend for herself, she would be cast out from the tribe. He was a firm believer that the fox shifters should keep with their own kind, and consequently no other races could be a part of their culture.

Only the females of the tribe could have fleeting relations with humans, as the risk of Vulpini men impregnating outsiders and revealing the tribe's secret was too great. Shifter blood was so dominant that a fox cub would be a guaranteed result for any human-shifter relations. However, although the Vulpini lifestyle afforded a casual approach to intimacies, the women were not allowed to marry outside of the tribe.

Ayse's eviction did not warrant much opposition from the tribe as many considered her a troublemaker simply due to her being a werewolf. Ayse had been part of only a small group of friends, and the only father figure she had ever known was Wilamir, the old chief. With his passing, she had lost everything. Although not all the Vulpini had been welcoming to her, it had been all she had ever known and setting out alone had been a daunting task at first.

One of the older tribesmen, Rojas, had taken her from the tribe after her goodbyes were made. Though he didn't have to, he had travelled with her for a while and showed her the best places to find contractual work, introduced her to individuals in various towns that could help her replenish her equipment, and showed her how to fend for herself on the open road. Those weeks with Rojas had been gruelling, but necessary. Suddenly, she had become a pupil to Rojas's life lessons in surviving as a loner.

Ayse had heard whispers of Rojas before she had truly grown to know him. He took the most prominent contracts the tribe were given, sometimes taking him away from the Vulpini for years at a time. He had fought in civil wars, travelled to some of the furthest places and back, always being celebrated on his return for bringing in large payments and great honour. But now Ayse realised how lonely he must have been out on his own all those times, and she was even more grateful that he was choosing to share his experiences with her.

That was one of the hardest lessons, as a Vulpini member there had been safety in numbers, but now she was alone. Though it was tempting to take up with like-minded travellers she met, Rojas warned her of the dangers of not only trusting strangers, but also about how easily her secret could be mistakenly revealed by journeying with non-shifters. After all, her ability to shift was one of her key talents. It allowed her to hunt for food, travel inconspicuously and she could defend herself better. Those traits would be a big loss in the name of companionship.

Rojas taught her to save her campfires for the coldest nights only and to keep them small and easy to extinguish when she did. He taught her to treat her food and key tools such as lock picks as a precious commodity that she should be frugal with, more so than money. On the open road, she could travel days without seeing another town or village and the gold in her pocket would not fill her stomach. Being a gypsy, gold didn't even guarantee you an inn room on the stormy nights any way, but a lock pick could get you shelter in any town.

During her travels, Ayse had never met another shifter and had never even known of any werewolves at all in her lifetime, at least that she knew of. When shifters were in human form they smelt like any other normal person, and when she was in human form, she lost all her extraordinary heightened wolf senses to be able to scent out others of her kind. She had asked the Vulpini about her own ancestry, but werewolves were as much of a mystery to the foxes as shifters were to the outside world. All that was known was that werewolves were rumoured to come from the northern country of Oror, were wolves were native. Considering that the northern neighbouring country was not exactly a hospitable place to southerners, Ayse had never even considered discovering her roots.

The crowd began to disperse, and Reuben began to collect the money and clear away the props as Nell disappeared to shift back into her human form. As the corner of the square emptied, Reuben caught sight of Ayse and flashed a wide toothy grin at her. She returned the sentiment with a warm smile, but deep inside of her she felt a cold weight that she hoped would soon be lifted as her mind raced with unanswered questions as to why they had sought her out.

Chapter Two

The moon was out in full magnitude; its white body being caressed by the passing clouds. The heavens were dark and secretive, with only fragments of starlit night sky peering out from between the veil. Ayse felt uneasy. The evening was eerie enough to cause her to shudder even when the cold night air could not. Before her lay an ancient oak wood that stretched as far as the eye could see. The black silhouette of the bare trees against the moon conjured up memories of being read frightening stories as a child. Their branches reaching upwards like gnarled hands with twisted fingers that clawed at the sublime vision of the moon.

She had finally reached the end of the flatbeds, the plains that were the outermost limits of Nevraah. The weather had turned fouler as she had travelled and now it truly felt like winter's arrival was imminent. The dark mass of trees that marked the border stood before her like ominous guardians of the north. She imagined numerous eyes watching her from the darkness, waiting for her to step foot on their land before they struck. A breeze whispered out from between the trees and she lifted her nose to reassure herself that there were no enemies secretly lying in wait. Standing before the impressive ancient forest, Ayse recalled the pleading faces of her Vulpini companions as they had begged the impossible of her, "Go north".

Oror was unknown territory. There was not one southerner that had ever stepped foot north of the border and returned. Nevraahn soldiers told tales of borderline skirmishes with the fearsome northerners; warriors who were well trained, ruthless and incredibly territorial. The lack of information that

Nevraah held about Oror was a testament to how exceptionally capable the northerners were of defending their own. Yet here Ayse was, about to tempt their wrath by stepping foot on their land.

Again, Reuben and Nell's pale faces flashed before her eyes. Reuben had squirmed under her gaze at first; uncomfortable with the news he had been made to bear. Ayse should have known by the way Nell's lip had quivered when she had spoken that there was something amiss with her old friends. But she had been too preoccupied with the way they had begun their tale to notice the couple's peculiar behaviour. They told her how they had been instructed to find her by Chief Solomon.

Reuben had sighed and fidgeted uncomfortably as he had explained. "The chief believes you owe the tribe for all the years that we looked after you. Not that that is by any means the belief of everyone within the tribe, we all know Chief Wilamir would turn in his grave at the thought, but nevertheless, it stands as his reason."

Ayse's temper had risen, voices were raised, but her anger had abated quickly when the full account of why the tribe sought her so desperately was made known to her.

"Six of the tribe have been held captive by Duke Remus since the beginning of the summer. They were on a job that we thought would be pretty straightforward... but the client had lied somewhat about the high-risk nature of the assignment." Reuben leaned back in his chair with his arms folded across his chest. "The duke means business, Ayse. When we tried to free our people, he killed one of them. The remaining five have been moved to an unknown location. After the last fiasco, the chief would not even risk another attempt to get them out."

Ayse had felt a knot twist in her stomach, she had never expected such a turn of events. The Vulpini were like smoke evading a grasping hand, they could never be caught, or so they had always presumed. A dozen questions had sprung to her mind; what had they been asked to steal? Who was the client? What had gone wrong? But there was only one question that had formed on her lips – "Who was it?"

Reuben had leaned forward, his hands going to his forehead before sweeping his hair from his face. His fingers rested on his temples as if he were suffering from an acute headache. His eyebrows were furrowed and the lines around his eyes and mouth were accentuated by the shadowed room they had convened in, making him suddenly appear older than he really was. He was unable to answer.

"It was Paya," Nell whispered sadly.

Paya. That one name sent flashes of memories through Ayse's mind. A happy go lucky character, Paya had been blessed with beautiful blonde curls that had framed her ever-smiling angelic rounded face. But now the world would never be gifted with Paya's smile again. Once the prisoners had been relocated after her execution, no amount of digging had uncovered their new location in Bremlor.

The Vulpini tribe was no stranger to tragedy. Many of the tribe were lost on various contracts, some presumably killed in fox form and not even given a proper burial. It was just a sad, but accepted, facet of their life that the way in which they earned their coin brought with it certain risks. However, no Vulpini had ever been captured and kept alive before. Their imprisonment risked exposing the tribe's dual nature and could potentially cause the normal folk to hunt their kind down like the world had never seen before. Ayse could easily imagine how it would currently be tearing their community apart.

"He'll release them at a price." Reuben had told her, pausing as he raised his head, his tearful eyes meeting hers. "The area in which they were apprehended was under maximum security, so the duke was intrigued as to how they had even entered such a place-" Ayse's mouth fell open as if she were about to interject but Reuben waved his hands to stop her, reassuring her as he spoke, "He doesn't know our secret. I guess that's one small blessing, when you take everything into consideration. Because we were able to infiltrate the duke's estate, he believes we can gain access to somewhere equally, if not more notoriously difficult to reach." There was another pause as Reuben cast a quick sideways glance to Nell before continuing. "The chief believes that you will be more capable of achieving this than anyone else."

And so that was how Ayse had found herself staring into the unknown. After all, who was better equipped to sneak into Oror than a werewolf? The many weeks it had taken to journey to the border had felt brief, but she knew that was only because she had been distracted, her mind consumed with doubt and fear of the expedition that she was undertaking. She had zigzagged along the border line, avoiding areas occupied by Nevraahn soldiers, until she had finally found a safe place to cross the flatbeds. Ayse had left all her belongings and her horse with Reuben and Nell in the city of Brankah, choosing to depart under the cover of darkness in wolf form.

As a wolf, she could travel light, eat when needed from what the land offered, while also having the perceptive senses that her canine body afforded her. The plan was to rendezvous with her old Vulpini kin in Brankah on her return. However, thinking of this just caused Ayse's stomach to twist with dread as she considered how unlikely a return journey would be. The churning knot in her belly made her regret her last meal of plains hare, even if the hunt had been a welcome distraction from what lay ahead.

The dukes of Nevraah had united to form an alliance headed by Duke Howell. Sick of battling over the border; they planned to take Oror by force. Duke Remus had requested that the Vulpini obtain information that would guarantee a successful assault on the north, as well as expanding their knowledge of the enemy.

The lives of the Vulpini were dangling on the thin thread of hope that with Ayse being a werewolf, she would be their best chance at infiltrating the north. Wolves were native to Oror and, legend said that werewolves once roamed the cold country. The odds were stacked against her, she looked and talked like a southerner and knew nothing about the north, but she had no other choice. With a sudden burst of energy, she propelled herself forward, maintaining a hurried spring to her gait as she breached the line of trees and entered the northern territory of Oror.

The earthy smell of the damp woodland surroundings filled her nostrils, her ears swivelled at the sound of prey in the distance, while movement in her peripheral vision caused her to start only for her to realise it was a stray leaf falling to the forest floor.

Ayse knew that she needed to calm herself before her nerves got the better of her. She stopped to compose herself, crouching low to the ground and closing her eyes to take in all her surroundings by scent and hearing alone. She shifted her paws in the dirt, feeling the earth stir beneath her, and when her heartbeat slowed to a steady pulse, she took off with silent speed, keeping her senses trained on every little thing around her.

The further north Ayse travelled, the more she enjoyed the freedom of the forest. She would snap playfully at every rabbit that fated to fall into her path before pelting onwards. Ayse found that the ground was increasingly on an incline and she was sure that before long the region would become more mountainous and rockier, making it harder for her to navigate.

***

Her journey further into Oror had brought great change to her surroundings. It was colder and her breath arose in a steamy cloud of fog before her. Frost could be seen clinging to the trees, crowning the branches with glistening adornments, and further on she even saw snow sheltered between large roots that had escaped the confinements of the ground. Ayse had never felt so far from the more moderate climate of Nevraah, where even in winter snowfall was seldom seen.

This new land intrigued Ayse and it brought even more excitement for her to watch it thrive in the daytime. She had been roused that morning as the birds awoke, heralding the new dawn with their song. She caught glimpses of regal stags and deer wandering proudly through the trees, completely oblivious to her. The urge to chase them was tempting as she watched their sleek forms pass by.

The forest remained dense and enclosing, yet rock began to mark the terrain more often. Granite protruded from the earth covered in moss and creeping ferns. A couple of times Ayse had come across well-worn paths, and although she caught no scent of any recent activity, she chose not to linger long near the trails, instead moving back into the thick of the wood so as not to risk being seen by anyone.

Ayse could feel herself tiring once again. Hunger had set in and her stomach was rather audibly making itself known to her. As the sunlight dimmed, so did her fortune, as the deer had since become scarce. She picked up rabbit tracks as the sunlight wavered in the sky, giving way to the evening and prompting Ayse to begin the thrill of the hunt. The night had a penetrating chill to it and the cold air brought with it a damp that hung around the foliage creating an even deeper primal earthy scent.

Hunger and excitement burned within Ayse, her mind was overcome by the wolf within her and her thoughts were focused solely on her prey. Driven by instinct, Ayse enjoyed letting her inner nature take over, she forgot her worldly worries and all that mattered was the here and now of the chase. The experience was exhilarating and liberating.

She could feel the blood pumping throughout her agile body. Her ears were flat against her head as she raced forwards while her nose stayed trained to the scent of the rabbit. The night seemed still and silent as she slowed to a stop and crouched low to the ground on the outskirts of a small clearing. There, she could see the rabbit on its haunches, as quiet and motionless as the night around it. Its beady eye glinted in the moonlight and Ayse could see the quick twitch of its nose. She could feel the saliva building within her mouth. She let her jaw hang slack and her tongue lolled out as she inhaled deeply, preparing herself for the finale. As the rabbit turned away from her, apparently content that it was alone, she moved.

She barrelled into the rabbit with such ferocity that she ended up close to the other side of the clearing by the time she had stopped. The large rabbit was clamped securely within her jaws, its body still twitching and writhing as its life drained from it. As she flopped leisurely to the ground with her kill, her nostrils flared, and she froze. As she scanned the area around her, the thought crossed her mind that the rabbit had been in her position not that long ago.

Suddenly the small clearing felt too open, she felt vulnerable and threatened. Tentatively Ayse raised her nose to the air. She was not the only predator that had been following the trace of the rabbit. It was a scent like her own, yet somehow different. A mixed breeze reached her, and her heart quickened. There was more than one of them.

The moonlight moved within the clearing and the glint of an eye in the darkness was all she needed to begin picking out the figure of a wolf. Undoubtedly, there were more around her, camouflaged in the shadowed forest. She dropped the limp form of the rabbit and remained close to the ground so as not to appear aggressive, yet ready to defend herself should they attack. Her heart began to pound within her chest; she had been careless in her hunt. The north had enthralled her with its new surroundings, and she had let herself run free, forgetting the peril she was in.

She watched as the wolf cautiously moved forwards, it sniffed the air as if examining her kill from afar. The wolf stopped and eyed her once more; there was no challenge to its gaze, only curiosity. Ayse slowly stood, the rabbit abandoned at her feet, but still the wolf made no move. Its pale eyes were bright and intelligent, yet Ayse felt they were lacking in some quality that she couldn't quite place. It reminded her of when she had encountered other animals in her wolf form.

As soon as she realised this, she knew that these were not werewolves before her; they were her first encounter with real wolves. She couldn't help but admire the beauty of the beast. She had seen her own reflection before, but seeing another wolf in the flesh, a truly wild wolf, was completely breath-taking for her. It felt like she had found some long-lost connection somehow. The wolf was larger than her, his coat a darker shade and his shaggy fur mane was untamed, yet regal at the same time. While admiring the beauty of the fierce and proud creature in front of her, it struck Ayse that wolves were surely the epitome of the north.

The wolf seemed as inquisitive about her as she was about it, but when she moved towards it trying to maintain a passive stance, it turned and fled, disappearing into the night without making a sound. She made no attempt at following the wolf, it would only have been perceived as hostility, and she did not want to pick a fight with the local pack, especially when they outnumbered her.

It was not an unfamiliar scene. Any animals that she or the Vulpini tribe had encountered in the past were the same. Even though the Vulpini fox shifters smelt similar, wild animals knew that they were not the same. Although some animals could be curious, most regarded the shifters as a threat and quickly left. Ayse had known Vulpini members that had experimented with this strange occurrence, trying to see if and how they could establish themselves with real fox skulks, but to no avail.

Alone once more, Ayse collected her rabbit from the forest floor and moved into the protection of the trees to eat it. The meal was sobering; the elation of the hunt and her meeting with the wolf had passed, leaving her to reflect on the reality of the situation that loomed before her.

As the north was uncharted territory for the people of Nevraah, Ayse had no clue in which direction she should head to try and accomplish her task and so thus far she had continued due north, hoping to chance upon some type of settlement as a starting point. As she swallowed the last of her rabbit, the first signs of snow fall began, small snowflakes drifting in spirals and delicately landing wherever they fell to dissolve into nothingness. One settled on Ayse's nose with a faint cold tingle before she instinctively licked it away.

Somehow her respite had made her feel even more tired than before, all the adrenaline within her had dissipated and she suddenly felt exhausted. As the snow continued, Ayse decided to find shelter for the night. She casually loped through the woodland, the snow falling ever thicker and faster, blanketing the world around her in perfect white. She continually shook her head to dislodge snow from her ears, snorting and sneezing as the flurry of snow attacked her senses. Inhaling the snow stung her throat and nostrils and she longed for shelter and warmth.

It wasn't long before Ayse found what she was looking for as she came across a rocky outcrop that had a small hollowed cavity at its base. It was just large enough to house her for the night; the space was reasonably dry, safe, and sheltered from the relentless weather. She shivered and shook, dislodging as much snow from her coat as possible, before creeping in and curling into a small ball.

Ayse lay with her face buried in her tail, keeping her nose warm from the cold night air. Above the bushy fur of her tail, she could see the growing blizzard raging outside of her hiding place. As she watched the snowstorm, she could feel her eyelids drooping. The repetitive fall of the snow lazily falling diagonally through the air had a hypnotising and calming effect. Sleep crept up on her in the same way she had stalked her own prey earlier that evening; darkness overcame her without her even realising it.

***

Low grumbling and throaty growls reached Ayse's keen ears, harshly pulling her from her sleep with fevered panic. It was still dark outside, but due to the season Ayse could not tell how long she had been asleep for. She could hear no bird calls on the air and safely assumed that she had only slept for a few hours at most. The snuffling amongst the snow continued outside and an agitated deep-throated exhale made her realise the sounds were getting closer.

Sheltered as she was, Ayse was unable to catch the wind to identify the intruder by scent. She knew that it was not the northern wolves returning, whatever it was sounded larger and had a deeper tone to its voice. She slowly crept forwards, her belly brushing against the ground and peered out. The tempest had ceased, yet only a small distance away the white snow was marred with large tracks that criss-crossed all over the place, constantly backtracking on themselves as if searching for something. A large brown bear lumbered into view and Ayse hastily retreated into the shadows.

The bear looked agitated, sniffing the air and ground continuously whilst moaning to itself. She knew that it could smell her; it just hadn't found her den yet. Ayse had only encountered bears a couple of times in her life whilst travelling near the Gustafrik Mountains; she would never forget the beasts. These brutes were strong enough to break a dog's back with one swipe of their paw and were faster on their feet than their lurching, ambling gait led anyone to believe. Bears did not hunt wolves, but they were incredibly territorial.

Ayse realised that in her hasty search for shelter, she had most likely stumbled into the bear's territory and somewhere it had picked up her scent, considered her a threat, and had sought her out. Generally, bears rested more often during the winter; however, she remembered warnings from the mountaineers of Gustafrik that you should never be fooled by a sleeping bear in winter. Many a man had met his fate by assuming bears were not a threat in the harshest season, only to find that getting too close to a hibernating bear could end in tragedy.

The bear was getting closer and closer, it was only a matter of minutes before it would pinpoint her location. Although the hole was too small for the bear, no doubt with the bear's longer reaching arms an investigating paw would find Ayse and do some serious damage. She knew that she had no choice, before long the bear would be upon her and it would be too late to run, she had to act now while she still had a chance.

She darted out of the cover of the rocks and began to run away from the direction of the bear as fast as her paws could carry her. Her muscles immediately ached, the trek had been too long and her rest too little. The cramped condition of the rocky crevice and the cold had caused her legs to seize up and the sudden exertion was painful.

Noticing her escape, the bear let out a drawn-out, yawning roar and gave chase, charging after her at full speed. She could hear it crashing through the undergrowth behind her, snorting and grunting with its own laboured efforts. Ayse was not accustomed to running through deep snow, and she found that the bear was quickly gaining ground on her. She darted through trees and veered off randomly to lose her attacker or confuse it, but all she managed to achieve was to disorientate herself, making her unsure whether she had doubled back on herself in her panic. She could feel the bear's thunderous pace through the earth beneath her paws, the whole world around them seemed to be vibrating with their chase. The bear tackled trees as it tried to catch her, forcing snow from the tree boughs on impact and sending showers of ice to the forest floor.

The trees scattered out, ending suddenly without warning, and Ayse found herself at the edge of a verge with a steep twenty-foot fall to the ground below. She skidded to a halt, snow cascading in a flurry as she slipped and slid onto her side. Straining to get to her feet quickly, she saw the bear was almost upon her. As she turned to run, the bear swung out at her with a heavy blow of its paw, catching Ayse on her hindquarters and sending her flying towards the edge of the ridge. She yelped in pain as the bear's claws raked through her flesh, and unable to stop herself she tumbled over the rock face, half-rolling, half-crashing to the ground below.

Her head was pounding, and her body was crying out to her that it was injured in a dozen different places, but the groans of the bear on the verge above her held all her attention. She shook her head, as if trying to shake away the aching pain and confusion and watched for a moment as the bear tested the rock edge with its forepaws, seeing if it could follow Ayse down to the lower ground. It grunted and began to make its way along the ridge looking for a way down.

Ayse didn't want to waste any more time, as she stood up one of her back legs gave way and she knew that she had no hope of outrunning the bear now. She had to escape quickly before the bear managed to find its way to her. Gingerly testing how much weight she could place on her damaged limb, she limped off hurriedly, whilst desperately trying to ignore the agonising pain torturing her body as she forced it to move.

The pain was fogging Ayse's mind, her body was becoming numb to everything around her and her footing was awkward and uneven, causing her to stagger and step into deep snow drifts. All the while, she feared her pursuer; all surrounding sounds were drowned out by the noise of her own throbbing heartbeat that echoed within her ears. She blundered through the forest in panic, not even thinking —just reacting. She staggered onwards knowing that she had to keep going forward to save herself.

Ayse felt the snow shift beneath her paw more than usual, an audible crack resonated through the air, like the quick flick of a whip the noise defogged her mind instantly. Her breath caught on her lips and she felt her eyes go wide as her thoughts raced to catch up with what had just happened. The scent of blood and iron reached her nose, agonising pain was spreading through her back leg, and she felt bile rise in her throat as she saw the jagged metal teeth of the bear trap biting through her skin and raking at her bone.

The ground around her was already turning crimson, the crisp white snow succumbing to the warmth and colour of her blood. She considered shifting but feeling the metal grate and jar against her bone was warning enough for her to remain still. Not to mention, her naked human body would not last long within this climate.

There was no time for panicking, or further consideration on how to get herself out of her predicament, Ayse's body was already giving in to the fatigue and pain. The cold air suddenly seemed to strike her deeper, and with each passing moment the world was caving in around her. The snow felt somewhat soothing as she slowly lowered her body to the ground, unable to hold herself up any longer. Ayse's vision began to tunnel in on itself, the trees in front of her seemingly stretching further and further away from her, until they blended into the darkness completely.

✱✱✱

Disembodied voices floated to her through the fog of her mind. Some of the words were lost amongst her fractured consciousness as the pain rolled across her body in waves. With each sharp ache that hit her, the darkness threatened to swallow her whole once more and leave her in silence.

"...surprised she even had the strength to howl."

"...a bad omen for the Wolfriks..." one muttered.

The shock of sudden vibrations through her body caused her to heave and inhale deeply, the smell of humans filling her nostrils. She tried to open her eyes, but she was unable to do so. It was as useless as trying to awake from a nightmare, her lids felt heavy and her body would not respond to her in its frozen state. Someone was tapping the trap that still held her leg and the agony was unbearable. Ayse could hear herself whimpering before her brain had even registered that she was the one making the noise.

"This bitch is lucky that the trap's seen better days, it could have broken clean through that bone."

Ayse tried to force herself awake once more; her eyelids fluttered sending bright, painful flashes into her vision, but ultimately, she failed to rouse herself. She could feel the call of the mist that filled her mind beckoning her back into unconsciousness; the voices were fading into oblivion once more as she slipped away from the world. Ayse knew she should be panicking, but she just felt numb.

"...out of her misery..."

A myriad of thoughts blazed through Ayse's mind, the Vulpini, then poor Paya... Would she be waiting in what lay beyond the mortal realm? Her last sobering thought was for herself, selfish, yet human. *I want to live.*

Chapter Three

Ayse's world lay in shadows. Her whole body was bathed in a halo of pain and she felt as if death stood before her, waiting just on the other side of the veil of life for her to give in. Her throat was dry, and she could feel her swollen tongue, numb and lifeless, as it lay in her bottom jaw. There was pressure on her muzzle, and she had a constant dull ache in her skull. Her whole body felt heavy, as if she had been weighed down with stones in the tide, unable to resurface. She struggled to move but a heavy hand clamped down on her to restrain her. Ayse flicked her eyes open in alarm.

"Easy, girl," a man said, his accent was unfamiliar to her and his voice was gruff from age.

Ayse's eyesight was blurry. She waited for her vision to focus, but the dizzying feeling continued. She was laid out on her side on a reed mat and she could feel the warmth of a brazier at her back. Someone was beside her, he smelt of dogs, sweat, and ale, but she couldn't move her head to see who he was. There was another hidden from her also; she could smell him somewhere else out of her line of sight.

Her muzzle was bound with rope and in front of her was a bowl of water, herbs, and bloodied cloth. She inhaled deeply, the sharp scent of the spices stinging her nostrils, but not enough to mask the smell of her own blood that stained the rags before her. Once she had stopped wriggling, the man beside her moved his hand to her belly and she let out a raspy growl from her parched throat.

"Calm down," he said as he patted her gently, before continuing his examination. "Well, you won't have a whelping bitch on your hands, that's for sure. Pity really, it would have been really nice to have some wolf pups to train."

"I don't think the dogs would appreciate having wolves in their midst," the other responded, he sounded younger than the first man.

"More like the wolves wouldn't take kindly to the dogs and rip their throats out," the older man chuckled. Ayse heard a scuffle as he leaned forward and then she could hear him pulling something that sent movement to her neck — she was chained and collared. "She's very weak, but while she's chained, I'd say you'd be safe without binding her muzzle as she needs to keep hydrated, but don't take too many chances. She's a wild one, after all."

"The men think we should have ended her when we found her."

The dog-scented man sighed. "That depends on your outlook. If I found a dog out in the street in this condition, I probably would have put it out of its misery. But, if it were one of my dogs, well, I can tell you that I have done, and would do again, pretty much everything I can to nurse it back. Dogs are loyal; the least you can do is give them the same loyalty."

"She's no dog."

"She's certainly not that. She's a beauty, though. I wonder how the hell she ended up so close to camp. Wolves stick together, but by the looks of it, she had a run-in with a bear and was left alone... very strange."

"Perhaps they left her for dead."

"I've known wolves to stay by their mates long past their last breath. They don't have that many young bitches that they can just throw one away." As he spoke, his hand gently brushed Ayse's fur and it sent tingles through her body. "Don't let her lick her wounds; damn animals can do more harm than good that way."

A blurred outline of an arm appeared in her view and she was softly held by the muzzle. Ayse didn't attempt to shake the man off. Another hand appeared with a blade, then the rope binding her was gently cut, before the hand reached for the water bowl and placed it close to her nose. Ayse opened her stiff jaw and her swollen tongue lolled out, but she couldn't reach the water.

She tried to shift her body so that she was on her stomach, but it was hard going. As she moved her back leg, she felt sharp pains of protest, but it wasn't until she put pressure on it that agony sparked through her body and she whined uncontrollably. A gentle helping hand on her far side aided her in positioning herself, and she dipped her face to the bowl and drank deeply from it. The water was cool and refreshing but leaning forward was causing her head to pound even more. She didn't care if she could drink. The water dribbled from her jaw as she drank, the cool feeling of it flowing down her throat was refreshingly welcome.

"I could spend all day with this beauty, but the dogs won't keep without me," the older voice sighed wistfully while helping her back onto her side, leaving her in the heat of the brazier. "I'll check in on her every morning and see to her wounds. Just make sure she drinks a lot, eats what she can, and don't forget, don't -"

"Don't let her lick her wounds. I've got it, Bernd," the other man responded, the amusement evident in his voice.

"All right, all right, I'll leave you to it," Bernd relented, getting to his feet. "If you need me, you know where to find me."

Ayse could feel a draft as Bernd made his exit. She moved her head to try and take in more of her surroundings, but the sudden movement caused her head to throb even more. Her already impaired eyesight was dimming, and she knew that she would faint at any moment. She slowly placed her head back down on the floor, closed her eyes, and tried to will the unrelenting pain within her tortured body to ease.

✳✳✳

Time became meaningless to Ayse, her body drained and injured as it was, she was in and out of consciousness. Every time she awoke, she wasn't sure whether it was a new day or whether just mere hours had passed. Her body remained painful and sore, while her mind became numb, trapped within a broken body. She witnessed little, she was unable to move far, and she was conscious even less. The water before her was replenished while she slept, her wounds were seen to out of sight, and a brave hand would venture to feed her whatever strips of meat she could manage.

Even though she was unable to move enough to take in her surroundings, she heard much in the short interludes that she was awake. Outside, she could hear the clash of metal and shouts as northern soldiers trained relentlessly in the discipline of warfare. The noise of dogs barking and horses whinnying would carry into the tent, and the smell of leather, mud, metal, and cooked meat seemed to constantly permeate the camp.

She recognised Bernd's voice; he came often to check on her. She also recognised the voice of the tent's occupant and she knew him to be an authority figure. The other men that came and went referred to him as 'lord', but she had no real idea what kind of hierarchy the north had. Most lords that were native to the south would be set up in some extravagant estate, not roughing it in a camp geared up for war.

Another frequent visitor, who seemed to be the second in command within the camp, went by the name of Markus; he was the only person to refer to the lord by his given name of Caleb. The two of them often spoke about battle strategies, of locations that she did not know, names she didn't recognise, and of failed attempts that Nevraah had made to attack them. They were fastidious in their battle plans; it was obvious that they were experienced in conflict, although their voices sounded younger than Ayse would have expected for men so familiar with battle.

✳✳✳

Ayse lay on her side, staring at the water bowl in front of her. Her eyes were half-lidded from sheer lack of energy as she listened to the men in the tent. The Nevraahn army had been sending in groups of soldiers to breach the north and return with information on the enemy camps, but they were just throwing their lives away. The Oror soldiers picked them off easily on their own territory, and the Orians ensured that no survivors crossed back over the border. She didn't understand how the northern men hadn't tired of this game yet, here they were all ready for battle, but from what she had heard, all it took were some well-trained scouting parties to keep the south out.

"They're attempting to cross all along the border. Lord Ulric and Lord Tomas have confirmed the same. We think they're trying to find a weak spot, but it won't happen," one soldier reported in.

"I wish they would give up already. I'm sick of dealing with their corpses," another soldier snorted with derision.

"If they want to keep our soldiers well trained with all these practice opportunities, then I'm not going to complain," the northern lord responded dismissively.

Most of the conversations Ayse heard were all similar; they gave her no valid information and in her current state, even if what she heard was worthwhile, it would be useless if she couldn't get back to the Vulpini. Ayse wished she could think clearly, her head was foggy constantly and it was hard to string two thoughts together. She would try and think of something, only for her mind to deflect her to another thought entirely. She felt as if she were in a dream state, whether it was from the blood loss, the pain, or the herbs in the water she wasn't sure, but she did know that every hour she lay there helpless was an hour wasted.

Even now, as she heard the soldiers exiting the tent, she realised her mind had wandered once again and that she had missed the rest of what they had been reporting. Ayse tried shifting her weight to ease the discomfort in her body, but it just caused further aggravation and she let out an unintentional whine.

Her whimper didn't go unheard and immediately she could hear footsteps coming ever closer. Instinctively, she flicked her ears in that direction as she listened to Caleb approach. A hand touched her, and she let out a throaty growl. He rapped his knuckles against her playfully as if chiding her and then gently repositioned her on her opposite side. She groaned as her aching body was moved, the painful tingling telling her that the sensation of feeling was returning to her.

Now facing inwards, her eyes immediately went to the face of the man in front of her. He was crouched, his hand still resting on her as he regarded her intently with eyes that were the deep colour of evergreen. An eye colour that was rarely seen in the south. His feathered raven hair was long enough to flick into his eyes in a dishevelled manner, but not long enough to fall far past his ears. He was older than her by a few years, but still younger than she had expected for a lord, his clean-shaven face most likely making him seem younger than he truly was.

He patted her gently, before returning to the far side of the tent to a table that overflowed with various items such as ink bottles, books, and scrolls, as well as what looked like a carved chess set with intricate figures. She watched him casually flicking through paperwork for a while longer before absent-mindedly looking around the rest of the tent. The most notable items were the brilliant blue pennants with silver wolf heads emblazoned on them. The same icon featured on standards, tapestries, and adorned the breastplate of a beautifully patterned suit of armour standing regally in the tent corner. There was another section to the tent that she could not see into as it was covered by drapes, but she assumed it to be the sleeping quarters.

***

Ayse found that in the following days, her headache was slowly easing, and with it the fog of her mind was lifting. With each day that passed, she was granted longer respite from her dreamlike reverie and she began to feel more like herself again. It was only then that it dawned on Ayse that she was in the north, these were northerners around her, and for all intents and purposes, she had accomplished what she thought was nearly impossible – she had infiltrated the enemy camp.

Ayse had nearly died getting there, and chained as she was, it wouldn't matter if she found anything of use to her tribe, but she was one step closer to her goal. Determination burned in her belly. As she watched the northern lord sit down and take up a quill at the table as he often did, she felt some semblance of energy return to her as motivation began to pool within her.

One thought struck her, and it bothered her slightly, the northerners had immediately taken her for a normal wolf of the north, completely dismissing the option that she may be a stray werewolf. It was possible that the legend of northern werewolves had been wrong all along. Maybe werewolves didn't originate in Oror at all, in which case, Ayse wondered where she would find others of her kind. Perhaps werewolves were like the Nevraahn shifters and were therefore unknown to most of the population. Regardless, she would have to play it safe to keep herself and the captured Vulpini alive.

Chapter Four

Gulls were circling and diving against the pale sky. Their distant cries were calling out across the stretch of ocean, the sound mingling with the crash of the waves. The sea was dark and unrelenting, throwing itself about wildly, as if in throes of agony. Tobias sat overlooking the bay, he sighed, and the taste of the salty air calmed him. There was something fresh and invigorating about the coast, even when the weather was grey and miserable. Even so, his mood was still as sombre as it had been for the past few months.

A dark cloud had been cast over the tribe and no matter where they travelled, it had followed. They had stretched out the summer as best as they could down on the southern coast, but even there, the weather had finally turned and the skies were greying with the shadow of winter that loomed on the horizon.

Tobias left his lonely vigil of the ocean and began to make his way through the dunes back towards the camp, allowing the long grassy reeds to brush against his open palms as he passed by. He could hear the children at play before the camp even came into view and that simple sound of their laughter brought a small smile to his lips.

The tribal caravans surrounded the main fire pit in the centre of the camp, the wagons and tents rippling out in circles away from the blazing bonfire. It was there at the heart of the camp where Vulpini life was thriving. Many of the women were cooking dinner for everyone in a large stew pot over the flaming fire pit. They were busy peeling and chopping vegetables, throwing them into the worn pot with a careless, yet precise aim.

There were others fixing garments, darning holes of casual wear, and sewing together outfits for performance purposes. In a makeshift tent, there were men sharpening swords and sorting lock pick tools, whilst women leaned out of caravan windows to hang wet clothes to dry in the early evening breeze. All the while the children ran and played about the active camp without a care in the world.

Several weeks beforehand, the tribe had received word from Brankah that Ayse had been found. Ever since, there had been a new sense of hope within the camp that their loved ones would be returned to them unharmed.

Tobias could not help but feel irritated by the way that things had unfolded. If Ayse had never been turned away from the Vulpini in the first place, then they would never have wasted so much time seeking her out when they needed her the most. The duke expected his information by the end of spring and so the Vulpini were running out of time.

Thinking of Ayse made Tobias's heart feel like lead in his chest, dragging him down like an immovable weight. Tobias had offered to go with the werewolf when she had been cast out, but Ayse had refused him, telling him that his place was at home with the Vulpini. He knew that she had desperately wanted his companionship but had not wanted to abuse his affection for her and sentence him to her own fate of exile.

Tobias could remember the day that old Chief Wilamir had carried her into the camp as a small bundle cradled in his arms. Even as a child, Tobias was aware that the new baby was special, his young mind misinterpreting the talk of her being "different" as a good thing, not quite what the tribespeople had meant. Even though Tobias was a few years Ayse's senior, it had always been the young she-wolf that had led him around and taken charge, always coming up with plans for the adventures they would eventually have one day.

Tobias often wondered why he had managed to bond with her better than any of the other tribe, perhaps because he shared with her the keen emptiness of not having any parents. His own mother had died giving birth to him and his father had not been a member of the tribe, he didn't even know who he was.

It was as he became a young man that Tobias had realised that it was not sisterly affection he held for the werewolf, but a deep and sincere love. He had never told her how he felt, but they were close enough for him to know without being told in words that she knew how he felt about her and that she did not feel the same. Tobias also knew that was why she had not taken advantage of him when he had offered to turn his back on the tribe to leave with her, but he would offer the same again without a moment's hesitation, if only she would have him.

He took a seat near the fire, filtering out all the hustle and hubbub of the tribe while he stared into the flames. One of the youngest children, named Jona, toddled up to him and climbed onto his lap, content to share in his silence in front of the fire. Tobias stroked the youngster's hair affectionately and felt Jona slowly drift into slumber, the child's thumb wedged firmly in its mouth.

Tobias's thoughts quickly returned to Ayse, as they often did. He wondered how far into the northern territory she had made it. Now more than ever, he wondered if she was all right, if she was hurt, and whether he would ever see her face again. It had been five years since Ayse had left, shortly after her thirteenth birthday, in those intervening years they would have matured down their own paths and grown into different people.

He wondered whether he would recognise her, how much she would have changed, whether her personality would be the same, or whether her expulsion from the tribe had hardened her to the world. At the thought of seeing her, Tobias mostly wondered whether he would still feel the same for her when he looked into her eyes, and even dared to wonder whether when she looked into his eyes, whether she might have found her own feelings had changed.

By the time dinner was served, the sky had already begun to darken as night approached the camp. Most of the tribe had gathered around the fire and were passing out bowls and hunks of freshly baked bread, the rest of the tasty broth remained in the stew pot to await the return of the other wandering Vulpini. The meal was simple, rustic, and full of flavour, and the whole of the tribe tucked into it wholeheartedly. Damp wood that had been thrown onto the open fire hissed and spat, the air trapped within the wood popping as the flames reached it, hungrily seeking out its own sustenance.

The Vulpini were a close-knit community and looking around the gathered faces that were chatting animatedly, Tobias knew that he was blessed to be among them. Whilst finishing his own meal, he could hear Old Thom telling the children stories before bed, regaling them with tales of daring foxes who outsmarted evildoers with ease. The stories were old and often retold; Tobias could remember hearing them himself as a child, yet the youngsters still cheered with the same enthusiasm as though it was their first time hearing it.

Tobias left the camp and its merrier inhabitants to the warmth of the fire. Ever since Ayse had left, he found that he preferred his solitude rather than carrying on tribal life as if she had never been a part of it. Every meal and tribal council meeting were just another reminder to him that there used to be another place at the table and another face in the crowd. He considered how now they were permanently missing yet another member, and possibly even more before the end of spring.

As he reached the final line of caravans, Tobias stripped all his clothes from his body and placed them behind the wheel of one of the wagons. Like all shifters, Tobias had no sense of shame about his body. Being able to shift since birth, shifters viewed clothes as something to only keep them warm when not in animal form. Tobias considered that if it were not for non-shifters, the Vulpini tribe would happily spend many a summer without a thread on their bodies.

As Tobias crouched on all fours to start his shift, he could feel the last of the warmth from the sun-baked ground through his skin. The cool night air brushed against his naked body sending a shiver through him that ended only when he stood as a beast. Shifts were a natural part of life for the Vulpini, although they were swift and painless, they took a certain amount of control and concentration. Panicked or fatigued Vulpini found it harder to shift, and during puberty shifters found their frenzied hormones not only impeded a transformation, but sometimes unexpectedly triggered one.

The breeze gently ruffled his fur as if the mother goddess of nature herself was welcoming the arrival of his fox spirit. Tobias ran towards the sound of the ocean. He jumped and sprinted through the long grass that led down to the beach line, the sight of the grass swaying was a tell-tale sign of his movement to any possible onlookers. As he reached the coast, he could see that the tide was in, leaving only a fragment of the shore to run along. Under the mastery of the night, the black waters took on an almost malignant nature, seeming to eat away at the shore and cliff with an insatiable appetite. The wind was growing in strength as the night matured and clouds were rolling in across the ocean to swallow the clear night sky whole.

Tobias sprinted along the slim strip of sand, the ocean reaching out to him on one side, and the jagged cliff face looming on the other side. His feet kicked up the sand as he ran, weaving in and out of the wet shoreline as the waves temporarily retreated. The damp sand stuck to him and clung to his fur. He slowed as his energy finally left him and he fell to his belly panting.

Staring out into the blackness of the ocean, he was unsure where the water ended, and the dark night sky began. His vision was full of the dark void before him. Tobias knew that beyond the darkness of the Graegan Sea lay the country of Shohana; although there was active trade between Shohana and Nevraah, little was known about the exotic country. Tobias wondered whether the dukes would set their sights on this other neighbouring land if Oror fell to Nevraah's insatiable greed.

Tobias glanced back at the coastline he had covered, he could see his tracks dotted along the sand, though some had already been wiped clean by the waves, erasing the fact that he had ever been there. With less energy than before, he retraced his steps slowly, feeling somewhat calmer for having vented his inner emotions with his spur of the moment excursion. The late-night run had tired Tobias out, he felt as if he could hear the call of the campfire beckoning him to go and lie in its glow, inviting him to fall asleep in its warm embrace now that the cold night air had become unwelcoming.

Chapter Five

Horace was continuing to clean a tankard while standing behind his bar; he understood that smudges had long ceased to mar the item, yet he continued to clean it regardless. His sharp eyes were trained upon the travellers sitting in the corner of his pub and he watched them with unease. Two of the customers had become familiar to him now, as they were the original couple that had sought out Ayse. Since his favourite hired hand had disappeared without a word, more travellers had appeared in Brankah to speak with the strange couple, but their visitors never stayed long.

Currently, the travellers were sat with another man. Horace knew this one was also a gypsy. Something about them just seemed to click into place in his mind when he saw them, their clothes, their mannerisms... he just knew they were gypsies. Something was happening and it worried him that he didn't know what it was, it had to be something big and yet, oddly enough, he hadn't heard so much as a whisper about it. What worried him even more was that young Ayse was somehow mixed up in it all.

He sighed and placed the tankard with its fellow flagons below the bar. He didn't like the feeling of it one bit. Ayse had never arrived looking for work only to leave without taking on a single job, yet she had disappeared without even making her farewells. This didn't sit well with Horace. Ayse always spoke to him before leaving town and this time around she had just vanished overnight. Something must have happened for her to leave so suddenly, but he couldn't even begin to wonder what would have been so urgent to the young girl.

One thing was for certain, he didn't trust the shifty looking Vulpini that had taken to frequenting his bar, and considering his usual shady clientele, *that* was truly saying something. What was the world coming to when he decided that there were even some people who were too depraved for his liking? He had reached out to acquaintances of his and found that the horse Ayse had ridden in on was still stabled within the city, yet there was no sign of the girl, and no sign of foul play. She had either left on foot, although there were no settlements nearby to warrant that, or simply vanished. Neither option was comforting to him.

"Boss," It was his barman, Kitson, pulling him from his train of thought and demanding his attention. The young man signalled for his employer to follow him out to the back room, and with one last glance at the travellers, Horace reluctantly followed him.

***

Nell's pretty little face was wrinkled up in a frown and that made Reuben also frown as he looked from her to their companion. The person sitting opposite them was an older man, grey had begun to streak through the black of his sideburns and his beard was nearly completely silver already. He looked exasperated as he tried to reason with the younger couple.

"You don't have to deal with that git month in and month out. He's got us over a barrel, and he knows it. There is no compromising with him!" the older man grunted agitatedly.

"We need more time! Even Ayse realised that when she agreed to go on this fool's errand. If you just explained to him -" Nell argued.

"This is not a man you explain to, Nell. He gives orders and people follow them, anyone who disagrees meets an untimely end." The man shook his head and folded his arms in front of his chest.

Nell pouted and looked at Reuben, as if begging for him to say something, but his blank expression gave her no support. She continued alone, "Ayse will already be north of the border by now, if you tell the duke that-"

"Ayse could be dead already for all we know," the man responded fiercely as he interrupted her again, banging his fist upon the table and drawing the attention of some nearby patrons.

Nell went quiet, her lip quivering as if she wanted to scream at him, but she didn't dare to cause even more of a scene. Reuben placed a gentle hand on her leg to quell her fury.

He addressed the man, "Rojas. It wasn't that long ago that we were asking Ayse to undertake an impossible task and she agreed to do it for the good of the tribe. She isn't even a tribe member anymore. For the good of our tribe, can't you also be willing to try at your own seemingly impossible task?"

Rojas looked shamed.

"We're not asking you to make it happen. We're just asking you to try," Nell interjected more softly.

Rojas sighed heavily. They were right, of course, and he knew it. However, he also knew that Duke Remus did not negotiate. Rojas was the mediator in the business between the Vulpini and the duke. After they had received word that their people had been taken hostage and they received the demands for their release, it was he who had been sent to the duke's household as an emissary of the tribe.

When the Vulpini had tried to rescue their own and failed miserably in the process, it was Rojas who was made to bear witness to the consequences and relay the terrible news to the others. He would never forget Paya's face in those final moments, the way she had looked at him knowing what was about to happen and how she had wordlessly pleaded with him. Her eyes had still been looking to him for help as the duke's executioner had taken his sword to her neck. Rojas doubted that he would be able to stomach the same scene again if the other Vulpini hostages were forced to endure a similar fate.

He knew that the whole of the tribe was in torment, yet it felt as if he were carrying the main weight of the burden for the Vulpini. He was grateful that he could at least spare them some of the pain. If the rest of the tribe were aware of what happened in the duke's prison cells, then they would not be able to stop themselves from trying to tear the Bremlor estate apart stone by stone. It would be to no avail, the Vulpini were not warriors, and the only way they would be reunited with their loved ones was to miraculously meet the impossible demands of the duke.

Rojas thought how Wilamir would never have let things unfold as they had. Wolf she may be, but Ayse had been raised as a Vulpini and Rojas had always considered it a wrongdoing that she had been forced away from the tribe. Was she now just another victim of this whole affair? For all he knew, Ayse could have met a similar fate to Paya at the hands of foreigners already. It left him wondering how much more tribal blood would be spilt and whether any of the hostages would return to their family again.

"Is there anything you have to help me persuade him? Will Ayse send word, confirmation, or could she be a lost cause already?"

"No. We discussed it at length, but the risk seemed too great. If she made it north, sending word back could undo everything she would have accomplished. If they caught her, or the messenger bird, she'd be her own downfall," Reuben explained. "We just have to put our faith in her."

"And give her whatever extra time we can," Nell emphasised.

"I could lie to him... Tell him we have confirmation of the infiltration. But if he suspects we're lying..."

"Appeal to his greed, the longer he gives us, the better the information we can give him. Tell him it's a guaranteed victory with the knowledge we'll gain," Nell proposed.

Rojas looked at the couple; their faces stared back at him with desperate determination. To them it all must seem so easy. He couldn't blame them as they were too distant from the horrors that he had seen first-hand. He leaned back in his seat and frowned, afraid at what he was about to ask next, "And if Ayse doesn't return?"

"If Ayse doesn't return, then all would have been lost regardless," Reuben responded bitterly.

The trio sat in silence; all pondering what the outcome would be if Ayse were to never return. Nell was making a feigned effort to look out through the dirtied windows. Her eyes brimmed with tears that would fall if she so much as looked at either of her companions. Reuben watched her with a pained expression on his face, afraid that even an attempt to console her would cause her more grief and so he just left her in her melancholic reverie.

He turned back to face Rojas, who returned his look with a grim smile though his brow was still furrowed with concern. The older man sighed once more before rising wordlessly to leave the couple to share in their sorrow in silence. Once Rojas had left, Reuben softly placed his hand over Nell's and as anticipated, she broke down into tears. He pulled her towards him, and she buried her tearful face in his chest to hide her pain from the world.

***

Horace was back behind the bar. One of his regular patrons was prattling on about something or other, but the barkeep wasn't paying them any attention. Instead, he watched with unease as the man left the gypsy couple and exited The Black Sheep. These people were not likely to give him any answers should he question them, but he felt that he needed to know what was happening, and more importantly where Ayse had disappeared to.

If the young girl was in trouble, he was more than happy to help her. Ayse's impressive skills had seen to it that business for him had boomed and she was a valuable asset whenever she was in town. However, he knew the real reason for his apprehension was that Ayse had become dear to him. If he had ever had a daughter, he would have bet good money she would have turned out like Ayse.

Every time the girl left Brankah, there was always the doubt in his mind as to whether she would return or not. The anxiety stayed with him through the months until she would eventually walk back into his bar, ready for anything he could throw at her. But this time felt different, it wasn't just a worry, it felt like a reality waiting to happen and he was afraid that even thinking such a thing would tempt the fates to see to it that his fears would come true. It was time for action. Horace felt he had spent enough time twiddling his thumbs and finally he knew what he had to do.

"Kit!"

The barman came hurrying at his call, his hair plastered to his brow with sweat where he had been moving that day's delivery of kegs into the back room.

"Yeah, boss?" he asked as he yanked a cloth out from under the bar and casually dabbed at his forehead.

"You said Raphael was in town?"

"I saw him in the markets yesterday, said he'd just arrived and that he'd be paying you a visit in the coming days."

"I need him to pay me a visit *today*. Find him for me and tell him I've got a contract for him that he won't want to refuse." Horace grabbed the cloth from his employee and flicked it at him to shoo Kitson from the bar. He then returned to his vigil of the gypsies. They might not want him to know their secrets, but one way or another he was determined to find out what they were hiding.

Chapter Six

The flames danced in brilliant burning ribbons of light. They entwined and cavorted as they softly embraced the wood and blackened it with their touch. The smell of smoke and burning timber was a comfort; it reminded Ayse of many a night spent around a Vulpini campfire. If she stared into the flames long enough, she could almost imagine herself sat there now with the Vulpini all around her, enjoying the pleasantries of normal tribal life.

A cold chill brought Ayse to her senses and she turned with a strained effort to watch as Bernd entered, bringing in the winter cold with him in a flurry of snow-laced wind. He always had a smile across his face when he came to visit her, and she was always happy to receive the meat scraps he brought with him. She would let him stroke her without much fuss as she ate but would shake his hand away on finishing her treats. Much like the Vulpini shapeshifters, she did not enjoy being handled by strangers in such an intimate way.

Ayse was healing well, but the better she became, the worse she felt for it. With her returning health came her full consciousness and the full feeling of her aching body. She constantly felt tired, yet unable to sleep because of the pain. Her body permanently felt stiff from lying inactive for days on end, and though she had begun standing and attempting to move about what little she could, it was extremely slow going.

Her hind leg was especially a torture to her, and the wound still felt raw to the touch. Ayse was unsteady on her paws, attempting to walk brought unwanted attention from the northerners, especially in Bernd's presence. They would try to aid her, but she would snap and growl at them in warning. She was always irritated as she struggled with her body, the heavy chain strung around her neck rattled and tormented her with every move she made. More than once she had bitten at it in frustration, only to hurt her jaws by doing so.

Ayse had recently made some small achievement in that she could make it to the tent entrance, where she could survey much of the camp. She often chose to keep herself inside and close to the wood burner, as with her body weakened, she felt the cold more than ever. On the few milder days that were afforded to the north, she would lie in the tent's opening watching the Orian men at work.

The northerners were a strange crowd. Not only were they loud and rowdy, but they were fierce with short tempers. Despite their fiery natures, they could be rather surprisingly easy going at times. Their sense of comradeship was strong; if the soldiers fought amongst themselves, they would generally end up laughing and cheering each other on, then bruised and with split lips they would eventually share a drink at the end of their brawl.

"I wish we could take you hunting with us, girl. I wonder what you would make of that," Bernd commented wistfully.

Ayse had grown accustomed to the northerners going on their hunting trips. A large group of the soldiers led by the northern lord would regularly hunt once a week or so, staying out most of the night and heralding in the morning by bringing in their fresh kill of deer to the delight of the others. On rare occasions, Bernd would accompany the hunting party with his hounds. Ayse had to admit, even she enjoyed when the hunting party returned as they would give her a small raw cut to enjoy.

"Bernd."

Both Ayse and the dog keeper turned to see Caleb stood in the tent entrance.

"You care more for that wolf than anyone else in this camp. I should feel unwanted, as you never visited this many times before her arrival," he mocked as he strode in. The snow fell from his fur cloak as he removed it and tossed it onto a nearby chair.

"Don't think that I don't know that you spoil her as much as I," Bernd retorted.

The northern lord smiled wryly, but did not turn from his task of examining papers on the table as he spoke, "How do you think she is healing?"

"She is getting there slowly," Bernd sighed. "Once she has more energy, we will need to start exercising her more. Her limbs will lock up if she stays cooped up in here."

"As if I do not have enough to do already," Caleb responded dryly.

"You will find the time, I am sure of it," Bernd chuckled as he left the tent.

The mere prospect of being expected to move around even more exhausted Ayse, but she knew that as her strength returned, she would need to prepare herself to finish the task she had been set. With the Orians intent on seeing her recover fully, they were unwittingly enabling her to eventually betray them.

While the thought was not a pleasant one, Ayse reminded herself that the northerners were never so accommodating to strangers of human form. Had she wandered into the north as a woman, she would have been cut down before she could even have spoken a word. Furthermore, the lives of people she knew and cared for were on the line and that mattered more to her than the kindness Bernd and the others had shown her.

Ayse shuffled closer to the brazier, the chain slinking behind her like a great metal snake. With a groan, she laid her weary body down and let the warmth of the fire fall over her. Even with her aching wounds, Ayse felt a continuous urge to stand and stretch every limb. However, she knew that what her body was really calling out for was for her to return to human form. She had never spent this much time as a wolf before, now she wondered how much longer she could continue with four paws.

Even in the Vulpini community, no shifter had pushed itself to its furthest limits as there was never any need to. Shifters could inadvertently transform at times, for instance if they were too inebriated. However, from experience, Ayse had learned that fatigued bodies were unable to shift as they simply did not have the energy to do so. Fortunately for her, her own exhaustion had prevented the northerners from randomly encountering a naked woman in their camp. As she recovered, Ayse wondered whether delaying her return to human form would eventually take its toll and force her to change.

She started out of her musing as a hand reached out and touched her, her body tensed and she growled, but Caleb was quick to shush her. The northern lord had a habit of sneaking up on her with cat-like quietness. His hands moved to her collar and he paused momentarily, before slowly removing it. Ayse was motionless, not wanting to stir and cause Caleb to change his mind.

"Bernd would probably disagree, but I don't like keeping you chained. If you want to recover, I wouldn't go running off if I were you. Although in your condition, I don't think you'd be hard to fetch back." Caleb rose to his feet and sighed as he shook his head. "Not that giving advice to a beast ever got anyone anywhere, least of all the beast."

Caleb returned to his paperwork but was shortly interrupted by two of his men entering the tent. Stopping briefly to salute him, Markus and the accompanying soldier continued forward as Caleb took a seat in front of them.

"You have news?"

"Nothing too unusual, my lord. The southerners have begun fortifying camps along the border here, here, and here," the soldier reported, detailing the areas on a map atop the table.

"Well, we can't have that, can we?"

"Should we proceed as usual?" Markus queried.

"Yes. Ready your men and attack the camps. I don't want those bastards getting comfortable right on our doorstep."

"Yes, my lord."

Ayse rose to her feet. She eyed the soldier as she padded softly over to the bowl of water and began to drink from it. She didn't recognise this northerner who was now pouring over plans with Caleb, but then she didn't need to, she just had to remember as much information as possible. However, the locations of the southern camps were not exactly useful to her. The soldier looked up from the tabletop and watched her with unease.

"M-my Lord, the chain is-"

"Yes," Caleb responded dismissively.

Markus looked up from the paperwork to survey this new development; his gaze went from Ayse to the man beside him. The soldier's mouth stayed agape for a few moments more as he stared at Ayse before regaining his composure and returning to his work. He continued to glance at the wolf from time to time and it gave her some small satisfaction to stare him down every time. Ayse gingerly sat on her haunches and continued to simply watch the men at work.

With his growing discomfort becomingly increasingly evident, it wasn't long before the soldier made his excuses and left the tent. Caleb and Markus shared a wry smile, evidently finding the soldier's fear amusing, before continuing with their usual reports. Ayse yawned before returning to her spot near the brazier, curling up so that she could watch the northerners planning their battle strategies. She settled down to hear a long conversation that would most likely yield no information of importance to her.

∗∗

The rain had turned the ground into a thick slop that Ayse's paws sunk into with every step. The downpour was unending. It was soaking Ayse through to her very skin and she could feel the water running down past her ears. However, all the muck clinging to her fur did not bother her. Her hind leg had strengthened considerably, and it was finally able to bear weight well again. Her more superficial wounds were long forgotten, having healed quickly with the aid of the Orian men.

As Caleb strode through the camp checking on his men and attending to various matters, Ayse stayed at his heels, forever playing the faithful hound. The northerners had grown accustomed to her presence and Ayse was able to traverse the camp largely unnoticed whenever she wished. However, she usually chose to stay close to the northern lord, as not only were the most interesting bits of information relayed directly to him, but it strengthened the trust she had gained to have the people think of her as nothing more than a lapdog.

The wet did not dampen the spirits of the Orians; after all, they were used to such weather. Not much had changed in the camp during Ayse's stay. Reports of fighting along the border had been constant, but then the soldiers from Oror seemed to relish the warfare. All the northern soldiers were male. In fact, surprising to Ayse was that there were no women in Caleb's camp at all.

Duties such as cooking and cleaning were given to the youngest boys, those still learning to wield a blade properly, and those too old or infirm to fight as well as they once had. From what she had overheard from the northerners, it was the woman's place to stay at home and look after the children. Ayse much preferred the combined partnership of the Vulpini tribe, where men and women were equal, rather than Oror's way of life.

Ayse found herself nearly colliding with Caleb as he came to an abrupt halt when some of his men stopped him to discuss requisitions. Finding the conversation stale, and the weather increasingly unbearable, Ayse decided to continue without him and find somewhere warm and dry where she could rest awhile. She could feel eyes on her as she left, and turning back she found Caleb watching her, but his face remained expressionless.

Ayse weaved her way through the mud-soaked camp at a leisurely pace, even in this wild weather there were men still training outside, the sweat indistinguishable from the rain on their faces. She couldn't help but admire the tenacity of the northerners. They were certainly a remarkable people. The guards on watch outside of Caleb's tent paid her no heed as she quietly padded into the warm and shook herself to clear as much rainwater from her coat as possible.

Whilst the idea of laying down beside the fire was tempting, Ayse had found that she should take her enjoyment wherever she could whilst in the north, and so instead, she decided to nose her way through the heavy drapes and into Caleb's private sleeping quarters. She carefully jumped onto the bed before curling up into a ball right in the middle of the embroidered quilts and furs. Content that Caleb wouldn't be able to shift the wet-wolf smell from his bedding for quite some time, Ayse drifted off to sleep.

***

"Damn dog!"

Caleb cuffed Ayse on her hindquarters to dislodge her from his bedding, though the blow was not hard. She slowly stretched and watched Caleb's disapproving face through half-lidded eyes, taking as much time as possible to vacate the comfort of the bed.

"Every time..."

Feigning innocence, Ayse yawned and padded softly into the main tent with the sound of Caleb's footsteps following close behind her. A soldier was waiting there for Caleb to return, he was unfamiliar to Ayse, but she could smell the stench of sweat and horse on him as if he had ridden there from a distance. Something about his posture and presence exuded a sense of authority and it made Ayse wary of him.

"I am sorry to keep you," Caleb stated formally as he glanced sideways at Ayse. "There was something I needed to attend to. You were saying?"

The soldier raised an eyebrow at Ayse before pulling out a cylindrical leather tube from his satchel. He unlatched the top and pulled out a thick coil of manuscript paper. Unrolling the paperwork onto the tabletop, he grabbed some of the nearest map markers from the war table to use as paperweights, preventing the curling corners from closing in on themselves.

"I have word from Stormdown. Lord Ulric and Lord Tomas have both laid out their territories for the coming months. The winter is ending soon and as the snow thaws we will need to change our patrols around Oror. The milder weather may allow the southerners easier access into our land and we cannot allow that to happen. Those Nevraahns are becoming increasingly determined."

"The High Lord wishes for us to change position?"

"Your camp is to remain here. The other Lords will be moving to these new locations come the spring, as you can see. Their new patrol routes, here, so you should match yours accordingly."

"What of Lovera?"

"All is quiet on that front, my Lord."

"Good. I will see to it that the new patrol arrangements are made when it is time. You've travelled a long way. I trust you will be staying with us this evening?"

"Please." The man responded graciously.

"Perfect timing, we are going hunting tonight. That is, if you are not too tired."

The man looked up at Caleb with a wide grin that seemed unfitting for his character, before replying, "I'd be delighted to join you."

The men fell into discussions that disinterested Ayse and so she lowered her head and skulked over to the brazier. Ayse huffed at the idea of the northerners and their hunts. They didn't know what a real hunt was until they had chased down their prey on four paws.

She didn't begrudge the humans their sport. After all, she too enjoyed the thrill of the chase. However, she couldn't help but be envious of their excursions, she had spent so long in the northern camp unable to run and hunt freely that she sorely missed the experience, as well as the quiet of her own company. More than once the men had made mention of taking her along on a hunt, but Caleb had always dismissed the idea. Ayse liked to think that the northern lord did not want to be outplayed by a wolf at his favourite game, and Ayse was healed enough to know that she would be capable of doing just that.

Chapter Seven

Raphael had seen some dives in his travels, but Lower Bremlor was one of the worst. He looked at the bargirl that lay sprawled in the bed beside him. She was still sound asleep, her freckled skin barely covered by the sheets and her hair dishevelled from the previous evening's activities. Raphael sighed. The girls here were not up to his usual standards but seeing as he was forced to spend his time there, he had decided that he may as well pass it eventfully.

He silently swung his legs out of the bed and grabbed his trousers from the floor, quickly, but quietly pulling them on without bothering to button them all the way, before softly padding over to the small window. He looked out into the small narrow streets of the crowded slum town. Morning was always late this time of year, and so the roads remained under the cover of darkness. Raphael could see the dull glow of lantern lights in windows as workers began their day, though they were swallowed into the darkness of the town as they left. No doubt passing the street walkers as they retired from their long night of work, as if pulling shifts to keep Lower Bremlor as a constant turning wheel.

Bremlor was a hilly region with a large farming community that had once prospered well, but under the command of the new duke ten years prior, the town had been split into two districts. High Bremlor was for the rich aristocracy of the land. Perched high in the hills, the duke had spent most of his money fortifying it and separating it from the lower townsfolk, the entrances were guarded extremely well and those without High Bremlor work permits were not allowed to enter.

Furthermore, the duke had increased all taxes within Lower Bremlor by a tremendous amount and had added taxes to just about everything in the city. The duke was trying to re-create High Bremlor as one of the most prosperous cities in the country by bleeding its own commoners dry. He had all but forsaken the lower district and the authorities didn't even bother to police there any longer. All those who could afford to leave had already migrated, but those unfortunate enough to have to remain found their lives a constant hardship.

Raphael shivered as the cold winter air bit at his skin. He glanced back at his shirt that lay discarded on the floor and considered retrieving it, but his mind soon wandered to more important issues. Horace had hired him to follow a traveller in the hopes of finding the whereabouts of his favourite agent, Ayse. Raphael grinned at the thought of one contractor hired to find another.

He knew Ayse well enough, their relationship was that of sporting rivals and after getting into trouble with her own assignment, he would make sure she would never live it down that he was the one that had been sent to fetch her. He would become the top sought-after hired hand after this fiasco. The problem was that the traveller he was following had disappeared into the glittering high life of High Bremlor. On the other hand, Raphael had been forced to resign himself to the slums, keeping an ear out for any news that could be beneficial to him whilst trying to find some way of entering the exclusive upper city.

Raphael had only seen his target in the slums a handful of times, using the aviary to send word to someone or another. He knew he had to get into High Bremlor to proceed with his assignment, but that was proving harder than he had anticipated. The guards for the upper district could not be bribed whatsoever and the whole of the elite were protected by walls that were impenetrable. The only way through was via the gates, and to get through those he needed a pass. He clicked his tongue in irritation and furrowed his brow as he contemplated how he would achieve his goal.

***

Rojas journeyed back into the city before the sun rose, slipping in between the narrow bars of one of the grates at the bottom of the impressive walls that encompassed High Bremlor. He padded along one of the dark passageways that served as an overflow tunnel in the rainy season. Rats darted about in the gloom, but he paid them no notice. As he returned into the twisted world of the despicable duke, his sombre mood returned also. The only respite he had these days were the nights he stole out of the city in fox form and ran wild, forgetting his mortal worries for a few hours at least.

At the beginning of his stay in Bremlor, Rojas had started by exploring whatever he could of the duke's estate in the hope of finding the captive Vulpini. Regrettably, he had found no sign of them whatsoever and even if he had, Chief Solomon had decreed that no further rescue attempts were to be made given the consequences of their last attempt.

Now, Rojas resigned himself to just escaping to the outer limits of Lower Bremlor where the farmland seemed to sprawl endlessly into the horizon. There he could run without being noticed and while away the hours before he had to return to human form.

Rojas desperately wanted to see the Vulpini prisoners, just to make sure that they were as unharmed as the situation would allow. They were all youngsters; three young lads and two of the girls remained. If the tribe had known the real dangers of the contract, none of them would have been sent. In fact, the job itself would have probably been refused entirely. He shook his head dismissively —hindsight was a brilliant yet bitter thing.

He reached the other end of the tunnel and saw the sky had a dull glow about it as the morning sun sleepily arose from its slumber. Squeezing out between the bars, Rojas continued into the gutter. He ran silently through the guttering alongside the paving, unknown to the guards that walked just above him. Rojas returned to his own simple bedchambers without any trouble, nosed his door open, and slid inside to begin his transformation.

He slowly stretched as he stood, his aching limbs protested with pain. Rojas knew he needed more rest, but sleep was a luxury these days. As he dressed quickly, he could already hear the morning calling forth the inhabitants of High Bremlor as the sound of servants scurrying down the hallways reached his ears. Running his hand through his hair in a half-hearted attempt to make himself look less dishevelled, he emerged from his room once more and with a heavy heart he made his way towards the duke's audience chamber.

There were already men ahead of him, waiting for their own chance to appeal to the duke. All of them bore the same worried expression. The duke was known for his volatile temper and even more so for his sinister sense of punishment. These men had most likely waited an age to be granted such an opportunity to have the duke hear their pleas, but in doing so, they risked their own lives by tempting his wrath.

Even Rojas had been made to wait, despite the fact he had told the duke's men that it was a matter of importance regarding the mission in the north. The line progressed slowly. Each man that emerged looked less happy than when he had gone in. Clearly today the duke was not in a merciful mood.

A squad of Bremlor soldiers were making their way through the corridor and Rojas gritted his teeth when he saw that they were being led by the duke's right-hand man, Lord Frewin.

"Well, well, if it isn't the Vulpini emissary," Frewin sneered.

Rojas averted his gaze, knowing that seeing the man's gloating face would tempt him into actions he would later regret.

The lord took it as a sign of weakness and continued, "You're looking a little tired there Rojas, have the lovely ladies of Lower Bremlor been keeping you up at night? It's only fair I suppose, considering we have your women to see to our every need should we fancy slumming it for the night."

Rojas's head snapped round to face his tormentor. It wasn't the first time he had heard this from more than one of the duke's men. Given the chance, Rojas would gladly drown the whole of High Bremlor in its own blood.

Seeing his target take the bait, Frewin continued, "I paid them a visit only the other night, you see. We know exactly how those gypsy sluts like it, a bit rough and a bit bloody. Although the little red head bruises far too easily, I think."

Frewin laughed and the soldiers around him chuckled and guffawed. Rojas saw red. He wanted to rip their throats out with his teeth and watch them bleed out. His hands twitched in anticipation of action, but he was quickly brought to his senses as his name was called from the audience chamber.

"Best hurry now, Rojas. You know how the duke does not like to be kept waiting," Frewin spat as he turned on his heel and left.

Rojas controlled his breathing and composed himself. He just had to wait, it would be painstakingly hard, but if he was patient enough and if he was careful, one day he would make all these men pay for their crimes on his people. He was lucky, if he had indeed lost his composure then it would have been the tribe who had paid for it. Right now, he needed to keep the duke in a good mood to ensure he agreed to extend the deadline.

The audience chamber was far too grand for a city such as High Bremlor; the duke had completely redesigned the whole of his estate, so it was fitting for that of a king. The duke sat with a bored expression, slouched to one side of his overly large throne-like chair, surrounded by expressionless officials. The few servants within the room looked dirty and unkempt compared to the pristine room, Rojas found it hard to believe that the man before him could be so blind to the poverty he was inflicting on his own people, all for his taste in decadence.

"Rojas of the Vulpini tribe, my lord," someone announced as he entered.

Rojas gritted his teeth and performed an elegant bow, if he was going to convince the duke to give the tribe more time, he might as well start buttering him up now.

"Please tell me you are not wasting my time again with your pleas to see the prisoners. I will not continue to repeat myself," the duke scowled, he was most definitely in a foul mood this morning.

"Of course not, sire." Rojas smiled. "I simply wished to report that I have excellent news... our agent has crossed the border into the north and has begun work to uncover any information of use to you."

The duke sat upright at this revelation and stared the Vulpini emissary down for a moment. Rojas wondered whether he had seen straight through his lie, but then the duke broke into a wide grin, "Excellent news, simply excellent!"

"Indeed, it is. They didn't say much in their message for fear of being discovered, however, they did confirm they were in the north and wished to make a request of you." Rojas responded as casually he could make it.

"A request of *me*?" the duke was already frowning, his eyes narrowed as he stared the Vulpini down. Rojas knew he had to handle this carefully.

"Yes, sire. It seems that in order to infiltrate an enemy camp of note, they must travel further into the northern territory than anticipated. They wish to secure valuable details for a strike to ensure that not only will you have an absolute victory, but to compile much-needed information on the enemy to ensure this is done with as few casualties to your men as possible," Rojas continued to remain as nonchalant as possible, while the duke listened intently, "An extension of time, by only a few months of course, would ensure intelligence such as this can be retrieved."

The duke seemed to reflect on this for some time, never looking away from Rojas, his eyes were dark, and they gave away no clue as to how he would respond. The Vulpini could feel his mouth going dry. He swallowed awkwardly to try and lose the uncomfortable swollen tongue feeling.

"I consent," the duke responded flatly after some time. "However, if you are speaking falsely and I do not get the information that you promise me… I will hunt down and punish every one of your people." His tone was firm and absolute, Rojas solemnly nodded in acceptance of this new condition. The duke's mouth widened into a wide grin once more as he said, "I am feeling generous today, so I will give you until the summer. I want my soldiers armed and prepared with full knowledge of the north to make a strike then. Do not fail me."

Chapter Eight

A distant tapping sound caught Ayse's attention. Her ears swivelled about her head until they could pinpoint the location of the noise. She raised her head and immediately her eyes scanned for the source of the noise. There was movement on the tabletop, a fat dusty moth had been attracted by the warm glow of the oil lamp and it was repeatedly colliding with the glass covering, not understanding the futile nature of its actions.

Ayse watched it for a few moments longer before she laid her head back down and continued to enjoy the warmth from the brazier. Even as she could feel the heat stroking her body, easing her muscles and lulling her into a drowsy state, the dull thud of the moth's body against the lamp continued to plague her. Disgruntled, she lifted her head with a groan and eyed the moth once more, but it was completely oblivious of the irate wolf by the fire.

She half-heartedly rose to her feet. Before she could gather enough energy to chase away her winged annoyance, another sound distracted her. The alarmed shouts of men could be heard from outside, quiet at first, but then quickly the sounds erupted into chaos.

Ayse hurried to the tent entrance to see what was happening. The camp was swamped in several inches of thick soupy mud from the previous night's rainfall, it flew in all directions as Orian men rushed across the camp to help those that were calling out to them. Ayse had seen many men come and go to the camp, often she had watched soldiers return from their excursions, but never had she seen what was unfolding before her. Beaten and bruised, their faces swollen beyond recognition and clothes stained with blood, the men that returned looked half dead as they staggered back into the camp. The few who were standing were helping to carry their brothers, but as soon as aid came to them, they too collapsed and had to be supported.

All the injured were swept away by the more able-bodied and taken into one of the larger tents where a physician could attend to them properly. Ayse ran through the slick without a care, the mud clinging to her fur as she rushed inside after the northern men. Caleb was already in the thick of it, barking out orders and helping to heave the wounded onto cots. The northerners were hurrying about the place, stripping the men of their bloodied clothes and shouting for more bandages. All the while Caleb was demanding answers. No one noticed the wolf amongst the madness.

As she watched the Orians battling desperately to save the lives of their comrades, the smell of blood filled her nostrils. Ayse could feel trepidation worming its way through her gut. In the time she had spent in Oror, she had never seen the northern soldiers so badly beaten.

"What happened?" Caleb demanded again.

"They're getting smarter," one of the injured soldiers answered through gritted teeth as his wound was being stitched together.

"What happened?" Caleb repeated as he moved closer.

"Those bastards... We thought we had them on the run, hunting them down... but they were just herding us into an ambush all along."

Caleb nodded in acknowledgement and placed his hand on the shoulder of the injured man to console him. The soldier gripped at Caleb's forearm and his voice became quiet as he hurriedly whispered, "Some of them are still out there."

Caleb stilled and stared at the man before nodding again, "I will take care of it."

As the northern lord strode from the tent, his face was set in a grim, determined expression and his eyes were alight with silent fury. Ayse could feel the invisible rage emanating from his tense body. As she followed Caleb out, she realised she wasn't the only one who noticed the change in his mood. The men distanced themselves from their lord as he stalked through the camp in anger. Ayse followed close enough behind to keep up with Caleb yet gave a wide enough berth so as not to irritate him.

Caleb went straight to his own tent, entering with Ayse close on his heels.

They found Markus and another man examining paperwork on the tabletop. Markus took one look at his lord and his face became just as sombre, causing the lieutenant to quickly look back to his work.

"After the men returned, I took the liberty of speaking with Nathaniel about where they had been dispatched to," Markus stated, indicating towards the maps in front of him.

"There are survivors," Caleb stated firmly.

Markus and Nathaniel exchanged troubled glances.

"We'll get a team together immediately, my lord," Nathaniel said, bowing his head briefly, before swiftly leaving.

Caleb moved towards the brazier. His face was implacable as he watched the flames writhe before him. He stood with his arms folded across his chest, his body tense and unyielding, and his knuckles white from how tightly he clenched his fists. With a lowered head, Ayse watched with unease, she had never seen the northern lord so affected by anything... never seen the Orian men so humbled in battle. It all seemed too surreal.

She looked to Markus, he seemed as concerned for his friend as much as she was. Ayse could tell by his expression that he was conflicted as to whether to disturb Caleb from his thoughts. Markus sighed as he ran his hands through his hair and fidgeted uncomfortably. Eventually, he spoke, his feigned light-hearted tone was clear, "First time for everything I guess."

At first, it didn't seem as though the words had made it through to Caleb. He was silent for some time before he looked over his shoulder and nodded to his companion. "We need to deal with this quickly before it gets out of hand," Caleb said flatly.

"Of course," Markus agreed, "Nathaniel is recruiting our best men and we'll set out at once."

"Increase the patrols. We cannot let this happen again."

Before Markus could respond, Nathaniel had returned, his face flushed and breathing heavy, no doubt from running about the camp gathering men together. He stood in the entrance and looked from Caleb to Markus before simply saying, "We're ready."

The northerners took no time in acting, following Nathaniel back outside where there were men preparing their horses. As Caleb climbed atop his horse, he motioned for his men to move out. Ayse instinctively began to follow.

"Stay," Caleb commanded, bringing Ayse to an abrupt halt.

All she could do was watch as the men left the camp, keeping her eyes trained on them until they were completely out of sight. The sky was greying, a mixture of the onset of evening coupled with the promise of more dismal weather.

Ayse could not bring herself to check in on the injured men, the smell of blood and broken flesh bothered her. Instead, she stood outside in the cold, keeping vigil and waiting for the return of Caleb and his men, unable to escape the groans of pain that emanated from the medical tent.

As night fell, the rain returned with a vengeance, pelting the camp and all those brave enough to face the weather with its heavy torrential deluge. The cold and wet reached down into Ayse's very bones and caused her still-healing wounds to throb and ache. There was only so much she could bear before she was reluctantly driven back inside to the familiar warmth of the fire.

***

Still drying out from the downpour, Ayse lay before the fire with her eyes impatiently trained on the entrance and her ears upright and alert. The rain had relented as dawn had broken, the dim glow of the sun chasing away the gloom and damp. Encouraged by the brightening weather, the morning birds had begun to sing their opening chorus in earnest. Other than the birdsong and the gentle crackle of the dying flames in the brazier behind her, Ayse could hear nothing. All was quiet within the camp. No voices, no shouts, just the peaceful calm of the early hours. Yet the tranquil morning did nothing to quiet Ayse's restlessness.

When the long-awaited sound of the return of the riders and their horses reached her ears, Ayse was wary as to whether she had been waiting so long that she was simply imagining it. Springing to her paws and quickly shaking to try and shift some of the damp sensation from her fur, the wolf rushed outside and was relieved to see the northerners as they arrived back to the camp. While the faces of the men were tired and grim, their bodies were more relaxed than before, and their mannerisms showed that they were weary more than concerned. This led Ayse to believe that they had been successful in their task. Ayse swiftly made her way across the camp to where the men were dismounting the horses, stretching their limbs and groaning from their aches and pains as they did so.

Ayse slipped between the bloodied and muddy Orian men until she found the one that she was looking for —Caleb. His eyes were still dark and brooding, but the gleam of anger that had been there the night before had finally been extinguished. From head to toe, his entire body was slick with a mixture of gore and muck, a testament to the vengeful wrath he had bestowed upon the intruders. Beside him, Markus was already beginning to relieve himself of his sopping wet clothing and attempting to clear his face of the grime with the soaked garments.

"Get clean and get some rest," Caleb ordered the men around him, handing his horse off to a young stable boy before adding, "You fought well."

The men dispersed to receive their well-earned rest and Caleb was no exception, he returned to his tent as soon as he had dismissed the northerners. Caleb began to extract himself from his dirtied clothing, dumping much of it onto the floor as soon as he had entered, before disappearing into his quarters. Not long after, Markus appeared in his half-dressed state and began to rekindle some life into the dying fire. The flames were hungrily erupting around the fresh wood that Markus had piled into the brazier by the time Caleb re-emerged clean and dressed.

"The medics say the men will live, though it was a close call for some of them. Many have a long recovery period ahead of them," Markus said as he heard his friend approach.

Caleb grunted in acknowledgement as he poured himself a glass of wine and slumped into a chair.

"We may have secured the breach in our defences for now, but we should warn the other lords and send word to Stormdown in case it should happen again," Markus continued.

When he still didn't get a proper response, Markus rose to his feet and turned to face his friend. Caleb simply nodded in agreement. The lieutenant moved towards the table and helped himself to the wine. Both men shared a few moments of silence as they drank, before Markus spoke again, "They were close to a settlement... If they ever reached the civilians-"

"I know." Caleb interrupted flatly.

From what Ayse had seen of the maps detailing the northern territory, the villages, towns and cities of the Orian people were further north than their current position. The various battle camps and the patrol routes to stop the Nevraahn threat were positioned between the border and the more populated areas of Oror. It made Ayse wonder how it was possible that the southerners had circumvented these and managed to make it so far into enemy lands.

Even though Caleb and his men had eliminated the threat, the muted natures of the men made her apprehensive. Perhaps the north was weaker than she had first assumed, was there a way for the Nevraahn dukes to win this war after all? She slunk to the floor, her own fatigue of keeping watch all night finally taking hold as she watched the two men drink their wine in reflective silence.

Chapter Nine

The sound of jovial voices carried down into the cold air of the stone prison. The noise grew as the men drank and the two girls knew that before long, their captors would stumble down into the darkness and find them. In the dim lighting that she had grown accustomed to, Lorie watched the wide-eyed look of fear on her younger tribal sister grow with each minute that passed. Ana's jaw was clenched tightly. She was sat with her knees up below her chin, her arms wrapped so tightly around her legs that her fingernails dug into her flesh. Looking at Ana, her face darkened with dirt, bruises, and dried blood, it made Lorie contemplate that she must look much the same. Ana's red hair was dirtied and unkempt, but then appearances weren't exactly foremost in their minds.

Poor Ana hadn't spoken since Paya had been taken away, and nothing that Lorie did could coax her out of her shell. The Bremlor men had broken Ana as if she were a wild mare in need of taming, and once they had crippled her sense of self, she had become nothing more than a hollow object that existed only as a source of enjoyment for them.

Knowing that she was running out of time, Lorie gave up on her attempts to shift and began to dress quickly. As she did so, she noticed just how skinny she had become since their imprisonment. Her body had become so rakishly thin that she could count her rib bones with ease. It had been some time since she had successfully transformed into her fox form as her body no longer possessed the required energy to do so. At first, they had managed to sate their compulsion for shifting by snatching time in fox form when left in the darkness alone. Despite her body being unable to transform, every fibre of her being felt the urge deep within her that she had gone too long without being on four paws, like an insatiable itch that she could not scratch.

Looking to Ana, Lorie wondered whether she still felt the same craving to shift, or whether every feeling other than fear had been obliterated from her body. Lorie couldn't remember the last time that her friend had even attempted to shift. Now she was just a shadow of her former self. Lorie shuffled closer to Ana and clutched at her.

"Keep your eyes closed, don't think about what is happening, just pretend we are safe somewhere else, safe at home," Lorie whispered the mantra over and over until the sound of the door above them unbolting caused her to fall silent.

Light showered into the darkness as the door was thrown open. Blinking against the harsh light, she could see the silhouette of Lord Frewin as he stood barring the entrance, the light shining down from behind him. As her eyes adjusted, Lorie could distinguish his leering face as he looked straight at her.

"Oh girly, are you not pleased to see me?" he sneered as he leisurely walked down the steps. His speech was slurred and his gait awkward as his body was laden with drink.

Behind him followed another man, but then it wasn't uncommon for Frewin to bring some of his party guests down to meet them. As handsome as the newcomer was, Lorie was immediately disgusted by his presence. She had tried pleading with some of the men Frewin had brought with him in the past, but they were all the same. Some of the men just liked to push them around, their real excitement coming from the damage and fear they could inflict on the girls, yet some of them had even darker desires. Lorie felt the bile rising within her at the thought.

Frewin noticed her eyeing the man next to him and chuckled. "Ever greedy for more aren't you. They put up a fight, but it is all for show, they love a bit of rough and tumble," he explained to the newcomer as they descended the last few steps.

The stranger's lips twisted up into a devilish smile that made Lorie shudder. She made a pitiful attempt to stay between Ana and their visitors, but as ever, it was futile. Frewin lurched forwards at Lorie and gripped her upper arm, pulling her up and thrusting her forwards at the other man as an offering. "Now, my good man, I promised you a reward and here it is. Be careful though, that one bites."

Lorie reeled away from the stranger, but he caught her before she could regain any sense of balance and trapped her with an iron grip. She looked back at Frewin closing in on Ana. The coward always chose the younger of the two girls as he knew she would put up no resistance. Ana was frozen with fear as Frewin grabbed her, pulled her to her feet and began to ascend the stairs with her in tow. Before Lorie could even contemplate struggling, her own captor had effortlessly picked her up and slung her over his shoulder. She kicked out her legs and dug her nails into his back, but the man was seemingly unmoved by her actions as he followed Frewin into the brightly lit corridor above.

Lorie could hear more men drinking themselves into a stupor in an adjoining room, but that was not where they were headed. Instead, she was carried down the hallway and into a small dark room while Frewin disappeared with Ana into another chamber.

The man dumped Lorie unceremoniously onto the small bed, the only furnishing in the room, before turning back to the door and bolting it closed. She sprang up from the bed as he turned to face her, Lorie could feel her face distorting in anger, ashamed of the tears that threatened to fall from her eyes. The man's face was calm as he watched her wordlessly as if gauging how she would act. He casually leaned back against the solid wood door and folded his arms in front of his chest. Lorie stood her ground, glaring at the man with her fists clenched, ready to fight. The man exhaled loudly as if put out by the whole event, then shook his head dismissively.

"I have no interest in you, girl, so do yourself a favour and get some sleep. We'll be in here for some time." Lorie glanced at the metal bolt on the door, but the man's gaze followed her own and he failed to hide the amusement in his voice as he advised her against causing trouble, "I might not have an interest in you, but that doesn't mean I'm not prepared to put you in your place if you decide to do anything foolish."

He motioned for her to get on the bed with a nod of his head. Suspicious of the strange turn of events, Lorie backed towards the bed without taking her eyes from him. His lips twitched as if fighting a smile and her eyes narrowed as she tried to second guess how the man was trying to trick her. She pulled herself onto the mattress, it was old and uncomfortable, and there was a stale damp smell about it that was so strong Lorie could taste it, yet even still, it was better than a stone floor. Lorie lay down on her side, bringing her knees up defensively in front of her so that she was almost curled into a ball. She refused to take her eyes off the man guarding the door, but he just stood there impassively and unmoving. Lorie fought the need to sleep, afraid that should she close her eyes something awful might befall her.

***

Lorie woke slowly, content that she was in no hurry to rouse herself any time soon. She turned her head to see Isaac sitting in front of the door. His knees were up, his arms resting on them casually, and his head was bowed, leaving her unable to see his face and tell whether he had fallen asleep or not. It was the fifth time in only a few weeks that Frewin had brought his new companion to visit the girls. As always, Frewin would steal Ana away, and as always, Lorie's mostly silent companion would instruct her to get some rest while he stayed motionless by the door.

Frewin had called the man by name on the second visit, and after the first uneventful night, this had prompted Lorie to attempt to engage in conversation with Isaac to seek his help, but he had simply ignored her. On the third visit, Lorie had begged Isaac to request Ana the next time he came, to save her tribal sister from suffering any further at the hands of Frewin. Isaac had simply stated that Frewin was a man of habit, and that he would not take kindly to having his routine disrupted, before falling silent for the rest of the night.

Moving as quietly as she could, Lorie sat up and carefully swung her legs over the side of the bed. The flagstone paving was cold against her bare feet as she softly approached Isaac and crouched beside him. She held her breath as she studied his face, afraid she would alert him to her presence. His eyes were closed, and his face was peaceful. His cropped curly dark hair was framing his face, making him appear almost angelic as he rested. His skin was more bronzed than that of a local man, in fact, it was unnatural for a man to be so tan at this time of year.

It was possible that he originated on foreign shores, yet his accent was that of a Nevraahn. Lorie wondered whether one of his parents had travelled to Nevraah from another country, imagining an exotic beauty of a woman travelling to a distant land and finding love. Once it hadn't been a great rarity to see foreigners in Nevraah, but in recent years, the war between the two neighbouring nations had become so heated that Nevraah had become less attractive to outsiders. Isaac was slim built, but he was well honed, he carried no weapons and did not wear a military uniform, leaving Lorie to ponder on what kind of career path the man had followed.

The sound of a door closing somewhere in the hallway caused Lorie to jump, when she looked back to Isaac she found that not only was he now awake, he was staring at her in a way that told her he was not happy to find her so close to him. She scooted backwards to give him space as he got to his feet.

"Come on, girl. It's time to get you back to your quarters."

"Are you *really* referring to the prison cell that way?" she scowled.

Isaac smiled, but did not respond. Instead, he took her by the arm and opened the door. As they travelled back down the corridor, Lorie could see a guard on watch, which meant that Frewin had already returned Ana to their cell. At the sight of Isaac and Lorie approaching, the guard unlocked the door and stood aside. Isaac guided her through the doorway before releasing his grip on her. She turned to face him, and he gave her a softened look before closing the door and leaving her in utter darkness. The sound of the guard locking the door seemed to resonate loudly in the shadows and Lorie waited until her eyes grew accustomed to the gloom before descending the stairs, feeling her way down by running her hand along the stone wall.

Her eyes were still adjusting, but she could just about make out the small pale form of Ana hunched over in the corner. Lorie swung her arms around the smaller girl and hugged her tightly. Ana's body stiffened at the touch of her friend. She was still refusing to speak, barely moved, and was just wasting away into nothingness. Left in the darkness to be forgotten, Lorie was worried that one day her friend would be swallowed up by the shadows and simply cease to exist completely.

Lorie hadn't told Ana about Isaac. She wasn't even sure that Ana was taking in anything of what she said any longer, and she didn't dare speak out in case someone heard her. Somehow, the stoic man had given Lorie some small glimmer of hope, even though he had refused to help her thus far. Whatever happened, she knew he was her best bet at being able to do anything to help their situation, as he was the only one that had ever shown her compassion in that vile city. She just had to keep trying to convince him to help them.

Chapter Ten

The city was alive. The festive drums were a rhythmic heartbeat that pulsed through the floor beneath the feet. Spring was well under way in Brankah, the days were growing longer, and the weather was finally beginning to turn for the better. The spring festival was enveloping the city in its celebratory embrace as Brankah welcomed in the season of rebirth. The streets were heavily crowded. Tobias was rubbing shoulders with people on either side of himself, noble and pauper alike, and everyone was moving constantly in a steady current.

The only paving stones free of footfall were occupied by street stalls. The merchants were selling various items, from steaming dishes that flooded the streets with aromatic scents, to wooden toys for children. Tobias stopped at the carpentry stall to appreciate the small menagerie of brightly painted animals on display. Tucked away at the back of the stall he could see an orange face with a crooked grin poking out between a lopsided horse and a purple cow. Tobias reached out and felt the varnished wood beneath his fingers as he stared at the small fox in his hand. From beneath hooded eyelids he glanced at the vendor who was busy in conversation before casually walking away; still gently holding the wooden animal that now resided in his pocket.

Every few metres along the street there was a new form of music or entertainment, but no matter how far he drifted through the town, the resonating drumbeats could still be heard. The energy of the people was infectious, and Tobias could feel it warming his very soul.

He wondered where Nell and Ben would be. Whether they would be taking advantage of the generous crowd and performing somewhere in the chaos, or whether they would be taking the time to appreciate the festival themselves. Tobias couldn't remember the last time he had been amongst so many strangers. He hadn't been out on a contract in years, instead, always staying close to home, wherever home happened to be at the time.

Attempting to find his fellow tribesman was proving to be nigh impossible, at least in human form. Tobias backtracked along the street and headed to the inn where he had managed to secure a room. It hadn't been easy. The festival had attracted people from all around and Tobias had reluctantly paid more than what the ground floor room was worth to claim it. Returning to the inn took longer than he had anticipated because of the constant waves of people flowing around the city. Whichever way he went, it felt as though he was going against the tide of bodies.

The sight of the humble inn was a welcome sight to him, and once he was safely inside the sanctity of his own room, he pushed the door to, leaving it slightly ajar, and slung his bag under the bed. Tobias then placed his newfound wooden friend on the bedside table before swiftly undressing, tossing his clothes onto the floor and taking to his knees to begin his transformation. He quickly glanced up at the wooden fox watching him and returned its toothy grin as he felt the change overcome him. Once he had fully shifted, Tobias leisurely stretched out, enjoying the feeling of the muscles move beneath his furred skin. It always felt good to change into fox form.

Nosing open the door just enough that he could squeeze through, Tobias slipped out of his room and bounded down the dimly lit hallway and towards the open window. He effortlessly jumped onto the wooden sill and glanced out at the alleyway before jumping down and taking to the streets. Not wanting to be trampled underfoot, Tobias slipped along the very edges of the buildings, unseen by the people in the street. The festival was a whole new world to him in fox form, the scents and sounds were so much more vibrant and overpowering. While as a man he had enjoyed the crowds and noise, as a fox it was a complete pain to his senses, the spicy foods made his nostrils itch and the loud music hurt his sensitive ears.

The more Tobias explored of the brimming Brankah, the more he realised that the city centre was simply too full for any real kind of street performance. If Nell and Ben weren't enjoying the festival, they would most likely be slipping their hands in various pockets and relieving the people of some of their property. After all, on a night where you grow accustomed to being bumped and jostled by the crowd, stealing becomes child's play.

Weaving amongst crates and baskets, Tobias's ears swivelled on his head as he kept his head low, constantly alert should his senses stumble across a familiar sound or smell. He ventured further away from the bustling city centre and traversed some of the outer districts to sample the area for evidence of his friends.

It didn't take him as long as he expected to find a sign of the traveller couple. He picked up the faint, but recognisable smell of the lilac flower perfume that Nell favoured. Following the trail meant daring to step into the path of celebrators, but fortunately, in fox form, Tobias was especially nimble. He was able to move with such ease that the people of Brankah were not even aware that he was jumping about their feet.

The trail led him to a bar and even under the distinct scent of stale ale, Tobias could tell that the Vulpini had recently passed through. The door was firmly shut, not that nudging it open and entering as an animal would have been a wise move. Tobias slipped down a side alley that was permeated with the stench of urine and was grateful to hear the flap of fabric somewhere close by.

***

Many faces turned to watch him with the same suspicious gaze as he entered the establishment. With one quick glance, Tobias evaluated that it was an utter shit hole. He didn't know whether the cautious stares he was receiving were because he was a stranger, or because the clothing he had borrowed from the makeshift washing line nearby didn't fit as well as he would have liked.

Smiling awkwardly, Tobias left the safety of the doorway and headed towards the bar, a man who refused to move out of his way eyed him with contempt as Tobias shuffled past close enough that he could smell the man was in need of a good wash. Catching the eye of the barkeep, Tobias smiled and politely asked for a drink. The young man behind the bar looked at him with narrowed eyes, pouring the drink in such a sloppy manner that the alcohol spilled all over the floor, before thumping it down in front of Tobias without a word.

Deciding that charm was lost on the man, Tobias elected to pay for the drink without thanking the barkeep. He turned around and began to sip from the tankard. He winked at the man who had refused to move, silently thanking the guy for his drink considering the coins that he had lifted from his unsuspecting pocket had paid for it. He scanned the rest of the bar and was happy to see the fiery red of Nell's hair in a corner booth. Still being eyed up by some of the locals, Tobias glided over to the table and sat down before the couple even realised what was happening.

"Tobias! What are you doing here?" Nell squeaked with excitement as she flung her arms around him and hugged him with more strength than her small size should possess. She looked down at his clothes and frowned. "What are you wearing?"

"I borrowed them from one of the neighbours." Tobias grinned.

"I hope you have your own clothing somewhere. You look awful." Reuben laughed.

"Thank you for that Ben, but yes, I have my things stored at my inn room."

"So, has the chief sent you?" Nell chatted away casually.

"Actually, no he did not."

The couple stared at him with a sudden unease. Nell looked from Tobias to Reuben and gave him a meaningful glare as if silently instructing him to say something.

"Does he... know you're here?" Reuben asked awkwardly.

"I imagine he's noticed that I have left, and I know him to be smart enough to work out where I have gone." Tobias sighed. He saw Reuben opening his mouth once more as if to say something, but Tobias carried on before he could venture an opinion, "I know what you will say, but I am not going anywhere. I have been miserable for such a long time, I just... I just need to be here. I need to be doing something to help. Even if it means waiting here for Ayse to return or waiting until the point we know that she won't ever return. I *must* be here. Please."

Nell and Ben looked at each other, reminding Tobias that the silent communication that bounced back and forth between the two Vulpini was like nothing he had ever seen before. Not wanting to start a serious debate on whether he should or should not be in Brankah, Tobias decided to distract them with a slightly different path of dialogue, "Have you heard anything from her?"

Nell shook her head solemnly. "It's now spring. Ayse knew we needed the information around now, but she has sent no word. Nothing... I'm so worried, I just..." she trailed off as tears welled in her eyes and began to run down her cheeks, yet she made no other sound.

Tobias's heart sank. People often spoke of 'heartache', but it was all too easy to forget how literal the phrase could be as the pain within his chest grew stronger. It was a sobering thought, everyone knew that Ayse was heading into danger by going to Oror, but the reality that she could be hurt, or even worse, that she could be dead, was beginning to dawn on him properly for the first time.

"We have until the summer now. We just need to have faith," Nell spoke softly as she regained her composure and reached out across the table to clasp Tobias' hands in her own. "We have asked Ayse to do the impossible, she's charting new territory, and it was unrealistic to set a deadline for that. There are just too many unknown factors. I am sure she is doing the best she can, she will come back to us when she is able to."

Tobias gave a weak smile, but even Nell's encouraging words weren't enough to lift the heavy weight from within the pit of his stomach. He knew that the odds of being reunited with the werewolf were slim and it made him feel physically sick to think of it.

"Nell and I have become pretty good at this waiting game, and as hard as it is, you just have to take each day as it comes, Tobias. If you don't, you'll be even more miserable here than when you were waiting with the tribe."

"We were just about to go and check out some of the festivities when you showed up, do you want to come with us?" asked Nell.

"It will take your mind off things, for a little while at least," Reuben added.

Tobias shook his head, but he tried to look as though they had at least managed to raise his spirits somewhat, giving them both a wide smile that disappeared as soon as they had left. He stared at the drink on the table in front of him without really registering that he was looking at it all. His mind was beginning to wander to dark places; he imagined mysterious woods with innumerable secrets that housed just one that he desperately sought the answer to – where was Ayse?

"Is my ale not good enough for you?"

The voice pulled him out of his daze, and he looked up to see a portly man looking down at him. Tobias expected to see a disgruntled expression, but the older man's face was kindly and the smile in his eyes made Tobias realise that he was jesting with him. Tobias wanted to respond, but he could only manage a sad smile as thoughts of Ayse still haunted him. The man raised an eyebrow as if surprised by the silence but took the seat opposite Tobias regardless.

Realising that the older man was going nowhere soon, Tobias ventured into the realm of conversation, "I take it you own this bar?"

The older man nodded. "I didn't come over here so you could compliment me on my fine establishment." The man paused to smile before continuing, "I am going to be honest with you. I am deeply worried about a friend of mine who appears to have vanished. Now before you ask what this has to do with you, the person in question happens to be friends with that rather interesting couple that just left."

Tobias could feel his stomach turn with unease, but he made sure that his face did not betray his discomfort. Instead, he took a swig from his drink and maintained a calm expression as he nonchalantly eyed the bar owner.

"I mean you or your friends no harm. I have tried to speak with them myself, but they haven't been very forthcoming... My friend, Ayse, she is very important to me. I just want to know that she is safe."

At the mention of Ayse's name, Tobias took a renewed interest in the man before him. While the barkeep didn't appear very threatening at first glance, Tobias found himself wondering whether there was more to the older man than met the eye. If Ayse was an acquaintance of his, then it stood to reason that there must have been something that brought the two of them together. Tobias couldn't imagine her striking up a friendship with a tavern owner otherwise.

The Vulpini had given Ayse the taste of travelling, something that was not easily forgotten, and the skills she had learnt to survive also meant that finding fresh opportunities and targets would be a necessity. That meant that it wasn't likely that Ayse had ever resided in Brankah long enough to culture a real friendship, which in turn meant their friendship had grown from some form of mutual cause or association. While he could mull it over and try and decide the most reasonable answer, Tobias instead decided to cut to the chase, "How do you know Ayse?"

Horace's eyes narrowed as he contemplated the question, with a sigh he decided that if he hoped to get any truth from the traveller, he had best start by being honest himself. "I help her find clients, those in need of her special skills and who are willing to pay for them. She was quite the popular choice amongst the people."

Tobias nodded knowingly. His mouth quirked up at the thought of what kind of interesting jobs Ayse must have experienced. With her more unique ability to go undercover as an animal combined with her thievery skills, it was highly believable that she had excelled as an agent of underhanded jobs in the city.

"You know her." It wasn't a question, but a statement. Tobias nodded in response and so Horace continued, "Can you tell me where she is?"

"She is currently working a job, a personal one."

"That doesn't tell me where she is."

"No, but it is all I can give you."

"Is she safe?"

Regret seemed to lodge in Tobias's throat, he lowered his eyes, his response was throaty and raw, "We don't know."

"What do you mean? Did something go wrong?"

"Not as far as we know. I can tell you care for Ayse, really, but I can't go into the details. You will know when she returns as soon as we do, as this is where she will be heading. If she wants to tell you what happened then, that will be her decision."

Horace wasn't happy with the vague answer, but it was more than the traveller couple had ever given him and so he appreciated it, nonetheless. However, he wasn't prepared to just wait it out and see if Ayse returned in one piece. The sooner Raphael managed to unearth some real information, the better.

"Let us hope that Ayse returns soon then," Horace said firmly as he rose from the table, leaving the traveller to finish his drink alone.

Chapter Eleven

The evening air was particularly mild for Oror. There was no downpour of rain, no storm of snow falling, and the wind had lulled into a gentle breeze. While Ayse still found the climate to be distinctly cold, it was clear that the northerners were finding the weather to be rather balmy, as some of the men were bare-chested as they enjoyed the festivities. Ayse inhaled deeply, enjoying the delicious smell of the hog roast rotating on the spit above the bright flames before her. The meat was glistening as it turned; the pig was criss-crossed with score marks, parts of the meat already looking crispy, while other portions oozed with golden juices. The mere sight of it was causing Ayse's bottom jaw to pool with saliva.

There was a variety of food and drink being prepared, and multiple kegs and barrels had been rolled out especially for the occasion. Ayse had spied a heavenly looking rabbit pie earlier amongst the dishes of delicacies, and even while she watched the pork twirl above the flames, the breeze brought with it the scent of venison that was cooking elsewhere in the camp, attempting to lure the wolf away from her object of desire.

It had been somewhat of a surprise for Ayse to see the Orians lay down their weapons for a day to celebrate the onset of spring with such earnest; even Caleb was more light-hearted than usual. Ayse had caught sight of him singing along with some of his men to a bawdy northern ditty and was grateful to have been in wolf form, otherwise she would have burst out laughing at the sight.

Ayse pulled herself away from watching the roasting meat with some regret, instead choosing to be distracted by watching with amusement as the Orian men drank themselves stupid. More than one of the northerners was drenched with ale from chin to chest, as they participated in drinking contests that were usually followed by drunken fist fights to see which man could handle his drink better. Despite some of the bloody results, there wasn't any discord in the camp that evening. All the men were enjoying themselves immensely and the merriment was clearly contagious, as Ayse felt her own spirits lifting.

It was easy to become enamoured with the casual nature of the northerners, the Orian men were so full of life that Ayse felt envious of their happiness. As she looked around at the grinning red faces of the soldiers, Ayse could hear the clack of tankards meeting mid-air as men drank to whatever excuses they could think of. All the while, the hearty, upbeat music vibrated through the camp with an accompaniment of gruff northern singers. Even the thick veil of night could not pierce the cocoon of warmth and revelry that enshrouded Caleb's camp.

The northerners had accepted Ayse as one of their own. As she drifted about the camp sharing in the jovial atmosphere, the soldiers would toss her scraps of meat, reach out to stroke her head, and one particularly drunk Orian had even tried getting her to sample some of the mead. Ayse's ears pricked up as she heard one of the men talking about her, she paused and watched the man as he raised his drink towards her.

"See, here she is!" he announced with slurred words. "I once said she was a bad omen for the Wolfriks, but look at her now, proof that the north can endure anything."

The soldiers surrounding him all cheered and toasted to Ayse's speedy recovery, causing her to feel a sudden sharp pang of guilt as she considered how she was deceiving the lot of them. The festive mood dissipated from her as quickly as smoke on the wind as Ayse remembered why she was in Oror in the first place. She headed for Caleb's tent with the intention of retiring for the night, no longer feeling that she deserved to be a part of the happy crowd.

There were no guards at the door as she entered, but she could hear the happy banter of men inside before she had even made it through the entrance. Sat at his table, Caleb, Markus, Bernd, and two of his men were busy playing a game of cards. The tabletop had been cleared of all battle plans and missives, and now was laden with plenty of drinks, plates with half-eaten food, and dog-eared playing cards.

Ayse watched Caleb with interest as she realised that the northern lord, along with the other card players, was far from sober. He sat casually slouched in his chair, his eyes half-lidded with drink and his shirt open, displaying his broad chest beneath it. There was a crimson blush about Caleb's cheeks from the wine he had consumed, and his eyes were bright with laughter.

Markus was managing to look a little more sober than the others, though he was still far from his usually subdued countenance. Bernd was swaying in his seat, but Ayse wasn't sure that the old dog keeper was even aware he was doing so. One of the guards was relaying a tale of a girl he knew back in his home village that apparently had an ass as large as that of a bear, and the other guard had his head rested on his arms atop the table as if he had already passed out.

She padded in quietly, not wanting to disrupt the men as they played. Caleb spotted her first and whilst still talking to the others he reached out for some of the food that had been abandoned on the table before offering his hand out to her. Noticing this, Bernd turned to see Ayse, almost falling from his chair completely in doing so, and broke into a wide grin.

"Here's my good luck charm!" the old man barked cheerfully.

While Ayse felt strange about being fed by hand, she was keenly aware that it would be entirely unlike any canine she knew to refuse such a tasty treat. She gently took the pork meat from Caleb's hand, after which he ruffled the fur between her ears.

"Let's see whose good luck she is," Caleb said confidently as he smirked at Bernd. "Deal again, Markus."

"I don't need a wolf to bring me luck." Markus smiled as he gathered the cards from the table and began shuffling them. "I think you've got more chance of the old gods bestowing fortune upon you than a beast."

"You must be the only non-superstitious northerner," mumbled the guard that had his face down on the table, evidently still conscious.

This statement caused Caleb to begin grinning from ear to ear as he gave his second in command a mocking look and winked at him. Markus shook his head at his friend with a smile and sighed.

"It's not that I'm not superstitious," Markus corrected, "I just don't see how a wolf can bring good luck."

"Ah, but she's not just any wolf. She's *our* wolf," Bernd replied, slapping his palm onto the table as he emphasised his words, causing the bottles of wine to shuffle slightly with each bang.

"Well, let's just see how lucky she is then," Markus said as he began dealing the cards.

Ayse sat on her haunches to watch as the card game unfolded. It was a game she was unfamiliar with and even by watching it she was unable to grasp the rules, so she couldn't tell which of the northerners was winning. All the men were past any point of sobriety to maintain their poker faces; instead, they would openly mock each other and give glances and smiles that betrayed how good their hands were. It didn't take long for the guard who was taking part to admit defeat and fold his hand. As the game appeared to reach a close, Caleb was winking at Bernd as all the men watched Markus frowning at the hand of cards he was left with. Frustrated, the lieutenant threw his cards to the table and looked at the smug faces that surrounded him.

"Luck not with you then?" Bernd asked as all the men broke into laughter.

"You can all sod off," Markus replied sulkily as he leaned back in his chair and folded his arms across his chest.

"That still leaves us with the question of whose good luck charm she really is," Bernd said turning to Caleb.

"Well let's see your cards then, old man," Caleb taunted with a raised eyebrow.

Both men revealed their cards at the same time, laying them flat on the table so Ayse was unable to see clearly what they had held. She looked between their faces trying to discern who had won the game, but the northerners were simply grinning at each other.

"All that proves is that the bitch is wise enough to know to be loyal to her master," Bernd sighed.

"Is that all?" Caleb scoffed.

"Let's see how well your luck holds then, my lord," Bernd suggested.

Markus sighed and shook his head, but a smile was playing about his lips as he leaned forward and gathered the cards up once more. "This is going to be a long night."

Ayse continued to watch with amusement as the northerners progressively became more intoxicated and played hand after hand of cards with mixed results. They went from arguing over who she brought luck to, to who had the worst tell, to taunting Bernd with the fact his mother could likely wield a blade better than he could, to all manner of strange discussions. It was a rare glimpse into Caleb's personality as he removed his persona of warlord and simply became one of the northerners drinking to the arrival of spring.

As she sat beside him, Caleb would occasionally stroke Ayse affectionately, his touch lingering more often as drink got the better of him. When it got to the point that she had simply become an armrest, Ayse shook his hand from her head, causing Caleb to stare at the brightening sky outside of the tent.

"Gods, I think we've had enough for one night," he muttered as he rose to his feet unsteadily and downed the last of his drink.

Markus turned to follow his gaze and chuckled, "You mean because it's no longer night?"

At this point, Bernd was sat upright, but his eyes were firmly closed, and he was snoring loudly. Markus clapped him heartily on the back, causing the poor man to startle from his sleep.

"Come on, Bernd," Markus said as he helped the man to his feet.

Bernd was muttering something, more to himself than Markus, but Ayse couldn't discern a single word of it. The lieutenant gently led the dog keeper from the tent while Bernd was still sleepily rubbing at his bleary eyes. The other man at the table roused his companion, putting his arm about his waist and hauling him up before they also took their leave, supporting one another as they staggered out into the fresh morning air. Caleb slowly stretched and stumbled towards his sleeping quarters, pulling off his shirt in one lazy movement and letting it drop to the floor as he pawed his way through the curtains and disappeared into the adjoining room.

The sight of the bright morning sky stung Ayse's eyes and she realised just how tired she was. She slunk over to the brazier but seeing that it had burnt out quite some time ago she decided to leave the draftier portion of the tent and followed Caleb into his darkened chambers. The northern lord was face down on his bed, sprawled over the top of the covers as if he had walked in and just collapsed on top of it. Already she could hear his deep breathing; sleep had clearly come to him quickly, aided by the wine he had consumed, no doubt. Ayse curled up on the floor beside the bed, and as she began to drift off, she could hear the faint sound of birdsong as the world outside awoke to the new day.

Chapter Twelve

Raphael was getting a headache. It wasn't from the copious amount of drink he had consumed either, it was from having to listen to the moronic man sat in front of him night after night. The man's weasel-like face irritated him beyond reason as he continued to brag and chuckle about his latest endeavours. Raphael tried to ignore the man while simultaneously appearing as though he was utterly engrossed in what was being said. As he sat in the dimly lit room over-packed with furnishings that would have looked decadent if they weren't so damn filthy, Raphael realised that High Bremlor was just as much of a dive as Lower Bremlor.

It had taken a lot of careful planning to come as far as he had, not to mention a lot of money spent on bribes and purchasing information, as well as a lot of time spent gathering his own material too. Raphael had found his perfect target in the pitiful, conceited man that sat before him guzzling wine to such a slovenly point that his whiskers were beginning to stain red. As a Bremlor lord and an officer in the Bremlor infantry, not only did he have access to High Bremlor, but he had been able to add Raphael to the exclusive guest list of those allowed there. Gaining the man's trust had been another job entirely. Men such as this didn't just give anyone their confidence, Raphael had been forced to earn it and then maintain it.

Raphael was brought to attention as the officer downed the last of his wine and slammed the glass onto the table. He was inebriated so much that his eyelids no longer seemed to be blinking in unison and he had the most sadistic grin plastered to his face.

The lord's words fell out of his mouth in a slur, "Come on, boy. Your lady friend is waiting." The man rose to his feet with little grace and beckoned for Raphael to follow.

With Lower Bremlor in the depressing state that it was, it hadn't been hard for Raphael to find a man willing to do just about anything for some coin. He'd paid a local to attack the lord when he next stumbled into an alleyway for a piss and then all Raphael had to do was be ready and waiting to swoop in and save the day. Raphael had bloodied the "attacker" somewhat to make his rescue truly believable, but the man in question hadn't cared if he was paid for the trouble. The plan had been quite simple. Raphael had almost been surprised that it had worked so well.

The lord was so quick to thank Raphael that he had practically tripped over himself in the process, going so far as to invite him for drinks with his fellow High Bremlor cronies. Then Raphael had put his charms to good use and built up a rapport with the soldiers. There were many nights of drinking and betting, and the men had especially liked the ease in which Raphael could woo a woman. and He had even attempted to teach them a few of his tricks with the ladies to cultivate more trust. He should have known better that the lecherous cowardly men he had been associating with would have their own twisted methods of getting a woman to bed, methods that they were all too willing to share with Raphael eventually.

And so here they were again to visit Bremlor's dirty little secret. Raphael obediently followed the man in front of him down into the darkness of the prison cell. The light from the hallway above illuminated the two pale and pitiful forms of the girls kept prisoner there. It hadn't been easy to restrain himself when he had first been invited to partake in Lord Frewin's nocturnal activities, more than anything Raphael had just wanted to smash his fist into that sneering face until it no longer resembled a face at all. But he knew that doing such a thing would help no one, least of all the two girls.

The prison cell was deep below the city in the subterranean catacombs. Above them, many more soldiers were stationed, then above that was Lord Frewin's estate, which was not only full of guards, but servants too. There was no way that Raphael would be able to escape if he allowed himself to fall victim to any notion of heroism. Raphael looked to the familiar face of the girl he had tried so hard to not become close with and she returned his stare with fierce eyes. Lorie was a fighter, she would survive this ordeal providing that help got to her eventually, however, looking over to the other girl, Raphael was not so sure that the younger one would make it. Frewin grabbed at his usual victim and dragged her upstairs, all the while Raphael just watched Lorie. Her jaw was clenched shut as she watched her friend being taken away.

"Come on," Raphael spoke softly, beckoning for Lorie to follow him.

Once they had reached the top of the stairs, Raphael made sure to take her by the arm so that the guard on duty would believe she was being taken unwillingly and he didn't let go until they were in the privacy of the closed room. On entering the now-familiar room, Lorie immediately went to the bed and sat down quietly, she watched Raphael as he took his usual seat on the floor in front of the door. She lowered her eyes and began to impatiently twiddle her fingers, weaving them through one another, it made Raphael smile.

"Spit it out, girl. You obviously want to say something, so say it already."

Lorie looked surprised for a moment before regaining her composure; Raphael noticed that she was pouting, sulking because he had been able to devise her intentions.

"Why are you here?" Her tone was demanding, but Raphael just tutted and shook his head with a smile. "You're not a friend of Frewin's, not really. If you were, you would be just as sick as he is." Raphael still didn't answer, prompting Lorie to continue, "I can see it in your face. You hide it from him, but I can see that he disgusts you. I know that you say you can't help us, but surely you can tell me why you are really here."

"I am looking for... a friend... I guess you could call her that."

"Do you think she is being kept here? Like us?"

"No, I doubt that is the case. Have you seen any other women here?"

"No. It's always just been me and Ana. If you don't think your friend is here, why are you in Bremlor?"

Raphael considered whether there would be any harm in divulging such information to the girl, he doubted anyone would believe her if she spoke out, but he also didn't think she would betray his trust. "Someone I believe to be an associate of hers is here. If I can find out why he is here, maybe I can find out where she went."

"If she knows any of the men here, then I think your friend needs to associate with better people."

Raphael smiled as he explained, "He is not a local man."

"Oh. Well, did you try just asking him about her?" she asked, but Raphael shook his head in response. "Why not?"

"He is a secretive man. He does not know me and therefore he will not trust me. He and his people approached my friend. I believe they tasked her with something. They knew her by name too. But too much time has passed now, something must have happened to her for her to have been gone for so long. We just want to make sure she is found."

"His people?"

"Gypsies." He replied, as he did so a chill ran over Lorie and she shuddered. Misinterpreting her reaction, he asked her, "Are you cold?"

Lorie shook her head. She bit her lip as she wondered whether she should continue with the conversation. Was this all a ploy? Was Isaac just here on Frewin's behest to get information out of her? It was possible, but it was also possible that Isaac was telling the truth. She had to know for sure, but she had to be careful. "This man, what does he look like? I will tell you if he has been here."

Raphael looked sombre, clearly uneasy with the idea of making Lorie speak of men that may have hurt her. "You don't have to do that."

"Just tell me."

Lorie could feel a knot coiling in her stomach as Isaac described Rojas perfectly. If he was in Bremlor, it meant that he was the go-between for the tribe and the Duke. This information was not a surprise to her as Rojas would have been the obvious choice for such a task. It pained her to know that the older Vulpini man that she missed so dearly was in the city, so close to her and yet completely out of reach. It didn't answer her question as to whether Isaac was who he said he was, or whether he really was just a pawn of Frewin's.

"Frewin has not brought that man here." Lorie wasn't lying, but she felt as though she was cheating by not telling Isaac that she knew who he was talking of. "How can you be sure that he knows your friend?"

"Because he was seen with the people that we believe hired her. My friend possesses a particular skill set, she is often hired to perform certain tasks and undertake delicate jobs. She was approached by two gypsies in Brankah, as I said before, we believe they knew her. But after meeting with them she disappeared without telling us anything."

Lorie couldn't help but smile, this friend of Isaac's sounded like she would have fitted in rather well with the Vulpini. If Isaac was telling the truth, part of the tribe had reached out to this woman for some reason. But it just didn't make sense to her. The Vulpini were close-knit, they wouldn't have turned to an outsider so readily. Unless it wasn't really an outsider they had turned to. As her brain pieced together all the fragments of information, she could feel herself on the edge of a revelation, Lorie could hear herself speaking before she had even made a conscious decision to do so, "Her name?"

"What?"

"Your friend, what is her name?" Lorie's voice had risen. She seemed impatient, her eyes had grown wider, and she appeared on edge. It made Raphael suddenly unsure of her, causing him to wonder what had elicited that kind of response and so he did not answer. Lorie's restlessness overcame her, "Is it Ayse?"

For the first time that he could ever recall, Raphael was speechless. His mouth hung open, but no words came forth as he tried to piece together how Ayse could possibly know the poor soul in front of him. Seeing his reaction, Lorie knew the answer to her question without him having to say anything. She breathed a sigh of relief as many things began to fall into place in her mind. Ayse had been recruited to help the Vulpini; she was the solution to their captivity. Furthermore, Frewin had no knowledge of Ayse, meaning that Isaac had been truthful and that he was an ally, even if he was a somewhat reluctant one.

Knowing that finally there was a real glimmer of hope filled Lorie was a sense of purpose, her courage had been slowly waning, but now she could feel it come flooding back to her. Tears began to fall down her face as she broke into spontaneous laughter, Raphael looked at her worriedly, but she waved away his concern and tried to calm herself.

"So, you know Ayse?" he asked cautiously.

Lorie nodded, her cheeks were still wet from her tears, but the smile on her face was unwavering. "I haven't seen her for some time. How is she? Before all of this, I mean."

"She was well when I saw her last. She travels often, as do I, but when we meet-" a smile came to Raphael's lips as he said, "Well, let's just say we have a bit of a rivalry going on. Whoever has been doing the best gets to crow over the other and buy them a drink. If I recall correctly, Ayse is winning."

"She sounds like she hasn't changed."

"So, tell me, where is she? What is happening here?"

Lorie paused, while she perceived Isaac as an ally, there were some truths that needed to remain untold. "Ayse used to be one of us."

"One of you?"

"Part of the Vulpini tribe," Lorie clarified.

"A gypsy then," Raphael snorted.

"Is that so bad?" she responded defensively.

"Actually, it explains a lot." Raphael chuckled. "But what do you mean she *used* to be one of you?"

"She left the tribe. That is a story for another time, maybe. In any case, the tribe got into trouble with Duke Remus, we're being held to ransom, so to speak."

"So, your tribe has to pay up before the duke will release you and your friend?"

"No, it isn't that simple. And it isn't just the two of us either. Three of our men are here somewhere too... You haven't seen them?"

"Shit... No."

"The duke doesn't want money. He wants to take control of the north. The tribe has to get him information on Oror for him to agree to release us."

"You do realise how ridiculous that is?" Raphael paused in disbelief, expecting her to correct what she had just said, but she simply stared at him mournfully. "No one has ever made it back from the north. I get that gypsies are known for being stealthy and underhanded, you're a people after my own heart, but some things just can't be done."

"There is one person who is capable of getting into the north undetected..." Lorie trailed off, looking at him as he understood what she left unsaid.

"Please, don't tell me you mean Ayse-" Raphael began.

Lorie cut him short before he could finish, "I know why my tribe would go to her and they have their reasons for why it had to be her. After what you've told me, she is almost certainly in the north at their behest."

"Then your people have sent her to a death sentence. Didn't you stop to think that there would be an easier way than sending Ayse into enemy territory?" Isaac's voice had taken on the tone of a lecturer and Lorie did not appreciate it.

"They did try another way and a friend of mine paid the price. There were six hostages to begin with. Now we are five." Isaac did not look content with her response, but he bit his tongue none the less. His face looked tense as he processed all of the information she had just given him. "What will you do now that you know of Ayse?" she asked.

"I will return to Brankah, to a friend of mine who is also very worried about her. He will have a better idea of what to do next."

It pained Lorie to hear this, to know that Isaac would leave without a second thought and abandon her to her fate. She knew that he had no responsibility towards her, but it still hurt to be cast aside so easily. Her eyes began to water, and not wanting Isaac to see, she decided to lie down on the bed with her back to him as she muttered, "We should both get some rest."

Chapter Thirteen

Ayse's heart was pounding. The adrenaline was pumping through her blood like fire, preventing her from feeling the cold northern air on her bare skin. The transformation back into her human form had been bittersweet, it was a release that she had wanted for so long, but it had not come easily to her. She had never experienced such a painful transition; her body was still in the echoes of discomfort and she was not relishing the idea that she would soon have to shift once more. Ayse did not have the luxury of time to wait for her body to recover, every moment that she remained in human form increased the risk of her being discovered.

Her hands felt numb as she fumbled with papers and quill, desperately copying information to parchment, making rough sketches of the lay of the land and copying down patrol routes as best she could. It wasn't the cold that caused her fingers to fail her. The feeling had simply become foreign to her as she had spent too long in wolf form. The sensation of pins and needles was over every inch of her body and every move that she made was painful.

While Ayse's body had healed well, she doubted whether she was truly healthy enough to make the trip back to the south. In human form, she could see the puckering skin on her leg where the trap had bitten through. The wound looked red and angry, but it pained her far less now. Regardless of the state of her health, Ayse was not prepared to wait any longer. Spring had already begun, and she knew that she had to make it back to Brankah and hand over the information before the summer arrived. The northerners were out hunting once again, and while it was rare for anyone to enter Caleb's quarters while he was away, Ayse was aware that she could be interrupted at any moment.

She could have just simply stolen the paperwork, however, if Caleb suspected that information on Oror may have fallen into the wrong hands, it could cause the northerners to re-evaluate their entire plans for that year. She had to be careful and ensure that they did not suspect anything was missing. Ayse grabbed a bag that had lain forgotten in the tent for some time and began to pack the paperwork into it. There was a noise just outside causing her to freeze, but after a few moments of bated breath, there was only silence. Ayse slung the bag over her head, secured it as tight against her body as she could, then dropped to the floor and began her change.

She had hoped that her earlier transformation would have paved the way for the next, regrettably she had been wrong. Her whole body coursed with burning pain, protesting her own shifting nature. Ayse could feel herself contorted between two very different forms and yet her body did not seem able to make that last push back into a wolf. Panic began to stir inside of her, but she desperately fought to keep it from overcoming her. Giving in to alarm would only distance Ayse even further from being able to complete her transformation.

She took a deep breath and attempted to clear her mind by focusing on the trivial things around her. She breathed in the familiar scent of the north and glanced around the interior of the tent, the furnishings had become commonplace to her, she knew where they would be without even having to seek them out. As she evaluated her surroundings, Ayse came to the realisation that she would never return to Oror and she was suddenly overcome with a peculiar feeling, as if she were leaving behind something important. Had she been there so long that the northern camp had become to feel like home? She ridiculed herself for even considering such a notion, after all, she had been nothing more than a pet, there was nothing to miss.

As her thoughts wandered over the life she had known in Oror, Ayse could feel her muscles relaxing and transitioning, hen her skin prickled as fur rippled all over her body. She shivered and shook, as much as she had wanted to be human again, it strangely felt more normal to be back as a wolf once more. Promising herself that she would remain in human form for a few months without shifting to balance herself out, Ayse padded over to the tent opening and stuck her nose out. There were still soldiers of Oror milling about the camp, but it would be easy enough for her to escape undetected under the cover of darkness. It was a dry night, the wind was stirring, bringing the trees to life as they shook and rustled at its touch.

Ayse silently loped through the shadows of the camp, ensuring she kept to the gloom, before disappearing into the cover of the surrounding trees. She was confident in the direction she was headed and after being cooped up in the camp for months, she was excited to be running free through the woods once again. Ayse had to remind herself that she was not alone in the beautiful northern landscape, and it wasn't the bears that were foremost in her mind. Somewhere, Caleb and his men were hunting, and she didn't want to chance an encounter with them, especially with a bag of information on Oror strapped to her body.

While quieter than the bustling wildlife of the day, somehow the night-time imbued the forest with a greater feeling of life and energy. The moon was so bright that night that it illuminated all the stray clouds that dared to cover it, making it appear as if someone had left large, light grey brushes of paint across the sky. The distant hooting of a solitary owl echoed through the trees causing Ayse to pause. She breathed in the damp and earthy smell of the land, sending her wolf senses into a spiral of instinct as she picked up traces of different scents.

She continued onwards, recalling how her first journey through the north had been so exciting and distracting for her. It was even worse now, after spending so long as an animal, Ayse was finding it increasingly harder to curb the urge to unleash her wolf. It wanted freedom and it wanted to run, hunt and become one with the forest. But then she would remember the strained faces of Ben and Nell as they had sat there, asking her to do the impossible, knowing that the lives of the Vulpini depended on her. Ayse was so close now. It was exhilarating to think of what she had accomplished, she just had to stay focused for a little while longer. Once in Brankah, and once the Vulpini had what they needed, she would take some time by herself and regain some semblance of normality.

Her nostrils flared as she caught the distinct scent of horses. She crouched low to the ground and froze, expecting to hear hooves crashing through the undergrowth as the men hunted, but she heard nothing more. She carefully crept further forwards, her belly against the ground, expecting that at any moment she would hear men talking, movement, anything. Yet still there was nothing. Continuing at a slow and steady pace, Ayse heard soft movement, but it was too quiet to be that of a hunting party.

Ayse stayed hidden in the undergrowth as she approached and surveyed the scene before her. There were ten horses tethered in a clearing, all of which were calmly waiting for their riders, who were nowhere to be seen. Ayse raised her nose and breathed deeply, she was certain that these horses belonged to Caleb's hunting party as she could smell the lingering traces of the men that she had become familiar with.

Her head was telling her to leave this place, to continue her journey to the south, yet worry gnawed at her. This scene was a long way from being normal. Something must have happened. She circled the clearing, remaining out of sight of the horses so as not to startle them. There appeared to be no sign of a fight, no blood, and all the saddle bags were accounted for, she could even see the quivers and bows.

The memory of the beaten and broken Orian men flashed into her mind. Concerned that some of the southerners had once again managed to penetrate this deep into the northern territory, Ayse picked up the scent of the hunting party and began to follow it. She heard the frantic sound of a rabbit disappearing into the bushes nearby, but the playful nature of her wolf had been forgotten; now her only focus was in finding Caleb and his men.

The Orian men were strong and capable fighters, Ayse found it hard to believe that they would have been so easily overcome by Nevraahn soldiers without any evidence of a skirmish. It troubled her that the horses and weaponry had been left in such an orderly manner, as if left by choice. What could have happened for the men to abandon their belongings and take off on foot?

The wind was picking up as the night grew, it tried to force Ayse back as if warning her to leave the north and go back to Brankah, but she stubbornly continued onwards. The gale did not give up so easily, it carried with it a deep primal scent that stopped Ayse dead in her tracks. Her heartbeat began to thump and pound as if throwing itself around in her small chest and she realised that she was trembling as she breathed in the foreign scent. It was like nothing she had ever encountered before. It was strong and powerful, and it triggered feelings of vulnerability within her; that sense of being preyed upon, of being in the presence of a true predator.

It was entirely new to her, nothing like her own scent and nothing like the Vulpini shifters, just the thought of what the creature could be filled Ayse with dread. Desperate to find the northerners considering this new threat, Ayse veered off from the trail so as not to leave her own scent anywhere near where the creature had been. It wasn't often that Ayse felt as though she were the underdog and the memories of her encounter with the bear were still fresh in her mind.

She weaved through the trees, catching snatches of the creature's scent as she travelled, but ensuring that she kept her distance from the route it must have taken. The scent was overpowering, it made every nerve and feeling in her body tingle and scream. The woodland tapered off as the land gave way to a small valley. She remembered it from the maps within Caleb's camp, yet the insignificant ink markings on a scrap of paper did not do justice to the beautiful landscape before her.

The moon had wrestled control of the heavens away from the clouds and was casting its gentle touch down into the valley, highlighting the tendrils of river water that snaked across the ground. The sky suddenly seemed entirely cloudless; a thousand different stars were blinking against the darkness, ever watchful of the world below. Ayse had often thought of the night as a dark and mysterious time yet seeing how illuminated the world could be from the pure white light of the celestial body above her, she realised how wrong she had been.

A sound broke the calm quiet of the evening. It reverberated through the valley, making it impossible to pinpoint its location. The wolf howl was clear and unwavering, before long it was joined by others. The sound should have reassured Ayse, knowing that elsewhere in the north, the native wolves were on the prowl, but instead the sound chilled her to the very core. While it was like her own howl, there was something hidden in the depths of that sound that called to some deep part of her, like some form of dominance that was causing the wolf in her to cower. This was not the sound of normal wolves. This was something more powerful, something unnatural.

Movement down in the valley caught her eye. There were large shadows quickly gliding over the ground in unison. Based on the sheer size of them, Ayse initially mistook them for horses, but as they travelled nearer Ayse realised that their movement was different, more like that of dogs. She moved forwards and from her new vantage point she could see them more clearly as they unknowingly travelled closer to Ayse. They called to one another, vocalising their excitement as they hunted, and it dawned on Ayse that they were wolves of incredible size and stature. They were playful, barrelling into one another, snapping mischievously at the tails of others, and bounding all over the place. The sight of such large and powerful beasts took Ayse's breath away.

Despite her fear, Ayse was in awe of the majestic beasts before her. They were of an ancestry that was so old it had become nothing more than a fable, yet here they were in the flesh – werewolves. Her legs felt wobbly and she would have collapsed to the ground if she wasn't so enthralled by the scene before her. They were monstrous, yet beautiful, and possessed an unnatural size and speed. Ayse found herself lost in their presence, content to play the voyeur for a little while longer.

Her eyes were enraptured with the impossibilities before her, yet her mind was embroiled with thoughts about herself. The wolves before her were giants of an ungodly nature, they were a distant cry from what she became when she shed her human skin. There was no possible way that she was akin to these behemoths of the north. Everything she had come to believe about herself had been utterly disproved, if she had only known that she was not a werewolf, would her life had been different? Would the tribe have allowed her to stay? There were so many questions bouncing around her head, but she knew that she would not discover the answers so easily.

Her thoughts wandered back to the northerners. She questioned whether they had met their fate with the wolves before her, but the idea would not hold in her mind. As soon as she had considered the notion, it was quickly torn from her as she realised the reality of the situation. There were ten wolves running through the valley. She thought back to the ten horses awaiting their ten riders, riders who had not needed their weapons for their hunt.

Ayse was in disbelief. For months she had dismissed the idea that there were werewolves in the north, no one had ever suspected her to be anything more than a normal wolf, and she had never seen any sign of people with dual natures. Not until now, at least. As Ayse thought back to the frequent hunting excursions the men would take, it all suddenly made sense to her. She wondered why it was such a secret; she had never heard it been mentioned in the camp, and the majority of the Orian soldiers never went hunting, so when were they allowed to enjoy their second nature?

No longer concerned for the safety of Caleb and his men, Ayse faced the cold reality of what she was getting involved in. She was betraying the northerners, they were dangerous and brutal beasts, and that was whilst in human form, she didn't even want to imagine how much more savage they could be as wolves. Furthermore, it reduced the chances of the Nevraahn soldiers successfully assaulting Oror from slim to pitiful. While she knew it was imperative that she told the Vulpini of the werewolves, telling the duke was another matter entirely, as shedding light on these legendary creatures could potentially uncover their own shapeshifting community.

It was difficult for Ayse to tear herself away from watching the werewolves. They were impressive, intriguing, and utterly captivating, from a distance at least. Ayse imagined that up close she would not be so enamoured with them. The mere thought of what they would do to her if they discovered her was enough to drive her back into the safety of the trees and send her running full pelt in the direction of the border.

Chapter Fourteen

Kitson watched the last few stragglers leave The Black Sheep. They stumbled out into the darkened streets of Brankah, the door slamming shut behind them as the last to exit had left it swinging in the wind. With a sigh of relief, Kitson threw down his bar cloth and went over to the door and bolted it shut to ensure no last-minute drunkards entered and attempted to stretch the bar's business hours to its very limits.

Kitson looked about the bar, there were dirty glasses left on tables, some still housing ale, and there were a couple of items abandoned by patrons, as well as the noticeable sticky layering of old ale clinging to each tabletop. Knowing that ignoring the grime wouldn't make it disappear, Kitson moved back behind the bar to grab a bucket and cloth. He set it down on the nearest table, the already-dirty water sloshing out of the metal container as he did so. He mopped up the spillage with the cloth and began washing down the counter.

The sound of footsteps reached him. He didn't need to turn to know that it was Horace finally emerging from his office. It was rare to see him in the bar these days, as the older man had taken to shutting himself in his room most of the time. After hiring Raphael to seek out Ayse, Horace's hope had waned when he had received no word from either of his agents. Ayse was still in the wind, there was no word on where she had gone, and now it was becoming increasingly worrying that Raphael had also disappeared without a trace.

The two most talented agents on Horace's payroll were gone. It had struck a nerve with the barkeep and he just hadn't been himself of late. When it became obvious that Horace had no intention of striking up any conversation, Kitson turned to see him pouring himself a pint with a sombre expression on his face. As if feeling the eyes of his employee on him, Horace looked up from what he was doing, but his expression didn't change.

"Boss," Kitson said by way of greeting, not wanting to probe into Horace's melancholy.

Horace did not respond, instead he lowered his gaze back to his drink and moved around the bar to take a seat, turning his back on Kitson completely. Kitson sighed and resumed his work. The sudden loud banging of a late-night reveller trying to gain access to The Black Sheep interrupted him, yet Horace remained seated and completely indifferent.

"We're closed!" Kitson yelled in the direction of the door, but the banging continued causing him to add, "Give it up already!"

Whoever was at the door must have been drunk enough to have not been deterred by Kitson's shouts, that was if they were in any state to even hear his calls. Frustrated, Kitson threw his cloth down and headed to the entrance. He unlatched the bolt and yanked the door open with a ferocity that didn't suit his usually quiet demeanour. He opened his mouth to reprimand the drunkard, but when he saw who was at the door, the only sounds that came from his mouth were garbled gibberish.

"Eloquent as always I see," Raphael said with a smile.

Horace was up and at the door before Kitson could even welcome the man into the bar. His whole demeanour had changed, and the relief was clear on his face. At seeing his employer regaining some sense of self, Kitson felt his own wave of relief flowing over him. Some good news was long overdue, and it didn't matter how late it was, this was something he and Horace needed to hear now. Standing aside, Kitson let Raphael into the building and then re-latched the door behind him. Horace was already beckoning for the visitor to sit with him at an empty booth and so Kitson went to fetch some fresh drinks.

"It's good to see you, Raph. I admit that I was beginning to worry."

"Only *just* beginning? It looks like you haven't slept properly in some time," Raphael chuckled.

Horace smiled, but it didn't linger for long as his face gave way to concern. "You're not looking too great yourself."

Raphael shrugged it away. "Being on the road always takes its toll. It's not like I stopped to ensure I was looking my best. I came here as fast as I could."

"Please tell me you found her," Horace pleaded desperately.

Kitson returned with the drinks and set them down with a familiar ease, before taking a seat himself. Pulling his own drink closer, Kitson looked to Raphael expectantly. Raphael's face was troubled, and it made Kitson nervous that he wasn't the bearer of good news after all.

"I didn't find Ayse, but I have a fairly good idea of where she is."

"Is she all right?"

"I can't know for sure how she's doing, but I can tell you now, you're not going to like where she is."

"Tell me everything you know," Horace commanded.

"That gypsy you paid me to follow led me to Bremlor, which believe me, is not an ideal holiday destination." As Raphael jested, he realised that Horace was glaring at him, he was clearly not in the mood for jokes. Rolling his eyes, Raphael continued, "So, it turns out Duke Remus has five Vulpini members captive and has done for quite some time. The duke has told the gypsies that he'll release them if they manage, by some miracle, to obtain information on Oror for him, so that he can successfully breach their borders. It's no secret that many of the dukes of Nevraah have banded together to form an alliance, I guess now we know why."

"What has this got to do with Ayse?"

"Well, unbelievable as it may be, our little Ayse used to be a part of the Vulpini tribe."

"*She was?*" Horace spoke with disbelief.

"That she was, according to the gypsy prisoner I spoke to. So, when the Vulpini needed someone to go north of the border, they turned to an old friend to get the job done."

"They sent Ayse to Oror?!" Horace's voice bellowed out in anger as he rose to his feet, unable to contain his incredulity.

"I'm afraid so. While I was assured that the Vulpini had their reasons for believing that Ayse was their best chance for pulling it off, I never did get any real explanation as to why," Raphael shrugged as he spoke, "There was something she wasn't telling me, but it didn't feel right to push her about it."

Horace was shaking. His eyes had grown so dark that they looked black and his face was trembling as he listened to Raphael speak. As his jaw clenched and his teeth ground together, the veins on his face visibly began to throb. Raphael had never seen Horace so bothered by anything in all the time he had known him, it was disconcerting to see the barkeep so at odds.

Raphael dropped his eyes and sighed. His whole body appeared to change as he dropped his normal carefree charade and spoke in such a serious tone unlike him that it made even Horace turn his head to pay attention. "Horace, if it is the last thing I do, I will see this through to the end. If we can't find Ayse, we'll at least discover why it had to be her that went there. I promise you that."

***

Raphael tossed and turned in his bed, the bed sheets were twisting around him and constricting his limbs as he attempted to get comfortable. He had lain awake for quite some time, unable to drift off to the realm of dreaming. The Brankah inn bed was most definitely an improvement on his previous sleeping quarters in Bremlor, yet he just couldn't seem to get comfortable. Even though it was only spring, the room felt too humid and close and he found the air was heavy and dusty, leaving his throat dry and making him feel thirsty. The bed sheets were sticking to him from his own sweat and they irritated him so much so that he decided to extract himself from their clutches entirely.

Throwing his bedding aside, Raphael arose from the mattress as he gave up on any notion of resting. Walking over to the window, Raphael almost expected to see the streets of Lower Bremlor through the glass, but as he stared out, all he saw were the dusty red buildings of Brankah. He closed his eyes and leaned forward. As his forehead touched the cold glass in front of him, it gave him some mild relief from the heat.

Understandably, Horace had not been happy with the news of Ayse. Cursing out the gypsies who had ensnared her in their problems, Horace had stormed from the room without another word. Kitson had then taken Raphael to the side and quietly informed him that the old barkeep had not been in the best of health in recent months. Sick from worry and refusing the help of anyone, Horace's fitness and temperament had both waned. It made Raphael desperately wish that he could have brought the man better news.

As if sensing Horace's deep loathing for their kind, the gypsy couple had not been seen within the bar for days. Raphael had attempted to track them down within the city, but no one had seen any sign of them for quite some time. Raphael wasn't even sure what he expected to gain from a meeting with them. If they had told Horace nothing, they would have likely given him no further information. But he knew that deep down it wasn't that he wanted to receive anything from them, really. He had just wanted to tell them he had seen Lorie, and possibly reassure them that there was still hope for her.

Just thinking of Lorie unsettled him. While it was true that Raphael could be selfish at times, it went against his nature to knowingly abandon a young woman in need. Leaving Lorie and her friend behind had pained him, especially knowing what they would have to endure all the while they remained there, but he had ultimately had no choice. Frewin's estate would have to be dramatically understaffed, and then there was still the issue of getting in, getting past the guard with the only key, before finally getting the girls out in one piece without being detected. Not to mention that Lorie had also told him that there were three other gypsies being held somewhere, and Raphael didn't have a clue as to where they could possibly be.

Raphael had wanted to return to Bremlor, confident that he could spin a tale to Frewin about why he had been gone and resume their friendship without question. However, when he had voiced his intention to Horace, the man had vehemently refused to allow it to happen. Normally Raphael wouldn't allow himself to be so commanded so easily, especially when he had a personal interest in what it was that he wanted to do. However, with Horace not acting like his usual self, Raphael also felt he should remain in Brankah to watch over the old man. When Raphael had told Horace that Ayse was most likely in the north, it seemed as though the barkeep had taken it as confirmation of her death. Raphael had seen people grieving before, whether Horace realised it or not, he had given up on Ayse the moment he knew where she had gone.

Every night Raphael found it difficult to sleep, kept awake by imagining what Lorie might be going through. At best, she was cowering with the other gypsy girl in that darkened prison cell, at worst… well, it didn't even bear thinking about it. Raphael was haunted by the possibilities.

Chapter Fifteen

The wind was in a rage that night. It was clawing its way into the run-down hovel with a vengeance, howling and whining in a high-pitched tone as it entered the building through every crack and cranny. The few remaining panes of glass that remained in the old windows shook each time the gale blew, causing them to shiver and shake like the rattling of old bones. Huddled in their wicker baskets, the messenger birds were doing their best to ignore the storm, but the horses were not so easily calmed. They could be heard in the accompanying barn when the wind paused in its tirade, and going by the uproar they were making, the riotous weather was clearly unsettling them. The wind reigned supreme in the flatbeds as there was no vegetation to shield its force. There were no other buildings or landmarks to be seen for miles, and so it was in the dilapidated cottage that Reuben and Nell had taken refuge from the weather.

Desperate to do all they could, the Vulpini couple had travelled to the expansive plains that marked the outermost territory of Nevraah, while carefully avoiding Nevraahn encampments. Between the two of them, the Vulpini couple travelled along much of the border at regular intervals in the hopes of picking up Ayse's scent. They had not had any success so far. Tobias had remained in Brankah in case Ayse managed to slip by unnoticed, but they had received no word from him either.

While Rojas had managed to convince the duke to extend their deadline, Reuben was aware that Ayse was not privy to that information and that really, she should be on her way by now. The Vulpini couple knew that even if Ayse ran late, she would still do all she could in the vain hope that it would amount to something. While in the wolf's mind, their time was running out, the couple knew that they could still be camped in the flatbeds awhile longer before the hourglass truly began to empty for the tribe.

Reuben awoke from his reverie with a start as Nell returned to the cottage. The wind had quickly taken advantage of her unlatching the door and had thrown it open with a resounding bang as it ricocheted off the outer wall. With no small effort, Nell managed to close the door and secure it behind her as she entered the building. She smiled softly at Reuben as he got up from the floor. His blonde hair was dishevelled, and she could tell that he must have lain awkwardly as he was rubbing his neck and pulling it to the side. Getting close to him, Nell stood on tiptoes and cupped her hands on both sides of his head, pulling his face down to her own and gently brushing her lips against his. With a sigh, Reuben took Nell's hands from his face and clasped them tightly in his own.

"No sign of Ayse?"

Nell shook her head sadly. Shivering, she reached for her clothing and began to dress quickly. "Nothing. The Nevraahn soldiers are still stirring all along the border, but there was no scent of Ayse having passed through." The sound of immediate and heavy rainfall besieging the landscape offered an excuse for Nell to steer the conversation in a new direction, "Looks like I returned just in time."

Reuben grinned and pulled Nell close, embracing her in his arms and affectionately stroking her hair as he whispered in her ear, "A little rain doesn't hurt anyone."

***

The rain was unrelenting. It was soaking Ayse down to her very skin so much so that she could feel it running through her fur in cold rivulets. With every soggy minute that passed with her plodding onwards through the cold, her mood grew as sour as the weather. Although cursing its swift arrival, Ayse realised that the rain might aid her in some way after all, as soldiers along the border would most likely have taken to scurrying for cover. Still, it didn't make Ayse any less miserable for having to bear with it herself. Seeing the extensive view of the plains before her was relieving, she was still some distance away from

Brankah, but it felt as though she had already made it home.

The downpour was waterlogging the grasslands, creating a layer of grimy soup for Ayse to slosh through as she ran. Knowing that it was inevitable that she would have to eventually spend a considerable amount of time removing the caked-on mud from her body, Ayse was aware of every splash and speck of muck that touched her. She kept her head hunkered down, ears flat against her head, as she persevered through the unending wall of rain.

Ayse heard movement to the side of her, but she reacted too slowly to prevent her attacker from barrelling into her, throwing her into the dirt and causing the two of them to roll and slide through the thick mud. Snarling and snapping, Ayse kicked them off and rose to her feet. She was angry at herself for having not heard her assailant approaching sooner and she could now feel the mud lodged in her nose and ears, and she could even taste it in her mouth. Blinking away the grime, Ayse's body relaxed as she saw the goofy, panting face that stood in front of her, covered in its own coating of sludge.

Despite its clumpy mud-covered appearance, the fox looked ecstatically happy to see her. Skipping around Ayse and snapping playfully, Reuben wagged his tail and brushed against her affectionately, which just further smeared muck along the two of them. At this point Ayse didn't care about the mud. She was so relieved to see a friendly face after so long that she quickly responded in kind.

The rain started to fall even heavier than before and began to strip the animals of their camouflage. Ayse could see the bright red of Reuben's fur followed by traces of white as the filth washed away. Undeterred by the rain, Reuben continued to scamper about energetically. Ayse snorted water from her nostrils and butted Reuben's hindquarters with her head, indicating for him to lead the way. He did so with continued vigour, the pelting rain unable to dampen his high spirits.

It wasn't long before Ayse spotted their intended destination in the distance, the weather was casting a grey haze over the landscape, but the darkened shape of a building was clearly distinguishable. As they approached, Reuben made many calls and yips of delight to alert Nell to their arrival. The fox and wolf went their separate ways around the cottage to shift as Nell opened the door, bracing against the weather as she waited for them both to enter.

Reuben finished shifting first. Entering the cottage with a wide grin across his face, he bent down to give Nell a firm, muddy kiss as he passed her by to find his clothing. Exhausted as she was, and still finding her transformations difficult, Ayse's change had taken longer for her to complete. She was grateful for the blanket that Nell passed her as she entered, offering up a smile in exchange as she moved inside. Once Nell had closed the door, the small room seemed far too tiny to contain the electric atmosphere emitted by the two Vulpini. Both were beaming with delight and it was infectious. Ayse could feel her own face hurting from smiling as they all dumbly grinned at each other.

"You have no idea how good it is to see you again," Nell gushed.

"Oh, I think I have a fairly good idea. I imagine it's the same feeling as seeing two familiar faces after being stuck in the north all winter," Ayse chuckled. Weary from her journey, she slid down against the wall and sat on the floor, pulling the cover about her for warmth. Mud was still slicked across her skin, but she no longer cared as she stared at her two companions. "I'm so glad to be back."

"It's good to have you back," Nell answered as she rummaged in a backpack for some clothing for Ayse to wear.

"I'm cutting it close though, spring is almost over." The regret was evident in Ayse's voice as she spoke.

"There's more than enough time, Rojas managed to convince the duke to give us an extension, and even without that we would have made it," Reuben reassured her. "If we had thought of some way of telling you, we would have. But it's not like you left a forwarding address."

Ayse accepted the clothing from Nell and rose to her feet, making some small attempt to clear away some of the mud before she pulled the clothes on. As she dressed, she noticed the eyes of the Vulpini resting on the bag she had put down by her side, yet the couple respectfully waited until she had finished dressing and resumed her seat to question her.

"Tell us what happened," Nell said quietly. Ayse reached for the bag, but Nell motioned for her to stop. "I don't mean the information. I mean tell us everything that happened to you, starting with that," Nell said as she pointed to Ayse's leg.

"Oh, that. I met with a bear trap, whilst running from a bear." Ayse laughed gently at how silly it sounded. "It's not so bad now." The smiles had disappeared from the Vulpini's faces as it dawned on them that Ayse's journey north had not been without its issues. Not wanting to lose the good energy, Ayse was quick to reassure them, "Don't look so glum, I'm here in one piece, aren't I? Besides, you will never believe what I discovered... about me, about werewolves, about everything."

***

Ayse was tucking into the cold food wholeheartedly, grateful that Nell and Reuben had brought provisions with them so that they weren't forced to hunt off the land in such foul weather. Nell was sat close beside Ayse, while Reuben paced the room. They were both still digesting all what Ayse had told them.

"I can't believe you're not a werewolf. The sole reason we sent you north was entirely unfounded. If they had found out-"

"They didn't, Ben. I made it back."

"But if they had, I just—I don't know what to say."

"It's alright, really. I always knew the risk was high, I agreed to it anyway," Ayse said dismissively, but with a tone of amusement. She washed down her meal with a swig from her flagon of water and continued, "Besides, aside from the fact that going north meant saving the lives of our friends, I discovered something about myself that I might never have known otherwise."

"It's all very interesting," Nell mused, "Does that mean you're a wolf shifter? Do you think there are others? In Oror, do you think?"

"I really don't know," Ayse replied as she swallowed her food. "If wolf shifters are anything like the Vulpini, they would be native to the same land as the animal they become. I saw natural wolves in Oror, but no shifters, and I didn't scent out anyone like me. Then again, I only saw a small section of the north. Just look at these maps, the land is extensive, and the terrain is so different from what we are used to."

Reuben resumed pouring over Ayse's stolen paperwork with interest. "The werewolves pose a problem for us. We obviously can't tell the duke, but when he attacks the north, who's to say he won't find out for himself?"

"I don't think the northerners are that careless, they keep their true nature locked down. It was only by chance that I discovered them, and I spent months there. Besides, it's not like we have much of a choice here, it's a risk we're going to have to take. We have to hand the information over."

"I know, I know. We'll take all you have to Rojas in Bremlor immediately.

Nell can send word ahead by bird. You might want to send one to the tribe too, they will want to know."

"I'm on it," Nell said as she scrambled to her feet and moved towards the birds.

"I'll come with you."

"No, Ayse. You need to get to Brankah for a long overdue reunion," said Reuben, receiving a quizzical look from Ayse as he did so. He smiled at her as he explained, "Tobias is there."

"I'll send a message to him first, so he'll be expecting you." Nell cheerfully chimed in.

Ayse could feel her stomach knotting, her recent meal no longer settling well with her at all. She didn't understand why the prospect of seeing Tobias once again suddenly made her so nervous. They had once been so close. Was she worried that time would have erased that and reduced their relationship to nothing more than a memory?

Biting her lip, Ayse knew that there was only one way to find out, but that didn't make the idea of facing him any easier. She was grateful to feel so exhausted after her journey. Sleep would come swiftly to her because of her fatigue. Any other night, she would have been kept awake by the thought of having to reunite with her once close friend.

Chapter Sixteen

Ayse anxiously hovered outside of her inn room door, Reuben and Nell had continued renting it and had kept her bags safe within, but right now she knew that there was more than just her belongings waiting for her inside. True to her word, Nell had sent a message to Tobias, informing him that he should expect Ayse's return in the coming weeks. When the couple had left Brankah, Tobias had taken up residence in Ayse's inn room to await her return. Ayse continued to linger outside the room with bated breath, unable to bring herself to open the door.

Saying goodbye to the Vulpini couple had been difficult. She had found it comforting to be in the presence of friends and so the idea of returning to travelling in solitude had been disconcerting for Ayse. Fortunately for her, Nell had given Ayse her horse, as well as supplies for the road so that Ayse could make the last leg of her journey in human form. That small act of kindness was customary of Nell, but Ayse sensed there was more to it as if Nell had noticed the troubles she had been having with transitioning. Ayse hadn't mentioned it to either of the Vulpini. While they were also of a shifting nature and so would be the most qualified to listen to her problems, Ayse was feeling vulnerable enough lately without her having to voice her fears out loud.

Gripping the handle of the door, Ayse closed her eyes and willed herself to open it before the last of her courage failed her. As she stepped inside the room, her eyes went straight to the face of the man she was expecting to see. His large cocoa-brown eyes watched Ayse carefully and he offered her a soft smile as she closed the door behind her. She could feel her heart beating quickly as his eyes stared into her own. Their expressions must have reflected one another as they stared at each other, evaluating how time had changed the person they once knew.

Part of her had imagined him to look the same, unsure what to expect, she had simply imagined that same gangly lad with his usual boyish charm. However, before her was a grown man in the prime of his life. Tobias had filled out considerably with age, and his once lean physique was now well toned. He had grown his hair a bit longer, causing brown locks to now fall into his eyes, and he had the shadow of facial hair about his chin. Tobias wore a nervous expression. It was clear that he had been feeling anxious about their meeting too. She could see his eyes appraising her, no doubt he was noticing how much she had changed since their last meeting also. Back then she had been just a girl, but now she was a woman. As if realising that he had been staring too long, Tobias's face flushed crimson and he met her eyes once more.

"It's been a long time, Ayse," he greeted her before his eyes darted to the side of the room and he cleared his throat. "I hope you don't mind, but I invited someone else to your welcome back party."

Ayse followed the direction of his gaze, she had been so preoccupied with seeing Tobias after so many years that she had been completely oblivious to the fact that another person was in the room with them. Horace was sat patiently. He looked older than Ayse remembered him being, his face was tired, his pallor paler than that of his usual complexion and more flashes of grey seemed to streak through his hair. As Ayse looked to him, he smiled warmly at her and she felt the sudden urge to run and hug him.

Embracing her tightly, Ayse could hear the threat of tears in his voice as he spoke, his voice coming out quiet and cracked, "You have no idea how much I missed you, girl."

Tobias felt awkward with the sudden display of affection that he had not received himself. He looked away and spoke casually, "Horace was concerned about your disappearance, while I couldn't really tell him much about what you were up to, it seemed the right thing to do to tell him that you were on your way back."

Pulling out of Horace's embrace, Ayse laughed, "So the two of you have just been camping out in an inn room, waiting for me to return?"

"More or less," Horace replied.

"You were worth the wait," Tobias added with pointed sincerity.

"Aren't I always?" Ayse joked awkwardly to clear the unease.

Horace's face grew stern as he turned to the matters at hand, "Is it true? Were you in the north?" Tobias's face flushed, surprised that the old man knew where Ayse had been, he opened his mouth to speak, but thought better of it. Noticing the younger man's reaction, Horace added, "Did you really think I'd just sit and wait for her to return, boy? I have my own way of doing things."

"Don't tell me you've been wasting your time and money on trying to track me down?" grimaced Ayse.

"Well, is it true?" Horace asked again, ignoring her question.

Ayse nodded in response.

"And you went there at the behest of the Vulpini? Was it because you felt that you owed them because you used to be one of them?"

Ayse nodded once again, whilst Tobias shook his head in disbelief, he found himself wondering if there was anything that the bar owner hadn't uncovered about their situation.

"You could have died. Was it worth the risk? It's a miracle you even returned. How did you do it? Did they force you into this?"

"Horace, this was more than just a job, this was important to me. I wasn't forced into anything. I chose to do it. As for how I managed it, do you really doubt me so much?" she jested, aiming to lighten the heavy conversation somewhat.

It was Horace's turn to shake his head, he sighed reluctantly, but gave up on lecturing the girl, "Well, don't expect me to add Oror to the list of places we'll take contracts for any time soon."

Ayse smiled at her small victory, already the mood in the room felt as though it was thawing, and the awkward atmosphere was lifting. Ayse was grateful that Tobias had invited Horace.

"Well kids, as fun as this is, we've got other matters to attend to," Horace announced as he rose to his feet.

"We do?" Tobias asked with a confused expression on his face.

"I know why you went north, Ayse. I know about the gypsies being held captive, but more importantly, Raph knows where some of them actually are."

"We've been shacked up in this inn room for over a week and you're only just mentioning this now?!" Tobias exclaimed in disbelief.

"Well, I didn't hear you telling me the ins and outs of why Ayse was traipsing around up north," Horace chuckled as he walked through the door.

Tobias looked to Ayse, but she simply smiled and followed Horace out of the room. Exasperated, Tobias had no choice but to follow them.

***

"Stop it," Ayse demanded.

"Stop what?"

"That smug look on your face. Remove it, or I will," she warned.

Raphael smiled even wider causing Ayse to groan. "Is it so bad that I'm happy to see you?" Raphael asked meekly.

"You and I both know you're taking more pleasure from having been sent after me than from my return. Might I point out to you that you failed to track me down."

"A technicality, I did actually find out where you were."

"Please. If you had even tried to cross the border into the north, you would never have found me, or even survived for that matter," she snorted.

Raphael's eyes narrowed. "Yes. I don't believe you really explained that. How exactly was it that you managed to survive?"

"Are you two squabbling again?" Horace interrupted. "You're like two bickering siblings."

As if to prove his point, Ayse stuck her tongue out at Raphael as Horace joined them at the table. He brought a tray of brimming drinks with him. Horace had decided to empty The Black Sheep of all other patrons and had relegated Tobias in helping him to move some of the less sober carousers out onto the street. Raphael continued to smile with a self-satisfied look about his face as Ayse frowned and reluctantly chose to drink her ale instead of speaking her mind.

Tobias returned to them with a vexed look, clearly removing some of the customers had been more troublesome than he had first presumed. Kitson returned to the table with a much happier demeanour, relishing the one time it hadn't been him that had been conscripted to empty the bar of drunkards. Tobias took a flagon from those on offer; he drank deeply from it before leaning back in his chair and looked at his companions expectantly.

"To business then," Raphael acknowledged. "As I'm sure Horace has mentioned to you by now, I came across some friends of yours while in the delightful town of Bremlor. There were two girls, Lorie and Ana. Lorie told me that there were three men from your tribe being held captive also, unfortunately, I never saw those poor souls."

"Were they all right?" Ayse asked.

"They're prisoners. Suffice to say things aren't great for them." Raphael paused with a pained look on his face. "But they seemed to be enduring, for the time being."

"Where are they? Can we get them out? What did Lorie tell you?" Ayse leaned forward as she peppered Raphael with questions.

"They're being held by one of the duke's closest friends, a man by the name of Lord Frewin."

Tobias grimaced, "Frewin? Rojas has mentioned him before, and he didn't have anything good to say about him either."

"I'm afraid your friend is correct, Frewin is a disgusting snake of a man," Raphael sighed, recalling all the times he had been forced to endure the awful man's company. "As for getting them out, they're just too well guarded at the present. Believe me, I considered it. But it would be a lost cause with the way things are."

"Not to mention, if you only managed to retrieve the girls, the three men would most likely be punished, or worse," Horace added. "If you want to hatch an escape plan, it has to be one that gets them all out at the same time."

"We might not need an escape plan at all," Tobias explained, "Ayse delivered, we have the information on the north that the duke wants. If he keeps his word, he will release all of the prisoners now."

"That's *if* he keeps his word," Horace muttered, shaking his head.

"I don't think it's wise to rely on that man being honourable," Raphael stated. "At the very least, it won't hurt to do some more digging and find out whether we can discover the location of all of the prisoners, only as a backup plan, of course."

"Rojas hasn't managed to locate the men," sighed Tobias.

"Neither did he manage to find the girls, but I did. I think it will be easy enough to assimilate back into that group of scoundrels, and then I can start to track down the three other prisoners."

"If the duke suspects that we're making attempts at finding or freeing his captives, he'll renege on our deal for sure," warned Tobias.

Raphael laughed, "I'm more discreet than you imagine me to be, gypsy. You can wait on the duke to fulfil his promise, but in the meantime, I'll be returning to Bremlor and finding your friends. When the duke fails to uphold his end of the deal, and I do mean *when*, then you'll know where to contact me so that I can sort out this whole mess for you."

"You're very sure of yourself, aren't you?" Tobias sneered.

"That's just Raph," Ayse sighed, speaking from experience.

"Why exactly are you interested in helping my people?" Tobias's tone was growing sharp as if an argument was brewing.

"Any friend of Ayse's is a friend of mine, and I don't like the idea of my friends lounging in some dank pit, especially when they are damsels in distress. Why exactly are you turning down my help?" Raphael said with a self-assured expression on his face, his eyes narrowed at Tobias as he silently attempted to goad the gypsy into responding.

Before Tobias could speak, Ayse interrupted and ended the quarrel before it could even truly begin, "As much as I hate to admit it, Raph is right. Having him in Bremlor as something to fall back on really can't hurt."

"Ayse admitting that I'm right? That must be a first! Horace, we should commemorate this occasion with more drinks!"

Raphael was absolutely beaming with satisfaction, causing Ayse and Tobias to grimace somewhat. Horace smiled as he looked around at the three young people, and for once he chose to acquiesce to Raphael's request and rose from the table to fetch more beverages. Raphael could call it whatever he wanted, but Horace was more than happy to drink to the safe return of his two favourite employees.

Chapter Seventeen

It was a wonder as to how solid stone could smell damp, how exactly that it was the wetness could penetrate such a solid object was a mystery. Even the air itself was humid, the smell of mould and mildew clinging to the very atmosphere around them. Pale shafts of light fell into the dingy stone prison cells, just enough to highlight the beaded eyes of rats that hid in the shadowy recesses. Each cell housed far too many occupants for its size; men were practically on top of one another in filthy conditions that bred disease and despair. On the other side of the rusted bars ran a long corridor and all along the walls there were brackets that housed torches, which sputtered and spat as the flames fought to stay alive in such damp air.

The prison of Bremlor was overflowing with captives. When the current duke had taken over, he had begun to rule the land with an iron grip and an unquenchable greed. With the city in the sad state that it was, it was only natural that poverty had become rife, and so the townspeople had been forced to resort to pilfering from the rich aristocracy of High Bremlor. Unfortunately, the duke reserved no mercy for petty criminals or crimes of desperation, anyone caught breaking the law was thrown into prison without any real form of trial or judgement. There they would languish, all but forgotten as soon as they had left the duke's sight. Doomed to remain there until they died.

It was here that the three Vulpini men had been housed, hidden in plain sight in the most obvious confinement that Bremlor had to offer. Duke Remus was not as foolish as some would believe, he knew that the Vulpini would not mount another rescue attempt unless it would yield freedom for all the tribal captives. By ensuring that the two gypsy girls were locked away somewhere more secure meant that it didn't matter where he imprisoned the men. Even if by some miracle Rojas ever managed to enter the prison undetected, the Vulpini were entirely indistinguishable from any of the other prisoners as all of them bore the same appearance. Rake thin from their meagre diet of stale bread and water, the once close-fitting clothes of the prisoners now hung from their bodies in tatters. Every man had the same unkempt and overgrown mass of hair, dirtied faces, and hopeless sunken eyes.

Owaiin was the eldest of the captive Vulpini men and it was he who had overseen the team when they had left the tribe to pursue their job contract. He cursed himself for having not realised the folly of the plan sooner on that fateful day. The warning signs had been there, but it was all too late when he had finally realised the dire situation that they were in. Before he could even react, the guards had discovered them and had already taken the two tribal members who had been on lookout duty into custody too. He also cursed the client who had lied to them. The plan had seemed so straightforward when explained to them, and all the man had wanted was to retrieve some paperwork that could prove his rights to his family's estate. However, he had failed to tell the Vulpini just how well-guarded the duke's estate was, not to mention how precious the duke was about his belongings.

Destined to relive that day over and over in his mind, Owaiin sat with his back against the slimy cold of the stone wall and distracted himself from his guilt by watching as his younger tribal brothers slept. Aiden and Mason looked even paler and pitiful sleeping than they did when they were awake. The two of them lay curled up next to one another in a way that reminded Owaiin of how the Vulpini children would huddle together for comfort on a stormy night.

Throughout the winter, Mason had suffered from an incurable cough that had racked up from deep within his ribs and left him breathless. If they didn't get him out of Bremlor soon, Owaiin wasn't optimistic that his friend would see another season. He didn't believe the duke would blink at the loss of another Vulpini life while at least one of them were still alive to use as a bargaining chip. The duke knew that the tribe would do whatever he asked of them if at least one captive lived.

Seeing the state of his immediate companions made him wonder how much worse off the girls were, wherever it was that they had been taken. He hadn't seen either Lorie or Ana since the group had been separated. Paya had been dragged away without much warning and all they could do was stand there and helplessly watch her disappear. They had all been told what fate had befallen her, it was a warning to the tribal members trapped within Bremlor as much as it was to the Vulpini outside of Bremlor.

It was hard not to speculate as to whether they were already ill-fated as spring had made itself known a few weeks prior and yet Owaiin had heard nothing as to whether the Vulpini had successfully met the duke's demands or not.

While it was hard to maintain any real measure of time within the darkened prison cells, Owaiin had made somewhat of an ally out of one of the prison guards who was kindly to those who were respectful and did not cause any disruptions. The guard in question, Hudson, had been friendly enough to keep Owaiin apprised of the goings on in Bremlor and whether he had heard any news regarding the Vulpini. While the guard was not privy to the innermost workings of the duke's estate, big news somehow always managed to trickle its way down the ranks to even the lowliest of workers within the city.

As if on cue, Owaiin heard footsteps echoing in the corridor announcing the approach of Hudson as he began his shift. Moving closer to the bars, Owaiin waited patiently for the guard to come into view of his own cell before hailing him, "Morning."

"Morning," replied the guard.

"Any news?" asked Owaiin, fighting yet failing to keep the desperation from his voice.

"As a matter of fact, there is. Although, I'm not sure that it'll be what you were hoping for," Hudson said apologetically as he drew closer.

Owaiin could feel a weight forming in the pit of his stomach as he began to fear for the safety of himself and his companions. Preparing for the worst he asked, "What's happened?"

"It seems as though your friends came through after all, the duke got what he wanted." Hudson was speaking in a light-hearted tone, but given his warning of bad news, Owaiin knew better than to celebrate at this latest revelation. The guard sniffed and wiped his nose on his sleeve as he looked about the place. "Problem is, it seems the duke isn't being as straightforward as he promised he'd be. He's set your people another task that they must complete before you get your freedom."

Owaiin clenched his fists and bowed his head against the bars in frustration. They had all known that it was a possibility the duke would not relinquish the control he had over the Vulpini. Yet they were faced with no other choice but to play his games until he had had enough of using them as pawns in his plans.

"What does he want us to do now?" Owaiin asked.

"Well, now that they have enough information on Oror to strike, the dukes have formulated a plan to hit the north as hard as possible. Apparently, your tribe will have some role to play in whatever strategy they've devised."

"My people aren't fighters; they're not trained for combat in that way," Owaiin protested.

"I don't think the duke cares, mate. I am truly sorry. I had hoped to bring you better news when I heard the duke had received his information. There's still hope for you yet, it's better than knowing your people have already failed you, right?"

Owaiin managed to nod in agreement before Hudson left to continue with his rounds of the prisons, yet deep down it didn't feel as though that small silver lining amounted to much in the grand scheme of things. For all he knew, the duke would continue to utter demand after demand, never actually releasing any of them when the terms were met.

Returning to his companions, Owaiin slumped against the wall and contemplated what he had heard. He couldn't even begin to comprehend how the Vulpini had managed to get information on Oror. What worried him more than the thought of the tribe having the information was the thought of at what cost they had gained it. He became haunted by the idea that some of the tribe might have perished in their efforts to breach the north.

Mason's heavy breathing rapidly turned into wheezing, and his eyes flicked open as he began to heave and cough the phlegm up from his lungs. Rolling onto his stomach, Mason dry wretched as he fought to breathe properly. Owaiin quickly moved to his side and began rubbing his friend's back to help him clear his chest. The commotion caused some of the other prisoners to begin mumbling and muttering, but Owaiin paid them no attention. The other occupants of their cell had grown accustomed to the ailments of the Vulpini, even before Mason had been plagued by his cough, the Vulpini men had been forced to help restrain one another from fits as they fought to keep their bodies from shifting amongst strangers. It was a miracle that no mishaps had occurred. A man turning into a fox amidst humans would have certainly caused an uproar to which the Vulpini would have had to answer for. The one upside to being so weakened was that their bodies had stopped trying to force them into fox form.

Aiden had also awoken and was staring at Mason with wide eyes as if fearing that he was about to see his brother breathe his last. While it felt like an age, Owaiin knew that it couldn't have been that long before Mason's breathing calmed once more and he lay down, his throat so hoarse that he was unable to speak. Owaiin comforted him as best he could, staying beside him and running his hand over his back in a gentler motion than before. Aiden visibly looked more relaxed as Mason drifted off to sleep, but the concern was still very much there.

"The cough is getting worse," Aiden whispered.

"I know," Owaiin sighed.

"Do you think we will be allowed to leave soon?"

"No, I don't think we will," Owaiin responded bitterly before realising that he did not wish to alarm the younger man, "But I think we are safe in the meantime. The tribe managed to get the duke what he wanted, they just have to do one more thing and then he'll let us go."

"Will it take long?"

"Let's hope not," Owaiin responded, even trying at a reassuring smile, but going by the look on Aiden's face, it hadn't been that effective.

Aiden moved next to Mason and laid beside him. Owaiin also chose to lie next to the weakened man so that he was cushioned between his two friends in some attempt to warm him with the heat of their combined bodies. All they could do was lie there and wait, hoping that one day they would finally be able to leave that awful place.

Chapter Eighteen

The Vulpini camp was alive with an infectious energy that it had not possessed for months. The bonfire was stacked high and sparks were flying into the air and disappearing into the night as their brief existence burnt out. A luxurious spread of different foods was on offer as the Vulpini had pulled out all the stops to celebrate the homecoming of their people. The moon had honoured them with its full brilliance, its light chasing away any sign of clouds that might dare to come into sight, forbidding them from ruining the festive occasion. The renewed happiness was evident from the faces of the tribal members, no longer marked by shadows of sleepless nights, the Vulpini were radiating with joy. Each person wore a smile as they danced and celebrated long into the night.

Rojas stopped his horse while he was still some distance from the camp, seeing everyone so carefree made it even harder that he was about to break the terrible news that their friends would not be returning home as expected. He waited some time longer; unseen in the shadows beyond the light of the camp. Rojas watched and savoured the look of the tribe in such a contented state, fearful that it would be some time before they returned to such happiness. Reuben and Nell had travelled back to the Vulpini camp immediately after delivering the information to Rojas in Bremlor, and, expecting him to soon follow with the released prisoners, they had begun the celebration early.

The revellers were so engrossed in their festivities that no one noticed Rojas's approach until he was among them. With a long face, he dismounted from his horse and scanned the crowd for the chief. As the tribespeople noticed that he was alone, they all stopped and turned to watch him, their smiles disappearing as quickly as the airborne sparks from the fire had died. Like a slow wave, the sound of laughter and chatter gave way to silence as more and more people stopped to look at the arrival of Rojas. Everyone began to crowd around him, but no one uttered a single word. They all just stood silently staring at Rojas and waiting for him to break the news they already knew to be true. The crowd parted for the arrival of Solomon as he came to investigate what was happening. He stopped in his tracks as he too noticed that Rojas had not returned with the missing Vulpini members.

"Rojas?" Solomon asked with apprehension, his face paling as he saw the man before him lower his head.

Ashamed of the bad news he had to bear, as if it were somehow his fault, Rojas couldn't even bring himself to look the chief in the eye, nor any of his tribal family for that matter. "He will not release them, not yet. He has asked yet another task of us. He promises that *then* he will free them," he spoke softly, not daring to say it too loudly, but in the deathly silence of the camp his words reached every ear and a murmur of disappointment and sobbing swelled among the people.

Solomon's hand went to his brow, then shakily he ran his fingers through his hair and agitatedly he began to pace as he digested the news. His body was trembling, but Rojas wasn't sure whether it was from worry or rage. Solomon's voice was bitter as he spoke, "He promised that he would free them last time. How is this time any different?"

"It's not, chief. But what other choice do we have?"

Solomon did not answer. He just shook his head in disbelief and resumed his pacing. Fear was spreading amongst the tribe. People looked to one another with wide eyes as they wondered what trial would be set before them this time. Rojas contemplated whether he should tell the chief what the duke had requested of them in private, but feeling as though hiding the truth from the tribe would ultimately do no good, he loudly cleared his throat to speak, the noise bringing everyone to attention as they waited in anticipation of what he would say.

"The dukes have formulated a plan to attack Oror with the information that Ayse managed to retrieve. However, just knowing the enemy and the territory does not guarantee them a victory. Ayse reported that the men of Oror are fierce warriors, trained in the art of battle. Therefore, the dukes do not wish to attempt to tackle them in a straightforward battle. They mean to set up a diversionary tactic, drawing most of the northern soldiers away from their true target. They will believe the south is attacking from one position, while the real Nevraahn force will be targeting a key location elsewhere in the hopes of securing a foothold in the north."

"How do the Vulpini come into this?" Solomon asked.

"The dukes need every man to ensure this plan works. They want all their best fighters striking hard at their intended location. But that means they still need a lot of manpower to build the force that will draw the Orians away. They are recruiting every mercenary band they can, enlisting all manner of people, even forcing prisoners to bear arms... The duke expects us to send every able-bodied man and woman of age to bolster his ranks."

"Barely any of our people are trained for combat, with most having never even wielded a real weapon," a woman in the crowd objected, causing the rest of the tribe to erupt into commotion and panic as they all tried to make themselves heard at once.

The chief motioned for them to calm down and asked for quiet, when order was restored, he looked to Rojas to continue.

"I know that this is a lot to ask, but we all know that it must be done to save our people and our secret. Anyone who is able, is to return to Bremlor with me. Training has been prepared for those who are to assist in the northern strike. I'm not going to lie to you, this is a dangerous task, but just learning enough to defend yourself could be the difference between life and death on the battlefield. We will be just a small part of a larger force, among us will be veterans of battle, so it's not as though we are simply sheep being sent to slaughter."

Rojas meant to continue but found that he could not. That last thought that had crossed his mind stuck with him and he suddenly felt as though he had just spoken an untruth to the tribe. According to Ayse, the men of Oror were experts at warfare, they were likely to be a challenge for the most experienced of warriors, never mind gypsy folk forced onto the battlefield.

Rojas was fortunate that as a younger man he had suffered a rebellious streak that saw him leave the tribe for many years and take up with sell-swords overseas. As a result, he was no stranger to a blade and could wield it well. He planned to train the Vulpini as much as he was able to and not just rely on the training that the duke would provide.

Noticing that Rojas was wavering, Solomon continued to speak to the tribe in his stead, "I know what you all must be thinking... many lives could be lost to save the five Vulpini left in Bremlor. But we are not the type of people to forsake our own. Those men and women languishing in their prisons are counting on us. If that wasn't enough, every day they spend there is another day that our secret might come to light. There is a bigger picture here. We must protect the future of our kind."

There was more murmuring in the crowd as the Vulpini whispered amongst themselves. While no one wanted to speak out to argue, there was clearly some discontentment among the tribespeople as fear grew in their hearts.

Not wishing to see if anyone was brave enough to test his authority, Solomon quickly ushered everyone to go and rest with their families while they were still able. "Tomorrow we will have to decide who is to go to Bremlor with Rojas, take this night to sort your affairs and see to your families. We must remain strong for our people."

As the crowd dispersed and the gypsies retired for the night, Solomon motioned for Rojas to follow him away from the main body of the camp and somewhere quieter so that they could speak in private.

Before Solomon could even begin, Rojas began to babble his apologies, "I am so sorry, chief. I tried. I really tried. Even when that bastard had made it clear that he wouldn't be keeping his promise I tried to get him to release at least one of them as a goodwill gesture, but he would not have it."

"It's alright, Rojas. I know you would have done all that you could. Let's not waste time on things we cannot change, we must look to the future." Solomon placed his hand on Rojas' shoulder. "We can get through this. Together we must unite our people for the challenge that lies ahead."

Rojas nodded in agreement.

"Now tell me, what of the other players in this? Where is Tobias? And Ayse?"

"Both of them are still in Brankah," answered Rojas. Solomon frowned at this response so Rojas tried to reassure him, "Tobias will join the fight, without a doubt. Ayse on the other hand... I'm not so sure. Nell told me that she was sporting some nasty injuries that hadn't fully healed."

"No, no, it's best not to drag Ayse into this any further," Solomon was quick to get that one important detail out. He didn't want Ayse joining up with the majority of the Vulpini tribe once more. It had been difficult enough getting rid of her the first time, he didn't fancy having to do it again now that the Vulpini saw her as a hero. "After all, we've asked enough of the poor girl. Tobias, on the other hand, he will want to be a part of this, you should send word to him immediately. Be sure to tell him to not allow Ayse to accompany him, after whatever it was that she went through in Oror, she deserves her rest. But we all know she'll be too damn stubborn to realise it herself... Tobias will have to convince her to stand down on this one."

"I'll take care of it, don't worry. Tobias knows how to handle Ayse, he will make sure she remains in Brankah. You never know, we might need her at some point in the future."

"I hope we don't ever have to ask for her help again," Solomon muttered, his tone becoming softer as he continued, "Is it wrong to hope that soon we can return to more peaceful times where we don't have to ask people to risk life and limb for the tribe?"

"It's not wrong, chief. It's that very same hope that keeps us all going."

"Tomorrow will not be an easy day." Solomon sighed, already dreading the prospect of separating Vulpini from their family members to send them off to fight a war they might not return from.

"I will take care of our people in Bremlor as best as I can, just concentrate on taking care of the rest of the tribe here at home."

"How is it that this conversation began by me comforting you, and now it is you that is comforting me?" Solomon laughed.

"Such is the way of the world," Rojas smiled. "And as you said, we must get through this together."

"That we must," sighed Solomon. "Come, Rojas. We'll be foolish to not take our own advice and get some rest."

The two men retired for the night, both in the knowledge that they would not fall asleep easily. High above the Vulpini camp, the clouds had finally wrestled for dominance over the sky and the moon had been captured in their advance. No light shone down upon the earth as the night grew colder. The wind was picking up strength as it prowled the land that had succumbed to the darkness.

Chapter Nineteen

The sun-baked ground beneath her paws was warm from the heat of the day, and if it wasn't for the distinct lack of salt air and sea, Ayse might have been fooled into believing that she was on the sun-warmed sands far south of where she truly was. The weather was so perfect that you could be forgiven for mistaking that summer had arrived early. The sky was of the softest blue and there wasn't a cloud in sight to stop the sun from cascading onto the earth with full force.

Ayse was panting heavily as she collapsed to the ground, her movement sending small dust clouds billowing up into the air. Safe in the shade of a lone weather-beaten tree, she surveyed the view before her. While the land surrounding Brankah offered many ideal places to run in animal form, she regretted that they had not chosen somewhere closer to a stream or body of water. Licking her dry lips, she knew that she would have to wait to quench her thirst until they returned to their horses.

Ayse heard the approach of Tobias before she saw him and turned to watch him arrive, his tongue was lolling out of his mouth as he ran to catch up with her, saliva dropping in heavy, frothy clumps from his jaws as he sped forwards to join her beneath the tree. He collapsed besides her panting, the whole of his small body shaking with his rapid breathing.

He rolled onto his side playfully and began rubbing himself in the dust causing more dry earth to erupt into the wind. Ayse snorted as the dust clouds found and tickled her nostrils. She batted the fox with the flat of her head to discourage him from making such a mess. Tobias stopped rolling around only to nip at Ayse playfully, grabbing hold of one of her ears and pulling at it. She rolled onto her back, effortlessly pulling the fox over herself and leaving him sprawling on the ground on the other side of her.

It had taken her quite some time, as well as much prompting from Tobias, to agree to partake in a run while in animal form. Ayse had not relished the idea of shifting back into a wolf so soon, but Tobias had reminded her how much freedom and enjoyment could be had from a run with friends. Eventually, she had given in and joined him on one of his excursions. Now it had become a regular occurrence for the pair, and without even realising it at first, Ayse had soon found that she had lapsed back into the familiar comfort of Tobias's company.

Ayse's initial transformation had been slow going and distressing for her body, but she found that the more often she transformed, and the more she relaxed about doing so, the easier it was to change form. It would have been improbable that Tobias had not noticed that her transformations were taking longer than they used to, but he had not yet mentioned it to her. Part of her hoped that he would never bring it up, especially now that she finally seemed to be getting better with it.

Having grown accustomed to spending time with her childhood friend once more, Ayse was not looking forward to the day that he would leave her. In only a few days' time, Tobias planned to head to Bremlor to regroup with Rojas and the others. It had not surprised her to learn that Duke Remus had reneged on his deal with the Vulpini. Ayse had offered to join the Vulpini ranks, but she was also unsurprised when Tobias had promptly rejected the idea. Of course, she hadn't let the argument drop that easily, but Tobias had been unrelenting in his decision that she should remain in Brankah to rest.

From the very first time that she had shifted in front of him, she had known that he had taken in every scratch, scar, and scrape on her body. His face had said it all as they had dressed afterwards, a worried frown line working its way across his forehead as he had imagined all that she must have endured in Oror. It didn't seem to matter to Tobias that Ayse had told him that the north had been an experience she would never regret as she had learnt so much about herself. It made her heart ache to see him so tormented over some of the things she had told him, it was the same look that he sometimes wore when they spoke about old memories they had shared, memories that had since become tainted by Ayse's expulsion from the Vulpini.

As Ayse lay there contemplating recent events, she was aware of a large shadow that suddenly fell in front of her. Tobias had returned to human form and was stretching out after his transformation. Ayse couldn't help but admire his muscles as they rolled under his skin as he stretched.

Once he had shifted, Tobias sat with his back against the tree and looked out at their surroundings. Ayse yawned and rose to her feet. She stretched lazily before beginning the process of her own shift. Losing her fur coat and returning to bare skin was a welcome relief considering the heat of the day. She laid back down and enjoyed the sensation of the breeze as it softly tickled its way over her body.

"I'm going to miss this," Tobias sighed wistfully. "I don't know how often we'll be able to get away for a run in Bremlor. Rojas managed it, but with there being so many of us, it'll be harder to keep it hidden."

"Not to mention, with all the other soldiers flocking to Bremlor, there's more chance of people stumbling upon you completely naked," laughed Ayse as she tilted her head to wink at him.

"That would definitely be hard to explain," Tobias chuckled.

Ayse rolled onto her side so that she could look at Tobias as they conversed. Her tone becoming more serious, she asked him, "Will you look for Raph when you get to Bremlor?"

"Yes," Tobias said with a twinge of agitation, "While he is a pain in my ass, I have to admit that he appears to be good at what he does. With any luck, he might have found out where our men are being held."

"If anyone can find them, it's Raph. He can charm his way into anywhere."

"Is that so?" Tobias asked. A smile played about his lips as he raised an inquisitive eyebrow at Ayse.

She snorted in response, "His charm never worked on me. Besides, I don't think he could ever be with a woman that was more proficient at his career choice than he was. He would never live it down."

They both chuckled at the thought, but it didn't take long for Ayse's mind to wander back to more serious topics once again, "And if he knows where they are? Will you try and get them out?"

"If we can manage it, then of course I will. It all depends on whether we would be able to get them all out successfully. I don't want to throw another

Vulpini life away on a 'maybe'."

Ayse understood Tobias's sentiments on the matter, but it was difficult for her to contemplate leaving Lori and Ana there if there was a chance at freeing them. Raphael had taken her aside and confided in her what cruel torture the girls were being forced to endure. She had agreed with him that keeping it from the other Vulpini was wise, as if they knew what was happening, they would lose all rational thought and act rashly. Ayse couldn't help but think of all the other Vulpini lives that might be lost soon. Sadly, she asked Tobias, "When Nevraah attacks Oror, how bad will it be for the Vulpini?"

"I wouldn't like to say. We're basically being used as a giant target for the incredibly skilled Orian soldiers, while most of the real trained Nevraahn soldiers are sneaking up to some fort elsewhere in the north. Even if the dukes' plan succeeds, it's not like they're going to take control of that camp and ring a bell that magically ceases all warfare. The north will still be attacking us on our front."

Ayse grimaced. "Do you think the dukes really stand a chance at taking Oror?"

"You tell me Ayse, you were there."

"I don't really know. I haven't seen the strength of Nevraah, but it seems overly optimistic to think we can take the northerners in their own territory. Even if the duke successfully takes Lord Ulric's fort, they must survive there still. What's to stop the northerners ousting them straight away?"

"I'm not trained in the art of warfare, Ayse. Hell, I don't even think you can call it an 'art', but I must assume that Duke Remus has measures in place for such events. They wouldn't be going forward with this ludicrous plan of theirs unless they thought it would actually pay off."

"But how many Vulpini lives will be lost in the process?"

"We don't have any other choice, Ayse," Tobias sighed, the weariness becoming evident in his voice.

"But what if we did?"

"Did what?" he asked confused.

"Have a choice. What if we could limit the amount of damage that the tribe take on the battlefield?"

"Why do I think I'm going to regret asking what it is that you're trying to tell me?" Tobias said grimly.

"If the northerners knew what Nevraah has planned, they can defend the correct camp, meaning that there won't be anyone there to tackle the diversionary force."

"Let me get this straight. You want to tell Oror that we're about to attack them?" Tobias looked at Ayse with incredulity and when her resolute expression didn't change, he became frustrated, his body tensed as he realised the full gravity of what notion had been at play within Ayse's mind.

"Just hear me out, Tobias. The northerners are not bad people. They saved my life. We can help them and help ourselves in the process."

"They saved the life of what they thought was just an animal, Ayse. They would have killed you if they had seen you for what you truly are. Is this really about helping *us*, or is this more about helping *them*?" Tobias asked bitterly.

"Are you really asking me that?" Ayse barked, sitting upright and glaring at her companion. "Why must it be one or the other? They are not our enemy, the duke is."

"What are you going to do, Ayse? Stroll back into the north and tell them that the south is about to attack based on information that you stole from them in the first place? How well do you think they're going to take that news?" Tobias asked her mockingly.

"If there's even a small chance that they will listen, that it could save the lives of the Vulpini and the northerners, then isn't it worth trying?"

Tobias was fighting the rising anger that was building within him, Ayse's expression had softened as she attempted to plead with him, but he couldn't help but judge her for wanting to help the Orian men. Calming himself somewhat, he tried to reason with her, "What of the Vulpini in Bremlor? What do you think the duke will do when his attack fails? Who do you think he will blame for Oror learning of his well-laid plan?"

"The Vulpini would have done as he asked, what reason would he have to blame them for his plan failing? It's not impossible for the northerners to have discovered the plan, or seen through the diversion, anything could have happened. I don't think the duke would suspect the Vulpini. Not after everything they've done for him. Besides, you said yourself, if you can get the prisoners out while you're in Bremlor, then you will."

Tobias shook his head. His eyes were ablaze with fury as he faced the reality of what Ayse was proposing. His tone became quite cold as he confronted her about her idea, "*If* I can get the prisoners out. This isn't even a discussion is it? Not really. You've already decided."

Ayse looked down at her hands and nodded. "Did you really think I would just wait in Brankah while the rest of you are risking your lives on the frontline?" She looked up at Tobias once more, the resolution was clear on her face and it made him all the more irritated.

"I can't stop you, Ayse," Tobias said as he rose to his feet. "But ask yourself this: who are you doing this for?"

Without another word he left her there and it was clear from the tone of his voice that he did not expect her to follow. Ayse bit her lip, the conversation had not panned out the way she had hoped it would. While it was true that the idea of being able to help the northerners had played a role in her decision, the Vulpini had been at the forefront of her mind. She didn't understand why it was so wrong for her to want to help both groups of people at the same time. She had seen how powerful the men of Oror were, the Vulpini and whoever else the duke managed to scrounge up would be no match for them in a fight.

Then there were the northerners, Ayse hadn't really considered what would happen to them after she had left Oror. She hadn't thought about the consequences of her actions, not at first in any case. She had been too focused on what she had to do next and ensuring that the Vulpini had everything they needed. Once in Brankah, when everything was out of her hands, it was then that she realised that she had played a pivotal role in the possible slaughter of many of the people she had met in Oror. It wasn't just a matter of those at Caleb's camp either, if the duke's plan was successful, it would draw out the three main warlords of the north and deal a critical blow to their perfect defence.

Ayse couldn't bear to think of what the battlefield would look like, the bodies of Vulpini men and women lying in the mud, their eyes open but unblinking, and their faces marked with blood. Then there were sure to be casualties on the northern side too. If she were there, would they be faces she recognised also? Bernd, Marcus, Caleb... was it possible that these people who had been so full of life could succumb to death so easily?

Just thinking about it made her feel depressed and she could feel the tingly sensation prick at her eyes and knew that tears were threatening to fall soon. She chided herself at feeling pity for the northerners. It was all too easy to forget that she had grown attached to them for whom they really were, but the attachment they had for her was for that of a pet. When they found out the truth and discovered what she had done, there would be hell to pay. Somehow, the prospect of what they might do to her when they learned the truth didn't deter her from her plan. This was something that she felt she had to do, and her single life was a paltry sum to pay if it ensured the safety of many others.

Chapter Twenty

The duke of High Bremlor's audience chamber featured the same ostentatious décor as it had the last time Rojas had entered. However, now it was full of well-dressed dukes from across the whole of Nevraah. It wasn't just the nobility in attendance that day either, each duke had brought with them the leaders of any companies they had each managed to enlist for their impending battle. Rojas even recognised some of the more renowned sell sword group commanders, most of which liked to wear their colours with pride on their armour. While Duke Remus had the least amount of military support, as it was he who had secured the information on the enemy, he sat with a smug expression on his face in the seat of honour beside Duke Howell of Bronzeheath.

It was Duke Howell who had begun this coup in the first place. He had gathered dukes from across the nation and had made them realise that they should unite against their common foe – the north. While Nevraah and Oror had always been hostile to one another, it was only in recent years that the warfare had erupted in earnest along the border. The promise of new land and rich rewards had been enough to tempt many dukes to fall into line at Duke Howell's command, including Duke Remus. The meeting room was swelling with occupants. Noticeably, even more dukes had joined the cause now that there was a tangible reason to believe that the scheme could be successful.

Duke Howell was discussing the battle strategy once again as the gathered men planned how best to divide their forces. As well as choosing which men would fight to draw the Orians out, and which of them would be moving to take the fort, Duke Howell was also in the process of positioning men who would follow up shortly afterwards to supply their newly taken camp with supplies.

The fort in question was an ideal location to capture based on the layout of the land they had received. Even with most of its soldiers removed, it would still pose a challenge to claim. The plan was to scale the wall with grapple hooks and take the remaining men by surprise. Once inside, they could secure the place properly and see to it that their supplies were brought in to ensure they could outlast any siege the north might throw at them. The fort was in an ideal location that offered a path back to Nevraah with the least hazardous terrain. With time and strategic planning, the Nevraahn army could potentially secure safe passageway for their men through Oror, allowing a link between Nevraah and their anchor in the north.

Thanks to Ayse's reconnaissance work, the dukes knew that the northerners scouted their territory frequently, especially along the border. If they gathered a considerable army on the flatbeds, it would be sure to get the attention of the northerners and prompt them into action. They would have no choice but to rally their own troops near the border line in anticipation of Nevraah's attack, and unbeknownst to them, the other half of the Nevraahn force would be entering their territory further west and heading to the fort.

The heat in the room was becoming unbearable. It made Rojas shift from foot to foot uncomfortably and pull at his shirt collar to bring himself some relief. The summer was shaping up to be one of the fiercest they had seen in some time, as if the sun was sharing in the same angry bloodlust as the men on the earth below.

Rojas couldn't help but think of his fellow tribe members who would be hard at work on the fields of Lower Bremlor as they trained in the unrelenting warmth. There were many Vulpini who had shown much promise, but far too many of them were finding it hard to master a weapon. All too soon, the dukes were preparing to march, taking with them the Vulpini whether they were ready to fight or not. It was not a pleasant thought.

Hearing chairs sliding and people shuffling to their feet, Rojas realised that the meeting had been adjourned. As all the people filed out of the room, Rojas caught sight of someone who was watching him intently with steely eyes, as if trying to get his attention. The man in question followed closely behind Lord

Frewin as they exited, he walked with a noticeable limp as he left, all the while watching Rojas to ensure that the Vulpini man knew that he wished to speak to him afterwards. Rojas nodded casually to signal his understanding, and then waited for most of the room to empty before leaving also.

***

Rojas sat at an empty stall and waited, his drink sitting before him untouched. He didn't have to sit there long before the man he had seen with Frewin approached and took the seat opposite him. He was young, handsome, and looked every bit as depressed as Rojas felt.

"You must be Raphael, Tobias has told me about you," Rojas said with a slight air of disinterest.

"Oh, I've known you for some time, Rojas. It was you that led me to Bremlor in the first place," Raphael grinned.

"So, I've heard," Rojas muttered, not one to admit he had been unknowingly followed for any measure of time. "I figured you'd know where to find me if you were so keen to speak to me."

"Well, there are worse places you could have chosen to meet. But let's cut to the chase, old man. I'm trying my hardest not to be seen with any of your people for the time being now that Frewin has promoted me to an officer. It wasn't easy regaining his trust to that extent, and it's not easy maintaining this deception." Raphael rolled his eyes as he spoke, clearly disgusted with the company he was keeping and based on his knowledge of Frewin, Rojas wasn't surprised.

"So, tell me already, why we are here?"

"Did Tobias tell you that I now know where all of the prisoners are being held?" Raphael asked with a lowered voice.

"He did."

"We're about to have the perfect opportunity to get them out of this shit hole." Raphael was grinning once more, despite Rojas beginning to shake his head.

"Did Tobias not tell you what happened the last time we attempted to free our people? I will not consent to another attempt."

"Tobias didn't have to, Lorie told me," Raphael said gravely. "And to be quite honest with you, whether you consent to it or not, I'm not going to leave those poor girls in there any longer than necessary. Don't take me for a fool, gypsy. Did you think I would come to you without a plan to get them out that would leave these Bremlor idiots none the wiser until it's too late?"

"So, tell me this brilliant plan of yours," Rojas sighed.

"It is brilliant actually. You see, I took a leaf out of the duke's playbook and it all fell into place really," Raphael was not even trying to contain his smugness, "Think about it, they're drawing the northern force out to leave their sought after prize ill-staffed and vulnerable. The brilliant part being, that's exactly what they're doing to Bremlor when they empty every bed to take every able-bodied man that they can in order to fight for them in Oror."

"Do you really think it's that simple? Frewin will have measures in place. His estate will still be well guarded."

Raphael grinned even wider. "Of course, he will. He will turn to one of his most trusted friends, someone who is unable to accompany him to Oror because of an ill-timed riding accident that, unfortunately, has left him with a leg injury."

Rojas couldn't help but smile as he realised what Raphael was saying to him, Frewin was unwittingly allowing the fox to rule over his chicken coop while he was away. "All right, I admit this is beginning to sound more promising. What about the men in the prisons? Will your leg impede the escape?"

"Firstly, my leg is fine. Didn't anyone ever teach you how to fall from a horse properly?" Raphael could see that his pretentious speech was falling on deaf ears and so he relented on his lecture, "Remind me to show you that one day, then. No wonder your people got captured, you're not teaching them half the things they should know."

Tobias had been right that Raphael was not an easy character to like, but Rojas was prepared to ignore the man's shortcomings if it helped the Vulpini in any way. He prompted him to continue, "You were saying?"

"The prison isn't the problem here, with most of the real authority riding around the north like idiots, when I walk in there in my officer garb, I will be able to get them released to me without any questions being raised. We will just have to act quickly. We have to get them all out simultaneously, and then get them as far away from here as possible."

"But we'll be in Oror with the others. No Vulpini will be left in Bremlor to help you."

"We're not going to get a better opportunity than this. I was thinking of enlisting Ayse's help, but I wanted to make sure that she wasn't already entangled in something else to do with your tribe. I haven't seen her around Bremlor, where is she?"

"Ah… Ayse won't be able to help you," Rojas replied, his mouth pulling to the side as he spoke as if the topic was an awkward one.

"Why not?" asked Raphael, the confusion clear on his face.

"According to Tobias, Ayse was planning on heading back to Oror. Chances are she's already there by now."

"Please tell me you're joking. It was a miracle that she even returned the first time, what madness would make her return there?!" Raphael's normal jovial personality had been stripped away as his innermost emotions boiled to the surface. *"And you just let her go?"*

"I think you know Ayse well enough to know that she does what she wants. Tobias tried to convince her to stay, and clearly he failed on that front."

"Clearly," Raphael muttered.

"You know what the dukes have planned. You know where my people are supposed to be… Ayse didn't want them being cut down by the Orians. She went to tell Oror about the attack in the hopes that their main force won't go to the flatbeds and will instead rally at the fort."

"That's a dangerous game to play, on both sides. If one nation doesn't kill her for it, the other just might," Raphael said grimly.

"I'm aware of that, as I'm sure she is too, but this was her decision. We have to respect that."

"I suppose I shouldn't be surprised. After all, if she went running up there to save five of you, why wouldn't she go running back there to save even more of you?" Raphael's voice had taken on a mocking tone as he slowly regained his composure.

"That's Ayse for you."

"That's a problem with the plan, is what it is. I can't pull this off alone and I can't trust bringing any strangers into this. It's too risky. Can none of your men stay behind?"

"The duke has detailed lists of our numbers. If any of them back out, he won't be happy. I can't risk his wrath. We all must leave with them."

"All right, you all have to leave with him. But what if some of you came back early?"

"You mean leave the battle?" Rojas whispered as if afraid to say it too loudly, "I can't abandon my people there."

"This isn't going to be an easy fight. Regardless of whether Ayse manages to warn the north, it doesn't matter to us who wins, you just need to get back here before they do, before the news even breaks of what happened there ideally. If Nevraah loses, the duke might have orders in place for someone to see to the prisoners. I need some of you back here to help me before the Nevraahn forces are even gearing up to leave. I only need a couple of you, maybe even one. I just can't be in two places at once, not to mention a lone officer moving about with five prisoners will be suspicious. Do you think you can manage that? Can I count on you?"

"We have Nevraahn officers keeping us in line all the way to Oror, but once the fighting breaks out it will be easy for me to slip away. I don't want to pull any more of my people away, the more of them that are there, the more they can help one another."

"Do you think you can travel back fast enough, old man?" Raphael smiled.

"I have a fast horse and an impatient nature. I think I'll do just fine," Rojas retorted.

"Let's hope so," Raphael sighed. "I don't believe the duke is going to honour this deal any more than he did the last."

"Me neither," Rojas agreed regretfully.

Raphael rose to his feet as he said, "I best get going before Frewin wonders where I am."

Rojas nodded and watched as he left, once the man had disappeared, he looked to his drink that still sat atop the table as full as it had been when he had ordered it.

Chapter Twenty-One

The weather was milder, even in the depths of the colder northern lands. As Ayse travelled deeper into werewolf territory, she found that small parts of the landscape were still glistening with wet snow, but now they were simply ornaments to distract her from an otherwise largely brown and green world. There were no sudden snowstorms and no torrential rain this time. The journey could even have been pleasant, if it wasn't for Ayse being keenly concerned for her safety the entire time.

Ayse wasn't the only one that felt uneasy, her horse had formerly been quite the steadfast character, yet ever since they had crossed the border it was as though the animal knew it was somewhere it shouldn't be. Her mare had become so nervous that Ayse was afraid it would startle at any moment, buck her from its back, and race off into the woods alone.

It hadn't been an easy decision deciding whether to journey back to Oror on horseback or not, in the end, she had been made to realise that if Nevraah had increased its patrols, then the north most likely would have done too. She was unsure as to whether the northern soldiers would have suspected her to be a shifter once she had disappeared from their camp, if that were the case, then they wouldn't be so quick to overlook a seemingly ordinary wolf a second time.

There was also the matter of the werewolves, surely such beasts capable of hunting and scenting out foes so perfectly were used for patrols, and so not wanting to get stopped short in wolf form, where she couldn't plead her case, she had opted for travelling in her human form. Ayse had tied a large white piece of cotton fabric about her mare's neck, in the hopes that someone would see it before deciding to attack. Worst case scenario, she carried with her all that she knew about Nevraah's plans to attack in the same satchel she had brought back with her from the north. Even if someone were to take her out before she could speak to them, she hoped they would at least find the paperwork she carried.

Returning to Oror had proven trickier than her first journey north, the border was patrolled with greater detail and so she had been forced to cross into Oror further west than anticipated, meaning that she was farther from Caleb's camp than she wished to be.

The thought of having to face Caleb in human form was particularly daunting. She had grown used to his somewhat affectionate mannerisms towards her as a wolf, but she knew that when he saw her now, his eyes would be as cold and harsh as the northern winter. She could feel a knot coiling in her stomach as her nerves began to get the better of her. While she was committed to her desperate plan of action, she knew there was a good chance that even if Caleb heard her out, he would have absolutely no reason to trust her. If she could just manage to convince someone to listen to her, then that might be enough.

It was strange being back in Oror, both exciting and frightening at the same time, somehow the northern landscape was a comfort to Ayse. It was calling out to some deep and hidden part of her soul that she hadn't realised had felt so disconnected from the rest of her until now. Her mind wandered through the possibilities of wolf shifters in the north and she wondered whether the tugging on her heart that pulled her further north was the call of the wild bringing her home.

Of course, the land was anything but homely to her. She had to be watchful of her surroundings and take great care each time she rested, ensuring that she chose the most hidden and secluded spots to keep her out of sight of anyone that might happen to pass. Sheltering as a human was a great deal more difficult than as a wolf, and safe havens had been few and far between. This meant that Ayse often found herself pushing onwards into the night in order to find a better place to rest. That night, she had been faced with the same problem, and having not been able to find a camp for the evening, Ayse had continued. Her horse was becoming more and more disgruntled with each hour that passed. More than once she had heard the very distant call of wolves, though whether they were natural or werewolf, she did not know. Fortunately, they were far away enough to not give her cause for alarm. The horse, on the other hand, was becoming increasingly spooked with every howl it heard.

The forest was alive with sound, all manner of birds and beasts had made themselves known in the darkness, creating a chorus of animal calls that echoed through the trees. As the night wore on, Ayse realised that she would probably be welcoming in the dawn before she even managed to find a place to lay her head. Pulling a flagon from her bag, she swigged at the bitter tasting drink inside and shuddered as she felt the fiery liquid reach her belly. Horace had sent her away with some of his finest whiskey. Ayse couldn't stand the stuff, but even a sip of it was enough to warm her somewhat.

Her mare stopped and began to shuffle from hoof to hoof. Something was troubling it, but in human form Ayse had lost her keen wolf senses. Calming the horse as best she could, she strained to listen to the world around her. There were no longer any bird calls. The night had fallen as still and quiet as a graveyard. A breeze whispered to her, bringing fragments of shouts and snarls with it before dissipating into the still air around her.

Dropping from her horse, she walked it back the way they had come and tethered it to a tree, hopefully far away enough from the noise that it would remain calm. Ayse then began to hastily remove her clothing, not wanting to be caught in such a vulnerable position or bear the cold northern climate on her skin for too long. She shoved her clothing into her saddle bags and moved away from her mare to shift. It watched her with a strange gleam in its eye as she left, as if wondering what craziness the human was up to.

As she stood on all four paws, the wind whispered about her and ruffled her fur affectionately as if realising that she was an old friend returned once again. The commotion of a brawl not too far away was breaking harsh against the otherwise perfectly quiet night. She followed the noise, ensuring that during her approach she remained hidden from view. She could smell the stench of what smelt like rotting meat before she even came upon the source of the excitement.

There, the forest gave way leaving the view of the four or five bodies strewn about the ground completely unmissable. There was blood everywhere, even worse than that, there were innards everywhere. Long trails of guts unravelled across the earth, causing the once brown and green world of the north to be stained red. None of the dead men were whole, either large chunks of flesh were missing, or even entire limbs.

Their armour marked them as Nevraahn soldiers, but the condition of their clothing was like nothing Ayse had ever seen before. The metal breastplates were dented inwards, their helmets had been caved in by sheer force, and some were still crushed atop of glassy-eyed heads. Finally, she drew her eyes away from the carnage and surveyed the two surviving Nevraahn soldiers. Bloodied and panting from their labours, they stood with their back to her as they approached their enemy with halberds raised high, ready to strike.

On the ground before them, a spear already protruding from between its ribs, a werewolf was clawing at the earth as it fought to get to its feet. It failed to do so. Too badly injured, all the werewolf could do was snarl as the men drew ever closer. Its muzzle dripped with blood. As the beast snapped its jaws at the men, foaming red saliva dribbling out as it did so. Ayse quietly circled them, carefully remaining hidden in the shadows. Once alongside the men, she could see their faces ashen from fear as they faced the unthinkable. Their eyes were wide, their faces dripping with mud and blood and there was the distinct smell of urine coming from one, or both. Closer now, she could see the true size of the werewolf, it was slightly smaller than she had anticipated based upon her previous sighting, but it was still monstrously large, almost the same size as her mare.

"What is that?!" one soldier asked breathlessly as they inched forwards still, each step was painfully slow, both men too scared to get closer to the beast.

"Some ungodly monster, that's what. We have to kill it," the other responded fearfully.

Ayse looked back to the werewolf, unknown to the men it had fully understood their conversation and it heaved as it tried to rise with even more desperation than before. Its dark eyes gleamed with anger, its hackles were bristling, and it growled from deep within its chest in a futile attempt at scaring the men away. Without even thinking, Ayse was moving. Her body was reacting without any predetermined thought, just instinct. She wasn't even sure what she was doing until she tasted the blood in her mouth as she tore the first soldier's throat out. He fell to the floor gargling and grabbing at his missing gullet until he moved no more. The other soldier had spun around at the sound and now his halberd was pointing in Ayse's direction. He looked from his dead companion to Ayse and sobbed in terror.

Ayse gained ground on him slowly, her ears pinned back and a growl ripping out from her throat as she kept her head low while stalking forwards. In his haste to get away from her, the soldier made the fatal mistake of forgetting about the other beast that was present. With one small step he had moved too close to the werewolf and it made one last heave of its body to snap at his leg and haul him to the ground, where it dragged him closer and bit into his neck with such ferocity that it nearly tore his head asunder entirely.

With the Nevraahn soldiers now dead, Ayse immediately changed her demeanour so that the werewolf would know that she was not there to antagonise it. It watched her with large unblinking eyes, but its ears remained flat against its head as it growled a warning to her. She tilted her head as she watched the werewolf attempt to move, but it slumped back to the ground with a large thud that caused it to whine in pain. She moved forwards, but once again it growled at her to stay back.

Ayse knew that the werewolf was losing blood, she could smell its strange exotic scent in the air and the smell of its blood made her own blood pound in her veins. She crouched low to the ground and the werewolf watched her intently as she did so, not understanding what she was about to do. As she rose to her feet as a woman, the werewolf shuffled backwards and yelped as the movement caused it further pain. It looked confused, alarmed even, but it didn't last long. Survival instinct took over and it quickly resumed its snarls and growls as Ayse attempted to move closer. However, Ayse was undeterred. In that small moment she had seen the alarm of the werewolf and she had understood that fear. It was the fear of the unknown.

"Can you shift?" she spoke loud and clear, her voice strong and commanding, "I have a horse so that I can get you back to your people, but you are far too large as you are. You have to turn back into a man."

The werewolf seemed at odds with itself as if thrown off by her kindness. It looked away from her as if abashed to see her in such a way.

Raising her hands to show she meant him no harm, Ayse continued trying to convince the werewolf to accept her help, "You're badly injured. We must get you back to your camp, but you must shift back into human form for me to be able to help you. I am going to get the horse. If you can turn back into a man, please do so."

She crouched on the floor and shifted once more, before turning on her heel and disappearing back into the thick of the forest, hoping that her no-nonsense attitude was enough to spur even a werewolf into action. She ran back to the horse with a desperate energy, returning to human form and dressing more speedily than she could ever remember doing so before. The horse had quietened down, most likely due to the sounds of fighting having abated, but Ayse was sure that if she led it back to the werewolf and it was still in wolf form, that it would be the last straw for the mare. Praying silently that the werewolf was not as stubborn as she had known some of the other northerners to be, she made her way back to the grisly glade.

The bodies of the Nevraahn soldiers were just as they had been, but the wolf was gone. In its place was the prone, naked and bloodied body of a man lying face down in the grime. Jumping down from her horse, Ayse rushed to the man's side and heaved him onto his back. She noticed that the spear was on the floor beside him, it had either come loose while he had transformed, or he had pulled it out after shifting. Either way, it had caused an even greater amount of blood to begin spilling from his wound.

Removing her cloak, Ayse wrapped it about the man's torso and tied it tightly. As she pulled the material taut, the man groaned and regained consciousness, drawing Ayse's attention to his face. He was young, just a teenager. Ayse could imagine that he was only just barely on the cusp of becoming a man. His hair was a dirty blonde colour and she wondered how much of that shade was truly dirt from the forest floor. He stared at her with confusion, his eyebrows furrowed, and his lips parted as if he meant to say something. Instead, his body shook as he began to cough up blood, rousing Ayse into action.

"Can you stand?" she asked, attempting to haul him to his feet.

The young man gritted his teeth as he stood with Ayse's help. She put his arm over her shoulders and began to move him towards the mare, each step becoming more difficult than the last as he bore more of his weight onto her. Getting him onto the horse was another challenge entirely; the mare had become agitated by the scent of blood in the air and had begun to shift from hoof to hoof again. Getting the horse to stand still while Ayse helped the northerner onto her back was a testing time. At long last they managed it, although the rider was in a less than dignified position of being slung across the back of the horse like a hunting trophy. She grabbed a coverlet from her pack bags and threw it over him to allow him to save some of his dignity at least.

"Your camp, where is it?" she gasped as she fought to regain her breath.

The man made as if to answer, but ended up coughing up more blood instead, clutching at the horse's coat as he struggled to catch his breath. Remembering the rough lay of the land, Ayse recalled that there was currently another camp closer to them than Caleb's, of course, it all depended on whether the werewolf even hailed from one of the three main camps.

Moving around the other side of her horse, Ayse took the man's face in her hands and made him look at her to ensure she knew he understood the question she was about to ask him, "Lord Ulric's camp?"

The man continued to cough and splutter, but he nodded dumbly at her before his body gave in and he appeared to lose all consciousness. Lifting the coverlet, she could see that the cloak she had fastened about his waist was already turning crimson and Ayse knew that she would have to move fast to ensure that he lived to see the morning.

If her memory served her right, the fort that Lord Ulric had planned to set up camp in for the summer shouldn't have been too far, but there was no way she would get him there in time if she was forced to travel on foot. Moving quickly, Ayse pulled some rope from her saddlebags and attempted to secure her prone passenger as best she could.

The poor boy was beginning to look even more like tomorrow's lunch as she tied him to the horse, but it was the best she could do. Ayse pulled herself into the saddle, carefully moving the werewolf as best as she could as she did so. It meant that his body ended up lying across her lap, his legs dangling over one side of the horse, while his arms hung limply the other side.

She kicked her horse to spur it into a gallop as she gripped onto her passenger with one hand to ensure he stayed put. Hooves pounded into the ground as they thundered between the trees. Ayse had been expecting to have to face Caleb, not a stranger. She wasn't entirely sure whether facing Lord Ulric instead would boost her chances of success or squash them, but at that point her main concern was getting the boy to his people while he was still alive. After all, she didn't much like the idea of being the bearer of his body instead of the person who had saved his life.

Chapter Twenty-Two

Sweat and the stench of horse was all that Rojas could smell in the stifling heat as he walked beside his mount. If the training had been difficult for most, the march northwards was a burden to them all. With only meagre rations to sustain them, the Vulpini endured a brutal schedule that saw them pushing onwards until the point of exhaustion under the unrelenting sun.

All the Vulpini horses, bar Rojas's, had been requisitioned by the duke for the more skilled fighters that would be travelling to the fort, leaving all the other tribal members travelling on foot. Rojas had opted to allow different tribal members who were finding the advance difficult a chance to ride the horse, taking it in turns to ensure that whoever needed the rest the most received it.

They had been kitted out in whatever armour Bremlor had to spare, but it was nowhere near the quality of that worn by the Nevraahn soldiers. The weight of the armour in the hot weather was unbearable, and it wasn't as though the Vulpini could let loose on an evening and go for a run either. The duke had men watching them carefully, ensuring that they didn't flee from the battle before they had even arrived. It was causing tensions to arise among his already weary people, as they desperately fought to keep their second nature from getting the best of them.

Looking out and seeing armed men for as far as he could see was an impressive sight. Rojas had to give it to the dukes, they had really managed to gather an impressive number of fighters, even if some of them were inexperienced. Even more impressive was the knowledge that this was only half of the Nevraahn force. Further west, the real threat to Oror would be mobilising and heading northwards too. It gave the Vulpini man some small hope that based on their sheer numbers there were enough of them that could keep the northerners at bay and keep casualties to a minimum.

A hand clapped on his shoulder, pulling him out of his daydream and back into the punishing reality of marching. As Rojas turned to see who had drawn his attention, Tobias gave him a wide grin before falling into line beside him.

"You are far too happy for a man on the march," Rojas muttered with a smile.

"It's not that. I just try to keep upbeat. The tribe are looking to us and if we look despondent then they will feel even worse than they already do," Tobias stated, gesturing at the Vulpini around them.

Every tribesman had their face down. Their eyes were dark and shadowed as they continued putting one foot in front of the other with the competence of a sleepwalker. It was clear to any onlooker that much like Rojas, all of them were brooding and simply following the crowd of people as they continued to march.

"You're right," Rojas sighed. "It's just so damn hard to stay optimistic when you're heading to battle. Especially a battle you don't even want to be a part of."

"As long as we stick together and help our people, we can get through this."

"There's something I need to tell you, Tobias," Rojas said quietly, turning to look at Tobias with sad eyes, "When the fighting begins, it will be up to you to keep our people safe."

"What do you mean? Where will you be?"

"I have to return to Bremlor." Before Tobias could interject, Rojas motioned for him to remain quiet. Dropping his voice to a low whisper, Rojas continued, "Believe me, I wouldn't abandon our people in the north if there was another way. Raphael has a plan to get all the Vulpini prisoners out. It's a plan that could work. But he can't do it alone."

"Are you sure his idea will work? We don't want to make another mistake. Is it really worth leaving the battlefield on Raphael's say-so?"

"He told me what he has planned, and we won't get a better chance than this," Rojas emphasised.

"What did the chief say about it?" Tobias asked.

"Actually, he doesn't know." Rojas scratched at his forehead absent-mindedly as he considered how angry Solomon would be if he knew that he was acting without his consent. "I don't think he would have approved. I worried that he would tell me to leave it, hoping that the duke would uphold his promise after the battle... but I don't think he will, Tobias. I think he will keep us on this short leash that has proven to be so useful to him."

"You? Going against what the chief would have wanted? That's not like you, Rojas," Tobias chuckled.

"I guess I've been spending too much time around you, boy. Your disobedience is rubbing off on me," Rojas said with a faint smile.

"You're sure of this then? If you're risking the wrath of the chief and leaving the tribe in the north, you must think it can really work."

"I do, Tobias," Rojas said solemnly, "I really do."

"If we manage to get our people back, we'll have to move the tribe somewhere far away, out of Duke Remus's reach. He won't be happy when he realises."

"With any luck, he'll have bigger problems on his hands. If Ayse is successful, that is."

Tobias shook his head disapprovingly. "You don't actually condone her actions, do you?"

Rojas looked at him with an expression that shamed him. "Of course, I do. How is this any different than before? She's travelled alone to Oror on the slim chance that something she does can save Vulpini lives."

"Not just the Vulpini, she wants to save the northerners too," Tobias muttered bitterly.

"Is that so bad? What quarrel do we have with them?" Rojas asked softly, but Tobias just shook his head in response. Rojas gave him a pitying look as he sought to comfort his companion, "Ayse spent a great deal of time there. It's not hard to believe she grew affectionate towards one or more of them. They saved her life. When someone saves your life, it's not something you forget in a hurry."

"They saved her because they thought she was just a wolf. They would have killed her otherwise," Tobias snapped.

It was Rojas's turn to shake his head. "Regardless of why they did it, they did it. Ayse has that debt weighing on her mind. Imagine how difficult it must have been to betray the people who saved her from certain death? That poor girl has more weight to carry than any of us marching in this infernal heat."

"And if they kill her for it?" Tobias asked.

"Ayse is aware of what consequences may lay ahead, just like before, just as we know what fate might befall us in the north. We can't always live our lives in fear, Tobias."

Tobias's grin had gone as soon as his mood had begun to sour. While part of him was telling him that Rojas was right, another part of him entirely would not be swayed on the matter. They continued to trudge onwards in silence, looking just as depressed as the rest of the Vulpini tribe as they marched.

✱✱✱

The night-time was the one thing they had to look forward to now. Not only did it give them relief from the tyrannical sun, but it was the one time they could curl up next to one another and pretend they were somewhere else entirely. Sleep generally overcame the camp quite quickly. The makeshift settlement was quiet, even the wind wasn't daring to creep amongst the soldiers as they rested.

Nell lay beside Reuben, not caring that it was far too hot for bodily contact as the comfort of her lover far outweighed the uncomfortable heat. She listened to his heartbeat, it was steady like the beating of a drum and the more she listened, the more she felt as though the whole world should be able to hear its rhythmic echoes.

"You're not sleeping," Reuben stated sleepily, not even opening his eyes to speak.

"How could you tell?" Nell smiled, looking up at him and stroking his cheek.

"Because your body is all tense," he answered, pausing to open one eye and look at her before closing it once more. "Now go to sleep."

"I can't sleep," she whispered in a frightened tone.

"Then you must be the only one. I'm so tired I could sleep for a week."

"I can't stop worrying..."

Reuben opened his eyes and pulled Nell closer to him and squeezed her tightly, speaking softly to her to reassure her, "It will be alright. I will look after you. We will all look after one another."

"I know that," Nell tutted. "It's not that bothering me."

"Then what is it?" Reuben asked, pushing her away slightly so that he could look at her face once more.

"I can't stop thinking of Ayse. After Tobias told us what she was going to do... I just can't stop wondering what she's doing right now, whether she's safe, whether she's hurt or worse even. You saw her when she returned. It made me feel guilty to see her in such a state because we sent her there."

"Ayse is a big girl, Nell. She knows what she's doing. Besides, if anyone can make it out of Oror alive again —it's her, having been the only southerner to ever accomplish it in the first place," Reuben jested.

"I know... I just can't help but worry."

"Well, worry while you sleep, because we need all the rest we can get," Reuben instructed with a smile.

Nell nodded and returned the smile. She cosied up to Reuben and began listening to his heartbeat once again, concentrating on the steady rhythm until the drumbeats faded away into nothingness as sleep overcame her. Reuben sighed as he realised that now he was cursed to be the one who could not fall to sleep. He gripped Nell's small body closer to him as he rolled onto his back and looked at the sky above them.

The skyline always seemed so much more benevolent in the summer. The black of the night had given way to a deep blue that was adorned with many twinkling spots of light. Not a single cloud was in sight, just an endless sea of glittering stars that swelled around the moon as it stood sentry over the world.

To pass the time, Reuben began to pick out the few constellations he remembered being taught as a child, first and foremost he recognised The Summer Fox, a favourite amongst the tribe. Others he could remember were The Great Water Steed, The Dancing Bear, and then there was The Wild Wolf... Reuben looked at the wolf far above him, the beast was prowling in the heavens without a care for the mortal world. Reuben pleaded with it, "Keep her safe."

Chapter Twenty-Three

Morning was finally breaking across the sky. The light was beginning to cast long shadows as the night-time crawled away from the world and hid in the darkened recesses of the netherworld. The dark stone building was an impressive sight against the backdrop of the dawn sky. It looked as though it had stood proudly for many years as its outer walls were crawling with vines and moss, making the fort look greener and more alive than any stone building should be.

Ayse was aware that there were sentries posted atop the walls, she could see movement as they reacted to her arrival. As they wandered well within the range of fire, she was glad to see no arrows hissing out at them from the battlements. Whether it was her mare's flag of white, or the limp body of the man atop the horse with her, she couldn't say, but it looked as though the northerners might listen to her. She hastened her approach. The boy had grown paler with every hour that had passed, his coughing had stopped altogether and while Ayse knew he was still alive, his breathing was shallow, and his pulse was faint. He surely wouldn't last much longer.

Stopping before the dramatic wooden gates to the fort, Ayse halted her horse impatiently. She was too close now to see any sign of life atop the battlements and so she was forced to wait. The loud rattle of a bolt unlatching signalled that someone was at the gate. A small panelling of the wood disappeared, and a face appeared in the peephole eyeing Ayse with mistrust.

"State your business," the voice growled.

Clambering down from her horse whilst trying not to send her passenger off balance, Ayse grabbed the reins and led her mare closer to the gate so that the man inside could see her better. Feeling her heart thumping against the inside of her chest like a bird beating its wings at a cage to escape, she answered with a shaky voice, "I have one of your men with me, he is gravely injured."

The sound of sudden movement both above her and inside the door echoed loudly as she answered, causing Ayse to wince and close her eyes, expecting some form of attack. But nothing happened. She looked back to the shadowed face at the door expectantly.

"You speak like a southerner, girl. We don't take kindly to trespassers," the man at the gate warned.

Ayse pulled her mare to one side and lifted the head of the boy on the horse so that the man at the gate could see him. Feigning her no-nonsense attitude again, Ayse ignored the warnings and continued, "I believe this is yours. If you want him to live, I suggest you fetch some help, *now*."

She heard the man at the gate muttering curses to the old gods as the wood panelling slammed shut and the bolt was re-latched. For a moment, Ayse thought that the man was choosing to ignore her, but then she heard the sliding sound of the gates being unbarred.

Northern soldiers spilled out and surrounded her. She had been near northern soldiers in full gear before, but she had never been at the centre of many men pointing weapons in her direction. It was disconcerting, to say the least. She swallowed with difficulty as her mouth suddenly felt rather dry. Ayse raised her hands to show that she was unarmed.

The soldiers were all watching her through narrowed eyes, but none of them spoke. The men parted to allow for another man to make his way to Ayse. He was dressed as a high-ranking northerner, wearing similar clothing to that of Caleb and Markus. He was tall and well built, striking an impressive figure against his soldiers as his hair was unnaturally blonde for a northerner. As he stopped in front of her, she saw that his eyes were a startling bright shade of blue also. He stared her down with such intensity that she wilted under his gaze. As soon as she had looked away from him, he moved towards the horse and inspected the boy quickly before signalling for some of the soldiers to remove the lad and take him inside the safety of the camp.

"You have some explaining to do," he commanded as he turned to face Ayse once more, his face was suddenly a lot darker than before.

She looked about her at the many stern faces of the soldiers and wondered whether she was expected to relay her version of events in front of them all. Certain that she was correct in believing that not all northerners were werewolves, she didn't think that telling a fantastical tale about men who turned into beasts would help her case considering her current situation.

"Would it be possible to speak to you in private?" she asked meekly, not daring to look up at the fierce lord again.

For a few moments there was no response, as if the lord was deciding whether to acquiesce to her request or not. With a sigh he finally spoke, but it wasn't to Ayse.

"Search her," he commanded, before disappearing back through the gate.

Soldiers moved forwards to search Ayse and once content that she was not hiding any weapons, they marched her forwards, leaving a handful of men to search her belongings on the mare. The inside of the fort was as formidable as the exterior and bore a similar resemblance to that of Caleb's camp. There were Orian men sparring together while others milled about the place with a sense of purpose. As she was escorted inside, they all stopped to watch her.

She had expected to be taken for an audience with the lord, but instead she was led down a spiralled staircase and into the darkened cells below. As she was prodded through a door non-too gently and heard it lock behind her, she stood in the darkness thankful to even be alive. The events of the night had been tiring and so Ayse collapsed to the floor, grateful that the cell was at least dry. She decided that if she was going to be made to wait, that she would at least get some sleep, after all, she wasn't going to sit there patiently for them like a dog awaiting its master. Those days were over.

✳✳✳

The sound of her cell door being pulled open roused her from her sleep and she bolted upright into a sitting position, watching with dazed eyes as the blonde lord made his entrance. She wasn't sure how much time had passed as she still felt incredibly tired, but she took some enjoyment from the surprised look on the lord's face, as if he hadn't expected to find her sleeping.

"It was a long night," she said by way of explanation, trying her hardest to reclaim some of her confidence as she spoke to him, yet still being unable to look him in the eye. "Is the boy all right?"

The lord raised an eyebrow at her question before answering her, "He will live."

Ayse let out a sigh of relief. She imagined that the chance of her being allowed to live would have been greatly diminished if the boy had perished.

"You are from Nevraah, are you not?" he asked her.

"I am," she replied. "But I'm not here as an enemy."

"All southerners are enemies," the northern lord retorted.

"If that were true, then I wouldn't have helped that boy, would I?"

"Yes... I am still trying to work out your motives behind that specific action. Tell me how it is you came to help him exactly."

Ayse bit her lip, unsure whether to speak the truth or not. She went with her gut instinct, "He was in werewolf form when I found him. He had killed a few Nevraahn soldiers, but he was badly injured, and the two remaining soldiers were moving in to finish him off. So, I helped him."

"You helped him?" the man questioned her, completely glossing over the fact she had mentioned the boy had been a werewolf.

"I killed one of them," Ayse stated flatly. "The other panicked and got too close to your boy and, well, that was the end of that. Then I told him to shift back so that I could get him to safety." Ayse paused for a moment before adding, "So you know about the werewolves then?"

The man flashed her a wide toothy grin that sent shivers through her body. "Oh, I know about werewolves," he answered, then smiled at her before continuing with his questions, "My men found no weapons on you. How did you kill the man?"

"I tore his throat out." Ayse swallowed after she spoke, her mouth was getting that dry feeling once again.

"I find that hard to believe," the man mused.

"I was a wolf when I did it," she responded stoically.

"Is that so?" he asked her with a raised eyebrow.

"Yes, but I'm not a werewolf," she explained.

The man broke into laughter. It was so unexpected that it made Ayse jump. Suddenly she got the feeling as though the northern lord wasn't taking anything she said seriously.

"If you don't believe me, ask the boy when he wakes," she said with a frown.

"Forgive me," the man said, regaining his composure. "It was just the idea that you thought I might have mistaken you for a werewolf was just too funny."

"Why?" Ayse said indignantly.

"For someone who seems to know a bit too much about werewolves, you do not seem to understand that there are no such thing as female werewolves," the man chuckled.

"Oh," she responded softly. This was news to her, if she had known that then she would never have believed herself to be a werewolf for most of her life. Everything she had presumed about werewolves was unravelling before her very eyes.

"I take it you are a shapeshifter," the man said, more a statement than a question.

"Yes, I suppose I am," Ayse said still in a daze.

"You mean to tell me you don't know?" the man said, the tone of his voice suggesting that he was about to break into laughter once again.

"In case you haven't noticed, we don't really get wolves in the south," Ayse responded sharply, "So I've never met another wolf shifter to compare notes."

"And you won't find any wolf shifters in Oror either," the lord said with an almost sad tone, "Other than you, of course."

"Wolf shifters aren't native to the north?" she asked with a confused expression.

"Oh, they were," he explained, "The Canini tribe were wiped out many years ago."

"The Canini tribe?" Ayse asked, feeling as though she was within reach of a revelation.

"You really don't know anything, do you?" he asked, just as bewildered by her as she was by him. "Tell me why you came to Oror.

"I came to warn Cal-, uh, Lord Caleb, of an impending attack from the south," she stuttered.

"Why would a southerner warn us of their own attack?"

"Nevraah isn't ruled as a nation, it's made up of different tribes, dukedoms, and cities… it isn't as though we're some united force standing in opposition against Oror."

"No?"

"No," she answered flatly.

"How is it you know of Lord Caleb?"

"It's hard to explain…" she mumbled, "I met him, sort of. Look if you just look in my bag then you can see the information on what the Nevraahn forces have planned, if you could get it to Lord Caleb and Lord Ulric quickly then you might be able to do something about the attack."

"I did and I have," the lord stated nonchalantly, breaking into a smile as he added, "And you've already notified Lord Ulric."

"You're-?" she asked, and he nodded prompting her to stop mid-sentence.

"I wanted to ask you about it in person. I'm finding it hard to believe that you have our best interests at heart by delivering this news to us. You must understand how this looks like a false play."

"Look, the truth is, the dukes that have rallied together to try and take the north have coerced my tribe into fighting alongside them. They don't have a choice in the matter. They're simply there to bulk up the diversionary force to lead your people away. They aren't fighters. They will be slaughtered in the battle. I thought if I told you about the attack, you wouldn't fall for their tactics and so the bloodshed would never come to my tribe."

"That sounds more believable," Lord Ulric said with almost a friendly smile.

"So, you'll deliver the information to Caleb as well?" she asked desperately.

"*Lord* Caleb will receive the information, yes." Lord Ulric corrected her with a frown, "So explain to me how it is you met my brother."

"Your brother?" she asked with incredulity.

"Does that surprise you?"

"You just don't look very alike…" she mumbled.

"We have different mothers," Lord Ulric explained drily. "Now tell me, where did you meet him?"

"Here, in the north I mean. I was here as a wolf, he saved my life," she responded, her voice losing its composure as regret and guilt prickled inside of her.

"He didn't realise you were a shifter." He said it as a statement, but Ayse took it as a question and shook her head.

"He would have killed you if he had known," Lord Ulric said with a deadpan tone.

"I know," she admitted.

"What were you doing in the north, as a wolf?" he asked, all humour gone from his face.

She shut her eyes and sighed, feeling as though she was about to take her last step off a steep precipice and fall to her end. She whispered the painful truth, "I was gathering information on Oror."

She flicked her eyes open to see his response, his eyes looked darker than before, but other than that, his face was as unreadable as a marble statue.

"It wasn't out of choice," she explained hastily, "I did it to save the lives of my friends. If there had been another way..." her sentence trailed off as she hung her head in shame.

The silence in the small room grew, and despite Ayse wishing that it would form a void that would swallow her whole, she remained there under the stern gaze of Lord Ulric. Eventually he sighed, his fingers going to his temples as if he suddenly had an acute headache.

"Fetch her horse!" He called loudly. There was movement outside of the cell as a soldier hastened to obey. "Get up, girl. It's time you were on your way."

"You're letting me leave?" she said with disbelief.

"What did you think I would do?"

"Northerners don't let southerners live."

"If that were true, then I wouldn't be releasing you, would I?" he responded with a smirk as he threw her own line back at her.

"I just told you that I stole information from you, the very same information that Nevraah is using to attack you-"

"And you saved my son's life," Lord Ulric responded firmly, "And I believe in repaying that debt in kind."

Ayse shook her head, "You don't owe me a debt for that. I already told you, Caleb saved my life, if anything we're now even."

"That is a separate matter. You'll have to square your debt to my brother yourself. I sent word to him as soon as I saw what you carried with you. He is most likely on his way to Fort Lyndon as we speak, so I would advise you to leave before he gets here. If you truly spent time with him, then you'll know that he has a short temper. Believe me when I tell you that he will not react well to what you have just told me." Lord Ulric's tone was stern, but not unkind.

"But you believe me, right? About the attack?" she asked as she rose to her feet.

"You sound sincere... but it is not something for me to decide alone. I will have to confer with my brothers when they arrive. We will reach a decision together."

Once he had finished speaking, Lord Ulric turned to leave, but Ayse called out to him, "Wait! Please tell me, what happened to the Canini tribe?"

Lord Ulric looked back and gave her a soft, yet sad smile. "I will save that story for another time."

"But what if we never meet again?" she asked as he turned his back on her once more.

"You want to repay that debt to my brother, don't you?" he replied as he began to walk away, "We will meet again, I am sure of it. I just hope for your sake that it is under better circumstances."

Chapter Twenty-Four

The candlelight was pitiful in the gloom, its glow could barely penetrate the thickness of the darkened prison cell and the flame shrank from the shadows as if afraid. Despite its small flame, it brought great comfort to Lorie that she did not have to spend her time in utter darkness. Ever since Lord Frewin and most of his men had departed for Oror, leaving Isaac in charge of his estate in doing so, Lorie and Ana had been afforded a few small luxuries such as candlelight and better food.

Isaac only brought what he was sure would go unnoticed, not wanting any of the remaining guards to sense that he was favouring them more than he should. He had also instructed the guard at the door to not allow anyone but him to enter until Lord Frewin returned, explaining that Frewin was possessive of his toys while away and ensuring that the Vulpini girls were safe from harm for the time being.

Even though their situation had been improved, Ana was still as reclusive as ever. Both Lorie and Isaac had attempted to get her to speak by comforting her and promising her that soon they would be far away from Bremlor, but Ana never responded. She just sat there, hunched over her knees, her bottom lip trembling as she stared into nothingness. It made Lorie wonder whether Ana would ever return to her old self, or whether Bremlor had broken her permanently.

As Lorie sat with her lone candle, watching the pale face of her friend staring wide-eyed at the bare wall in front of her, she heard the jingle of keys and the shift of the door above them opening. Isaac gingerly limped down the steps as the guard above him re-latched the door. Once the door was safely closed, he continued his descent without his feigned injury and smiled warmly at Lorie as he crouched down beside her.

"I've brought you some treats." He beamed as he pulled out a couple of handkerchief-covered slices of cake and a flagon of wine from his coat pocket.

"Well, don't you know how to treat a girl," Lorie jested.

"I try my best, given the situation." He winked at her.

After handing Lorie her slice of cake, he moved over to Ana and placed her slice in front of her. He watched her for a short time, but she didn't acknowledge his presence.

Lorie split her cake in two and offered Isaac half of it. He politely took it from her, although he wasn't hungry.

"How long do you think it will be before Rojas returns?" she asked him.

"It might be a while longer yet. I imagine that they're almost at the northern border by now, but they have to wait for the duke to send word before they can go ahead with the attack."

"Will it be a real battle?" she asked fearfully.

"I'm afraid so," he answered. "But with any luck, Ayse might have just pulled off her second life-threatening, nigh-impossible plan that involves the north."

Lorie smiled. "Well, if anyone could do it, it would be Ayse."

"You never did tell me why it had to be her that went north in the first place."

Lorie shifted uncomfortably and dropped her gaze. "It's not really something I can explain, you just have to believe me that she was the best one for the task."

"Mmhmm." he muttered disapprovingly.

"Next time you see her, ask her yourself. But I doubt you'll get any more out of her than you did from me," Lorie teased.

"I always get what I want eventually," Isaac said with a wink. "One way or another, I'll find out what makes Ayse so special."

"I wouldn't be too sure of yourself on that front."

"Oh, but I am always so sure of myself," Isaac said smugly.

"And don't I know it..." Lorie sighed. "What is the plan for when we leave Bremlor?"

"You know the plan," Isaac huffed.

"Just tell me again. I'm so desperate to leave, just talking about getting out of here makes me feel better," Lorie pleaded.

"Rojas will return when he is able. I've secured some Nevraahn soldier armour for him and I will send him with an order bearing Frewin's seal that the Vulpini prisoners are to be moved from the cells. Meanwhile, I'll be escorting the two of you from the premises and because I'm such a wonderful master of the house, the guards will just happen to have a night laden with drink and beautiful women to keep them distracted. We'll all meet in Lower Bremlor, where our horses will be ready and waiting for a quick escape. It's important that we leave as soon as possible, just in case any of the Bremlor soldiers grow suspicious and think to ask questions about why the prisoners are being moved."

"And then what?" Lorie asked watching him carefully.

"And then we will take you back to your tribe," Isaac concluded.

"What about the others? Those still in the north fighting?"

"There's not much we can do for them. We'll just have to wait for them to return on their own merit. Whether or not that will be marching back with the duke singing of his victories, or running with his tail between his legs, we'll just have to see on that front. Once your people are all reunited, I imagine your chief will want to disappear fast. Once the duke realises that your people got the better of him, he'll be howling for blood. Is there somewhere safe you can go?"

"The Vulpini are travellers by nature, we know plenty of places that we can lay low for a while."

"Good. You might need to stay hidden for quite some time. I don't know how far-reaching the duke's wrath will be, or how long it will take before it burns out completely."

"Will you miss this when you're gone?" Lorie asked softly.

"This? As in, the disgusting city of Bremlor filled with its pig-headed, filthy idiots? I doubt it," Isaac laughed.

"I don't mean Bremlor," Lorie said.

"I know what you meant," Isaac smirked at her and whispered, "Why do you think I returned to Bremlor? It wasn't for the scenery."

Lorie smiled and lowered her head as she felt her cheeks grow hot, grateful that the solitary candle did not afford much light for her blush to be noticed. Changing the subject, she asked him, "What will you do after all this?"

"I will do what I have always done. Travel, find jobs, take jobs, and earn coin, before travelling on again," he replied casually.

"Sounds like the same life the Vulpini lead," she commented.

"Yeah, only there are fewer people to enjoy it with when you travel alone," he pointed out wistfully.

"Does that make you sad?"

"Not usually," he answered truthfully, "But sometimes it does."

Lorie tilted her head as she watched the shadows play on Isaac's face. His brow was furrowed as he considered the lifestyle that he led. His expression made Lorie's heart ache for him. She wanted to reach out and comfort him, but she felt that it would be too brazen. More than anything, she wished she had never asked him about what he would do once they parted ways.

Eager to see him smile again, Lorie changed the conversation to a lighter topic and made every effort to make the man laugh long into the night. Knowing that they would soon be leaving Bremlor was a bittersweet thought for Lorie, the sooner she was free, the sooner that Isaac would be gone from her life completely.

***

Raphael watched the people go about their morning from his window. The view from his room in High Bremlor was vastly different from when he had slummed it in the lower district, there were no women of the night returning to their children, and no farmers leaving home to work the fields for that day. Instead, there was the odd soldier roaming outside and kitchen maids and servants scurrying in all directions to ensure that the estate was running perfectly, despite their lord and master being absent.

He sighed as he drew the drapes together and pulled his shirt off. He had spent the night talking with Lorie and had only left when she had fallen asleep. By that time, even Ana was resting peaceful, though her cake was still untouched. He had been surprised to find that morning was rousing the inhabitants of Bremlor as he had left, not realising quite how long they had chatted away for. Time tended to pass easily when in the company of Lorie, it was something he knew he would miss when she was back with her tribe.

He finished undressing and climbed into his bed, his mind still afflicted with thoughts of the Vulpini girl. Raphael had known plenty of women in his time, yet he had never encountered one that had bewitched him so. He couldn't pinpoint what it was about her that attracted him. Of course, she was pretty, and being easy on the eyes was never a bad thing. He also admired her strength and attitude; despite her current predicament, Lorie was a fighter that refused to go quietly. Was that what attracted him the most, her tenacity?

Perhaps not being able to understand the exact reason why he held affection for her was what it meant to truly care for someone. In the past, he had always known why he had loved a woman, if you could call it love. It was either for her looks, her warm personality, her money, or sometimes it was just because he was bored and she had been there.

But this was different. This was something more to him, something he held dearer than any of those other women from his past. And yet he was cursed with the knowledge that Lorie was not his. She would return to her people and vanish from his life for certain. Her chief would stow their people away somewhere safe, somewhere out of reach, even from him. Once again, he found that he was haunted by thoughts of Lorie, only this time it wasn't in fear of what terrors she was enduring, instead, he was plagued by the thought of a terrible fate... of a life that didn't have the Vulpini girl in it.

Chapter Twenty-Five

Rojas remembered that the first time he had visited the flatbeds he had been in awe of the expansive green space, impressed with the beautiful emptiness that had stretched for miles and miles. It was a far cry from the view before him now. As far as the eye could see there were men camped out, makeshift tents, smouldering campfires, and all manner of weaponry and supplies crowded onto the back of carts. The once burgeoning landscape was now marred with churned up mud tracks and blackened, gutted remains of fires from days past.

Different factions of men would periodically break out into brawls as they argued over the smallest of things. The only thing keeping utter chaos from erupting throughout the settlement were the officers from Bremlor who had been charged with overseeing the forthcoming assault. The fear of them reporting any major mishaps to Duke Howell and Duke Remus was enough to keep the men in line, for the most part.

When they had finally reached the plains, it had been a relief for the tribe to finally set up camp and rest their weary feet. However, as the days had begun to pass, a sense of foreboding had started to grow among the Vulpini. To Rojas, it felt as though each new day that passed was vanishing quicker than the one before as the impending warfare loomed before them.

Once they were given the signal, they would have to march towards Oror's outermost border to face the northerners in battle. Tensions were still high due to the lack of opportunity for the tribespeople to shift, but Rojas had reminded them that the prisoners in Bremlor had suffered much longer without a transformation than they. It had been a sobering thought for most.

As judgement day hovered on the horizon, Rojas had begun to fear for the safety of his people more than ever. Most of them had been average at best when training back in Bremlor, but under the pressure and horror of a real battle, he was sure that nerves would get the better of many of them. Tobias may not have agreed with Ayse's plan to warn the Orians about what lay ahead, but Rojas was praying desperately that she had succeeded in her task. As far as he was concerned, anything that could potentially limit the damage done to the Vulpini was worth attempting.

The air was growing cooler as the evening sky began to dim, a breeze was whispering its way through the crowded camp and crickets could be heard harmoniously chirping in the grass. A few of the Vulpini were beginning to settle down for an early night, while some of the more studious tribesmen continued to practice their swordplay with one another. Rojas lay down with the intention of simply resting his eyes as he listened to the clash of blades, but it didn't take long for sleep to take him in its embrace.

✳✳✳

Rojas woke with a start. The camp was quiet and dark as night-time reigned, yet something was stirring in the shadows. He couldn't hear it, but he could sense it, something was causing the hair on his arms to stand upright, sending prickles of unease rippling across his skin. He laid motionless on the ground, feigning sleep as he listened intently and strained his eyes to pick out any shapes in the gloom. Then he heard it, the soft rustling sound of someone drawing ever closer.

Rojas waited until he knew that they must have been within touching distance before he lunged at them and tackled them to the ground. The person yelped in surprise, causing nearby Vulpini to stir from their sleep, but as Rojas' eyes accustomed to the dark in order to see the person that lay pinned below him, the would-be assailant broke into laughter.

"I was expecting a somewhat different greeting, Rojas," they chuckled.

"Ayse? Is that you?" he gasped, hurriedly scrambling off the poor girl as quick as he could and helping her to her feet before explaining, "I didn't know who you were with all that creeping about."

"It took me some time to find the Vulpini part of the camp," Ayse responded, "And I didn't want to attract any unwanted attention, so I had to move carefully."

"It's good to see you again," he said embracing her fondly.

It was hard to see Ayse clearly in the darkness, but Rojas could see her well enough for stirrings of familiarity to creep into his mind. His heart was telling him that he knew the person before him, even if his eyes weren't yet sure due to the darkness. The last time he had seen her, she had been a young, skinny girl that was more boyish than most of the other girls her age. She had grown into her features, her large eyes and full lips were once a cute characteristic of the child he had known, but now they added to her beauty as a woman.

Something about the way she looked struck him as odd, but he couldn't quite place what it was about seeing her that was rekindling something in his memory. Shadows were known to play tricks on your sight in the limited light, so he dismissed the notion as a trick of the night.

He dropped his gaze as he spoke more seriously, "I had hoped to get a chance to thank you personally for what you did for us. It will not be forgotten."

He spoke with such gravity and emphasis that it was impossible for Ayse not to feel the full weight of his sincere gratitude. Smiling at him awkwardly, she could feel the heat on her cheeks as she flushed red. She wasn't sure how to respond to such a statement and so just settled with, "Any time."

"I thought you were in the north?" he whispered.

"I was," she stated as she sat beside the smoking remains of the fire, the dim embers did not afford a better view of the girl Rojas had not seen in years.

Rojas moved closer to her for them to speak quietly with one another, in hushed tones he asked her, "What happened? Did you tell them about the attack?"

"I tried," she explained regretfully. "But I don't know whether they believed me. As you can imagine, part of what I had to tell them didn't exactly make me sound trustworthy."

"You did the best you could, that was all we could hope for," Rojas comforted her.

"I know. I just wish I knew what Oror was planning to do now."

"Do you know where they are? Did you encounter their forces when you crossed the border?"

"I made a point of travelling along routes where I knew there wouldn't be people. The Orians have scouts that prowl their territory and I didn't like the idea of accidentally being found by one. When I left their camp, they had only just summoned their lords together to discuss what I had told them. I imagine they wouldn't have mobilised the full strength of their force until they reached a decision."

"You're probably right," sighed Rojas.

"Is Tobias here?" Ayse asked.

"He's somewhere around here, still sulking no doubt. It really didn't sit well with him that you were returning to the north."

"I know," Ayse replied with a slight tone of exasperation.

"It's just because he cares about you so much-"

"I know," she interrupted, not wanting to discuss Tobias's feelings for her.

"It really is good to see you," he said earnestly as he smiled at her affectionately.

"So, you said," she smiled back at him. "Tell me, is there any news from Raph?"

"Oh yes. Your rather colourful friend," Rojas chortled, "He's quite the character, not to mention he manages to rile Tobias up something fierce. He's in Bremlor. He managed to trick that dimwit Frewin into promoting him to the rank of officer, so he's stayed to run Frewin's estate in his stead."

"Leaving him in charge of Lorie and Ana?"

"Exactly. He also managed to discover the location of Owaiin, Mason, and Aiden. We have a plan in place to get them out, but it won't be without its troubles and Raphael can't free them all by himself. Once the battle begins, I must return to Bremlor to help him. We have to ensure they are released at the same time and get them out of Bremlor as quickly as possible, before anyone notices that they are missing."

"Wouldn't it have been easier just to leave someone back in Bremlor with Raph?"

"Of course, it would have been, silly girl," Rojas chided her. "But we didn't have that luxury. The duke knew our numbers, it would have been impossible for one of us to remain behind unnoticed. I don't like the idea of leaving our people here to fight without my guidance, but this needs to be done. The chance of the duke finally honouring his promise isn't exactly high."

"I agree. If he backed out before then it's likely that he will back out again.

It's hard for people like that to relinquish control over others."

"I just hope we can pull this all off, Ayse. It will be heart-breaking if we manage to free those trapped in Bremlor only to discover that many Vulpini fell on this damned battlefield." Rojas paused, before quickly trying to change the subject. "Now tell me about these werewolves I've heard so much about."

"Oh, they are really something else. Monstrously large, unnaturally strong… they could strike fear into the heart of any man."

"Actually, this probably isn't the best topic of conversation given our forthcoming battle," Rojas admitted with a frown.

"I don't believe they fight in wolf form," Ayse reassured him, "Not on the battlefield at least. Patrols are another matter."

"You've seen them patrolling in wolf form? Nell told me that you saw them hunting from a distance."

"I did. But during my latest visit to Oror, I came across a lone werewolf fighting Nevraahn soldiers who had been lucky enough to make it further into the northern territory."

"But unlucky enough to have discovered a werewolf," Rojas added.

"Visiting the north and seeing the werewolves, it makes me wonder about my own heritage. Everything I thought I knew about myself was false."

"I'm not surprised," Rojas replied. "It was a shock for all of us to hear that what we had presumed about you all this time wasn't true."

"Do you know why Chief Wilamir thought I was a werewolf? Why didn't he just presume that I was a wolf shifter?"

"To be honest, Ayse, I don't think anyone had ever heard of wolf shifters before you discovered that you weren't a werewolf. We had heard tales of werewolves in the north, so that just seemed the more likely option. Not to mention that it was here in the flatbeds that Chief Wilamir found you."

"It was?" she asked with surprise.

"I can't say for sure where, whether you were closer to the northern border or not, but he returned from these plains with you cradled in his arms. That much I do remember."

"I spoke to a werewolf in the north, he spoke about the wolf shifters to me and he referred to them as the Canini tribe. Have you ever heard that name?"

"I can't say I have. Did he tell you where to find them?"

"No. He told me that they were long gone, all of them have been dead for many years apparently," she added sadly.

"I see," Rojas said softly. "When we return to the tribe, I will ask the chief about your past. Perhaps Chief Wilamir told him something that he didn't share with the rest of us, or maybe he has heard of the Canini tribe."

"Thank you," Ayse responded politely, though it was clear from her pessimistic tone that she didn't hold out much hope that Solomon would have any answers for her either.

"We'll keep digging Ayse. Someone out there has to know something about wolf shifters."

"Even if there are any survivors other than me, they're probably just as secretive about their existence as the Vulpini. They won't be easy to find."

"Out of all the things you've done recently, how many of them were easy?" Rojas grinned. "I think you've proven that just because something seems impossible, it doesn't mean it actually is."

He winked at her and placed a reassuring hand on her shoulder before pulling her in for a hug, refusing to let go until she had smiled.

"I should make myself scarce," she said reluctantly. "I don't want the duke's men to see me here and make it harder for me to leave when the time comes."

"Is there somewhere safe that you can rest nearby?"

"My horse isn't too far from here. I can get back to it before morning arrives."

Rojas nodded and then watched Ayse disappear into the thick of the night. He still couldn't shake the nagging feeling that had attached itself to him on meeting the young wolf after so many years. Something was bothering him, but he couldn't quite place his finger on it. With a weary sigh, he pushed any thoughts of it from his mind. After all, if he didn't rest now, then he would be feeling it tomorrow for certain.

Chapter Twenty-Six

The once crowded prison cell had become quite sparse, as many of the prisoners had been released on the condition that they agree to join the duke's ranks of men to fight on the northern front. If they survived the warfare, they would be granted their freedom on their return to the city. The duke had been rather vague about what fate would befall those who managed to survive if Nevraah was not victorious. Naturally, the Vulpini men had not received such an offer, as they were to remain in Bremlor to ensure that their fellow tribal members on the front line continued to be obedient.

It had been an agonizing time for Owaiin when the Vulpini had been in Bremlor; knowing that his people were so close to them, yet so completely out of reach. Instead, he had reluctantly had to content himself with whatever news Hudson could bring him, describing how the Vulpini training was going and whether he thought that they were progressing well.

Of course, Owaiin knew that the tribe would not be proficient in battle, but it had reassured him somewhat to hear that most of them had learned to wield a blade with some level of competence. With there being fewer prisoners to watch over, the small number of guards that hadn't been recruited for the war roamed the cells with less frequency, leaving the prisoners in peace for most of the day.

The sound of footsteps startled Owaiin. He had memorised the rotation of the guards and knew that there shouldn't be any wardens checking in on them for some time yet. He waited with trepidation, wondering what cause there would be for someone to come to the prison on such a random visit. Two men walked into view, one he recognised as Hudson, the other was a stranger to him, but was clearly identifiable as an officer by his uniform.

Hudson didn't look pleased to be in the company of the man. The officer carried himself with some degree of self-importance and his head was held high, meaning that when he looked at the prisoners, he was automatically looking down his nose at them.

Still peering in at the prisoners with great interest, the officer asked, "Which ones are they?"

"Those three near the back, sir," Hudson replied, indicating towards the Vulpini men.

"I see. Bring them forward."

Hudson beckoned towards Owaiin, who in turn nudged Aiden and they both moved towards the bars to stand before the officer.

"What of the third man?" the officer asked.

"Sickness ails that one, sir," Hudson explained sheepishly, "He doesn't have the strength to stand."

Owaiin clenched his jaw as the men in front of him discussed Mason's current condition. His friend's health had deteriorated considerably. Even in the warmer summer weather, Mason had continued to suffer from an incurable cough. To make things even worse, a fever had set in, and so getting him to eat or drink anything had become quite difficult, further weakening the poor man.

"Sick, you say? Well why hasn't anything been done about it?" the officer asked.

"Sir?" Hudson replied with confusion, causing the officer to turn on him with a fierce glare.

"Did you send for the medic?" he demanded.

"Uh... no. I was never told to—I mean, the duke never showed any interest in ensuring they were looked after, sir."

"What do you think the duke will think when he returns victorious from the war, and one of the people he is supposed to be returning to the Vulpini is nothing more than a corpse? Do you think he will be happy? Do you not think you should see to it that they remain alive so that you do not make your duke look incompetent?" the officer admonished him.

"Yes, sir," Hudson gabbled quickly, "I will send for a medic straight away!"

"Well get to it!" the officer yelled when he saw that Hudson was still standing beside him, sending the guard tripping over himself in his effort to obey.

Once Hudson had disappeared in a flurry of heavy feet slapping on the stone flooring, the officer turned to Owaiin and Aiden who still stood impassively at the bars and winked at them. His whole demeanour changed as he smiled.

He whispered conspiratorially, "Now gentlemen, I must leave you to your own devices for some time. But please know that it won't be long before I come to fetch you." The officer spoke carefully, emphasising the last few words in a way that made Owaiin truly believe him.

The officer glanced about at the other prisoners in the cell, content that they had paid the conversation no real attention. He looked back to Owaiin and nodded at him before departing.

"What was that?" Aiden blurted out.

"I don't rightly know," Owaiin responded, "But I'm not going to complain if it means Mason gets some help."

Still bewildered by what had just taken place, the two Vulpini men returned to their friend's side near the back of the prison cell. Mason had paled considerably. He was barely conscious most of the time and just remained on the floor shivering and coughing. His arms were up in front of his chest to warm himself from a chill that only he could feel, while his knuckles were white from the force of the grip he had on his own clothing. Sweat beaded across his forehead, his hair was stuck to his face from his own perspiration, and his lips trembled as he slept.

"We need something for his fever," Owaiin commented. "I hope Hudson doesn't take too long in fetching the doctor."

"After that dressing down, I highly doubt it," Aiden responded. "Who do you think that man was? It's not usual for an officer to come down to these stinking pits."

"I'm not sure. It makes me wonder why they would suddenly take an interest in us now," Owaiin said with apprehension.

"Perhaps they've had news from the front line, maybe they're even *winning*. It makes sense that they would ensure that they can return us to the tribe in one piece."

"Something isn't right about it. The duke didn't even bother to check on us when he received the information on the north, why would he now?"

"Maybe it's because this time he really is going to release us?"

"I wouldn't count on it," Owaiin said shaking his head. "People don't change so easily. Something else is going on here, I just don't know what."

"That officer said he would return for us soon," Aiden said hopefully.

"Aiden, if we've learnt anything, it's that we shouldn't trust anyone in this damn hell hole."

The younger man reluctantly nodded in agreement. While Owaiin didn't want to dishearten his friend, he also didn't want to raise his hopes just for them to be dashed. As they both sat beside their friend in silent solidarity, all they could do was be grateful that Mason would soon be attended to by a doctor. Owaiin just hoped that it wasn't too little, too late.

***

Raphael walked back to Frewin's estate with a sense of unease. He hadn't known that one of the Vulpini men was afflicted with sickness, and if the man in question wasn't able to walk, then it could cause problems for their escape plan. Raphael berated himself for not thinking to check on the men sooner, he had been so preoccupied with not showing them any preferential treatment that he had completely neglected to ensure that they were alright. He had seen some of the prisons that Nevraah had to offer before, and he should have known better that the men would not be in the best of health.

Even with Rojas returning, Raphael was beginning to doubt whether the two of them would be enough to successfully pull off the escape plan considering that they would have to carry one of the men to safety. He doubted that any form of medication that the doctor gave the man would have such profound results in such a short time. It was almost a certainty that it wouldn't enable him to walk unaided when the time came, but at least the Vulpini would finally get some much-needed medical treatment.

He had seen to it that one of the stable masters in Lower Bremlor was keeping seven horses in reserve exclusively for Raphael's use, having told the man that it was in preparation for hunting expeditions. In order to ensure that his story was believable, he'd selected a few other soldiers on more than one occasion, taking them out into the land around Bremlor on the hunt for wild boar. They'd only been successful in catching their prey once, but the prize of the beast wasn't what Raphael was after.

He just needed the stable master to believe that at any moment he might return for another impromptu hunting expedition, thus ensuring that the horses were kept aside for his use only. Additionally, he had rented a room in the lower district that he had stocked with bags and provisions for their journey, as well as the spare Bremlor uniform that Rojas would need in order to gain access to the prisons without question.

As he entered Frewin's office, he noticed that there was a stack of paperwork atop the writing desk that had materialised in his absence. With a groan, he sat down to tackle the details of running a lord's estate. Most of Bremlor's assets had been claimed for the war efforts, meaning that supplies were running low on all fronts. As a result, Raphael was inundated with requests to help with the food shortages, as well as many other trivial matters that he couldn't even begin to think about.

Already he could feel a headache gnawing at the edges of his mind as he began to digest all that was required of him. Important affairs and working through paperwork were not one of Raphael's strengths. Knowing that it would be a long day, he rang the bell to call for a maid to bring him some refreshments.

Chapter Twenty-Seven

There was something empowering about slipping through a sleeping camp unnoticed, knowing full well that the occupants of the tents were completely unaware of her presence as they lay enraptured in their dreams. Ayse was carefully picking her way through the encampment and heading to where she knew Rojas should be with the rest of the Vulpini. Without any warning, a horn sounded loudly on the clear air, rousing all the soldiers around her from their sleep immediately.

Panicking, Ayse kept her head hunkered down and walked with a sense of purpose towards the tribe in the hopes that no one would think anything of her being there. All around her people were scrambling to arms, still rubbing the sleep from their eyes as they tried to react to the call of the war horn. Distracted by all the commotion, Ayse was taken by surprise when she felt a hand grip her upper arm and pull her to the side.

"Ayse!" Tobias exclaimed. "What are you doing here?"

"I came to see Rojas before I left. What is happening here?"

"Did you not hear the horn, Ayse? It means the northerners are on the march," Tobias said in alarm.

"They're coming here?"

"The scouts must have seen them approaching for the signal to be given. Everyone is being called to arms."

"I don't understand, I told them! I told them this was a ruse!"

"I guess they didn't listen," Tobias said gravely. "They weren't supposed to know we were here until we moved closer... They only know we're here because of you."

A pang of guilt stabbed at Ayse's chest. "You don't understand, I was trying to help. You can't beat them, Tobias. They will slaughter everyone," Ayse whispered fearfully. "If they could only see what was really happening. If only they could see the duke's forces west of here."

"It's too late for that, Ayse." Tobias hissed as he pulled her away. "You have to get out of here."

Ayse could feel her heart picking up pace and building into a frenzy as all around her there were shouts and movement. She stared around blankly, not able to process what she should be doing.

"Ayse," Tobias called her name, grabbing her other arm and shaking her to get her to pay attention. "You have to get out of here, *now*."

"No, Tobias," she whispered sadly as she shook herself free of his grip, "I have to do something."

"Ayse? Ayse! Where are you going?" Tobias called after her as she vanished into the crowds of moving people.

"I have to try and convince them they're marching the wrong way!" Ayse shouted over her shoulder as she ran into the crowd.

She disappeared amongst the soldiers who were rushing to bear arms in the darkness. Tobias felt his stomach tighten. This girl was going to cause his hair to grey at this rate.

***

Birds were singing sweetly in order to woo the morning as it arrived, not knowing that the land they inhabited would soon succumb to violence and bloodshed. After returning to her horse, Ayse had made her way back to the northern border in search of Oror's forces. She wasn't sure what she would do when she found them, but something inside of her was spurring her into desperate action.

As the flatbeds had been free from any northern presence, Ayse was led to believe that the scout who had alerted the camp must have travelled from within the Orian territory itself. Although she knew that she had asked a lot of Lord Ulric when she had told him to trust her and the information that she had brought him, she hadn't imagined that he would really dismiss the attack plans so easily. It left Ayse feeling angry at the foolishness of the northerners. Their stubborn pride had led them to the wrong decision. She galloped through the trees, ducking to avoid the low hanging foliage as she raced onwards in search of the Orian soldiers.

Without warning, her horse screamed and pitched Ayse off its back as it reared upwards, before falling to the ground with a sickening thud. Ayse winced as she pulled herself up. The horse lay there whining and snorting hot air from its nostrils. Its hooves were weakly kicking at nothing, churning the loam beneath its feet as Ayse scrambled forwards to see what had happened. An arrow shaft was protruding from the horse's neck, buried deep in its soft flesh and causing warm blood to spill out in thick dribbles down its velveteen skin.

Ayse didn't have time to think of the horse, as she realised that in her haste she had been spotted by the northerners before she had even noticed that she had stumbled too close to them. She ducked into the undergrowth and out of sight as she heard shouts and movement up head. A couple of Orian soldiers came into view. They looked to be scouts, most likely travelling in advance of the main body of their army.

Ayse hid further into the tangle of bushes and moved farther away from the horse as she heard it breathe its last few ragged gasps. Its wide eye stared at her with accusation as its body heaved one final time, before falling perfectly still. The men kept their distance, watching and waiting. Seeing them scanning the area about her, Ayse moved behind a tree and tried to calm her rapid breathing. The sound of hooves crashing onto mud reached her, more soldiers had arrived.

"Come out!" a northern voice bellowed at her.

Ayse bit her lip, but she did not move or dare to respond.

"If we'd wanted to kill you, we would have shot you and not your horse," the voice called again.

"That depends on how bad your aim is," Ayse called back tauntingly.

She heard the muted sound of snickering as some of the soldiers found her response amusing.

"You're just a girl," the voice called out to her, a hint of surprise and condescension evident in his tone, "Come out so we can see you."

Ayse was disgruntled at being called 'just a girl', but she knew that she couldn't hide behind the tree and simply hope that they'd grow tired and leave.

"Are you going to stay there all day?" the voice mocked her, as if capable of reading her thoughts.

"Are you going to keep marching your army the wrong way?" she mocked back at him.

"A southerner telling us we're going the wrong way? That must mean we're heading in the right direction," the voice said loudly, more to his men than to Ayse.

"I'd love to see your face when you realise how mistaken you are, but I get the feeling I won't be around long enough to see that happen."

"Come out where we can see you and we might let you live."

Doubting that they really would show her any mercy, Ayse was aware that they could easily cut her down should she try to make a run for it. Resigning herself to her fate of having to face them, she pushed her way out of the mass of vegetation and stood in view of the soldiers. From the looks on their faces, they were dismissive of her immediately. They clearly didn't see her as any kind of threat. There weren't too many of them, she counted maybe ten at the most as her eyes moved from one man to the next, possibly more if there were others on foot hidden in the trees, eight of them were on horseback.

"So, there you are," The same voice spoke, drawing her attention to its speaker.

As she looked to him, her breath caught in her throat as she was surprised to see that it was Caleb who hailed her. He looked much the same as when she had last seen him, only now he was sat astride his horse in the full splendour of his war armour. His sword hung from his hip, his breastplate was embellished with wolves and knot work patterns, while his fur-trimmed cloak was regally swept over one shoulder.

"You mean to try and tell me that we're heading in the wrong direction, when my men have already reported that Nevraah's forces are currently gathered on the plains?" he smirked.

Ayse was still in too much of a daze to answer him, instead, she was wondering how she had forgotten his voice so easily. Then again, it was not often he had used such a harsh tone with her, although she had witnessed his moods often enough towards others.

"Well?" he asked impatiently.

"That's not Nevraah's true force, they're just bandits, mercenaries, and ex-cons who have been scrabbled together to resemble an army," she finally replied.

"I don't care who they are, if they stand in opposition to Oror then they are our enemy."

"You should care. While you're killing those people, your own people will be getting slaughtered as Duke Howell and his companions take your fortress to the west of here by surprise. You're falling into the duke's trap."

"Give me one good reason why I should listen to you?"

Caleb's distrust and disapproval were clear on his face. Ayse couldn't think of anything that she could say that would make him suddenly believe her. She knew that the only way he would turn his army around would be for him to see the real Nevraahn army for himself. While there was nothing that she could say to sway him, Ayse suddenly thought of something she could do to entice him into action. She started stepping backwards into the bushes as she replied, "Alright."

As she disappeared from his view, Caleb called out to her, "I'm not really in the mood for games, girl."

But Ayse wasn't planning on playing any games. She just needed to get his undivided attention, and there was one sure-fire way she knew how to do just that. Ayse re-emerged from hiding and stood perfectly still as the northerners stared at her in wolf form. At first the men looked confused, then their mouths fell agape as they realised what had happened.

Caleb's face was another matter. Even from where she stood, Ayse could see the anger in his eyes and his jaw was clenched. While she had seen Caleb lose his temper before, she had only witnessed such ferocity from him only once, and it was at that point she could identify the likeness between him and his brother Ulric.

As Caleb reached for his weapon, Ayse took that as her cue to leave and began speedily loping off through the undergrowth heading west. She could hear the shouts of the men behind her, but she paid them no attention as she concentrated on staying ahead of Caleb's horse. Horses were quicker than Ayse in her wolf form, but with a little effort she was better able to navigate the meandering forest trails than Caleb's bulky war steed.

Whenever she felt that they were falling too far behind, she would stop and wait for them to catch sight of her once more before disappearing into the trees. Only those who had been on horseback had followed her, she assumed the other soldiers on foot had returned to their main unit, which was most likely still following its intended path towards the flatbeds. Ayse knew Caleb was no fool, he would have realised that she was leading him away from where he wanted to be, but she also knew how prideful he was and that he wasn't about to allow someone who had deceived him to get away so easily.

Chapter Twenty-Eight

The march towards the edge of the flatbeds was a solemn one with fighters wordlessly marching in unison. There were no rally cries, no cheers or orders, just the rhythmic sound of feet upon earth and the clinking of metal. They halted when the treeline of the northern territory was in sight, staying just out of range of arrows from any would-be assailants that could have been hiding under the cover of the forest. There was no sign of Oror's army, but they all knew that they couldn't be far away. Somewhere deep in the darkness of the wood, men were advancing upon their position to spill blood.

The day was fearfully still. Nevraahn standards hung stationary from banners, as not a breeze stirred amongst the men and women as they waited for the forthcoming clash of metal. With no relief from the heat, sweat beaded across the faces of the southern army as they all faced northwards. All eyes were on the horizon, waiting with bated breath for the first sign of the enemy.

Tobias looked to either side of him as he stood in formation with the rest of the Vulpini. He surveyed the familiar faces of his tribe as they prepared for the inevitable with a faint heart. Weapons and armour glinted in the bright sunlight, creating a sea of dazzling lights as he looked out across the crowds. Beyond the Vulpini units, there were lines of all manner of men and mercenaries that the duke had managed to procure for his war, most of which were more eagerly awaiting the battle than the Vulpini. Tobias could see the excitement on the faces of those closest to him, and it seemed the more grizzled and war-scarred the men were, the more blood-thirsty they looked. He could see the twitch of their hands as they restlessly played atop their sword hilts.

"Tobias," a voice called from behind.

The Vulpini man turned to watch as the ranks parted to allow Reuben through. He nodded as his friend approached, before turning back to resume his vigil.

"Tobias, have you seen Rojas? We lost track of him before the horn sounded."

"He's not here," Tobias responded quietly, "He had something important to do."

"Something more important than this?" Reuben asked, gripping Tobias's arm and pulling him back to face him as he spoke.

Tobias shook Reuben's grip away. "He wouldn't have left otherwise. You must know that already, Ben."

"I don't understand. Our people need him now. He's one of our most skilled fighters, we need him here."

"And five other Vulpini need him in Bremlor," Tobias responded with laced words.

"Do you mean to say-"

"Yes, Ben. If all else fails, at least they will be able to return home."

"I don't like your optimism," Reuben said sourly.

"I don't like our chances," Tobias grunted.

"Rojas found a way to get them out safely?" Reuben asked, adding with a graver tone, "We don't want a repeat performance of last time."

"He's got someone there to help him and with most of Bremlor out here, they're not going to get a better chance than this."

"I hope they succeed, we're long overdue some good news."

"I fear that even if we get some good news, we won't be in the mood for celebrating. After all, we'll be burying some of our fellow tribesmen before this is through, or being buried ourselves. I'm not sure which is worse."

"I've instructed the tribe to stick together as much as possible as hopefully they will have some safety in numbers. With any luck, the real warriors here will take the brunt of Oror's forces. Though going by the looks of them, I wouldn't trust them with my life. Some of these men look like they're gagging for a fight so much so that they'd be willing to kill any man, regardless of whether he's fighting by their side or not. If we're lucky, we can get through this."

"With our recent run of bad fortune, I don't think we should be counting on luck in this war."

"It's better than giving up before we've even started," Reuben said pointedly.

Tobias sighed, "I know. I know."

"Our people are looking to you, Tobias. Stand strong for them. They must have some form of hope to see them through this."

Tobias nodded, but his heart was still consumed with misgivings. The odds were just too greatly stacked against the Vulpini and their lack of experience on the battlefield. Death would be stalking amongst the men as the battle broke out, silently traversing the mortal realm, invisible to their human eyes. It was unfortunate that the reaper favoured no one in this world. It would take the lives of men from either side of the battle without bias, not caring which side of the map they were born on.

Reuben held out his hand to his friend. "Take heart, Tobias. We will take each day as it comes."

Tobias took his friend's hand and Reuben pulled him into a brief embrace before retreating through the lines of waiting fighters to re-join Nell. Tobias turned his attention back to the Orian border. Nothing stirred on the tree line as far as he could see, but that didn't mean that there was nothing out there waiting for them. He doubted that the men of Oror would shy away from a real battle. After all, they didn't seem the type to linger in the shadows.

Yet somewhere out there he hoped there was someone staying out of sight. Ayse had made the foolish choice to return to the north once again and he had to wonder how many times she could tempt fate before it ended badly for her. He didn't know how she hoped to change the flow of war, but Tobias prayed that she was being careful in how she went about it.

Somewhere in the distance a horn sounded, sending a shudder of anticipation amongst the southern forces. Some of the more inexperienced people looked about with confused expressions, before realising that the sound had not come from within their ranks, but from the thick line of trees that dominated the horizon before them. The northerners were finally coming.

✳✳✳

Rojas was driving his horse hard and fast. While he felt some sympathy for the beast, his mind was on far more important matters, such as reaching

Bremlor as soon as possible. At the rate in which he was travelling, he knew he'd be aching for days afterwards, however, a bit of saddle sore was a small price to pay in the grand scheme of things. When the horn had sounded that fateful night, Rojas had felt the disappointment wash over him at the realisation that the soldiers of Oror were still heading straight for them. He had hoped with all his heart that Ayse had been successful in convincing them that the true threat lay in the west.

It was this same hope that kept him from blaming her for her actions that had followed in the ensuring chaos. Tobias had found him and told him Ayse had decided to return to Oror in one last desperate attempt to convince the northerners to travel west. His heart felt heavy as he considered that now, more than ever, Ayse would be in grave danger. If Oror had so easily dismissed her claims, they must have decided that she was untrustworthy, and so they would not look kindly on her returning to their land.

In the frantic disorder following the call to arms, it had been easy enough for Rojas to slip away unnoticed by any of the duke's men. They were far too busy kicking the more undisciplined soldiers into action to notice that he had left in the wrong direction. Grabbing what little supplies he could, he had mounted up and rode out before the men had even woken properly. The sun was beating down on his back as he rode towards Bremlor, racing as if the god of death was snapping at his very heels.

Chapter Twenty-Nine

Her chest was burning as her breath left her body in hot ragged gasps, the pain was unbearable, but Ayse forced herself onwards knowing that it couldn't be much farther to go. Her pace had fallen as her body was nearing the point of exhaustion. As a result, the horses slowly gained ground on her, though she knew that they must also be feeling weary from the chase.

Ayse no longer had to stop to allow her pursuers to catch up to her and many stolen moments to catch her breath had resulted in being close calls with capture and arrows whipping past her head. Caleb had not relented in the hunt, not that Ayse wanted him to, but it was a bitter thought that he wanted her dead so badly that he would abandon the battlefield to do it. She silently wished that she lived long enough to prove him wrong and that there might still be time to help the Vulpini.

She slowed down as the ground she was covering began to incline, her paws felt heavy and cumbersome as she pushed onwards. Ayse was panting heavily, saliva falling from her jaws in thick, white strings. She stopped momentarily to cast a glance backwards. She couldn't see the riders, but she knew they couldn't be far behind. With great effort, she spurred herself into a slow jog once more, knowing that if she stopped for too long it would be even more difficult to find the energy to continue. Pushing her body to the extreme had made her realise how far from being fully recovered she truly was, as her injured leg was paining her far more than her other limbs.

Her ears pricked up at the sound of a distant shout. Alarmed that it had come from in front of her, Ayse began to panic that Caleb had outwitted her by moving ahead of her somehow and had trapped her between him and his men. Ayse's heart began to pound loudly in her chest. Unsure what to do, she began to veer off in another direction to avoid being caught in their pincer movement.

The land began to even out once more, enabling her to progress more easily. She loped through the undergrowth and remained close to the protection of the trees and bushes as she pressed onwards. Before long she heard more noises, the whinny of a horse, men shouting orders, and the overwhelming even beat of feet marching on earth. Once she realised that the source of the noise wasn't Caleb or his men, she barrelled onwards with a renewed spring in her step, suddenly hoping that her pursuer was not too far behind.

She skidded to a halt as she came to the edge of a small rise. Below her, she could see the columns of Nevraahn soldiers snaking their way through the trees as they marched towards Fort Lyndon. Seeing the perfectly armoured soldiers with their impressive weaponry further emphasised how much of a mockery those camped out on the flatbeds were. This was no riffraff of different groups and coerced tribesman, nor did they have an array of mismatched weaponry. Every soldier had a uniformed sword and shield and complimenting armour. There were spear carriers, officers on horseback, all of whom looked quite imposing.

Ayse crouched low to the ground to ensure she was not seen by the Nevraahn army but ended up just collapsing completely as she lowered herself. Her limbs cried out for respite as she lay there breathing heavily. Ayse struggled to calm herself, her body heaving from her exertions, while her eyes watched the soldiers moving below her.

The sound of branches being moved alerted her to the presence of her Orian pursuers. Looking a little worse for wear, they emerged from the treeline not too far from where she was. They looked tired and dishevelled, sweat was plastering the hair to their faces. It gave Ayse some satisfaction to know that she hadn't suffered alone in the hunt. Their expressions were grim and foreboding as they looked at their enemy, but they weren't looking at Ayse.

Being sure to stay in the shadowed cover of the trees, Caleb and his men watched the procession of the southerners with great disgust. Ayse was thankful that they had the sense to dismount and approach carefully on foot when the noise of the Nevraahn army on the move had reached them. It would have been a sad end to her plan had they charged out and found themselves quickly outnumbered.

With no small effort, Ayse hauled herself to her feet and slowly moved towards the northerners. She assumed a low body position, her ears flat against the back of her head and tail tucked between her legs as a sign of submission. She stopped when she was just out of reach of the men, not wanting to tempt an ill-tempered northerner into swinging his sword at her. Her approach garnered a few glances from the men, but they quickly resumed their watch of the soldiers below.

"Looks like the bitch was right," one of the soldiers spat with a depressing tone.

"Yes," Caleb admitted bitterly, throwing Ayse a contemptuous look. "Mendell, take another, take the two best horses we have and re-join Lord Ulric on the plains. Tell him to bring his men westward as fast as the gods will allow. Go now."

The men didn't need to be told twice. Two of them disappeared quickly leaving the rest to continue watching the Nevraahn soldiers with growing discomfort.

"What is our position at Fort Lyndon?" Caleb asked.

"Not good, my lord," one of the men answered him, "They're running on the bare minimum. Lord Ulric would have surely taken most of his men with him when he marched for the plains."

"We need to get there and warn them, if it's not already too late," Caleb said through gritted teeth.

He turned on his heel and retreated the way they had come with his men following close behind him. Ayse's ears stood upright as she watched them leave. With one last glance back at the grand lines of Nevraahn soldiers, she loped after Caleb and his soldiers.

Their horses were not too far away, each one saturated in sweat and breathing heavily from its recent efforts. The horses eyed her warily. Ayse found the men mounting up as she approached. Once again, she assumed a submissive pose as she moved forwards. Caleb shot her a disapproving look and she expected him to yell at her to leave, but instead he ignored her and motioned for his men to move out. She followed close behind.

***

By the time they had travelled the short distance to Fort Lyndon, they could see they were already too late. Tell-tale grapple hook lines were cascading from many of the battlements, a sign of how the southerners had gained access. The clash of battle emanated from within the fortress, but most of the Nevraahn soldiers that were continuing to arrive stood amassed outside of the fort, its gates still firmly shut and preventing them from entering. Men were still scaling the walls as there was no other way to gain access, but by the occasional sickening sound of men falling to their deaths, there were still defenders very much alive atop the walls.

"The fort has fallen," one of Caleb's men gasped.

"Not yet it hasn't," Caleb reassured him, "If the gates are closed then it means there are still men fighting inside to keep them just so."

"What should we do? Surely we must help them?" another soldier asked nervously. "We can't just walk through those southerners and knock on the front door."

"Maybe we could ask to borrow their grapple hooks," another soldier added with a snort.

"We don't need either," Caleb said with a smile, "Fort Lyndon has a well-kept secret. Follow me."

The men did as they were bid, with Ayse falling in line beside them. As she loped alongside Caleb like old times, she was suddenly bombarded with many memories of her time in the northern camp. She shook her head to regain her clarity. This was not the time to be nostalgic. Caleb led the men further north to a small shrine that looked as though it had survived since the dawn of time. It must have been hewn from granite, but it was hard to tell as a thick blanket of moss covered it in such thick swathes that it was possible to mistake the sanctuary for a small hill. If they hadn't approached the landmark front and centre due to Caleb's knowledge of the land, Ayse was sure that it would have been almost impossible to recognise it as a building. On the few segments of bare rock face, Ayse could see carvings of runes that she did not recognise.

"A place of the old gods?" a soldier asked as he gingerly touched the runes with his hand. "What are we doing here, my lord?"

"You'll see," Caleb said as he dismounted, prompting his men to follow suit.

As they followed the northern lord down the slippery steps into the entrance of the shrine, Ayse could smell the soggy sweat of the land as it embraced her. The air was thick with damp, its palpable atmosphere was almost suffocating and the soil inside was alive with all manner of bugs and insects that craved the wetness. Ayse could sense them squirming in the darkness, as if the earth itself was alive despite being such a dark and dismal place.

Caleb took a torch from a rusted bracket and lit it, though it took some attempts to tease the flame to life in such air. When the deed was done, the light cascaded brightly into the stone chamber. That was when Ayse realised that it was not a shrine at all, but a tomb. All along the walls there stood solid rock benches that housed the dead. Bones were piled atop of one another, skulls facing outwards in some grim form of greeting to any who entered, their discoloured teeth grinning at the visitors in a twisted welcome.

The tomb was deceptively large, the space more cavernous than Ayse had imagined based upon its exterior. There were seven sarcophagi evenly spaced on the floor in three lines, creating an 'H' shape. Each stone coffin was plain, their only decoration being half-worn runic patterns.

As they moved towards the centremost sarcophagus, Caleb's torch light reached the furthest limits of the crypt, unveiling a stone altar centred in the back of the room. Ayse wondered what kind of tomb required an altar hidden inside of it, but the thought was soon swept from her mind as Caleb passed the torch to one of his men and began to push at the heavy stone seal of the coffin. With bemused looks, the other men all pitched in to help him shift the colossal slab of granite, sliding it at an angle so that it turned on itself and ended up horizontal at the top of the grave. Caleb reclaimed the torch from the soldier and shone it into the dark pit, obligingly all his men peered into the deathbed.

"By the gods!" one exclaimed.

"We must move quickly," Caleb commanded as he hauled himself into the coffin and promptly disappeared, causing Ayse's ears to perk upright with alarm.

All of Caleb's men followed him into the void without question and Ayse ran forward to see where they had disappeared too. Standing on her hind paws, Ayse leaned her forepaws on the stone coffin and investigated it. There was a short drop that was followed by a stone staircase descending into darkened depths. The passageway showed the faint light of Caleb's torch slowly receding as the men disappeared into the mysterious pathway. Dropping back onto all four paws, Ayse took a few steps backwards and then took a running jump into the grave. She landed rather awkwardly at the bottom, causing jolts of pain to shoot through her legs. Undeterred, she ran after the northerners before the light of the torch vanished from her sight entirely.

As Ayse re-joined the group, Caleb cast an appraising glance her way before continuing to lead his men through the meandering passageways. There were a multitude of tunnels and different passages, but Caleb walked with unwavering purpose. Ayse suspected that the many runes that decorated the walls could lead any man to the correct destination, if they knew enough about which rune to follow. The air inside the subterranean labyrinth was even poorer than that of the crypt above. The light of the torch dimmed as it was choked by the oppressive air, causing a few of the men to glance about themselves nervously.

As if sensing their unease, Caleb spoke to them to distract them from their discomfort, "These passages will lead us directly inside Fort Lyndon. Ready yourselves for battle men."

Caleb led them up another stone staircase that ended abruptly; wooden planking had covered the ascent, blocking the way forward. Unsheathing his sword, Caleb passed the torch off to one of his men and then used the round pommel of his sword hilt to begin striking against the planks with great force. Aged as it was, it didn't take long for the wood to splinter and crack, and once there was a gap, Caleb replaced his sword in its scabbard and began ripping away the lumber with his bare hands. The soldiers and Ayse ducked out of the way of falling timber as Caleb made a large enough gap for them to continue their journey.

When they passed through the broken wooden panelling, they found themselves in what looked to be an old wine cellar. Large kegs lined the walls and the smell of wine and ale seemed to permeate every inch of the place. As they neared the door to the cellar, the sound of fighting could be heard faintly, it made all of Caleb's men stiffen as they unsheathed their weapons and prepared for what lay ahead.

Caleb placed the torch in an empty bracket on the wall and motioned for his men to follow him quietly. Opening the door, the northern lord led his men out through the building and headed into the courtyard where the clash of iron and steel rang out the loudest.

Chapter Thirty

The soldiers of Oror emerged from the trees as though they were a living embodiment of the forest coming forth as guardians of the north. They were so many in number that as they fell into line on the plains of the flatbeds, they looked as though they outnumbered the trees that lay behind them. They gathered in precise units that squared off against the less organized assembly of southerners.

The blue and silver pennants of the Orian soldiers stood out boldly against the shadowed green forest behind them. Just the sight of them was enough to shatter the nerves of many of the southerners waiting on the plains. Tobias could feel his stomach churning at the prospect of clashing against any of the stoic northern fighters. He noticed some of the Vulpini visibly shrinking away at the sight of their foe and realised that his people needed some encouragement.

"Stand fast!" he called out to the tribe, "Just because they look impressive doesn't mean that they fight impressively also."

His words felt utterly hollow as he knew that the Orians were highly skilled in battle, but the banter seemed to be enough to steel the men and women beside him to grit their teeth. There was a ripple of motion as the Vulpini unsheathed their weapons in readiness. Tobias could feel the sweat of his palms already as he gripped the hilt of his sword.

Although he knew that his nerves were getting the better of him, he convinced himself that the sweat was simply the result of the scorching hot sun. Elsewhere, he could hear other men throughout the Nevraahn ranks calling out to their troops, rallying them together before the final charge. As Tobias stood waiting with his fellow tribesman, he knew that there was no running from what lay ahead and that it was too late for anything Ayse could possibly do to spare them from the fated bloodshed.

***

The men parted to make way for their lord; Ulric rode out to the front of his troops and surveyed the enemy. Even from a distance, he could tell that they were not the military force that they had envisioned. It made him begin to doubt whether they had made the right choice in deciding that the information from the wolf shifter had been false.

Regardless of how much truth she had spoken, Caleb had been right that the sheer amount of men gathered by Nevraah required their attention. Rabble or not, they had marched on the north and would therefore have to pay the price. Ulric hoped that after quashing the attempted invasion, it would put the south in their place for a good long while as Oror had other matters to attend to.

Even still, Ulric couldn't quite shake the feeling that something troublesome was stirring in Oror somewhere. In the back of his mind, doubts had taken root and were riddling his brain with their possibilities. Ever since the scouts had returned to inform him that Caleb had chased off after the shifter girl, he couldn't help but wonder about her possible motives.

Leading only a few men away from the battlefield would ultimately do no good for the Nevraahn infantry, so why had she done it? Was it simply to taunt Caleb after he had not fallen for her lies? Or was it more than that? Was it that she had spoken the truth and so she was leading him away to prove it?

"Has Markus readied Lord Caleb's men?" he asked his lieutenant.

"Yes, my lord."

"And what of Lord Tomas?"

"He is ready and waiting also, my lord."

"Prepare the men," Ulric commanded.

At his signal, the soldiers of Oror drew their weapons and began pounding sword on shield in a slow, but rhythmic display of unity. The beat grew faster and louder until it exploded into a crescendo of war cries and shouts as the Orians began their roaring charge towards the enemy.

***

The ground thundered as the two armies ran at each other, blades drawn and voices crying out across the still air. There was a silent lull as the forces neared one another, quickly quashed when the Nevraahn and Orian armies collided with a loud eruption of noise. The sound of metal striking metal, screams, battle cries, and shouts, all of which seemed to reverberate across the whole of the flatbeds. The plains were overcome with a sea of moving bodies as men and women fought to the death, grappling one another, slicing, bludgeoning, and crying out for their country.

Tobias was already feeling the bittersweet reality of battle. For every northerner he managed to cut down, a Nevraahn fighter would fall somewhere close by. It felt as though they would simply carve each other out of existence. Unfortunately, warfare was a game for those skilled in battle, and it was already painfully obvious that the Orians were highly adept at fighting.

Tobias was immensely grateful for the time spent training in Bremlor. They had been pushed so hard that much of what was taught had become ingrained in the very fibre of their being. As a result, he found himself instinctively reacting on the battlefield. The Vulpini had been somewhat fortunate, as the foremost peak of the wave of Orian soldiers in their initial charge had broken hard against some of the mercenary forces further down the line of Nevraahn infantry.

Close by, Tobias could see Gabi, a young woman of the tribe, being beaten back by a northerner. Tobias closed in and swung out at her assailant. The soldier saw him coming and ducked aside, although not quickly enough to avoid Tobias's glancing blow to the back of his hand, which caused the Orian to drop his blade. Tobias made to cleave the soldier asunder while he stood unarmed, but the man punched out at Tobias with his shielded arm, striking Tobias in the face. The sharp edge of the metal shield scored a large cut along the Vulpini man's temple. The blood stung as it poured into Tobias's eye from his open wound and he could taste the salt of it as it reached his lips.

His vision began to waver. Quickly, he wiped the blood away from his face with the back of his arm. As he did so, he saw that the northern soldier had reclaimed his sword from the ground and was just about to strike him. Tobias dove out of the way, hitting the ground less than ceremoniously. He spun around to see his attacker looming above him, but before he could roll away, he saw a blade seemingly appear from nowhere out of the man's chest.

The eyes of the northerner went wide, and his mouth kept opening and closing as if wordlessly trying to speak. The whole manner of it reminded Tobias of when he had gone spearfishing and the caught fish would continue to flail and gasp in futility, unaware that its life was fading away from its body. The blade withdrew itself and the soldier crumpled to the ground in a twitching heap. Where he had stood moments before, Gabi now stood trembling with a shocked expression on her face. The bloodied sword still gripped tightly in her hands.

Tobias scrambled to his feet. Before he could even thank Gabi, he found he had to defend himself from yet another attacker. The two Vulpini were pulled apart in the current of battle, and the next time he looked beside him, Gabi was considerably further away. When he next sought to find her, she had disappeared amidst the sea of combatants entirely.

The continuous clash of blades sent shivers of vibrations rattling through Tobias's sword and into his hand. He could feel his grip becoming numb from his efforts and already his body was beginning to feel fatigued from all the fighting. Breathing heavily, Tobias gritted his teeth and persevered.

Each parry and thrust was becoming less about precision and more about desperately keeping his foes back. Blocking attacks and swinging out to catch the enemy where they were most vulnerable became a monotonous task that tested the endurance of every man and woman fighting that day. Those who were unable to maintain the energy to continue did not survive long enough to lament their failings.

**

The sun was still beating down on all of those embroiled in the fighting, glaring at them from on high with its fiery temper, like a parent scolding its mischievous children. Looking out across the battlefield, you could see the air shimmer and shift in the heat of the land, distorting the view of the fighting into some otherworldly illusion of battle. Ulric rode through the mass of swarming people, cutting down his foes left and right as he pressed further into the fray. As with every skirmish, the fighting was savage and bloody. Men were falling to the ground clutching at slashed throats as they choked on their last attempts at words. The only sounds coming from their mouths were gurgles as the blood boiled up from within their bellies.

Already there were broken bodies littering the battlefield, their weapons abandoned by their sides, and their limp forms being trampled into the mud as those still breathing fought to stay that way. Blood pooled in the downtrodden turf, soaking into the earth and forever tainting it with the sacrifice of war. There hadn't been such a great conflict between the two nations for as far as living memory could recall, but this was a war that would not be forgotten so easily.

The southern army had been surprisingly robust. Based on their less than satisfactory appearance, Ulric had expected many of their units to break ranks shortly after they had locked together in combat. However, they had continued to fight back with a fierce desperation.

Seeing the threat up close was enough to make him believe that the shifter girl had simply been another ploy by the southern state to coax them down the wrong path of action. Wherever she was, he hoped that his brother had finally caught up with her and was teaching her a permanent lesson about what happened to those who found themselves on the wrong side of the Wolfrik clan.

He could see his men making the most of every opportunity to gain ground on the plains and contented himself in the knowledge that the battle would most likely be over by the time the day was through. While the southerners were fighting bravely, they were simply no match for the well-trained soldiers of Oror. Ultimately, the northerners would win this battle, but as to whether it would end the war, it was hard to say.

Ulric wanted to ensure that any Nevraahn men fortunate enough to leave with their lives would limp back to where they had come from with their tails firmly between their legs. If he had to make this battle more bloody than necessary, then he was prepared to do so to ensure that the south would think twice before striking again. Then Oror would finally be able to return its attention to its northern shores, where it was needed most.

Chapter Thirty-One

When Caleb and his cohorts had emerged out into the courtyard, they had stepped directly into the midst of battle. Chaos reigned supreme as Nevraahn and Orian soldiers were battling to the death. Men fought atop the battlements to help or hinder those attempting to scale the walls, and more of the fighting had spilled out onto the lower grounds of Fort Lyndon.

Many of the northerners were gathered near the impressive wooden gates, working together to fiercely defend the entrance to the fort from the Nevraahn intruders that wished to invite in their comrades that waited just on the other side.

"There's more than just a skeleton guard here, my lord," one of Caleb's men stated with surprise.

"Yes," Caleb agreed. "It looks as though Ulric had some misgivings about marshalling all of his troops to the plains after all."

"It's a good job too," another soldier commented, "Without these extra men, the gates would have fallen long ago, and we'd be up to our necks in southern bastards."

"We're already up to our necks in southern shite," another soldier said as he spat on the ground and drew his sword, "So let's start cutting them down to size."

The men all looked to Caleb and he nodded his consent. Without another word to each other, the northerners drew their weapons and leapt into the fray.

All of them moved with the affinity of a pack stalking their prey, moving into position behind the southern soldiers attacking the men at the gates and suddenly forcing them to defend themselves from both directions.

Ayse watched them for a few moments, entranced at the sight of such skilled fighters in action. Caleb fought with a breath-taking fierceness, his finesse with a blade was mesmerising, his reflexes quick and sure, and he struck his foes with a flawless precision. Watching him move through the soldiers was like watching some elegant, yet deadly dance being performed. Caleb cut down his enemies where they stood with ease, deflecting the blows of others as they sought to strike him.

Ayse began helping Caleb and his men by picking off Nevraahn soldiers that were aiming to take the gate. She moved like a fleeting shadow amongst the men, unseen and unnoticed by her prey until they could feel her teeth biting the life out of them as she tore out their throats. Ayse had never been entirely happy with taking the lives of others, but as she considered what torment the Vulpini had suffered in the dark cells of Bremlor, she found that there was no room in her heart for remorse for her prey.

A desperate shout from the ramparts caused Ayse's ears to swivel round, catching her attention and causing her to glance upwards to see what was happening. An Orian captain of the guard was shouting at his men to reclaim the battlements, but for every grapple line they cut down, two more would hiss through the air and claw at the stone masonry.

The number of southerners atop the walls was increasing and they were pushing the northern soldiers back. This enabled even more of the enemy to ascend the ropes and gain access to the fort. If things continued as they were, the Orian men would be forced down into the courtyard, just waiting to be swarmed from those who climbed over the wall, or those who entered via the gate when it was finally overrun.

Ayse glanced back at Caleb. He was still deep in the thick of the battle, blood splatter was inked across his face, but there were no wounds to make her believe that the blood was his own. He fought with his teeth bared; snarling at his attackers as if the wolf inside of him was begging to be unleashed. Beside him, his men were fighting valiantly, bloodied and breathing hard, but still fighting. They had lost ground as the enemy had encircled them, forcing them back with their fellow northerners in front of the gate. Ayse knew that the men must be pushing themselves to the point of exhaustion. She was still suffering from the long chase, and likely they would be too.

Torn with indecision about where she would be best effective on the battlefield, Ayse silently wished Caleb and his men good luck as she leapt forwards and raced towards the battlements. She dodged the men fighting on the stone steps, weaving in and out of bodies, both alive and dead, as she made her way to the high balustrade above. At the far end, she could see the Orian soldiers being pushed even farther backwards. Nevraahn men were still hauling themselves onto the rampart, quickly moving into position to oust their enemy from the walls.

Ayse was unable to do anything about the metal hooks that dug into the masonry, so instead, she moved quickly and aimed for the Nevraahn men who were pressing against the northerners. Most of the men were facing away from her, their attention on the Orians attempting to hold fast at the opposite end of the parapets. Ayse stole upon them with quiet, but deadly accuracy, seeking out the soft of their flesh beneath their helmets and tearing their voices right out of them. Biting through the unprotected joints of armour, she gripped men by their limbs and pulled them off balance, releasing her teeth just in time to see the men topple over the edge of the stonework. They frantically tried to grab at whatever they could before they fell with a metallic crunch onto the terrace below.

Ayse's haste and diligence helped to clear many of the assailants from the battlements. The men of Oror who had found themselves cornered at the opposite end of the wall saw the wolf coming long before the Nevraahn soldiers could, and the sight of her striking down so many of their foes gave them a second wind as they began pushing forwards to reclaim the ramparts.

As the northerners spread out once more along the walls, extricating the stone from its tangle of hooks and lines with a new sense of vigour, Ayse drew closer to the captain she had heard and was surprised to find she recognised him. Pale in the face and less than steady on his feet, the young blonde man was continuing to fight alongside his brethren, despite the fact he had suffered a grievous wound the last time she had met him. The young werewolf, Lord Ulric's son, was commanding his men to take back the ramparts as she approached him. In a moment of respite on the wall, he caught sight of her and offered up a small effort at a smile,

"It's you, isn't it?" he said with ragged breath as he clutched at his side.

Ayse could see the wound still pained him. She whined at him and snapped her jaws to show her disapproval.

"I wasn't going to lie in my sick bed and wait for the end," he laughed, "That's not how we northerners do things."

Ayse realised that he was likely still resting when the Nevraahn army had attacked. It wasn't hard for her to believe that he had demanded his armour and gone out to fight alongside his brothers in arms without a second thought for his injuries. Though she admired the tenacity of the Orian men, it was a wonder as to how so many of them survived through sheer stubbornness alone.

A Nevraahn soldier charged at the young Orian man with his blade high in the air. The northerner managed to dodge the attack, but as he did so, his face contorted in pain, and he fell to one knee as he moved out of the way. The southerner went to attack again, and the young man managed to quickly brace himself as he deflected the assault with the flat of his blade. He was barely able to defend himself in his current position, and the southerner was giving him no quarter.

With a snarl, Ayse launched herself at the attacker, unsuccessfully trying to find any flesh to rip into, as her teeth met with metal wherever she sought out a weak spot. Fortunately, the weight of her alone was enough to send the man stumbling backwards and onto the floor. Abandoning his sword, the Nevraahn man guarded his face and throat from Ayse with his metal plated arms.

"Move, wolf."

She obeyed the command immediately and as she leapt aside the young Orian kicked the southerner as hard as he could, sending him skidding over the side of the stone ramparts with a yelp.

The young Orian was still on the ground. He heaved himself into a sitting position against the outer wall and breathed in deeply. His face was paling even more so than it had been before and Ayse could smell fresh blood. He had likely torn his wound open.

"Sorry about that," the boy grinned, "I didn't really know what to call you."

Ayse whined softly.

"My name's Jon, by the way," he offered offhandedly, ignoring her apparent concern.

Jon winced as pain twisted its way through his body, causing Ayse to whine even louder. His lips were growing as white as the pallor of his face as the blood drained from him. Another Nevraahn was fast approaching the fallen northerner, but Ayse jumped at him before he could strike, this time finding the bitter taste of blood with ease as she ripped into his jugular.

"We should have listened to you in the first place," Jon sighed. "But no one wanted to trust a southerner, and a shifter southerner at that," he added with a broken laugh.

Ayse looked about her at the bleak reality of their situation. While the Orian men had bravely fought back atop the walls, the Nevraahn army had an expendable amount of men to throw at the fort. The Nevraahn men scaling the walls were fresh fighters who were not tired from battling since the conflict had broken out. As a result, the men along the wall were once again finding themselves in a dire predicament, and with a quick glance Ayse could see that the northerners in the courtyard below were finding themselves in a similar dilemma. They were losing the battle.

As she looked back to Jon, Ayse could see he was also watching the scene before him and his face expressed a serene sadness. Ayse suddenly realised that there may be help closer to hand than she had initially thought. While there was no sign of the Orian forces showing up any time soon, Ayse recalled that there would still be northern patrols policing their territory in werewolf form. That was, if they hadn't already encountered the Nevraahn army in the forest and met with an ill fate.

From what she could ascertain, the existence of the werewolves was a secret, even to some of the Orian men themselves. It was likely that any werewolf that had seen the might of Nevraah marching on Fort Lyndon had not clashed with them for fear of exposing their true nature. But these were desperate times. If there was ever a situation that allowed for the rules to be broken, surely this was it?

Without a second thought, Ayse threw her head back and howled as loud as she could. Like a war horn summoning all men to arms, she howled with every emotion that swelled within her, begging for anyone who heard to heed the call and join the fight. The sound was powerfully primal. It sent a shudder amongst those who heard it, northerner and southerner alike, and some of the Orian men snapped their heads around at the sound, as if reacting to the noise on a deeper level. As Ayse finished her call to arms and lowered her gaze, she saw that she had garnered the attention of Caleb and his men, as well as other northern warriors in the fort. At such a distance, she was unable to perceive Caleb's reaction properly. Was he angry? Probably. But at that point, Ayse really didn't care. She looked back to Jon, who was shaking his head with disapproval, but a smile played about his lips.

"Probably shouldn't have done that," he said weakly, "They won't realise that you're not one of us. They'll think they really have been summoned here."

Ayse was glad to hear it and she let out a pleased yip.

"They will come, but there will be hell to pay when they do, wolf. If the southerners didn't have much of a reason to attack us before, when word gets out that Oror harbours monsters who hide in human skins, they'll be able to gather support from any nation of their choosing. Not to mention we'll have a civil war on our hands most likely, the normal folk will be afraid of us. If we survive that far, that is."

While his words were true, Ayse couldn't bring herself to worry about a future beyond that day. Right then, her only concern was ensuring that Fort Lyndon didn't fall to the Nevraahns. If that were to happen, and it ultimately led to the fall of Oror, then her actions in this whole affair would be irrevocable and she would have to live with the knowledge that because of her the northerners had been defeated. And for what? For the lives of the Vulpini in Bremlor that had been promised to them? They had been forced to reclaim the Vulpini themselves anyway, so Ayse's trip to the north had not helped them in any case. Not to mention, now more of their kin were fated to fall on a battlefield far from home. There had to be a better end than this. There just had to be.

Chapter Thirty-Two

The daylight was beginning to dim as the sun began its descent, vacating the throne of the heavens to allow its sibling to reside there for the night. The air was cooling as evening arrived and a breeze had grown in the last hour that was picking up strength as it roamed the battlefield. As it gained momentum, the wind whispered promises of a stormy night to all those who felt its touch.

Sweat, blood, and grime decorated the faces of the Vulpini as they strived to keep their ranks together. They had been pushed back across the blood-soaked fields and were making a last desperate stand together. All along the flatbeds, the situation was the same. Even the hardiest of the southern fighters had found themselves falling back due to the relentless assault of the Orians. The Nevraahn ranks were growing thinner as the day waned and before long, they would be broken, and their assault would be crippled. The northerners could sense the end was near, they were surging forward with the blood thirst of a beast moving in for the kill.

Tobias could see the battle souring fast, soldiers all along the southern line were falling quickly and if they weren't being cut down by their foes, then they were moving farther back and no longer pushing for a victory. The Vulpini tribesman could sense that soon the lines would break and cause chaos to erupt as every man inevitably fled for his life. When that happened, anarchy would reign. There would be no fear of retribution from ranking Bremlor soldiers as, without a doubt, they would be fleeing also.

Nearby, Reuben was defending himself against an attacker. The Vulpini was staggering as he fought to keep his footing and guard against his assailant. The northerner was beating him back; whipping his blade at him repeatedly with such ferocity that all Reuben could do was block the sweeping blade as it came, not once seeing an opening for retaliation. Bleeding from over a dozen different minor wounds, sweat stinging his eyes, and his breath short and laboured, Reuben gritted his teeth and held fast.

He didn't have to wait long. So preoccupied with his intended target, the Orian had failed to notice the small figure that stole up to him from behind. Nell appeared to almost embrace the soldier from behind as she gripped him steady with one hand, whilst simultaneously slipping a long thin blade underneath his breastplate with the other. With a cry the man shook Nell from his body and turned on her with a roar, but it was too late, Reuben had found his window of opportunity and had struck, cleaving the man's head clean from his body. It rolled away from them and down an embankment before coming to a standstill, staring upwards with unblinking glassy eyes as clouds converged on the dull sky.

"We're done for," Reuben panted, looking to Tobias as he spoke.

"We can't keep this up much longer," Nell added. "Once the troops begin to splinter away, the northerners will ride in on their mounts and cut us down as we try to flee."

"I know," Tobias said grimly. "We should get any who are willing to stay to remain and fight while the majority of the tribe try to flee."

"I'm not sure how far they'll get," Reuben said sadly. "Even if we manage to hold the bastards back for some time, eventually they will hunt down any runaways."

"It's the best chance we can give them," Tobias answered.

Reuben and Nell dejectedly nodded in agreement.

"Spread the word, any wish to stay and fight need to hold fast. We can't allow any Orian soldiers to break through. The rest are to flee immediately. As quickly as they can," Tobias commanded.

Nell and Reuben both parted ways, disappearing into the throng of fighters as they relayed Tobias's orders to the rest of the tribe. Weary and wounded, Tobias gripped his sword and looked to the nearest northerner. With an ominous foreboding, Tobias resumed his role of pawn on the battlefield. Tobias continued fighting a war that he had no desire to be a part of, and watching the lives of his tribal brothers and sisters being snuffed out before his eyes, their bodies falling to the floor like abandoned chess pieces.

***

Ulric could foresee the battle ending soon. The enemy was clearly weakening as their lines of defence began to fail. Already there were signs of pockets of men fleeing the battlefield and it wouldn't be long before they all broke rank and turned tail to run. The night was fast approaching, and he was keen to see his men well fed and rested before the break of dawn. They had wasted enough of their time on this southern scum.

The cold air swelled as the day finally broke under the pressure of the nighttime, the sun's last rays flailing weakly on the earth before fading completely. As the shadows lengthened and grew monstrous, revelling in the darkness of the late hours, the Nevraahn forces finally buckled under the strain of the Orian warriors. As predicted, once one unit had broken rank, the rest had panicked and began to scatter like leaves in the wind. The Orian mounted infantry moved in to run down their prey, showing no mercy as they cut down fleeing men without hesitation. Hounded by the northerners, men were being slaughtered as they attempted to escape the bloodshed.

As the blood and bodies were falling to the ground, a clear sound thundered through the cooling air. From within the forests of Oror a war horn sounded, it's deep drawn-out call resonated out of the trees and reached the ears of all those on the battlefield. Ulric waited with bated breath as the sound tapered off, then his eyebrows knitted together in a frown as he heard the second blast call out from the within the thick of trees. Gripping the reins of his horse, he turned his steed to stare back at the darkened horizon of Oror with trepidation.

"Lord Ulric!"

The northern lord turned to watch as the rider who had hailed him approached. Ulric greeted him with a grim tone, "Markus."

"The horn. It must be Caleb calling for our return," Markus said with concern.

"We must move quickly."

"So, it was true? What that shifter told you?"

"There's only one way to find out. Caleb wouldn't have asked the men to sound the horn without good cause. Let them leave with their lives. Ensure enough men remain to see that the southerners are sent running for the hills. We don't want them getting any ideas when we start to move out. Get the rest of our troops on their way to Fort Lyndon post-haste."

"Yes, my lord." Markus complied, kicking his horse into a gallop as he began bellowing orders at all the Orian men along the battlefield. Other officers took up his cries and they began marshalling their men into formation to move out.

Ulric could feel unease coiling within the pit of his stomach; it snaked its way through his guts and gripped at his heart until regret began to bleed out. He knew that Caleb would only have summoned the Orian army back for only one reason – Fort Lyndon was under siege.

They had been wrong about the wolf shifter. They had dismissed her warnings as lies and now they would be paying the price for their folly. His heart was beginning to pound hard in his chest, threatening to beat its way out of his body entirely as fear struck him, leaving him in a cold sweat. Jon was at Fort Lyndon and still gravely wounded. Caleb had taken only a few men with him when they had ridden after the girl, and even with the extra men that Ulric had left behind as a precaution, if any northerners still lived at the fort, they could well be breathing their last before the night was through.

Spurring his horse into action, Ulric began racing back towards his homeland as he shouted for his men to fall in line behind him. The majority of the Orian soldiers were hastening to return to the north, while those left behind continued to drive the Nevraahn army back. Darkness was falling as all manner of men and women abandoned the plains, running for their lives, or hurrying to save the lives of others.

* * *

"They're retreating?" Reuben gasped, limping up to Tobias and watching as the northern forces fell away from the plains in waves and began to vanish back into the darkened forest.

"Not exactly," Tobias responded, "They're moving to Fort Lyndon."

"You mean...? Ayse?"

"It must be." Tobias sighed with relief, "While the timing could have been a little sooner, I'm not going to complain that they saw reason eventually."

The northern fighters closest to them began to return, abandoning the fight without any qualms from the Nevraahn forces. While both forces were now retreating, it was still painfully obvious as to which army was running scared.

Reuben clapped a hand on Tobias's back. "Come brother, we have to get our people out of here before those northerners remove us from these plains, for good."

"We move as planned, keep a rear guard for our people as they leave. Just because the main Orian force is heading home doesn't mean those staying behind won't put a blade through our backs if given the chance."

"Of course, Nell and I will get everyone together."

"I'll take some of the tribe to look for any wounded survivors on the battlefield. I'll not leave them here to die alone."

"It's risky-" Reuben began.

"It's a risk worth taking." Tobias said firmly, "We've lost enough of our people as it is."

The battlefield was littered with bodies, crushed and mutilated, they lay where they had fallen, soaked in their own blood and filth, foe and ally alike. Among them, Tobias could already pick out some of his tribal brothers and sisters that were ill-fated to never return home. Calling out to those closest to him, Tobias sheathed his sword as he and his comrades began to pick their way through the carnage for survivors.

Reuben and Nell were busy bringing order to the other Vulpini who remained. With the battle now over, the gypsies were staring aghast at their surroundings as if in a state of shock about what they had just been a part of. The Vulpini couple hastily moved them along, allowing Tobias and his comrades to continue their grim task without onlookers. Searching for the wounded was a long and arduous task that was particularly painful to bear. Examining bodies of strangers still stricken with their last fearful expression was a sad situation by itself, but when discovering that the body was that of someone you had once known, it was utterly distressing.

Kneeling beside the pitiful figure, Tobias gently brushed aside the dark strands of hair from the pale face of Gabi. Her eyes were closed, and her face was surprisingly clean from the blood and mud of the battlefield. She looked as though she could be peacefully sleeping. He positioned her body better so that she was lying in a restful pose, her hands clasped on top of her chest like the statuesque marble tomb coverings that the nobles received in death.

"We should bury them." one of the Vulpini said sadly as he watched Tobias tend to the body.

"We should, but we can't." Tobias replied his eyes wet with tears, "We have to look after those who are still living first. It's not safe here."

It was a sad ending for many, simply left to rot on the plains of the flatbeds, but Tobias was sure they would think of a way to honour them properly when they had retreated safely, and after the wounded were tended to. Continuing with their depressing task, Tobias and his men stalked the fields, pulling those still breathing out of the slick of gore and muck and hauling them away to safety. There were no stars that night as the dark clouds had engulfed the sky in their suffocating embrace. The moon shone down with a cold light whenever it could be glimpsed between the rolling waves of the heavens. Its bright body acting as a beacon to the souls of the dead that wandered lost on the battlefield, summoning them to the netherworld.

Chapter Thirty-Three

The night had arrived with a roar. Claps of thunder boomed out above Fort Lyndon as if snapping and barking at the hostilities below. The Nevraahn army forced to wait outside of the main conflict had grown impatient, and so had begun to shower the fortress with bright hails of burning arrows, causing many of the buildings within to burst into tumultuous balls of flame. Brilliant flashes of pure white would grace the world momentarily as lightning carved its way through the sky, illuminating the pale figure of Jon as it did so.

They had moved to the cover of the gatehouse, with Ayse keeping close by to ensure that he reached safety without any Nevraahn soldiers attacking. It was easier to protect him through the narrow opening of the gatehouse doorway, and no southerners had been able to get past her. Ayse had considered shifting to try and tend to Jon's wounds, but the thought of being attacked while she was in her more vulnerable human form was enough to sway her against the notion. Jon's strength was fading fast. She could see it in his eyes as they grew dimmer with every passing moment. He sat slumped against the wall, listening to the sounds of warfare outside as his consciousness faded.

Another thunderclap echoed loudly, Ayse could even feel the vibrations through her paws. Yet another crack sounded far too soon after the first, the floor beneath her rumbling once again as Ayse looked to Jon who was staring back at her wide-eyed.

"The gates..." he gasped.

Ayse ran from the gatehouse and looked to the large gates where the meagre remains of the Orian guard were still courageously fending off any would-be attackers. With every booming noise, the gates quivered and shook from the impact, sending tendrils of vibrations through every stone nearby. The southerners had indeed grown impatient, as the gates were in the process of being assaulted repeatedly with a battering ram.

While the Nevraahn army wanted Fort Lyndon as intact as possible for when they assumed control of it, they were obviously growing concerned that their window of opportunity to snatch the camp from the northerners was slipping through their fingers. First, they had set it alight, now they were hammering at the front gates as if they meant to tear them from their very hinges.

Ayse helplessly watched as the gate began to splinter under the rhythmic boom of the ram. She could even hear the shouts of the soldiers on the other side as they maintained their fierce tempo. The few Orian guards on the battlements above the gate sought to attack those charging the gate from above, but their efforts were in vain. The thunder roared out and the fighting inside of the fort lulled as all the soldiers in the immediate vicinity of the gates backed away as the wood began to crack and fall away. The gate buckled under the attack and the ram ripped through a portion of the gate wide enough to fit two men abreast.

Ayse could see the wooden trunk of the tree that had been cut down to use as a ram. It disappeared back through the broken gate, ready to strike again, but before it could do so, a deafening howl sounded from just outside the fort. The sound was savage enough that it seemed to quell the thunder with shame. Before long, other voices joined in the call of the wild. The shouts of desperate men could be heard from outside and the battering of the gates had come to a standstill.

Screaming men attempted to find safety in the fort, entering through the breach in the gates and tripping over themselves as they fled. The northerners waiting inside quickly dealt with the terrified men, re-igniting the warfare between the Nevraahn and Orian men down in the courtyard. Chilling screams could still be heard from outside, long, drawn-out cries that struck fear into the hearts of those who could hear them. A dark shape stirred in the gap of the gates, its large hulking form clawing its way through with a snarl. When it emerged, it shook itself and stood tall. The sheer sight of it took the breath away from all those staring at it in terror.

The powerful wolf looked to Caleb and bowed its head slightly in acknowledgment, before it turned its attention to the southern invaders. It pounced into the gathered men with its jaws wide and its lips pulled back, baring its deadly teeth for all to see. Claws and teeth made short work of any men that stood in its way. The wolf tore into them, shaking its head as it pulled out entrails and guts, sending the hot stinking meat flying all over the place.

Before the southern soldiers could even contemplate reacting to the beast before them, more werewolves had entered through the broken gates. Their hackles raised and angry guttural growls emanating from deep within their throats. They prowled forwards ready to attack.

In one quick instant, the wolves had moved. Suddenly, they were amidst the enemy and were creating havoc as they mangled the men and left their bodies in pieces. One of the werewolves bounded up the steps and along the battlements, clawing at men and disembowelling them with quick, furious swipes. It barrelled into southerners, sending them scattering and falling, while others it forced to the ground as it tore into them.

As the werewolf ran out of men to attack, it began to stare down Ayse. She could see the blood and saliva dripping from its slack jaws as it slowly approached her. Its nostrils flared as it took in her scent, the scent of a shifter. Its ears flattened against its head and its nose wrinkled into a snarl causing Ayse to slowly begin backing away towards the safety of the gatehouse.

The wolf was picking up speed as it neared her. Its size was far greater than that of Jon when she had been close to him in wolf form. The wolf's eyes had a bright gleam to them in the darkness and Ayse could see the flames of the burning outbuildings reflected in them. Her heart was pounding as the werewolf approached. She darted into the gatehouse, running straight for the prone figure of Jon. Her quick movement caused the werewolf to roar as it tore after her.

As the beast ran through the gatehouse door, the door frame shook and strained under the pressure. The sheer size of the wolf in the doorway blocked out much of the light from outside. Ayse stayed close by Jon, her head lowered submissively as she desperately hoped that it would see her as an ally. Still growling, the wolf slowly approached her and the injured man, it moved closer to Jon, sniffing at him as it did so. It opened its jaws and without thinking Ayse snarled and snapped in its face to deter it from doing anything to the young man, but her attempts at protecting him were pitiful. She was like a mere puppy attempting to frighten away a grown wolf. The wolf gnashed its teeth at her briefly before snorting hot air at her in contempt and adopting a more passive pose.

"It's good to see you too, Reis," Jon laughed weakly, alerting Ayse to the fact that he was not unconscious after all.

The wolf growled at Jon, it wasn't in a vicious manner, but more of a reprimanding tone. It nosed at his breastplate, causing the young man to wince.

"Yeah, I know," Jon said through gritted teeth as he batted the werewolf's muzzle away. "I think I pulled my stitches."

Ayse saw her opportunity and she wasn't about to miss it. She crouched low to the ground and began to shift. It was a painful experience given the exhausted state of her body, and her muscles felt as though they were ripping away from her very bones. Once human, she shivered from the adrenaline rush of her transformation.

"If you guard the door, I'll see to his wounds," she breathed heavily as she spoke, the words rushing out of her, but the werewolf simply stared at her with wide uncomprehending eyes.

"For the love of the old gods, put a shirt on," Jon said abashed as he looked away from her. "Reis will be too busy looking at you to see any southerners attacking at this rate."

On hearing this, the werewolf snapped at Jon and turned its back on Ayse to watch the door, as Ayse rose to find something to cover herself with. Finding a discarded shirt, she pulled it over her head and was happy to see that it was large enough that it fell to mid-thigh length. Next, she set about finding something to see to Jon's wounds. Unfortunately, the gatehouse didn't offer much in the way of medical supplies, but by some stroke of luck, she found that someone had decided to spend their shift in the gatehouse repairing their clothing. She found a needle and thread, as well as more shirts that she planned to shred for bandages. Grabbing a bottle of old gin that stood abandoned on the table, she rushed back to Jon and knelt beside him.

With great care, she began to unbuckle his breastplate, though even the smallest movement caused him to go rigid with pain. Once removed, she could see that underneath his clothing was dripping wet with the red of his blood.

Ayse ripped his shirt open and removed the bloodied dressings to get a better look at the damage. Sure enough, the wound from where the spear had pierced through his skin had been split open once more.

Reis stirred just outside the doorway, his hackles rising and a growl escaping from his throat. Whatever he had reacted to must have seen him and taken off in the opposite direction as the large werewolf never strayed from his post at the door. Outside, they could hear the battle raging on. There were shouts and cries, the clash of metal, snarls, and screams, and all the while the storm seethed above them in the heavens. Feeling the need to hurry, Ayse doused the needle, thread, and wound with some of the alcohol, causing Jon to whimper and bite his lip.

"I'm sorry," she muttered as she threaded the needle.

"Just do it," Jon said unflinchingly.

She nodded and set to work as quickly as she was able to. Her hands were still shaking and every time she felt or saw Jon grimace, she could feel her nerves failing her even more. Ayse didn't have the finesse of a surgeon, but she managed to knit the wound up. It was far from presentable, but it didn't need to last, it just needed to stem the bleeding long enough for a real medic to see to him. Ayse then began tearing at the fabric and creating makeshift bandages, swathing it around Jon's torso and pulling the material tight.

"It's not perfect," she said when she realised there was nothing more that she could do, "But it should hold for now."

"Give me that," Jon rasped, motioning towards the liquor.

Ayse obliged, watching as he took a swig of the bitter alcohol.

"What's happening out there?" he asked her.

Ayse walked barefoot over to the door, carefully avoiding touching the large beast that guarded the threshold. Looking out, she could see the devastation clearly as the fires were still burning bright enough to illuminate the massacre within. It looked like a couple more of the werewolves had entered Fort Lyndon and were quickly seeing to the last of the Nevraahn soldiers that remained within its walls, while the Orion men defended the gate from any more invaders.

"It looks like the wolves have nearly secured the fort," she said with amazement. "If Caleb can keep the Nevraahn soldiers from entering through the gate or scaling the walls, we might just live through this."

"That still leaves us with that giant host of bastards on our front doorstep," Jon sighed, "We can't defend against them forever, they will think of another way in."

"We don't have to last forever," Ayse replied. "Caleb sent for Lord Ulric. We just have to keep control of the fort until he arrives with your forces."

Jon smiled. "Well, that challenge sounds more reasonable."

Ayse moved back towards Jon and shortly afterwards Reis returned to them, watching with interest as Jon took another drink from the bottle.

"We still have another problem on our hands though," Jon said bleakly, "They've seen us for what we really are. Our men, the southern men, everyone..."

"It was the only way," Ayse said softly.

"It's in the lap of the gods now," Jon replied. "There's not much we can do about it."

As if suddenly realising that their call to arms had not come from a fellow werewolf, Reis groaned and looked to Ayse with contempt.

"Don't blame her," Jon chided him. "If you hadn't shown up when you did, this place would be crawling with Nevraahns and we'd all be dead by now."

"Surely your own people will understand?" she asked.

"Oh? Does everyone in Nevraah know about shifters?" Jon mocked.

"No..."

"I didn't think so," Jon snorted. "But they're not the worst of it. It's the Nevraahns that worry me. When word gets out, they could rally many to their cause. This war would pale in comparison to what the future could hold."

Ayse's eyes were downcast as she considered the consequences of her impulsive actions and what that could mean for the future of the north. Yet given the chance to change things, knowing that the southerners would have broken through eventually, Ayse wouldn't have done anything differently.

"Reis, you should return and help the others. I'm safe enough in here now with the immediate threat gone. We just need to keep those bastards out of Fort Lyndon for now," Jon whispered, his voice growing even hoarser.

Reis bowed his head momentarily and then returned to prowling the battlements for any men foolish enough to attempt to climb the walls.

"You should go too. You're more use to them out there than to a sick man in here," he said as he grinned at Ayse.

She frowned at the thought of leaving him alone but realised the truth of his words and nodded wordlessly. Saving him the embarrassment of blushing once again, Ayse ducked out of sight to remove her shirt and shift. She found this transformation more difficult than the last. Before, she had the urgency of Jon's condition to drive her body onwards, but this time all she felt was her exhaustion. When she finally stood as a wolf, she doubted whether she would be able to shift back to her human form any time soon. She padded back over to Jon and butted his knee playfully with the flat of her head before following Reis out into the cold night air.

With the monstrous new threat now out of sight in the fort, the Nevraahn army outside had managed to reclaim some form of composure and was once again sending men over the walls. However, they didn't last long once they reached the top. Reis and the other werewolves barely let the feet of the soldiers touch upon the stonework before they stopped their hearts from beating in their chests. The werewolves were ripping the grapple hooks out of the stone with their bare teeth, occasionally sending men that had been climbing those ropes plummeting to their death.

Even with the hooks being removed, more would whizz through the air and clack against the wall, scraping into place to allow for more attackers to climb up. Down at the gate, the Orian men were stemming the flow of southern invaders with the help of yet more wolves. The Nevraahn forces were attempting to enlarge the gap at the gate, allowing for more of their men to pass through at a time. While the northerners were defending themselves well, the gate was slowly, but inevitably diminishing as it continued to be worn down by the attackers.

Ayse helped to defend the battlements, feeling that staying close to a werewolf who was aware that she was an ally was better than tempting fate in the courtyard below. It also meant she could stay close to Jon, should he need her. The thunderclaps were crashing less often against the clouds, the lightning becoming smaller and less vibrant with every brief pulse. It was going to be a long night. Ayse couldn't even remember the last time she had slept at all. Her body was functioning only because of her desperation to live. As she watched the other men fighting, she knew that they would also be feeling the same and she wondered how much longer they could continue.

Chapter Thirty-Four

The early morning arrived with such a sweet nature about it that you would never have guessed that the weather had been in a foul storm of a mood the night before. The fires had almost burnt themselves out, reducing stables and storehouses to nothing but smouldering ash. The front gate was now nearly non-existent; shreds of wood where its hinges remained were all that had survived of the once proud doors. Nearly all the northerners were at the front gate now, desperately fighting to stop the flood of Nevraahn invaders from gaining ground within the encampment.

Only Ayse and Reis remained on the battlements, although they were quickly becoming outnumbered by their attackers. The fatigue was taking its toll on all the Orian men and even the wolves were beginning to tire. On the other hand, the southern warriors were well rested, having simply been waiting outside for most of the battle. It was difficult to continue fighting with the same weary body when each new foe was fresh and ready for battle. Reis was becoming lazy with his kills, moving more sluggishly as he rounded on the men and flung them into the air, letting their descent to the courtyard below be their demise instead of his teeth. The men in the courtyard were also suffering. Their once beautiful dance of blade and blood had become a display of perseverance as they staggered about, panting heavily from their exertions.

Without warning, the werewolves began howling. It startled their attackers momentarily, but it was not enough to deter them for long. All the wolves took up the call, the sound becoming a deafening wild chorus as the long-drawn-out tone continued. Ayse tilted her head and looked at Reis with confusion as he howled along with his brothers.

When he paused in his howling, Reis saw Ayse's quizzical look and let his jaw go slack, his tongue lolling out in a lop-sided grin. He swivelled his ears on his head repeatedly as if trying to tell her something, but she wasn't quite sure what it was that he wanted her to understand. He shook his head and snorted as if laughing at her, before resuming his call. The werewolves only stopped their cries when something sounded out in response, it was the deep booming voice of a war horn echoing out from the woodland surrounding Fort Lyndon.

Suddenly, it became very clear what Reis had been trying to tell her, the werewolves had heard Lord Ulric's forces approaching. It didn't take long for Ayse to be able to hear them too, the drumming sound of the feet of soldiers marching on the ground, men shouting war cries, and the war horn still blasting out to announce their arrival. Ayse silently thanked the gods for their providence.

∗∗∗

Ulric breathed a sigh of relief when he saw that Fort Lyndon was still manned with northerners, although from what he could see, they seemed to be few in number. The sound of the wolves had been surprising, but it had served well as an indication of just how desperate the situation at the fort must have been for the men to have decided to fight in wolf form. While he was aware of the possible repercussions, his only current concern was ousting the southern scum from his land.

The Nevraahn army had been so concerned with throwing the lives of its men at the fort to overrun it, that they had not bothered to prepare themselves for an attack from behind. Ulric had sent his troops far and wide, encompassing the might of the Nevraahn army in their grip and ensuring that the southerners were trapped between Fort Lyndon and the vast forces of Oror. Already the men had joined in battle as the Orian infantry rushed those attacking the fortress, drawing their attention away from the weakened structure. The attackers had become the defenders as Nevraahn men had suddenly found themselves trapped with no option but to fight for their own survival.

"My lord," Markus hailed Ulric as he approached. "The men have circled the enemy as you requested. They're cut off from being able to retreat. They'll either hit hard against our soldiers or face the cold stone of Fort Lyndon."

"Good. It's more important than ever that we allow none to leave alive."

"They've seen the wolves…" Markus tapered off, unsure what to say on the matter.

"Yes, we can't let a single southerner that has seen our true nature reach Nevraah alive."

"What of our men?"

"We'll deal with that when the time comes," Ulric replied. "For now, just ensure that these bastards don't see another morning."

"My lord, do you want me to get a pack together? I can take a score of men and we can patrol the limits of the battlefield to ensure no stragglers or fleeing Nevraahn men escape."

"Good idea. But do it quietly. I don't want the normal folk knowing any more about this than they must. Stay out of sight. The last thing we need is anyone seeing you transform."

As Markus left to gather his men, Ulric turned his attention back to the action in front of him. These southern soldiers were of a higher calibre than those they had faced on the plains. As forewarned, he was witnessing the true force of the Nevraahn army. Their lack of forethought had left them open to attack from all sides and now they were surrounded. All Ulric had to do was to keep pressing his men forwards until they had squeezed the last ounce of life out of the southern troops. Kicking his horse, he cantered towards the fray to join in the bloody warfare, eager to see it end.

***

The Nevraahn soldiers had given up on scaling the walls now that they had a bigger threat to face, as a result Reis and Ayse had joined the rest of the northerners down at the gate. No longer hard-pressed to defend the entrance to the fort, they had moved outside and were throwing themselves into the thick of battle with an intense second wind now that they could see that victory was in sight.

Swords were blazing in the sun, slicked with blood and brains as they flashed through flesh and bones. Mounted soldiers were riding down the adversary, swinging out their blades and inflicting maximum damage on the poor sods grouped too tightly together to avoid the deadly assault. Werewolves were snarling and snapping in the crowd, biting through metal and crushing the enemy in their own armour, the blood spurting outwards as their bodies caved in.

The beasts were even more impressive by the light of day, somehow making them seem even more real. They were taking the brunt of the damage from the enemy, as they were the most hulking target to attack. Their hides were littered with arrows and they were bleeding from countless wounds. The southern men were attempting to swarm the beasts only to find themselves swept up in a deadly flurry of claws and teeth.

Ayse was pelting through the men, leaping onto unsuspecting southerners and ripping out their throats before they could even touch the ground. She heard a distant shout and it made her freeze. Her ears quickly swivelled round to try and trace the source.

"Lord Frewin! We must fall back! Lord Frewin!"

With a snarl, Ayse dodged around those locked in the throng of battle as she sought out her prey. It was a name she would never forget, and he had done things she could never forgive. Anger was burning inside of her. She could feel it making her skin itch and crawl with anticipation as she sought out the man responsible for hurting her friends. Surrounded by soldiers were two southern officers on horseback, one of them was pleading with the other.

"Lord Frewin, this battle is lost. We must retreat."

"We'll retreat when I say we will. I will not be defeated by these dogs," Lord Frewin spat in the face of his comrade.

This was confirmation enough for Ayse that her target was most definitely the man before her. She ignored the guards all around the despicable man, and a growl ripped from her throat as she ran at him. Her inner wolf took over as she snarled and leapt through the men, she could feel the saliva dripping from her jaw as the wild urge to rip flesh from flesh consumed her.

The horses screamed and reared at the sight of her. Frewin was thrown clear from his horse while the other officer managed to cling to his steed. The sound of sudden shouting reached Ayse's ears, but she wasn't listening. The words weren't even making themselves known to her as her wolf didn't comprehend language and it was her wolf that was prowling forwards with a desire to kill. Once on the ground, Frewin was fair game for Ayse, she bounded forwards and struck the man, but she didn't go for the throat. Instead, she tore at his limbs, biting into his thighs and dropping the hunks of flesh from her jaws as soon as they came away from his body. He was screaming in terror, shouting at his men for help and she was aware of movement all around her, but she ignored it.

As Frewin struggled to unsheathe his sword, she went for his hand, biting through multiple fingers, feeling the bones crack beneath her teeth and causing the man to howl and squeal as though he were a beast himself. Ayse was in a mad frenzy. Soldiers began to attack her, but she snarled at them and dodged their blades, only suffering from glancing blows. All the while she guarded Frewin as if she were a starving wild animal protecting her prey from other scavengers.

As the soldiers began to swarm her, a dark shadow leapt amongst them, scattering them in all directions as it bit and tore at the combatants. The officer on horseback had fled shortly after Ayse's attack, and with the arrival of Reis, the remaining soldiers either met a grisly end or ran screaming for their lives.

When there was no one left to challenge him, Reis approached Ayse and barked at her, reprimanding her. Ayse growled at him as she crouched low over Frewin in a guarding position, too blinded by her bloodlust to realise that the officer had stopped screaming some time ago and that his body now lay lifeless. Reis tried once more to assert his dominance over Ayse, snarling at her with such intensity that he expected her to back down immediately, but still the small wolf growled and spat at him as her fur bristled.

Someone was shouting again, but Ayse's mind was too deeply fogged by vengeance and the scent of blood to hear it. Reis, on the other hand, understood it perfectly. He moved towards Ayse to strike and, falling for his feint, she played straight into his hands. He gripped her by the scruff of her neck as she fought back. She kicked and snapped at him, so he shook her as if he were scolding a pup.

As Reis carried Ayse away, her energy evaporated from her body and her fury abated as she was unceremoniously removed from the battlefield. Two days of non-stop running and fighting had taken its toll and she hung there in his jaws like a trophy from a hunt. By the time he had entered the gatehouse, she was barely conscious. She could hear the murmur of Jon's frantic voice, but she couldn't distinguish the words. Reis gently laid her on the floor, and she could feel the warmth of Jon's legs at her back, she didn't even fight the feeling of sleep as it came.

Chapter Thirty-Five

Although the day was bright and cheerful, the mood in the camp was dismal and depressing. The weather would have been better suited if it was casting sheets of heavy rain onto the earth. The Vulpini, along with other surviving mercenary groups and Nevraahn soldiers, had returned to their camp on the southern tip of the flatbeds to lick their wounds.

They had managed to drag many injured tribesmen off the battlefield and so were staying in the relative safety of the camp until they were all fit enough to travel on. Unfortunately, even some of those who had made it back to the camp had later died from their injuries in the day that had followed.

There was no real plan of action any longer. Bremlor officials remained in their grand war tents discussing battle strategies, brooding on the lack of development and listening to reports that ultimately yielded them no new information. No one dared to disturb them and incur their wrath. That portion of the camp was given a wide berth.

There had been no word from the western fort and so no one knew whether the coup had been successful or not. There was still a good chance that the battle was continuing there, leaving many of the soldiers in denial of a probable defeat until they had heard otherwise. Because the Orian men had fallen back to defend their land, taking their great number of warriors with them, there was a growing sense of foreboding within the plains camp that the fort would be a loss.

Tobias didn't care whether the fort had been taken or not. They had lived up to their end of the deal and paid dearly in blood by doing so. All he was concerned about now was ensuring that his people rested long enough so that they were fit to travel, then they could return to the rest of their tribe and never have to concern themselves with accursed politics again.

As he sat with the rest of the surviving Vulpini in mourning, he couldn't even bring himself to think of Ayse, Rojas, or any of the Vulpini in Bremlor. He was too bitter and angry about what they had endured, and the loss of his tribal brothers and sisters was still incredibly raw in his mind. His heart was full of rage and sadness, even the brightness of the day offended him.

The blood-stained faces of his dead companions haunted him regardless of whether he was awake or asleep. He sat beside the campfire, staring into its flames with an aggravated look, and saying nothing to the others. The fire was blazing with a harsh light, but he sat there unblinking as he stared back into its heated gaze.

***

Reuben watched his friend with growing concern. Ever since they had returned to the camp, Tobias had simply fallen apart. Out on the battlefield he had commanded their people as if he was a born leader, surprising many in the tribe with his conviction. However, once they had retreated to safety and Tobias had washed the blood from his body, he had seemingly washed away all will to continue governing their people with it.

Would the Bremlor prisoners be released now? Reuben didn't know. Did their family members die for nothing? He didn't know that either. The rations were still thin on the ground, but with everything in such an uproar it was easy for the Vulpini to sneak out of the camp and hunt in fox form, enabling those still fit and healthy to bring back plump hares from the plains.

Reuben had also begun to plan for when the Vulpini would depart, collecting what supplies he could and commandeering a couple of wagons and horses to help the wounded to travel. They had claimed that they needed them to help move the dead from the battlefield and no one had bothered to challenge them on it thus far. Injured and wounded as they were, the journey back would be a treacherous one, but one worth taking. Every moment they lingered within reach of the other Nevraahn forces increased the chances of them being coerced into some new danger.

So lost in his reverie, Reuben was startled when he felt someone reach out and touch him. He turned around to see that Nell had returned. She smiled at him sweetly, but her expression was tainted with the horrors of war. In the depth of her eyes, there was a profound sadness that Reuben wasn't sure could ever be removed. As he pulled her close and held her tightly, he realised how lucky they were to have survived together.

They had both come away with plenty of minor wounds and bruises, as no one had escaped unscathed, but Nell had come away with a particularly nasty gash to her neck where a northern soldier had attempted to behead her. Reuben had pulled her away from the blade just enough to spare her life, but the wound was sufficiently deep that it would leave a significant scar. When Reuben had dealt with the attacker, the Orian had not been so fortunate as to keep his own head. Reuben traced the angry red wound with his finger, hovering above her skin and not daring to touch Nell for fear of hurting her.

"We need to redress your wound," he said softly.

Nell nodded in agreement, before hoarsely adding, "I had to remove the bandages when I shifted." She paused before asking, "Is he still the same?"

Nell pulled out of Reuben's embrace and glanced at the figure hunched over by the fire. Tobias was motionless and in the exact same position as when she had left the camp.

"He just sits there," Reuben replied as he led Nell to a quiet spot where he could see to her injury. "He won't speak to anyone."

"Many of our people are like that. They're still recovering from the shock of war... from all that killing, and on top of that they're all grieving. We just have to watch over them," Nell said gently as she sat and let Reuben fuss over her.

The Vulpini man bit his lip. Nell was right of course, but it felt awful to leave his friend in such a sorry state. Changing the subject, he asked her, "How was your run?"

"As expected, the northerners are still guarding their perimeters well, but there were other southerners picking over the battlefield that the Orian men didn't seem too concerned with. I think as long as we steer clear of them and their land, they won't bother us."

Reuben continued to dress her wound, taking great care to be as gentle as possible, something he found particularly hard with his rough callused hands. "Good. We should take all those who are willing and see to it immediately."

"It can wait until tomorrow. That way we will have the whole day to honour them properly. Besides, I think that it's best that you stay here." Nell held up a hand as Reuben went to protest. "We need someone to rely on here, that person is now you."

He sighed, "Alright. Just don't take any risks out there."

"I won't. I promise," Nell answered, pausing to kiss him sweetly, "I think this is what the tribe needs right now. Burying our brethren will give them some closure."

"I know. I just don't want to linger here too long. The more time that passes, the more anxious the dukes will become. I want to be gone from this wretched place before they think to bring us to heel again."

"How do you think the other forces are faring at the fort?" Nell asked.

"Only the gods know," Reuben replied. "The longer we wait, the worse it looks for the southern army."

"What of Ayse? Do you think she's still out there?"

"I hope so," he replied softly, his mind wandering to think of where the wolf could possibly be.

The northerners had turned their army around just as they were about to land the killing blow, something important had called them back to their land and the only possible explanation was the attack on the fort. It was the only reason that the remaining Vulpini had managed to survive. Many of them would have been cut down whilst fleeing, and those who they had managed to save from the bloodied ground and carry to safety would have otherwise surely died a slow death where they had fallen.

But where did that leave Ayse? Was she still alive somewhere? Reuben knew that if she were given the opportunity, she would return to ensure that the tribe was alright. But that thought left a heavy weight in his chest. If Ayse never returned to them, did that mean that she had perished out there alone?

Then there was Rojas to think of. He would still be travelling back to Bremlor as fast as his horse would allow. The sooner he arrived in that bleak place, the better. If the news broke that they had lost the fort, the dukes would no doubt regroup in Bremlor, taking the remnants of their army and their bitter tempers with them. Rojas needed to get the Vulpini prisoners away from there before Duke Remus could alleviate his foul mood with their punishment, or before he could call forth another favour from the tribe.

If all went as well as could be hoped, the tribe would still have to travel some distance to get away from the repercussions of the duke's fury after he discovered he had lost his bargaining chip with the tribe. There were plenty of places that Reuben could think of where the Vulpini could hide in safety, especially now that the summer had arrived, and the weather was milder.

Chapter Thirty-Six

Ayse was awoken by the sound of loud voices. The noise of the real world fought to reclaim her from the sleep that desperately sought to keep her in its heavy embrace. Even as she roused and clarity began to return, she could feel the fatigue engrained into each of her bones and muscles. She ignored her protesting body as she staggered to her paws. Brilliant daylight was cascading in through an open window, and outside the day was quiet and calm. The battle was over.

She found herself in a small, well-furnished room. Realising that she must have been carried there reminded Ayse of her last few moments on the battlefield and she felt ashamed. The memories of those moments were disjointed, but still clear enough for her to recall her careless behaviour. Behind her was a crackling fire, its heat rolling out from the hearth in waves and warming the stone room.

From the sour smell of salve, it was clear that while she had rested the northerners had tended to her. Ayse wasn't sure how long she had slept for, her body was so exhausted that it felt as though she could happily collapse and drift off into unconsciousness once again with ease. However, the sound of an argument brewing nearby snared her attention.

"She still has to answer for what she has done!" a voice she didn't recognise was demanding.

"She tried to warn us about the attack, we have no one to blame other than ourselves for not listening," Lord Ulric responded calmly.

"That doesn't change the fact that she infiltrated our land, spied on us, then fed the information to those bastards in the south," the same angry voice spat back.

"She saved my life," she heard Jon interject, "More than once, actually."

"She fought alongside us," another unfamiliar voice added pointedly.

"Neither of which would have been necessary if she hadn't gathered information on our people in the first place," the aggravated man continued.

"Nevraah was rising against us," she heard Caleb say flatly, "They would have attacked in force eventually, whether they had information on our lands or not."

"It doesn't change anything!" the man continued to fume, "The blood of Oror has been spilt because of her."

"And yet more blood was saved because of her," Jon retorted.

"Enough," Caleb said sternly. "If you so wish it, Tomas, I will take her before the high lord, and he can decide her fate."

"We should be dragging her out into that courtyard and making an example of her!"

The voices were close. Ayse had silently crept from her room and followed the source of the argument. She hovered unnoticed in the open doorway, watching the men before her arguing. They were gathered around a war table, completely oblivious to her presence as they continued their heated debate. She could see the familiar faces of Caleb, Markus, Jon, and Lord Ulric. There was also a stranger stood amongst them, tall with hair the colour of mahogany and amber coloured eyes. Lastly, there was the man still venting his frustrations, Tomas, he was red in the face and spittle was spraying out from his lips as he tried to assert his will over the others.

She had heard his name in the past and knew that he led one of the northern war camps. He seemed younger than Caleb, most likely the youngest of all three warlords before her. His dark hair and similar features to Caleb made her wonder whether he was yet another brother.

"Tomas," Lord Ulric was tempering the younger man, "Caleb was the one who took the girl in. She's his ward. You will do her no harm until she receives judgement from the high lord."

"This is a joke," the brunette man muttered.

"Shut it, Reis," Markus said sternly.

From behind her, Ayse could hear footsteps approaching. Not wanting to be discovered eavesdropping, she stepped out of the shadowed doorway and into the room where all the men turned to stare at once. Visibly turning a deeper shade of red with his veins pumping in his temple, Tomas stormed from the room at the sight of her. As he did so, Lord Ulric sighed and slumped into a chair.

A servant boy passed along the hallway. He glanced in and saw all the angry faces turned in his direction, so he quickly chose to hurry onwards. Caleb was watching Ayse with brooding eyes, the green of his irises looking more shadowed than she remembered them being. Ayse wilted under his gaze, her ears pinned flat against her lowered head, and wondered whether Caleb would reach for the sword at his hip at any moment. She looked to Jon and was happy to see that the colour had returned to his face. He gestured for Ayse to go into an adjoining room and she obeyed. The hairs rose on the back of her neck as she felt the gaze of the silent men watch her leave.

As she entered the small connecting room, she realised that it was some sort of washroom. There was a basin and a jug of water atop the plain wooden furnishings, as well as clean clothing neatly laid out ready and waiting. Realising why Jon had sent her in there, Ayse shifted as quickly as her sore body would allow and pulled one of the fresh cotton shirts over her head. As the shirt touched upon the cuts and scrapes on her body, the soft material suddenly felt too rough and sent tingles of aching pains rippling through her.

The man's shirt was large enough that it fell to her thighs once more, but as she held up the trousers, she realised that they would be far too big on her slim figure. Just the shirt would have to do. Preparing herself to face the collection of northerners, she returned to the meeting room and stood perfectly still, not daring to speak until some else did so first. Too afraid to face their scalding gazes, Ayse simply stared at her bare feet on the floor.

"See," Jon said light-heartedly, "I told you so."

Mistaking his meaning, Ayse looked at him and defensively replied, "What? I am dressed this time."

Her response made Jon flush a deep shade of crimson. Caleb's head snapped round to Jon's direction and his eyes grew dark as he glared at his nephew. Jon wasn't looking at Caleb, but it was as though he could feel his uncle's angry gaze penetrating into him as sweat began to appear on his forehead. In the background Reis was stifling a snicker and his eyes were bright with the threat of laughter.

"I—I meant how quick your transformations are," Jon stammered quickly with an apologetic tone.

If the speed at which she shifted impressed the Orian men so much, it meant their own transformations took a great deal more time than that of shifters. Ayse wondered what other differences there were between their two races.

"How much did you hear?" Caleb asked her curtly as he turned his attention back to her. He was assessing her as he spoke, his gaze lingering on the scarring on her leg, the kiss from the bear trap.

"Enough," she replied quietly, after all she couldn't blame them for wanting to punish her for what she had done to them.

"And you have nothing to say on the matter?" Lord Ulric asked her.

Ayse shrugged, she had come to the north prepared to die if that was what fate had in store for her. She hadn't really considered what would come to pass if she were successful. She hadn't thought about having to confront all the men before her at once.

Lord Ulric shifted in his seat. The silence in the room was growing into a void as no one else spoke. They were waiting for her to say something.

"What is there to say?" she said numbly, "You know what I did, and you know why I did it. It's not really up to me to say what happens next, is it?"

Lord Ulric looked to his brother as if gauging Caleb's reaction, but his face maintained the same dark expression.

"Well, isn't this lovely conversation the perfect way to celebrate reclaiming Fort Lyndon?" Reis muttered sarcastically, it earned him a stern look from Markus.

"What of the Nevraahn army?" Ayse dared to ask.

"Gone," Caleb responded coldly.

"After your involvement in calling the werewolves to battle, we couldn't allow any of them to leave alive," Lord Ulric explained as a matter of fact.

Ayse paled at the thought. She wouldn't lose sleep over the dead southern men, but the thought of the northern forces hunting down every man, especially when the southern numbers had been so considerable... it was unnerving.

"What of those on the plains?" Ayse asked.

Lord Ulric's eyes flickered as he remembered what Ayse had told him the last time they had met. "Ah... yes. There were survivors there, fortunately, none who are aware of our true nature. They slunk back to the far end of the flatbeds."

Ayse exhaled a breath she hadn't even realised she had been holding. There was hope for the Vulpini yet.

"Your people," Lord Ulric said softly, "They would have been there, yes?"

Ayse nodded dumbly.

"You fought alongside those attacking your own people?" Reis said incredulously.

It made Ayse pale when he phrased it that way.

"Perhaps Lord Caleb and I should speak to the girl alone," Lord Ulric said, and the other men immediately understood that they had been dismissed.

Markus, Jon and Reis all moved to leave the room. Reis was pulling a face indicating that he was not happy to leave.

"Reis," Ayse called to him. It caused all the men to stop and look at her. "Thank you... for, on the battlefield, you know..." she mumbled, keenly aware of the attention focused on her.

Reis grinned at her. "There's no need to thank me. It was Lord Caleb that ordered me to stop you from committing suicide with those southern bastards. I would have been enjoying myself far too much to notice your predicament otherwise."

Ayse could feel her cheeks burn as she realised that Caleb had saved her life, again. The three men left the room without another word. Jon offered her one consoling backwards glance before she was left in the sullen company of the two northern lords.

"Forgive me, I haven't yet asked you your name?" Lord Ulric asked politely.

"Ayse," she replied.

"I'm afraid I can't tell you how your tribe fared," Lord Ulric continued, "The battle was bloody on both sides."

"What will you do about those who fled?" Ayse asked.

"We'll let them live, if that's what you're asking," Lord Ulric responded, "As long as they stay on that side of the plains."

Caleb was leaning against the table, his gaze focused solely on Ayse and his arms folded in front of his chest, not saying a word.

"And what of me?" she asked as she looked away from his stern gaze, her throat dry.

"We haven't decided yet," Lord Ulric answered with a sideways glance at Caleb, "But I do recall that I made a promise to you that I would tell you of the Canini tribe the next time we met."

"You'll tell me about the wolf shifters?" she asked hopefully.

"I always honour my promises," Lord Ulric said kindly.

Caleb exhaled loudly. "What is there to tell? Surely your parents told you of your heritage?"

Ayse glanced down at her hands. "I never knew my parents."

A look flashed between the two men.

"She's never met another wolf shifter," Lord Ulric explained.

"So, this tribe of yours...?" Caleb asked.

Ayse bit her lip, not wanting to tell them about the Vulpini's secret. "They took me in when I was just a baby."

Caleb wasn't one to be fooled so easily. "They must have known you for what you really are. I've never known humans to be that understanding." Ayse said nothing in response, which was apparently enough confirmation for the northern lord. "So, they are also shifters of some ilk too then."

"You said you'd tell me what happened to the Canini tribe," Ayse reminded Lord Ulric, wishing to draw the conversation away from her friends.

"Yes, that I did," he replied. "I will tell you what I know of the wolf shifters, though I'm afraid it will most likely not give you the answers you were hoping for. The Canini tribe lived in Oror centuries ago, in secret, unknown to the normal folk, or so the stories claim. Our early ancestors hunted them down one by one and sacrificed them to the old gods until there was no living shifter left in the north."

Ayse recalled the macabre tomb with the shrine inside of it, the walls lined with piles of human bones, and she shuddered at the thought. "Why?" she asked.

Lord Ulric frowned as he thought of his reply. "Do you know what makes us different from you?"

She shook her head.

"Your second nature is a gift," the northern lord continued, "Ours is a curse. Legend says that back when the old gods used to roam the earth as men, one of our ancestors discovered the secret to immortality. This angered the old god

Soriven, the goddess of death. She was so embittered that he had managed to outwit her, that she cursed him and all his brethren. Every son born to their tribe would suffer the same fate. She granted them all unnaturally long lives so that their punishment would be prolonged, their existence filled with horror and pain as their forms would be twisted into that of a monstrous wolf. Our transitions are not... easy. Many of our young die within their first year, mothers returning to cots to find their babes contorted between forms, having perished during their first transformation."

Ayse found herself trying to swallow away the dry feeling in her throat at the thought of it. She had never considered how easily her second nature came to her, or the Vulpini. "But I don't understand. Why did your ancestors kill the Canini?" Ayse asked.

"We don't know the exact reason. Too much time has passed for the truth to have survived in its entirety. We can only assume that they sought to placate the goddess by honouring her or sought vengeance on her in murdering her gifted children."

"But if all of the wolf shifters were wiped out..." Ayse began.

"Evidently our ancestors did not do a thorough job of it," Caleb muttered, "Or we wouldn't be in the company of a wolf shifter now."

"Indeed," Lord Ulric mused, "It makes me wonder whether there are other wolf shifters that survived by fleeing to Nevraah."

The northern lord had not given Ayse much in the way of closure. Her heart felt heavy in her chest as she considered an ancestry that she had never known being wiped out of existence from every inch of Oror.

There was a rap at the door and a soldier stood framed in the doorway.

"I grow tired of reports," Lord Ulric said wearily, the soldier in the doorway blanched as if he were afraid that his presence had angered the blonde northern lord. "Come, girl," he said as he rose to his feet and gestured for Ayse to follow, "I'll leave my brother to deal with this while we find you some better accommodation, as well as some more suitable clothing."

Ayse followed in Lord Ulric's footsteps, not daring to look at Caleb as she passed him. She could feel his eyes on her as they left the room, but he said nothing.

Chapter Thirty-Seven

The only clothing that was small enough to fit Ayse well was a plain tunic from one of the young serving men. She got the impression from Lord Ulric that if they had happened to have a dress laying around Fort Lyndon somewhere, that the northerners would have made her wear it. That was apparently the role of Orian women —to look dainty and pretty and not get involved in the more important affairs, such as battle and espionage. Lord Ulric had claimed that if she were his daughter, he would have her housebound for months for gallivanting all over the country in men's garb. She had stuck her tongue out at his back as he told her this, disgusted by the idea of the submissive northern women.

They had given her a room for the night that was more comfortable than she would have imagined for a battle camp. However, she had been so exhausted that it was possible that the stone flooring would have felt as equally cosy. Before settling down for the night, she looked out of the window to where she could see the courtyard below her. The sky was a subdued blue as evening arrived, and birds were fluttering about the stone structure while a sweet breeze gently moved its way through the land.

The burned outbuildings had been removed and there were currently men hard at work repairing the gates as a guard of Orian soldiers stood watch. There were no longer any bodies in sight. Ayse wondered whether they had all been buried or simply hauled off and burned. She had slept soundly, her body too fatigued for worries to keep her from sleeping.

***

Ayse had awoken slowly. She had initially been disorientated by her surroundings until her mind had stirred from the shackles of sleep and reminded her where she was. She contemplated her future, what would the northerners do with her and who was this high lord they had spoken of? It wasn't a comforting thought to think she could be dragged before some strange and powerful leader of Oror and made to stand trial for crimes that she had regrettably had no choice but to commit. Though she feared the consequences, she understood them. The burden weighed on her heavily, of the lives lost because of her actions, of the even greater number of lives that could have been lost as a result.

A knock at the door startled Ayse and she stared at it fearfully for a moment before calling out, "Come in."

Jon entered with a sheepish expression, followed closely by Reis who closed the door behind them.

"We wanted to see how you were doing," Jon said awkwardly. He paused as if expecting for Ayse to reply and when she didn't, he continued, "It's good to see you... ah, better dressed."

Behind him, Reis shook his head in disagreement, a grin on his face and that same bright twinkle in his eyes.

"I never did thank you for saving my life," Jon continued, "So, thank you."

"For crying out loud Jon, just spit it out," Reis groaned as he rolled his eyes.

"Right," Jon mumbled, "We... well... We were wondering-"

Pushing the young man aside, Reis asked her directly, "What did they decide? They won't tell us anything. What do they plan to do with you?"

"They didn't tell me either," she replied.

"You didn't ask?"

She shook her head.

"Gods, girl!" Reis exclaimed. "Lord Tomas is baying for your blood right now. You should act like you give a damn."

"It's not that I don't care. But what else can I do?"

Reis rolled his eyes again and began to agitatedly pace the room.

"What would you have had me say? I'm not going to run away from what I've done. I endangered your people to save my own."

"If all you cared about were your own people, then you wouldn't have stayed to fight alongside us," Reis stated bluntly.

Not knowing what to say in response, she opted to change the subject, "What happened with the werewolves? What did you tell your men?"

"The normal folk? We claimed ignorance. No one had a better suggestion at the time. Fort Lyndon is currently rife with stories of protective Orian spirits taking on the guises of wolves. Who knows whether it will come back to bite us in the ass later, we must let things be for the time being," Jon answered dismissively.

"They believed that?"

"Is the truth not just as unbelievable? The north still remembers the days of the old gods, though probably not as well as we should. Tales of spirits and ghouls still linger in our villages. Everyone remembers the legend of Varg the White Wolf. It's not that much of a leap for them to believe this. They saw the wolves with their own eyes, after all. It's not as though they have a reason to think differently, no one saw the men transform."

"Varg?" she asked.

"A myth. A giant white wolf that presumably roams the land doing only the gods know what," Jon answered.

"A story to frighten small children into bed at night," Reis added as he came to a standstill.

"Who is the high lord they spoke of?" Ayse asked.

"He is exactly that," Reis responded as if it needed no explanation, "He is the high lord of Oror, Aneurin Wolfrik, and he rules this land. More specifically, he is the father of Lord Ulric, Lord Caleb, and Lord Tomas."

"And he will decide my fate?" she asked.

"Not if you can help it," Jon said. "He won't look favourably on your situation."

"He means to say that he will likely have you executed. Probably not a quick death either," Reis added offhandedly.

"He's never been... soft tempered," Jon said with a shrug.

"That explains where his sons get their personalities from then," Ayse retorted, causing Reis to crack a smile.

The prospect of meeting such a man was daunting, but Ayse was still resolved to face whatever punishment they deemed her worthy of. The guilt of what she had done was growing by the day. Regardless of what Caleb had said about Nevraah attacking eventually, the bloody battle between the two countries had been catalysed by her. So many lives had ended because of her, so many families ruined. The guilt bore a hole right through her heart that she could always feel, eating away at her from the inside out.

There was another knock at the door, causing Jon and Reis to exchange a worried glance. Ayse called for the visitor to enter and a small serving boy opened the door, his eyes going wide with surprise when he saw the two northern men inside her chambers.

"Lord Caleb has summoned you," the boy said, looking to Ayse.

"Well, it looks like we might find out what they've decided today after all," Reis commented as he strode from the room.

"Good luck," Jon said softly to Ayse as he left.

✱✱✱

Caleb was seated at the war table, his clothing more casual than before, reflecting the milder weather. His shirt was loosely open and Ayse could see bandages beneath it, likely covering wounds from the battlefield. He dismissed the servant boy as soon as Ayse had entered. She had hoped that Jon and Reis would have joined them, but going by the already tense atmosphere in the room, they had the foresight to avoid the awkward confrontation with the northern lord.

Ayse stood near the doorway, unsure what to do with herself as Caleb continued to sort through papers on the tabletop as if she wasn't even there. Just as she was about to grow impatient enough to break the silence, he spoke.

"Who would have thought the north could nearly be brought so low by a single she-wolf," he sighed as he laid the papers down and leaned back in his chair to look at her.

His eyes still had the shadows of anger lurking in their emerald depths, wallowing beneath the surface as if threatening to emerge at any moment. Ayse could feel a tremble in her hands. She clasped them in front of herself so that Caleb couldn't see how much he unnerved her.

"I trust you slept well," he continued casually, his gaze flicking back to the tabletop momentarily.

Ayse nodded in response.

"My brothers can't seem to reach an accord as to what should be done with you. If we can't reach an agreement, your fate will be decided by the high lord instead. You certainly have a few of the men championing your cause, but I fear that the decision will ultimately end up in my father's lap."

Ayse remained silent.

"With the current situation, the last thing I need is to have to make a journey to the capital right now. Fort Lyndon is still undergoing repairs, we have wounded to tend to, and a southern host remains waiting just outside the borders of our country. Tomas and I will have to move our camps now that Nevraah knows our positions. Understandably, we have more important matters to attend to than you."

Still Ayse didn't dare to say a word.

"I can't see us reaching an agreement in the next couple of days, after which Tomas and I will be returning to see to our own men. If that happens, I have asked Ulric to care for you here until I have the time to take you to Stormdown. Fort Lyndon is a more suitable place to keep you than my camp." Caleb paused as if recalling the amount of time that she had spent in his camp already and then quickly added, "It's no place for a woman."

Caleb rose from the table as if to signal that their talk was at an end.

"How long will I have to wait here?" Ayse asked.

"I can't say for certain. Our priority here is in defending Oror. Hopefully, your southern brethren will have the sense to return home and stay there. Ulric will take good care of you in the meantime. When I can return for you, I will."

"So, I'm just to sit here doing nothing until then?" she asked with an annoyed tone.

"I thought you would be glad of the reprieve, are you so eager to meet with the consequences of your actions?" he asked with a raised eyebrow.

"It just seems like a waste of time," Ayse replied sullenly.

"Do you have a better suggestion?"

"It's time that I could spend ensuring that my tribe are somewhere safe."

"You mean let you leave?" Caleb laughed, "Do you take me for a fool?"

"I have no intention of trying to run from what I've done, but I cannot simply wait in this place when I have no idea whether my people even survived the plains. If you allowed me to leave, I would return to answer for what I've done."

Caleb continued to laugh, and he shook his head. "It's out of the question."

"Surely it would make no difference to you whether I pass the time here or in the south."

"Do you honestly expect me to believe you would return?" Caleb said with an amused tone.

"You didn't believe me last time and look where that nearly got you," Ayse replied with a frown.

Caleb tilted his head, the fury dancing brightly in his eyes. "I believed you to be nothing more than a wolf and look where that got me."

"If I had any intention of running then I would have left the moment you reached Fort Lyndon and returned to my tribe instead of staying," Ayse proclaimed with frustration.

"So, you're suggesting that I just let you leave and rely on your good faith that you will return to face judgement?" he asked, his tone laced with antagonism.

"I know I don't deserve any favours from you, but I swear that I would return," she pleaded.

Caleb tutted and muttered, "The word of a wolf shifter."

Sensing that he was considering what she was asking of him, Ayse waited silently, not wanting to say the wrong thing and anger him further.

Caleb shook his head. "Once you are reunited with your people, your conviction to face your punishment will waver. You will want to remain with them."

Ayse squirmed and her gaze lowered. "I no longer have a place with the tribe, so that will not be an option."

Caleb's brows rose at this new revelation. "You risked your life for a tribe you are no longer a part of?"

"It's not so easy to forget the many years I spent with them. I care about them. I wouldn't have done it otherwise," Ayse replied defensively, folding her arms across her chest.

"If you care so much for them, then why did you leave them?"

Ayse's lips trembled momentarily as she answered with clipped words, "I didn't choose to leave."

Caleb's mouth had formed a thin line, but he didn't press the matter further.

"If you're that concerned that I won't return then you could always send someone with me," she suggested, steering the conversation back to whether he would allow her to leave.

Caleb smirked at the thought of it. "I don't think that would be wise."

He wasn't wrong, Ayse couldn't even begin to imagine what would happen if she went to see the Vulpini with a werewolf in tow, the mere thought of it made her cringe.

"The answer is no," Caleb said flatly. The hue of his eyes was alight with violent fury waiting to surface.

In that moment he seemed more akin to a predatory animal than a man, the look he gave her struck her straight to her very core. Her breath caught in her throat and all she could do was nod in agreement as words failed her.

Chapter Thirty-Eight

The world was awash with hues of black and blue as night had descended and covered the earth in shadow. The waning moon glimpsed out from behind its cover of passing clouds. Their ethereal bodies were fleeing the sky with the same desperate need that fuelled the urgency of the Vulpini tribe as they prepared to leave the flatbeds. The wagons and horses were packed. Those too sick and injured to travel on foot were climbing aboard, while the others readied themselves for the long march home.

Reuben had proceeded to send groups of the tribe away in staggered measures, hoping to attract as little attention as possible as the Vulpini portion of the Nevraahn camp began to empty. They had left their tents standing, fires still lit, and anything that wasn't utterly essential had been left behind, to ensure that no one would realise they had evacuated in their entirety until morning arrived.

Reuben hoped that even when their disappearance was noticed, that the Nevraahn forces would have more important matters to attend to than hunting them down and hauling them back to the battlefield. Another day had passed and there was still no word from the western fort, as a result, the atmosphere in the camp had become rather ominous and tensions were running particularly high. The Nevraahn officials had sent scouts to assess the situation, but so far none had returned. Reuben knew it was only a matter of time before it became crystal clear to the Nevraahn commanders that their attack had failed, and he planned to be well out of reach by the time they saw sense.

Tobias was still withdrawn, saying little and eating even less. He had ridden out with the first batch of Vulpini deserters, leading the way back to where the rest of the Vulpini tribe awaited. All those who had been too old or too young to be recruited by Duke Remus, along with a few able-bodied people to help with the day to day running of the tribe, had taken up residence just outside the lakeside town of Baluum. It was a safe location that offered a few reasonable ways of foraging for food for the tribe, such as fishing in Lake Tempest, as well as a friendly village nearby in case there was anything else that they needed.

In the faint light of the campfire, Reuben watched as Nell helped the last of the injured onto the wagons, dressing their wounds one final time before they hit the road. Other Vulpini members were milling about the camp as quietly as possible, taking what little they could carry and organising themselves into groups ready to head out together. Reuben prayed that their journey would be uneventful and easy going, and with any luck the weather would stay mild and they would reach their destination in a timely manner.

"Ben!" a voice called out to him.

Reuben watched to see Wren approaching. She was a large girl, not overweight, but broad shouldered and muscular, the opposite of her namesake.

"All of the wagons are ready," she confirmed. "They're ready to move out whenever you say the word."

"They'll be the hardest to move, we don't want to attract attention from any of the others," Reuben mused.

"Just leave it to me, I'll have them leave nice and quiet. We'll let them go one at a time."

"I trust your judgement."

"To be honest, some of the other mercenaries around here seem to be getting a little bit skittish themselves. I wouldn't be surprised if we weren't the only ones abandoning the flatbeds this evening," Wren said casually.

"I don't care what they get up to, I just want to make sure we're far away from here when that damn duke realises it."

"I heard some of the soldiers talking," Wren continued in low tones, "The commanders are in a foul mood, they're wondering what the hell is keeping their army in the west. Apparently, they've started squabbling amongst themselves."

"Good. Let them attack each other and leave the rest of us in peace," Reuben muttered.

"What do you make of it, Ben? There's no way an army of that size could have been defeated in its entirety, right? Maybe they are holed up in that fort and the northerners just aren't letting them get word out."

"You saw the size of the Orian army. Anything is possible. I wouldn't bet on Nevraah being the victor in this case."

"I suppose it won't matter to us who owns what spit of land really, as long as we're left alone."

"That's the idea," Reuben replied with a wink, "But things never seem to be that easy."

Wren heartily clapped Reuben on the back. "If we can make it through this, we can make it through anything. I'll see you in Baluum."

"Travel safe," he wished her as she walked away.

***

Time seemed to be passing far too quickly for Reuben's liking as he frantically gathered the last of the tribe. Nell had long since taken to the road with her company of tribal brethren and already the sky was beginning to lighten as it was whitewashed by the fast-approaching morning. As Reuben had said goodbye to Nell, he had felt his fear and trepidation creating a heavy weight in the pit of his stomach. She had promised him that she would stay safe, but there were many things out there in the world, and many cruel twists of fate that could force her to break such a promise.

Unlike the other Vulpini, Nell planned to branch off alone to visit Brankah as her group of people passed the city. There she could send word to Chief Solomon that they were on their way, as well as leave a note for Ayse in the bar they had frequented, detailing where they were going should she wish to find the tribe.

Thinking of Ayse made his stomach feel even queasier. There had been no sign of her after the battle. Reuben had hoped she would return to the plains after the northerners had been redirected to the fort, but then he still wasn't sure whether it was Ayse that had alerted them to the real threat or whether they had just figured it out for themselves. Reuben didn't like to consider that she may have met her end in the hostile country.

Men were beginning to stir in other areas of the Nevraahn camp. Morning campfires were being stoked and the smell of wood smoke and meat began to travel with the dawn breeze. Knowing that they couldn't linger for much longer, Reuben started motioning for the remaining tribe members to begin leaving the camp. He took one last look about their settlement, ensuring that no one had been left behind, before hastily following the others. As he reached the outermost edges of the encampment, the first few rays of sun broke out through the clouded sky.

The further they strayed from the camp, the more relieved Reuben suddenly felt. The delicate sound of birds trilling could be heard, and the air had a sweet freshness about it that invigorated Reuben's soul, filling him with hope for the future. After all the trauma and torture that they had endured, he felt somewhat foolish to think that they could soon be living a peaceful life once more. Yet with no hope there was nothing to dwell on but misery, so Reuben gladly clung onto his desire for happier times.

Chapter Thirty-Nine

It had taken Rojas quite some time to travel to Bremlor and he was feeling the wear from the long journey. His body ached and his head throbbed from lack of sleep, yet he was still persevering. He had been fortunate enough to have been able to barter for a fresh horse and new supplies in a small town that he had passed through, yet even with that advantage, time was still of the essence. He could hear the heavy footfalls of Raphael as he paced outside of the inn room. The steps were becoming quicker as the man grew impatient. Ayse's friend had given Rojas a clean shave and cut his hair, promising that between that and the smart Bremlor uniform, the guards wouldn't think of him as the gypsy that had been frequenting the city if by sheer luck they had ever witnessed him. Rojas fumbled with the last of the buttons on the officer uniform he had donned and left the room.

"Gods man, anyone would think you were a woman with the amount of time it takes you to dress!" Raphael exclaimed.

"Well, you could have found some better fitting clothing," Rojas muttered in response as he attempted to smooth out the rumples in the tight-fitting uniform.

"We have to get going. *Now*," Raphael stressed.

"It was less than an hour ago that I arrived. I'm still shattered from the ride and I have the sweat of that damn horse all over me. I'm going as fast as I can."

"The guards won't give a damn that you stink like a mare, gypsy. But your friends will mind if you fail to free them in time," Raphael lectured him. "Now take this, it's an order stamped with Lord Frewin's seal. With this, the prison guards will release the Vulpini prisoners into your custody. Once you have them, get to the stables as quickly as you can. We'll meet there. Now go." Raphael was physically forcing Rojas from the building as he spoke, hurrying the older man into action.

As they left the inn, the two men parted ways with a small nod to one another, silently wishing each other good luck in their endeavours. There were few to encounter on the streets of Bremlor at that time of night, meaning that it was easy for the men to move undetected. The quiet night promised them an easy return journey when they had the prisoners in tow. Of course, there were the usual strumpets and beggars lurking in alleyways, but the farmers were all in bed in preparation for the early rise the next day.

***

The night sky was clear of clouds. It wore its speckled cape of stars with pride as the full moon shone down upon the earth with its soft illumination. The evening was surprisingly warm. Raphael could already feel the sweat on the back of his neck, though he was unsure whether it was from the heat or his unsteady nerves. He was experienced in subterfuge and underhanded dealings and his confidence had never wavered, yet this time he could feel unease tickling up his spine as if tracing along his bones with one cold finger.

Raphael knew what the cause was, normally he had only himself to worry about, but this time he had a bigger concern – Lorie. His personal interest in this job was proving to be a hindrance, he couldn't quite steady his nerves as much as he would have liked. If he was too skittish when he approached the Bremlor guard, then it could potentially betray his true intentions.

After he entered Lord Frewin's estate, Raphael took a short moment to compose himself and mop away the beads of sweat from his temple with the back of his sleeve. He pulled at the neck of his stiff and unyielding uniform shirt, relishing the brief sensation of cool air on his skin. Raphael would be glad to rid himself of the uncomfortable Bremlor uniform as soon as they had fled the city.

He continued down into the deepest level of the estate, a path he had walked countless times since becoming entangled in the affairs of the Vulpini. He knew every step, stone, and wall tapestry he had to pass to reach his intended destination.

The guard that stood watch outside of the cell door watched as Raphael approached, but his face showed nothing but disinterest. He was far too familiar with Raphael visiting the girls to think anything of it, but this time Raphael had to swallow away the dry feeling in his mouth and plaster a fake grin to his face as he neared the man.

"Good evening," Raphael said courteously, but the only response he received was a grunt. "I'm here on orders from Lord Frewin. I'm to take the prisoners to the estate grounds."

"Orders from Lord Frewin? I'd not heard that he'd returned," the guard grumbled with a confused expression.

"That's because he hasn't, you dolt," Raphael reprimanded him. "We've received word that the assault on the north was victorious. Lord Frewin is on his way back with his men."

"I've not heard that either," the guard sniffed.

"You're hearing it now," Raphael growled. "Now Lord Frewin has instructed that he wants the girls clean and ready and waiting for him in his chambers so that he can give them a proper... goodbye, before they get sent back to their gypsy tribe. Now are you going to let me do my job or are you going to explain to Lord Frewin when he returns why his orders weren't carried out?"

The guard eyed Raphael for a moment with a squinted gaze before moving aside and shoving the key at him.

"Thank you," Raphael said curtly. "I can handle the two girls by myself. You're relieved of your post. I suggest you make the most of your free time before the Nevraahn forces return."

The guard nodded in agreement and shuffled off. Raphael waited until he could no longer hear the heavy footfall of the guard's footsteps before he unlocked the door to the prison cell and entered.

"Lorie?" he whispered into the darkness as he took a torch from the hallway and descended the stone steps.

For a moment, his heart froze as there was no response. As he reached the bottom step, the light illuminated the small room and Lorie stepped from the shadows.

"You scared me for a moment there," he sighed.

"I wanted to be sure it was you," she replied. "Is it time?"

"Yes, we have to move quickly," he hurried her.

Lorie glanced behind her then back at Raphael with a worried expression. "Help me get Ana up."

Lorie hauled her tribal sister to her feet, but she just stood there trembling with her arms clutched around her own body. Her eyes were wide, and her mouth was agape as she stared fearfully into nothingness. Try as they might, Ana could not be coaxed to follow them anywhere.

"Ana, please," Lorie begged. "We have to go."

"We don't have time for this," Raphael muttered.

"I won't leave her."

"I'm not suggesting you do," Raphael said with a wink as he moved forward and scooped Ana up. He slung her over his shoulder in one fluid movement.

The poor girl went rigid with terror, but Raphael couldn't waste time worrying about her state of mind now. If they didn't leave soon, then there would be worse things in store for her in the future.

"Follow me," Raphael beckoned as he began leading the way back up the stairs.

***

It had been a long time since Rojas had been made to go undercover on a job, and back then he would have learned his role inside and out. This time, he had been given just a few minutes of instructions from Raphael and would have to hope for the best. He had prayed to every old god he could remember, hoping that if they could still hear him that they might bless his mission and see that it was successful. While the guard at the prison gate had given Rojas a funny look, most likely due to his ill-fitting clothing, he had agreed to lead him to the cell that contained the Vulpini prisoners.

As the guard came to a stop and Rojas peered in at the filthy men inside, he was about to protest that the guard had brought him to the wrong prisoners, but then he saw two of the men perk up at his arrival. Unshaven and with matted hair, the prisoners were incredibly thin and gaunt looking, they stared at him with wide eyes as if he were a ghost.

Rojas's breath caught in his throat as he realised the pitiful creatures before him were his kin. He snapped his jaw shut as he felt his anger rising. He knew that if he dared to speak that he would say something that he would later come to regret. Instead, he wordlessly thrust the paper summons at the guard beside him without even looking at him. A vein was beginning to throb in his temple, and he could feel it ticking away under his skin as he waited for the guard to read the order. Time seemed to stretch to an excruciatingly slow pace.

When the guard had finally finished reading the scroll, he didn't seem to question the legitimacy of it at all, instead asking, "Do you need help moving them?"

Rojas shook his head.

"What about the sick one?" the guard enquired.

Rojas turned on the man with a fierce glare as he echoed, "*The sick one?*"

"Yeah, one of them is in ill health," the guard mumbled.

"I can manage," Rojas said with clipped words.

No doubt feeling the animosity rolling off Rojas in waves, the guard fumbled with the keys to the cell, his hands shaking and causing them to rattle against the lock.

"You there, gypsies. You're being moved," the guard called with a jittery voice.

Rojas painfully watched as Owaiin and Aiden struggled to their feet, supporting Mason between them. The stricken man was pale and barely conscious as his friends half-carried, half-dragged him out of the cell.

"Are you sure you don't need any help moving them?" the guard asked nervously.

"Look at them," Rojas snapped. "They won't be a problem. You're dismissed."

The guard relocked the cell far quicker than he had unlocked it and scurried away as if his life depended on it.

"Rojas," Owaiin breathed with relief.

"Not here," Rojas said softly, "We need to hurry. Here, let me take him."

Rojas gently moved Aiden aside and took his place in helping to support Mason. He could feel Mason's bones through his clothes. He felt so fragile that Rojas was afraid that every step they took would cause the man to shatter like glass.

"Where are we going?" Aiden asked.

"We need to get to Lower Bremlor," Rojas replied, "There are horses and provisions waiting for us there."

"What about the girls?" Owaiin asked.

"Hopefully they'll be waiting for us there too," Rojas answered.

✳✳✳

Lorie stared at the perfect night sky above her. She had forgotten what it was like to be outside in the fresh air, to see the world around her, but most of all, to feel free. She was suddenly so happy that she could feel a stupid grin stretch across her face. Isaac had to keep hurrying her onwards; she knew they had to move fast, but it was all too easy to get lost in the feeling of her new-found freedom.

The gentle night was interrupted by the loud booming sound of the bell tower in High Bremlor. Isaac turned around and stared in the direction they had come with a grimace. She heard him curse beneath his breath. Lorie looked at the concern on his face and suddenly lamented that she had not moved faster.

"Are they signalling our escape?" she gasped.

"No," Isaac muttered as a second toll rang out. "They're signalling that the attack on the north was a failure."

"That's all right then, isn't it?" Lorie asked, but Isaac's frown remained firmly in place.

"Not when I just told the guard that I was moving you because we were victorious," he explained. "Quickly now, we're almost there."

Isaac hefted Ana into a better position on his shoulder before continuing through the darkened streets with a new panicked vigour. Lorie followed in his wake, trying desperately to ignore everything around her as Lower Bremlor began to spring to life. As the bell had sounded, it had roused many of the occupants from their sleep and they were coming to their windows to see what was happening. Lights appeared behind windowpanes, the creak of opening doors could be heard, and there was a hush of whispers and mutterings as the townspeople awoke.

"There it is! Quickly Lorie, get inside," Isaac panted as they neared the stables.

Lorie did as she was bid, scooting in through the stable door that had been left ajar. She squealed loudly as hands clamped down on her, causing Isaac to appear in the doorway with a look of alarm. As Isaac opened the door wider, the light of the moon shone into the darkened stables and illuminated the Vulpini men.

"Rojas!" Lorie exclaimed as she saw the man who had hold of her. She threw her arms around him and cried with joy.

Owaiin and Aiden looked to Raphael with surprise, Owaiin's mouth opened as if to say something, but someone else spoke first.

"You didn't tell me about Mason, Raphael," Rojas growled.

"*Raphael?*" Lorie asked as she pulled out of Rojas's embrace, blinking back tears.

"One issue at a time, please," Raphael sighed. "Let's get you out of here first, you can all ask questions later."

"Mason is too sick to ride alone," Owaiin stated with a worried glance to his friend that lay propped up against the wall.

"He can ride with me," Rojas said. "What of Ana?"

Lorie shook her head sadly. "She's not in a good way."

"She can ride with me," Raphael answered. "Get saddled up, everyone. We can leave the other two horses behind. The guards will have realised that I lied to them, we need to get out of Bremlor before they alert anyone and lock down the main gate."

As Rojas heaved Mason onto the horse, he looked back to Raphael and said, "I don't know whether he will make it to Baluum in this condition."

"Of course, he won't," Raphael snapped as he tried his best to settle the petrified Ana atop his horse. "I have no intention of taking you to Baluum."

"That was the arrangement," Rojas glowered at the younger man.

"That *was* the arrangement, yes," Raphael answered with a sharp tone. "That was before I realised how ill your friend was. We can't travel far with him like that. I have a safe place we can go. There's a small village not far from here, hidden in the hills, hardly anyone knows about it. They will shelter us for as long as we need."

"How can you be so sure they will help us? What if they tell Duke Remus that we're there?" Rojas asked as he helped the other Vulpini onto their horses.

"They owe me," Raphael said as he pulled himself up behind Ana. "I helped rid them of a bandit problem, once upon a time."

"You don't strike me as the type to defeat a group of bandits in a fight," Rojas replied with raised brows.

"I'm not. The bandit leader was a betting man, I just had to beat him at a round of cards and he promised to leave the village in peace."

"You must be a dab hand at cards then," Owaiin mused.

"No," Raphael grinned, "I'm a dab hand at cheating."

"Remind me never to play cards with you, in that case," Rojas muttered as he kicked his horse into motion.

The Vulpini moved out in silent succession with Raphael leading the way out of the city. All of them were feeling the same gut-wrenching fear as they ventured forwards. Each shout and sound were enough to make them jump and twist in their saddles to see what was happening. When they finally reached the main gate of Bremlor, Raphael sighed with relief to find that it was still open. Spurring his horse into a canter, he headed straight out of Bremlor without another glance back at the dismal place, with the other riders following close behind him.

Chapter Forty

The familiar flap of flags struggled in the wind as Ayse entered Brankah. Dusty air that was stiflingly warm enveloped her, smothering her with the stench of the city. As usual, Brankah was bustling with all manner of people as they made the most of the summer sun. Despite the close crowds and unbearable heat, Ayse couldn't be happier to be back there. She dismounted from the beautiful horse that the northerners had given her and handed it off to a waiting stable boy. As she watched the small lad lead the black mare away, she reflected on her departure from Oror.

When Ayse had relayed the news of her meeting with Caleb to Reis and Jon, they had offered to help her leave. Jon considered it a repayment for her saving her life and Reis, well, he just wanted some fun it seemed. Ayse had left a note for Caleb promising that she would return by winter at the latest.

Reis had escorted her back to the safety of the flatbeds, and as the days had passed, Ayse realised that Reis was prone to talk often and at great length. She found herself almost wishing for the frosty silence of the northern lords instead.

"The tempers of Orian men are similar to that of a flame, they burn fiercely bright and with great heat to begin with, but eventually they are reduced to nothing but cold ash." Reis had explained. "By the time you return and face the high lord, they will be heating up over some new issue and will be less inclined to punish you so gravely."

Reis had made his farewells to her at the edge of the border, before returning to Fort Lyndon and expecting there to be 'hell to pay for his disobedience', as he had told her.

As Ayse had reached the area of the plains where the Nevraahn army had been stationed, she found that it had been completely deserted. There were a few remnants of belongings and assorted debris betraying that a camp had once been there, but there was not a single soldier in sight. Unsure where the Vulpini tribe would have travelled on to, Ayse had decided to head to the only place she thought they might have left word for her – Brankah.

As Ayse navigated the familiar streets, she found that the Rubah District was looking as grim and disconcerting as ever, yet its dismal appearance didn't affect Ayse's bright mood. She was eager to see Horace once again after being in the presence of the generally sullen northerners for so long. Not knowing whether to call them friend or foe, she was looking forward to seeing the cheerful barkeep who she knew she could trust. Ayse was hoping that not only would he have word about what happened on the plains, but perhaps Raphael would have been in touch about the Bremlor escape too.

Even with its dank and uninviting appearance, The Black Sheep was such a welcome sight to Ayse that she could have kissed it. She entered the bar and before she could even fully scan her surroundings, a booming voice shouted out from the back of the bar.

"Ayse!"

She turned to see Horace hurrying over to her. He swept her up off the ground and embraced her tightly, much to the surprise of his patrons. He was squeezing her so much that she could feel her ribs beginning to wince from the pressure.

"I feared the worst!" he exclaimed as he finally relinquished his grip on her and set her back on the floor. "When that gypsy woman said that they hadn't seen you at all after the battle, I was so worried."

"Which gypsy woman?" Ayse asked.

"Come into the back. I'll tell you everything," he said as he pulled her along, taking her behind the bar and into his back office.

As she sat down in the large seat in front of Horace's desk, which overflowed with paperwork and trinkets, Horace bellowed for Kitson to bring them some drinks.

"With the rate at which you play with fate, you should be careful that your luck doesn't run out soon," he mused as he dug through the stacks of papers atop his desk. "Now where is that note she left you…"

"Who?" she asked.

"That little red-head gypsy woman, you know, the one who roped you into this mess in the first place." Horace couldn't contain the bite from his voice.

"Nell?"

"Can't say I ever really caught her name," Horace replied as he pulled out an envelope from beneath a large tome. "Here it is!"

She took the letter from him and tore it open. Sure enough, it was in Nell's handwriting. It was a short message, simply detailing that the tribe would be in Baluum awaiting the arrival of the Vulpini from Bremlor. Nell was far too clever to leave more important details in the note, yet Ayse dearly wished there had been more information contained in that small letter. She was desperate to learn of how the tribe had fared during the battle on the plains.

"Did she say anything else?" she asked.

"Just that they didn't know where you were," Horace said with an apologetic tone.

"What about Raph? Have you heard from him?"

"Nothing, I'm afraid."

"He should have been out of Bremlor by now." Ayse frowned as worry began to gnaw away at her.

"You and Raph are both as bad as one another for keeping in contact. Just because we haven't heard anything, doesn't mean he's not doing fine," Horace comforted her.

"Still, I have to be sure," she replied. "What of the battle?"

"Well, I assume you know more on that matter than I," Horace scoffed. "The Nevraahn army came slinking back when their attack failed. The dukes are all holed up in Bremlor sulking by all accounts. They've lost the support of some of the other dukes, who have now returned to their own lands. Duke Howell hasn't given up though. If he had, he wouldn't still be in Bremlor with the rest of them. They're up to something."

"Will they attack again?"

"They returned with only a fraction of their original force; they don't have the strength to attack Oror again. Not at the present time, in any case. That's not to say they won't rebuild their strength and attack again."

"They'd be foolish to try again. The north won't be so easily tricked a second time."

"Likely they'll not have the aid of you and the Vulpini getting them inside information either," Horace said pointedly.

They were interrupted as Kitson brought in a tray with two brimming tankards atop.

"What took you so long?" Horace muttered.

"Sorry, boss," Kitson replied before looking to Ayse with a grin. "It's good to see you."

"It's good to see you too, Kit," Ayse said as she smiled warmly.

There was the loud eruption of an argument breaking out in the bar, Kitson rolled his eyes and sighed, "Duty calls."

Horace waited until Kitson had left the small office room before resuming their conversation, "Please tell me that was the last time you'll be venturing north of the border. This old man will die from his frayed nerves, if not."

Ayse fidgeted uncomfortably in her seat, she didn't want to lie to Horace, but at the same time she knew he wouldn't understand why she was willing to return to face the judgement of the northerners. In fact, she didn't think anyone would understand. If she told any of her friends, they would likely implore her to remain in the south, after all, the chances of the Orian men seeking her out in Nevraah were particularly slim. But Ayse couldn't live with the burden of what she had done.

"My plan is to find out what happened with Raph and catch up with the Vulpini," she replied, omitting the truth from her friend.

He nodded along, agreeing with her plan of action. "I'm guessing you'll want to leave as soon as possible?"

"Preferably."

"Stay the night and rest. I'll make sure you have all you need for the journey tomorrow. Just take care and travel safe. There are plenty of unhappy mercenaries along the roads now. I hear the dukes haven't exactly paid them their promised dues. You don't want to meet with a mercenary who's recently been duped out of some coin."

"Thank you, Horace," she said affectionately.

"You can thank me by promising me that next year you and Raph will work as normal, without any drama from outside sources. I think I've had enough of being entangled up with this tribe... and those dukes... and whatever else keeps coming our way..."

Ayse smiled as Horace animatedly complained about recent events, but she felt a dull heavy ache in her heart as she considered that she would never be able to fulfil that promise to him. Tears came to her eyes unbidden and she wiped them away, the motion causing Horace to stop mid-rant.

"What are you crying for, girl?" he gasped. "Are my complaints that hard on the ears?"

"I'm just so glad to know you," she said with a sad smile, "Whatever would I have done if I didn't have you."

"Careful now, Ayse," he warned, "I'll not be made into a blubbering mess today! Save your tears and let's drink to the future."

"That I can do," she agreed wholeheartedly as she raised her glass.

As the two of them drank to a happier future, Ayse could have sworn that she saw the barkeep's eyes watering ever so slightly, but she chose not to mention it. Horace was right; today was not a day for crying, and she was determined to enjoy the rest of her time in Brankah while she still could. She still had a long journey ahead of her and once that was complete, she didn't even know whether she'd ever be afforded the opportunity to revisit the city again.

Chapter Forty-One

The village of Angos was tucked away in the sweeping hillsides of western Nevraah. It was a sleepy little place that was fed by fresh mountain streams and managed to survive self-sufficiently because of its sheep and goat farming. If there was ever a lean year, the villagers would simply send a wagon of fleece to the nearest city or market to sell. Raphael and the Vulpini had been well-received in Angos, and even though the villagers had asked for nothing in return for looking after the travellers, those who were fit enough to work had pitched in with the day to day chores of the village.

The only condition that the villagers had set in place was that their visitors did not send word from the village, as they wished to protect their privacy and remain hidden from the rest of the world. Rojas had been unhappy about this arrangement as he was desperate to contact the rest of the tribe and confirm that they were safe and well. It had been hard for Raphael to keep the older man in check to begin with, but once Rojas had seen how much better his people were faring in the village, he had reluctantly agreed to their terms.

Once clean, shaven, and fed well enough to put some meat back on their bodies, the Vulpini captives were beginning to look less like corpses and more like people once more. Mason was recovering well under the care of the village healer, although his body was still frail. Ana, on the other hand, was still withdrawn from the others. She remained indoors and only really ate or drank when Lorie attended to her. They all hoped that once she was back in the comfort of the Vulpini tribe that she might be restored to her usual self.

Raphael was chopping wood for the villager who had been kind enough to share his home with them. He could feel the sun beating down onto his bare back and every now and then a breeze would whisper and cool him with its soft touch. He could feel the beads of sweat coursing down his skin, sending shivers of feeling throughout him. Raphael mopped his brow with the back of his arm, even his hair was slick with his own sweat as he continued to swing the axe.

"I thought you might like a drink."

He stopped mid-swing at the sound of her voice. Lorie stood watching him, her eyes roving across his torso appreciatively. In the weeks that they had spent in Angos, Lorie had healed well. Her face was no longer gaunt, and her body had more shape to it. She was a far cry from the starved wretch he had met in the pit of Bremlor's stomach. The villagers had given them clean clothing to wear and Lorie wore a simple white dress that was fitted at the waist and accentuated the shape of her figure. Raphael couldn't help but admire her.

"Thank you," he said as he dropped the axe and gratefully took the water from her.

Lorie watched as Raphael drank deeply to quench his thirst.

"I should be thanking you, should I not?" she said playfully as he finished his drink. "You saved us, after all. Or did you do it more for Ayse's sake than ours?"

"I've never really been one to do Ayse any favours, not unless I can get one up on her in the process." Raphael winked.

"So, this was about besting Ayse?" Lorie asked.

Raphael cocked his head to the side and gave her a meaningful look. "I wouldn't say that was my sole reason."

"Our tribe won't be able to pay you for your trouble."

"I never expected them to," Raphael replied, a hint of offense evident in his voice.

"Rojas says we will be leaving soon..."

"Yes," Raphael said glancing away from her. "Your friend is well enough to travel now, and Rojas is eager to return to your people. He worries that they will fear the worst about you all."

"Keeping our silence was a small price to pay for the hospitality we've received," Lorie said softly.

"Let's hope the rest of your people agree on that matter," Raphael said. "I don't want a whole tribe out for my blood because I kept the lot of you hidden."

"They wouldn't do that," Lorie chuckled. "I suppose I should let you get back to your work..."

"If you want something hot to eat tonight, then yes you should," he grinned back at her.

"Here, give me that," she said as she reached for the empty flagon.

As Raphael handed it back to her, Lorie's slender fingers enclosed around his and their eyes met briefly with a longing glance before he let his hand slide from hers. She was left holding the empty bottle. Blushing, she dropped her eyes to the ground and began mumbling about being needed in the kitchen as she made a hasty escape.

Raphael watched her leave. Something was stirring inside of him and he wasn't sure whether it was wanted or not. Even a powerful man could be brought low by his own emotions. Raphael wasn't sure that he wanted to be that man, but then he wasn't sure whether he still had a choice on the matter. With a sigh, he returned to his work. He picked up the axe and held it aloft to bring it down onto the wood, but once again his swing was interrupted.

"It won't work you know."

Rojas had appeared. The old man had a habit of sneaking around unseen and unheard. A habit that unsettled Raphael somewhat.

"What are you talking about, gypsy?" Raphael said feigning disinterest as he finally split the log in front of him in two.

"You and Lorie, it can't happen," Rojas said flatly.

"Oh? I didn't realise you were her keeper."

"I'm not," Rojas replied. "That girl has a mind of her own, so she'll do as she pleases. But she knows the rules of our tribe, and she'll stick to them because she knows they're there for a reason."

"The rules of your people, huh? What you're telling me is gypsies don't like non-gypsies sniffing around their flock," Raphael jeered.

"It's not without cause, we have our reasons. You wouldn't understand," Rojas replied, trying to soften his tone, but failing.

Raphael stopped chopping wood to face the Vulpini man, "Because I'm an outsider?"

"Because you're not one of us."

"Isn't that the same thing?"

"No," Rojas said, his brows drew together, and his tone grew more sombre as he added, "Even Ayse wasn't allowed to remain with the tribe and she was more than an outsider, she was one of us for years. Even now she remains loyal to the Vulpini."

"Wasn't allowed? I never did hear the full story about Ayse and your people," Raphael said with a bitter tone.

"And you never will," Rojas said curtly, "We keep things to ourselves."

"Until you need help, then you turn to anyone stupid enough to help you. Even the poor girl you kicked out of your happy family apparently," retorted Raphael.

Raphael expected the older man to hurl back an insult, but instead his tone softened even more and Rojas sadly said, "Believe me, if I could explain the details to you so you could understand that everything had to happen for a reason, I truly would. What happened with Ayse was... far from perfect. But there were reasons behind it. I sincerely appreciate all that you've done for my people, Ayse included."

Raphael sucked his teeth and shook his head, knowing that if he were to open his mouth that he wouldn't be able to stop himself from hurling more abuse at the man in front of him.

"I know we must seem ungrateful with all of our secrets and rules but know that I consider myself to be personally in your debt. If there was anything that I could ever do to repay you, you need only say the word."

"Anything but telling me what the hell is going on with that tribe of yours I take it."

"Anything but that," Rojas conceded.

"I'll hold you to that one day, gypsy," Raphael warned.

"I wouldn't expect anything less from you," Rojas replied, he grinned as he added, "At least this time you earned a favour from doing some real work, and not just cheating at a round of cards."

"Cheating is what I do," Raphael replied with a smirk, "Pretty sure I swindled those idiots from Bremlor out of five of their prisoners, after all."

"Well, when you put it that way..." Rojas sighed.

"Out with it then, old man," Raphael said as he continued to chop wood, "You didn't come here to exchange pleasantries. I assume you're here to tell me you want to head for Baluum."

"Not much gets past you."

"Just the odd gypsy creeping about and eavesdropping on the conversations of others," Raphael replied, looking at Rojas with a gleam in his eye.

A smile played on Rojas's lips.

"When do you want to leave then?"

"Tomorrow," Rojas replied. "Can you make sure we have provisions?"

"Is that it?" Raphael asked.

"Were you expecting something more?" Rojas said with a raised eyebrow.

"Actually, yes I was. I expected you to tell me that you intended to travel on alone. I thought you might be sick of outsiders by now."

"I'm not foolish enough to turn down your help after all this time. Besides, we still have a great distance to travel and perhaps your swindling will come in handy on the way."

"Perhaps," Raphael chuckled. "I'll see to it that we have everything we need for the morning."

"Then we set out at first light," Rojas sighed with relief, "Angos is indeed lovely, but I will be glad to return to the rest of the Vulpini. Thank you, again."

Raphael nodded to the older man as he left. He gladly resumed his work, welcoming the distraction and allowing the repetitive thump and thud of the splitting wood to block out all other thoughts. If he had to dwell on the fact that his time with Lorie was ending, he wasn't entirely sure what he would do. It was far easier to simply remain focused on the menial task before him. Raphael anticipated that after the day was through, the village would have no short supply of chopped wood.

Chapter Forty-Two

Ayse had expected the villagers of Baluum to tell her that the Vulpini had moved on by the time she arrived in the quaint fishing village. However, the people there had been kind enough to point Ayse in the direction of where the Vulpini had set up camp a small distance from the town itself. Ayse felt uneasy. The tribe should have been long gone by now.

There was a muted calm in the serene landscape, no birds sang out from the tree branches, no breeze ruffled through the leaves, and the only sounds were that of Ayse and her horse amidst the supreme stillness. It was a pregnant silence that made Ayse wary of her surroundings, as though nature itself was holding its breath in anticipation of something.

"Halt, stranger!" a voice called out.

Ayse scanned all around her, but she couldn't see the speaker. Removing her hood, she uncovered her face so that whoever was hidden in the undergrowth would see her. "I'm looking for the Vulpini tribe," she responded.

"Who are you to seek out the Vulpini?" another voice called out from another direction, Ayse realised that she was likely surrounded.

"Ayse," she responded flatly, she was already tiring of this situation.

From out of the trees four young Vulpini emerged, each was armed with a flat bow and had an arrow trained on Ayse's position. It wasn't the reaction she was expecting from the tribe.

"Forgive us, Ayse," one of them said, Ayse recognised the speaker as Bryant. "As you can imagine, we're wary of Duke Remus seeking us out."

"That explains the warm welcome," she muttered.

"We're under strict instructions to not allow any non-Vulpini through. I'm afraid that includes you."

It felt like a punch to Ayse's gut. Bryant was right, of course, technically she was no longer a Vulpini member, but it wasn't that long ago that she had risked life and limb to help them. Her face screwed up with anger as she realised how quickly the Vulpini were ready to discard her now that she was no longer needed.

Seeing her temper rising, Bryant quickly added, "I've sent someone to fetch the chief. He's the only one that can permit you access to the rest of the tribe."

"Right," Ayse said curtly.

***

While they waited, the tribal archers never once lowered their bows and time passed in awkward silence.

"Ayse," Solomon greeted her from horseback, before turning to the others, "Return to your patrols. You're no longer needed here."

The Vulpini archers materialised back into the surrounding woods at his command.

"It's been a long time, Solomon," Ayse said flatly as she looked at the Vulpini chief. He looked a lot older than the last time she had seen him; his hair had greyed considerably and the skin around his eyes was weathered with age.

"Indeed, it has," he replied. Solomon stared at her intently, studying her face and features more than she cared for. "Come, let us talk somewhere more private."

She expected Solomon to lead her to the Vulpini camp, but instead he took her back the way she had travelled through the woods. Without a word, he came to an abrupt stop. There were no markers to make the area worthwhile, but Ayse assumed that it was a safe distance from the Vulpini scouts. As Solomon dismounted from his horse, Ayse followed suit and they tied them to a stunted tree nearby.

"Walk with me, Ayse," he said, more of a command than an invitation.

"What happened with the Vulpini on the battlefield?" she asked, desperate for answers.

"We suffered great losses," Solomon said bitterly. "But many of our people managed to return to us and for that we are grateful."

"Is Tobias all right? What about Nell and Ben?"

"They all survived, though some are a little worse for wear."

"And Rojas?"

"We have not heard from Rojas at all," Solomon said as he came to a standstill and turned to look at her with accusing eyes. "All this time and no word... we can only assume the worst."

"I don't understand," she began, "They should have escaped with ease with Bremlor practically empty."

"They would have been returned unharmed by now if you had not instigated this absurd escape plan."

"You have no idea what they were going through in that shit hole," she spat at him, "It was cruel to leave them there."

"Not as cruel as getting them killed, surely?" Solomon asked, though she knew he expected no answer. "Tobias told me what you did, that you returned to the north to warn them of the attack."

"I did it to try and save those forced to fight on the plains!" she cried.

"So, helping Oror didn't even come into your decision?" he asked with narrowed eyes.

"Of course, it did," she admitted. "But the Vulpini were my main concern."

"You spent one winter there and already you owe the northerners your loyalty?"

"It wasn't like that. I owed them because they saved my life and I repaid them by betraying their trust."

"So instead you betrayed our trust," Solomon snapped. His eyes were dancing with malice and Ayse released why he had brought her out into the middle of nowhere for this conversation rather than in front of the whole tribe.

"I have never betrayed the Vulpini. I risked my life for you," she shrieked in anger.

"You put the northerners above the welfare of the tribe and, as a result, those in Bremlor have paid the price for your misdeeds."

"You don't know that-" she began.

"A foolish hope, Ayse," he reprimanded her as if she were still just a child. "They should have been here by now. I have held on for as long as possible, but the tribe must move on eventually. Every day we linger here increases the risk that Duke Remus will find us. Oh, how I was wrong about you," Solomon sneered, "I thought you would actually help the tribe, not send another six of them to the grave."

Ayse couldn't bring herself to think of the Vulpini in Bremlor, she didn't want to believe that they could be dead. Raphael would have been with them too. It felt as though she was so deep in denial that she could drown in it. Solomon was right. Too much time had passed. The plan to free the Vulpini must have failed.

"I didn't come here to argue with you," she said bitterly. "Just let me see Tobias and I will be on my way."

"Tobias doesn't want to see you. Do you think any of them do after what you've done to us?"

Ayse recalled Tobias's dislike of the plan to free the Bremlor prisoners, the distaste he had for her venturing north once more, and she could not forget the recent coldness of the Vulpini archers. A lump caught in her throat, and she could feel the heat on her face as shame gripped her.

"It's not like that. If I could just explain-" she began to protest.

"There is nothing you can say that will bring them back to us," Solomon interrupted with a harsh tone. He turned his back on her, but she could still see that his body was tense with anger.

Ayse lowered her head. She could feel the sting of tears in her eyes and she didn't want to give Solomon the satisfaction of seeing her cry.

"What will you do now?" Solomon asked her, his tone more even.

"I don't know."

"What of the north? Will you return there?" he pressed her.

She didn't answer him.

He laughed and shook his head. "I should have known."

"I still have to answer for what I did to them," she said firmly.

"And what about what you did to us?" Solomon asked her, his voice dripping with venom as he turned to glare at her once more.

"What would you ask of me this time, Solomon? Do you want me to go to some other hostile country to risk my skin for you?" she said sardonically.

"I want you nowhere near the Vulpini. I want you to have nothing to do with us and the tribe wants nothing to do with you."

Another feeling like that of a punch to the gut, Ayse bit her lip to stop herself from speaking out.

"Do you understand?" he asked her.

She nodded.

"Humour an old man, Ayse," he said, suddenly more softly. "It's been a long time since I've seen you in your other form. Let me see it one last time."

"Why?" she asked with narrowed eyes.

Solomon sighed. He ran his hands through his hair as he contemplated what he was about to tell her. "Wilamir told me something on his deathbed, something about you. He made me promise to never tell you, but... Some promises are made to be broken."

"I don't understand."

"Part of me never wanted to believe the story he told me. But ever since Nell and Reuben returned and told me about the werewolves, the real werewolves, I know that what he told me all those years ago was the truth. So please, show me your wolf form. I must see it one more time now that I realise what you really are. If we are to part for good Ayse, it's time you learned the truth about your parentage."

Ayse nodded in agreement. While she was far from modest, undressing in front of a man she detested was something she could not stomach. She took cover behind some trees to shift. While Ayse was inclined to believe that Solomon could simply be lying, something about the way he had spoken to her told her that he was being truthful. She couldn't help but wonder what Wilamir had kept from her all her life. What was so important that Solomon felt the need to tell her now and why had Wilamir sworn him to secrecy in the first place? As she stepped out into view once more, she looked to the man she hoped would give her some much-needed answers.

Solomon's face was pained as he saw her approach. "As always, your wolf form is quite breath-taking."

She huffed at him, telling him that she didn't want to hear his weak attempts at polite conversation.

"Right," Solomon sighed. "As you know, all the tribe has ever known about you was that Wilamir found you abandoned in the plains as a babe. He brought you back to the tribe and when you first shifted, well, that was a surprise to us all. Being so close to the northern border, we all just assumed..."

Ayse was growing impatient. A growl began to rumble in the back of her throat.

"Easy, girl. Have you forgotten how to respect your elders so easily?" Solomon lectured her. "As it turns out, Wilamir wasn't completely honest with the rest of the tribe. He confessed your real origin to me shortly before he died. He wasn't in the plains that day by accident —he was there to take care of you. You see, your mother was one of us, a Vulpini."

Ayse's body tensed, Solomon paused as he noticed her reaction, but then he continued.

"Your mother's name was Lyra. She left the tribe a couple of years before you were born. No one heard from her after she left. No one knew where she went... not until she contacted Wilamir asking for his help. Lyra begged for him to travel to the flatbeds, promising that she would explain everything when he got there. When Wilamir arrived, he found Lyra living with a man, a northerner. A werewolf." Solomon's voice was breaking slightly, his jaw clenched, and he closed his eyes, as if having to relive the tale hurt him personally. "You know, I cared for your mother. We were close before she left..."

Ayse's heart was pounding in her chest. The sound of the blood pumping in her ears was threatening to drown out Solomon's voice.

"She was frantic when Wilamir arrived. Lyra just thrust you at him, begging him to keep you safe for a while. Apparently, she had met the werewolf whilst on a contract for the Vulpini, they fell in love, gods know how... and so she had left to be with him. They tried to make it work, keep it secret, but there were people in the north that sought to use her to hurt your father. They had no choice but to flee to the plains. They managed to live there for some time, they had you, but... it wasn't enough. The Orians were hunting them, so they asked Wilamir to care of you while your father arranged to speak with those he used to serve. Wilamir did as he was bid but when he returned as planned, he found your parents murdered. He buried their bodies in the plains and returned to the tribe with you."

Ayse felt numb, her mind was racing as she struggled to digest all the information at once. Solomon moved closer to her, she could feel his hand hovering behind her neck as if unsure whether to console her or not.

"I know this must be a lot to take in," he said softly, "You must understand, Wilamir kept it from you to protect you. After what the northerners did to your parents, he was worried that if they discovered you existed, that they would kill you too. He didn't want you to go seeking answers in Oror. He wanted to keep you safe."

Still, Solomon's hand didn't move to touch her. She wasn't even sure whether she wanted him to comfort her or not. Ayse whined softly, it was an unconscious reaction to what she was hearing. Her heart swelled with sadness as she considered the parents she had never met and Wilamir's final wish to keep her safe.

"You look like her," Solomon continued, "Like Lyra." He sighed and his voice hardened again as he continued, "It pains me to see her memory in your features. I was right to expel you from the tribe when I did. Even though I wasn't sure how much of Wilamir's story to believe... I couldn't risk you becoming a woman and everyone in the tribe recognising you as Lyra's daughter. Can you imagine the shame of it? You're a monstrosity. You were born from the union of a fox shifter and a werewolf. You have no place in this world."

Ayse couldn't believe what she was hearing.

"When Tobias told me that you had met Rojas in the camp... Well, I was worried he would have realised who you were. Perhaps it's a good thing he never returned," Solomon was chuckling as he spoke, happy to have dodged such bad fortune.

His words made Ayse recall that dark night in the Vulpini camp on the plains, and the way Rojas had looked at her strangely in the dim light. It made her heart ache to think of the older Vulpini man. Where was he now? Had they at least buried his body, or had they all been thrown somewhere to rot?

Ayse finally felt Solomon's hands reach out to her, but it wasn't in a consoling manner. So lost in her grief and confusion, she was completely unaware of the threat right beside her until it was far too late.

Chapter Forty-Three

The air was filled with the sound of laughter, joyful crying, and happy chatter. The minute that Rojas and the others had returned to the Vulpini camp, they had been swamped by bodies, while the scouts ran alongside them whooping and whistling to announce their arrival. The tribal members had rushed to see their returning family members, their hands reaching out to touch them, to check that they were truly real.

It was an emotional upheaval amongst the people. They cried as they told Rojas and the others how they had presumed them dead after waiting for so long with no word. At seeing Ana still deep in shock, some of the older women of the tribe took her away to try and soothe her. Mason was helped down from his horse and stood on unsteady feet as he greeted his family and friends. The others all dismounted as the tribe surged around them asking where they had been.

"We had to stay in a small village while Mason recovered, we couldn't send word," Rojas explained.

Tobias pushed his way to the front, "What of Ayse? Was she with you?"

"You haven't heard from her?" Raphael interrupted with a worried expression.

"No," Tobias said with a pale face, "I take it you haven't either?"

"I'm afraid not," Rojas said solemnly. Tobias lowered his head, his shoulders visibly dropping as his last hope was dashed.

"Where is the chief?" Owaiin asked.

"He had business to take care of in Lutheran. He just left suddenly, but that was a week ago now," Tobias explained.

"He didn't say what business he had there?" Rojas asked.

"No," Reuben said as he moved to the front of the crowd with Nell. "He's been busy preparing to take the tribe to the Soma Valley. I assume it was to do with that."

"You can ask him yourself when he returns," Nell said as she took Rojas by the hand. "Come. You have travelled a long way and we are all so happy to see you, let's celebrate!"

As she suggested it, the Vulpini around her roared with agreement and suddenly they were all moving to prepare a feast worthy of the return of their family. Tribal members took up musical instruments, filling the woodland with beautiful music as the Vulpini began to celebrate in earnest. Even those still wounded from the battlefield were getting to their feet to greet the freed Vulpini and help to prepare a feast that would not be soon forgotten.

***

Although the mood in the camp was jubilant that night, Raphael felt awkwardly out of place amongst the revellers. He hadn't spent much time with any of the other Vulpini members and so he found himself in unfamiliar company. He could see Tobias sitting by the campfire, his face betraying the torture he felt inside.

Elsewhere, Rojas was being informed of what had happened during the battle in the flatbeds by a young couple. Raphael could only hear snatches of their conversation, but it didn't sound as though it was a pleasant topic. Ana was nowhere to be seen, but the other Vulpini who had been held captive were surrounded by friends who couldn't stop expressing how glad they were to have them home. Lorie had also been ambushed by well-wishers who were happy to see her again.

He had never seen her look as happy as when she was sat laughing with the rest of her tribe. The horrifying memories of Bremlor must seem so distant to her now. As if feeling his gaze on her, Lorie turned to Raphael and smiled at him. He returned the smile, but lowered his gaze quickly, not wanting to intrude on her time with the family she had sorely missed.

"You looked a bit lonely," Lorie said as she sat beside Raphael. "So, I thought I would come over and join you."

"I didn't mean for you to feel like you had to come over here," he smiled at her.

"I know, but I wanted to," she said with a grin.

"So, this is your life then," he sighed as he looked around at the happy people, "These are your people."

"Yes," Lorie replied proudly. "I'm so glad to be home. And it's all thanks to you that we even got here."

"What will you do now?" Raphael asked.

"It looks like we'll be heading for the Soma Valley. The plan is to stay out of sight until Duke Remus has bigger things to worry about, or hopefully just forgets about us."

"Unfortunately, the duke doesn't seem like the type of man to forget. It's wise of your chief to keep you hidden," Raphael paused for a moment before adding, "There are other places you could hide."

"There are not too many places that could house the entire tribe," Lorie chuckled.

"I meant *you*," Raphael clarified. "You don't have to run to the Soma Valley with the rest of the tribe."

"And where would you suggest I go?" she asked incredulously.

"You could come with me," Raphael said softly, staring at her intently with his large cinnamon coloured eyes.

Lorie looked shocked for a moment and her cheeks flushed red, she dropped her gaze and quickly mumbled, "I've only just managed to be reunited with my tribe, I can't abandon them now..."

"Is that really what you want? Is that really the reason?" he asked as he reached out to touch her hand.

As soon as his fingertips met with her skin, she recoiled from his touch, glancing about her as if afraid that some of the other tribal members might have seen.

Raphael's eyes hardened at this response, he started to speak, "I thought-"

"It's not what you think," Lorie interrupted. "I—I just can't—You don't understand because..."

"Because I'm not one of you right?" Raphael muttered with a shake of the head.

Lorie's eyes went wide, she looked distressed by what he had said, and

Raphael felt a pang of regret at the thought of hurting her. She lowered her head and as she blinked, a tear fell from her cheek. "If there was any way... But there isn't. You don't understand... This is the way things must be. We can't be together."

"Lorie, I-" he started to apologise, but she rose quickly and left with her face in her hands.

Raphael jumped to his feet to go after her, but a hand enclosed around his upper arm and pulled him back. He turned to see Rojas's grave face staring at him.

"Just let her go, Raphael," the older Vulpini said sadly, "This is hard on her too."

Raphael gritted his teeth. His heart was telling him to run after Lorie, but his head was telling him that her mind was already set on the matter. He slumped back down to where he had been sitting before. Rojas made a move to join him, but Raphael shook his head to indicate that he was not in need of the company. Rojas patted the man on the shoulder before leaving him in peace.

***

Morning arrived in a chorus of birdsong heralding its arrival. All around the camp the Vulpini were still sleeping or lazily rousing themselves from slumber after their heavy night of festivities. The tribe were so relaxed that they were completely unaware of the arrival of their chief. Solomon rode into the camp wondering why the scouts had not made themselves known to him as he had approached.

"What's going on? Why is there no one keeping watch outside of the camp?" he bellowed angrily as he dismounted, causing Vulpini all around him to start from their sleep and snap to attention. "You should thank the gods that it was me and not any of the Bremlor guardsmen."

"Chief!"

Solomon turned to see who had called out to him, but he was grabbed by the person before he could even get a look at them. As they allowed him to leave their embrace he gasped, "Rojas?"

"You're a sight for sore eyes, chief," Rojas said beaming at his old friend.

"And the others?" Solomon asked nervously.

"All here, all safe," Rojas replied as he motioned towards the Vulpini who had been held captive in Bremlor.

Solomon's face broke into a wide grin, his anger dissipating as he saw the happy faces of the Vulpini that had been missing from the tribe for so long.

"When did you get here?" Solomon asked.

"Yesterday," Rojas replied. "We had to shelter in a village while Mason recovered."

"We thought... Well, we thought the worst," Solomon admitted.

"What were you doing in Lutheran?" Rojas asked.

"I just had to sort out one last thing before we move to the valley," Solomon explained. "We're good to go now."

"Good. We shouldn't stay here long. The duke is a wrathful man, I dread to think what he would do if he found us," Rojas said quietly, not wanting to alarm the rest of the tribe who had gathered around them.

"We'll make preparations and leave today," Solomon said to Rojas before turning to the rest of the tribe and speaking loudly for all to hear, "Everyone, get ready to depart. Dismantle the camp and prepare your horses and wagons."

The camp sprang into action at the command of their chief, rushing to ready themselves for their impending departure. Solomon took Rojas to the side to speak to him as the rest of the tribe busied themselves.

"Ayse? Have you heard from her?" the chief asked.

"No," Rojas said sadly. "Tobias said you haven't heard from her either."

Solomon lowered his head. "It's likely she never made it out of the north. We'll probably never know what happened to her," he said regretfully.

"I don't think that will be enough," Rojas said as he nodded towards the man approaching them.

"Chief," Tobias greeted his tribal elder. "I wanted to ask a favour of you."

"Oh?" Solomon replied.

"I want you to grant me leave to search for Ayse," Tobias said flatly.

"Tobias... The poor girl probably never left the north-" Solomon began.

"I have to be sure," Tobias replied. "I just have to."

"I can't allow you cross the northern border, Tobias."

"I'm not asking you to. I just wanted to travel to Brankah, maybe a couple of other places that she might be laying low in. I just need to do something. Please," Tobias begged.

Solomon looked to Rojas who gave a small nod. "I suppose I should be grateful that you're even asking permission this time," Solomon sighed. "I can't spare anyone to go with you. The tribe must get to safety."

"I will travel with Raphael. He's returning to Brankah so I will go with him."

"Raphael?" Solomon asked with a frown.

"A friend of Ayse's," Rojas stated, quickly adding, "He's trustworthy. We wouldn't be here if it wasn't for him."

"Well, I guess that's settled then," Solomon said reluctantly as if admitting defeat.

Tobias nodded gratefully before hurrying off to find Raphael.

"Do you really think it's wise?" Solomon asked Rojas as they watched the young Vulpini leave.

"He needs closure. I hope he finds it," Rojas replied wistfully.

Solomon nodded in agreement, but as he watched his tribe preparing themselves for the journey ahead, his brows furrowed over his dark and tempestuous eyes. His happiness at seeing his tribal brethren returned to him was short-lived as his mood grew more morose. If anything remained of the gods to listen to the prayers of humans, he silently wished that Tobias did not find whatever he was looking for.

Chapter Forty-Four

Raphael was grateful to reach Brankah at long last. The journey had been lengthy and tiresome, made even more so by the dour companionship of Tobias. The man spoke very little and brooded endlessly. Raphael was trying his hardest to raise his own spirits, if he could have carved out his weeping heart in those woods and left it there, he would have done so. As it was, he had to live with the torment of possibly never seeing Lorie again.

Two love-sick men travelling together felt like the butt of a bad joke. Raphael couldn't help but find the idea both totally amusing and appalling at once. Many years ago, he had promised himself that he would never be so foolish as to fall in love with any woman. Yet somehow Lorie had taken him completely by surprise, and now her very existence felt tied to his own. He had hoped that with some distance, their tie to each other would waver and fade, yet as they rode into Brankah he could feel it pulling at his heart stronger than ever.

Wandering through the streets of Brankah, they found the stalls bustling with the fruits of the harvest. The autumn was mild that year, although when the wind blew through the streets there was a bitter bite to it, promising that the winter that followed would be a harsh one. It didn't take long for the men to find their way to the familiar location of The Black Sheep. So desperate for an alcoholic drink, the two travellers practically fought to get through the doorway. Kitson stared at them wide-eyed as they walked to a stall and collapsed into their seats. Raphael motioned for the barman to bring them some drinks. Even when the flagons were set upon the table, the great silence between the two men was not broken. Raphael didn't even look up at who was serving them until they spoke.

"Well, you two certainly don't brighten up my bar," Horace's gruff voice ridiculed them.

"Horace," Raphael smiled slightly, though his happiness at seeing his old friend was not enough to alleviate his sour mood.

The greying barkeep joined them at the table, it was enough to draw Tobias out of his reverie and greet the man.

"It's good to see you safe, Raphael. Now I can finally rest easy at night," Horace said with relief.

"I'm sorry if I gave you any cause for concern," Raphael said fondly, "But you should have known better that I wouldn't be defeated so easily."

"Of course, of course," Horace chuckled. "But what on earth has you looking like two men attending a funeral?" Horace asked.

Raphael looked to Tobias to see if he would answer, but from the flat unmoving line of his companion's mouth, he knew that it would be up to him to inform Horace of the bad news, "It's about Ayse…"

Horace's face paled and he set his drink back on the table before he had even taken a sip from it. "Why? What happened?"

"It doesn't look good, Horace. We fear the northerners have… Well, it doesn't look like she made it back."

Horace laughed so abruptly that Raphael was certain the old man had finally cracked.

"Gods, man," Horace chuckled, "You had me worried then!"

"I'm sorry?" Raphael enquired.

"Ayse made it back in one piece," Horace explained. "Haven't you seen her? She was heading for Baluum when I last spoke to her."

"What?" Tobias gasped as he bolted upright in his seat.

"Oh, yes. You don't have to be haunted by the thought of her having perished in the north. She was safe and sound when she visited last. Ayse headed straight out to find that tribe of yours. She was desperate to learn what had happened on the battlefield and Bremlor. But, I had no news to tell her."

"Forgive me," Raphael responded, "We found ourselves having to shelter somewhere unexpected for some time after we fled that dreadful place. I tell you now though, I will be glad to never set eyes on Bremlor again."

"What else did Ayse say?" Tobias asked impatiently.

"Not much, she seemed very happy to be back, said she would be leaving to find the Vulpini, and that she hoped to discover what had happened in Bremlor by doing so. Did she never make it to your tribe then?"

"No," Tobias said solemnly.

Horace's face grew serious. "Her journey should not have been that eventful to have taken her off course…"

"There are still lingering forces in Nevraah… perhaps she was unfortunate enough to happen across a mercenary group still reeling from the bloodlust of war," Raphael mused.

"I warned her of the remaining soldiers milling about. I don't think she would have been so foolish to have travelled near them."

"Maybe she didn't have a choice, or didn't realise," Raphael wondered.

"We have to find her," Tobias said desperately looking at both men.

Tobias found his heart lifting somewhat to learn that Ayse had made it back over the border, although he couldn't understand what would have distracted her from finding the tribe.

"I couldn't agree more," Horace nodded solemnly.

"Only Ayse can survive the perils of the north, only to get lost in the south," Raphael said drily. "Of course, you know I'll be more than willing to help find her."

"And even more willing to never allow her to forget it," Horace added.

Raphael grinned, "Of course."

Tobias looked a bit put out by the turn in conversation and opened his mouth as if to say something, but Horace waved his hand dismissively. "Raph's heart is in the right place, lad. Don't go getting worked up about it, lad. He wouldn't be Raph if he didn't seek out every opportunity to out-do Ayse at something. For a man with no family, some days it feels as though I managed to inherit two squabbling children, I swear."

Raphael was certain that Ayse would be found somewhere; he couldn't fathom how a girl who had survived so much would be so easily brought low on her home territory. He knew Ayse well enough to know that she was a strong woman and he also wouldn't consider a lesser person as a rival.

Raphael was also truly grateful to have a new cause to champion, something to keep him distracted from more heartfelt matters. If they managed to find Ayse, he wondered whether she would be more forthcoming about the tribe's secrets considering she was no longer one of them. Maybe then he would finally get a real answer as to why he and Lorie could not be together. The more Raphael thought about it, the more he clung to the desperate idea that finding Ayse would bring him his own form of closure.

"So, what are we going to do about Ayse?" Tobias asked frustrated.

"Everything we can," Horace replied. "I'll enlist as many agents as possible in the search to find her. Somewhere between here and Baluum, someone must know something."

"As much as I dread to admit it, we should probably pay a visit to Bremlor. It's not impossible that somehow the duke's wrath has fallen onto her," Raphael groaned.

"Or perhaps she went there to find you, Raph," Horace added. "But I think that would be best left to someone else. It wouldn't be wise for you to show your face there."

"You won't hear any complaints from me. The last thing I want is to have to meet with that snake Frewin," Raphael said with disgust.

"Oh, that wouldn't be likely in any case," Horace said casually, "From what I've heard, Lord Frewin was among the forces that perished at the western fort. Only those who survived the plains returned. Any who had stepped foot in Oror were not seen again."

"Good. I hope he suffered," Raphael spat.

"It's almost a shame that he wasn't on the plains," Tobias added darkly, "He most certainly would have suffered at my hands."

Both Tobias and Raphael drank deeply from their tankards as they reflected on the demise of a man that they had both hated.

"Come on, lads," Horace barked, "Less drinking and more thinking. We've got a dear friend to find after all."

Setting down their drinks, the men pooled their ideas on how best to search for Ayse. Before long, the autumn would be over, and the land would once again be in the cold grip of winter. The great winds would descend from the north, howling like wolves in a pack and ravish the land as part of their harsh winter hunt.

Epilogue

The darkness was shattered by blades of light that broke in through the cracks in the wooden crate. The inside of Ayse's head was victim to the hammering of a brutal headache and the light was a harsh addition to what fuelled her pain. Her memories of what had led her to her current circumstances were hazy at best. She had been talking to someone for certain, but then what? The answers eluded her.

Ayse had tried to shift but failed. She wasn't sure what was preventing her from returning to human form. It was as though she had lost the ability to shift entirely. Her unique dual nature that lay just beyond her sense of feeling was gone, there was nothing to reach out to, nothing to call on to cause her body to change, now there was only the wolf body that she inhabited. Her body had been through a lot, had it finally taken its toll? She wasn't sure. However, there were two things Ayse was positive about: firstly, she was trapped somewhere, and secondly, she was in danger.

Ayse could feel the weight of a collar about her neck, but no amounting of kicking or scratching would loosen the damn thing from her throat. The large box she was in stank of piss and blood. The stench of ammonia was burning in her nostrils. She had tried in vain to scratch and paw at the wooden crate, but it would not give an inch. Straining her eyes to peer between the planks, she could only make out a little of where she was being held captive. It looked like a wooden shed or outbuilding, filled with various junk and scraps. A window with a broken pane was the only source of light filtering into the building. There were no signs of life, no distant voices on the breeze – just silence. It was suffocating.

She was trapped in the body of her wolf, imprisoned in a crate, in an unknown location and with no clue as to who was holding her captive. However, Ayse knew that one way or another, she *must* escape.

Author's Note

I began writing *Vulpini* over ten years ago and it has gone through many, many revisions since with the help of a great many people who read it and gave me constructive feedback. The world of "traditional publishing" seems like an even harder nut to crack these days and, believe me, I've done my fair share of trying. While I've had some luck in placing short stories, my novel received positive feedback but never found a home. Ultimately, I just wanted to get my stories out there for others to enjoy, and fortunately self-publishing has made that even easier for people like me. A quote that has always stayed with me from a very young age is the following:

"If, when you wake up in the morning, you can think of nothing but writing... then you are a writer." — **Rainer Maria Rilke, Letters to a Young Poet.**

While I'd love to pretend that as a young kid, I was super cultured to even know of this, this quote was introduced to me by the way of Whoopi Goldberg in *Sister Act 2*. It's this quote that has kept me going all these years and kept me pursuing my love of writing even when it felt like nothing was breaking my way. I hope others see this quote and it gives them as much purpose as it did for me.

I had the whole storyline for *Vulpini* planned in my head before I even began writing it. As it turns out, when I started writing it, the story grew into such size that what I had originally planned to be the content for the first book became enough for the first two titles. It's because of this that one particular character has a bit of a question mark about them at the end of the book, as when planning the plot, the "end" of *Vulpini* was supposed to be a nice "middle" that paved the way into the second half of the story. Of course, that second half is now the second title, *Wolfrik*, which will be releasing in 2021. As I had already planned for this to be a series of novels, there are also other titles planned for after the release of *Wolfrik* too.

If you've read this far, I hope to ask one more favour of you – if you have a few minutes to spare, I would really appreciate it if you could leave a review of *Vulpini* on the website of the retailer that you purchased it from or Goodreads. If you have any queries or want more information on my other work, you can contact me via my website: www.megpelliccio.co.uk.

Acknowledgements

There are many people who I must acknowledge, as without them this book would never have been finished. First and foremost, my parents, for not only sharing their love of reading with me from a young age, but for also encouraging me to always be creative. I will always cherish the memories of my parents reading to me, putting on the voices of characters and sharing their favourite books with me.

My husband is my biggest supporter, not only putting up with being my number one beta reader, dealing with all my worries and concerns, but also encouraging me to never give up. Of course, I must especially thank Kadi Vowden-King for lending me her artistic talents and bringing my book cover to life, as well as helping me with graphics for my website, social pages, and more.

There are many people who I would also like to thank as they took the time to read my early writings and give me constructive feedback, such as Jaine, Elliott, Emma, Jen, and numerous others. I also wouldn't have had the courage to publish without the support of many of my friends, such as Steph, Sooz, Loz, Anna, Jay and Kate. Lastly, I must thank you, the reader, for taking the time to read my story – so thank you.